JOURNEY

TO

LOVE

A few words from Alvin L.A. Horn and Lorraine Elzia:

Dear Reader,

It has been a pleasure for us to write as a team creating timeless characters in a mixture of current times and historical perspectives which bind love and growth. *Journey to Love* is an emotionally moving novel of heritage, mystery, intrigue, and unpredictable love which transforms lives and liberty.

Within these pages, soulful music transcends several eras creating the backdrop for fictional behind-the-scenes historical events that have shaped our lives. As a passenger on a Greyhound bus, inhale the scents and be captivated by the sights while leaving the South in the 1940s. After WW2, inside a Chicago blues club, two lovers carve a new path for themselves from traditional norms, creating life-changing events and arising passions. From within the Apollo Theater, the expressive sounds and the unforgettable voices of 1960 can be heard. Fear, strength, and defiance are experienced while traveling from Memphis to Atlanta by car to hear Dr. Martin Luther King preach. Rebellion and free love connect in 1967 San Francisco as a Hippie and a Black Panther form a union and forge a new world. The heart and heat of Cairo, Egypt is relived through the eyes of a young Black couple in the 1970s. Traveling through layers of emotion expressed in the passage of several decades, discover: love, loss of love, rekindling love, and sensual grace lasting a lifetime.

Journey to Love is a depiction of romance in many forms of expression with deep passions giving hope for the future, as we peer back in time at the narrations of our past. Between the covers of the book, awareness of the rich history of the American Black man and woman can be found. The adventures along the way are composed of both joy and pain, ultimately leading to triumphs to thrive through the ages.

SHOUT OUTS FROM THE LITERARY WORLD

Words from our readers:

Journey to Love took me on a tour of life, love, infinity, and lessons. Reading through Blu Rivers thoughts and feelings regarding his retirement facility, "Blue Haven," showed me a man who was willing to sacrifice his personal life in the need to provide and care for others. That was until he met Serene May. Ms. May was the key, the secret, the fascination, and lesson Blu needed to explore the possibilities of what he didn't know he "needed"... LOVE!

Serene May is a complex woman who draws you in with her mystery, enlightens you with her wisdom, and keeps you guessing at every turn. She teaches you the "real" meaning of what love truly is. While Blu reads her journal, he takes a walk-through life's time portal that provides him with lessons, no school, no book, and no movie that could give enough realism.

Journey to Love guides the reader through several time passages while introducing you to significant life-changing figures of the time (Sam Cooke, Martin Luther King, John Lewis, Marcus Garvey, etc.) This book will have your imagination seeing interactions of individuals who are unsure of themselves. Still, they learn the value of self-esteem, beautiful people growing beyond their mental limitations, and following their hearts, leading to dreams fulfilled.

-**Andrea Landry,** CEO/Founder of Progressive Organized Wellness Empowering Recovery, LLC; *We are One* Talk Show Host, Award-Winning Mental Wellness Advocate/Author and Publisher/ National Public Speaker

This smart read weaves intrigue and romance against a beautifully vivid cultural landscape, to which the story is made tangible. The tranquility and passion of the lives of Serene, Blu, and company provide readers with a divine feeling of yin and yang, showcasing the authors' delight in duality.

These writers have a knack for the fascinating tug between tradition and tuition. I only wish a soundtrack may be included alongside the book.

-**Michelle Auwae-Lapilio**, Avid Reader/Book Reviewer

"Thought-provoking. Raw. Sheer poetry. Horn's writing will take you up and down the Pacific Coastline and more. Heart-stopping, jaw-dropping, and unmistakably an author you need to look out for. Flawed characters, realistic situations, and touching real-life moments, his books will positively leave you thinking after you put them down."

-Johnathan Royal, founder of Books, Beauty, and Stuff

Alvin L. Horn is a genius writer. His writings are poetry, a melody intro for a sensual, erotic thriller that leaves you wondering if you were there in the flesh—one of the characters. Alvin's poetry is just as poignant...tender, emotional, thoughtful, and erotic. I'm a true fan of this brother. I'd read anything he wrote. I'm looking forward to reading his works.

-Bestseller Suzetta Perkins,

Author of Two Down: The Inconvenient Truth and Hollywood Skye.

"Alvin L.A. Horn transports the reader into the past through this intricate and well-written tale. Unique and gripping storylines from this master novelist. Bravo, Sir."

-Justina Wheelock, Author of Knight Moves

Lorraine Elzia entices the reader from the very first page. Lyrical words and beautiful descriptions are interwoven to paint the beautiful world in all she writes. Her novel details an unorthodox tale of woo and passion while also engrossing the reader. The uniqueness of her novels is the addition of soulful original poetry that are sprinkled in... again, enhancing the realism of the characters. Lorraine has skillfully captured the essence of forbidden love while catapulting the reader into the realm of another world. Even paced story lines, intriguing interludes, and steamy remnants are only the tip of the iceberg with this sultry fiction novel.

Lorraine Elzia's writing is always an excellent read. The insight she shares in her characters is priceless. Ms. Elzia's storytelling skills are both captivating and enlightening.

Journey to Love – is an inspiration for all

As always, thanks to the supporters of the efforts of Alvin L.A. Horn and Lorraine Elzia. In this novel, we strived to bring you a fresh and ground-breaking page-turner filled with engaging stories that will jumpstart your mind and imagination as you visit different times and places. We thank you for the opportunity to share this book with you and we truly appreciate the love and dedication of our readers.

ALVIN L.A. HORN
Romantic Blues
Publishing
alah57@gmail.com
www.alvinhorn.com

LORRAINE ELZIA
Aveeda Productions
lorraineszone@gmail.com
www.lorraineszone.com
www.aveedaproductions.com

Alvin L.A. Horn
alah57@gmail.com
www.alvinhorn.com

Lorraine Elzia
lorraineszone@gmail.com
www.lorraineszone.com

ISBN: 9798537002451

Our editor on the project: Nicole Baker Editing Services
niquita1277@gmail.com, nicolebaker67@yahoo.com

Cover layout: Alvin L.A. Horn

Cover design and interior formatting: Waheduzzaman Manik, bookpattern.com

Female Cover model: Renee Mohead Davis, www.reneedavis.com, Facebook and Twitter

Male Cover model: Stock Art Image

ACKNOWLEDGMENTS

God, thank you for allowing us to write and to be read by many. You have blessed us with gifts and blessings. We thank you for allowing us to share, help, enrich, inspire, and bring peace.

The friends and family very dear to us; the song says, "We go a long way back." Each one of you somewhere along the way has loved and supported us in your unique way, helping us stay on course or get back to where we needed to be, and we thank you for that.

Our editor on the project: Nicole Baker Editing Services

niquita1277@gmail.com

nicolebaker67@yahoo.com

JOURNEY TO

LOVE

ALVIN L.A. HORN
&
LORRAINE ELZIA

CHAPTER

ONE

"This is not what I thought I was ordering, but whatever it is, I love the taste. I have to find out from the server what the name of this drink is."

"Mr. Rivers, I believe it's a mocha latte, and I think I have yours. You asked for vanilla flavoring in yours, and that's exactly what I taste in my coffee. Excellent choice. It's delicious and I want to thank you for treating me to coffee for this second interview. It took some of the tension off me and eased my nerves. I also want to thank you for the job offer. I'm really excited for the opportunity to be part of your team, and I know I'm gonna love working for you. Your staff seems to have a tremendous amount of pride in the work they do. I admire that trait in an organization. Although, Mr. Rivers, I have to say… your interview process is very different from any I've gone through before, especially this second interview. First, it was a bit unusual for you to walk me around the grounds of the complex and introduce me to your staff and the residents when you had not hired me yet. That was an unexpected treat that allowed me to get a real feel for the place. The history behind your organization is amazing, and seeing it firsthand allowed me to understand how you came into all you have and all that you do here. Then...oh wow, there was the classy ride here to the coffee shop in your restored Ford Thunderbird convertible. That was an added perk that sealed the deal for me. You said it is a 1961 model, right?"

"Yes, '61."

"My grandmother would love riding around in your car and listening to your music. "Going Out of My Head" by Little Anthony and the Imperials from the sixties was one of her favorite songs. That's the type of music she played all the time when I used to visit her. Hearing that in your car brought back really fond memories for me."

"Cassandra, older people love my car. I often enjoy sitting in it and listening to music while in front of Shady Pines Retirement Home. It releases stress for me...if I have any at the time."

"Shady Pines? Mr. Rivers, that's funny, you almost made me spill my coffee. I think the old ladies on the *Golden Girls* television show would have probably called your facility Shady Pines, just looking at the beautiful grounds and the ivy crawling the brick building."

"I often joke about my facility as being Shady Pines from the TV show. Some of my friends started calling it that a while back in jest and it stuck with me. Our residents actually love to tell their friends to come to the big sign that reads Blue Haven - Retreat Community."

I am completing a hire of an event coordinator. I have assembled a great team of caregivers, food service providers, and custodial maintenance personnel. "From the building and the grounds to every moment inside, we attempt to make our facility shine for the people under our care." I pause briefly and look out the windows of the coffee shop. It is near the waterfront marina of Long beach, and the hustle and bustle of city life feels a bit less here.

"Our staff and the families of our guests are welcome to enjoy right along with, or without, our geriatric tenants. We don't house the elderly; we offer a living experience as natural as it can possibly be. With each patient, we customize their living plan to their standards and wishes. This is where I know you will flourish as our new event coordinator making each resident feel they are living for each day."

I drive Cassandra, my new hire, back to the rest home and finish up the final details of her job orientation and paperwork, before leaving her at the front desk with my sister. Sherry is my administrative assistant who gave Cassandra her first interview over a lunch date. I know Cassandra is in caring hands, and Sherry will get her up to speed. My sister is my rock, and if anyone knows the facility as well as me, it's Sherry. She has been my right hand since the inception of this facility. Its success lays partly on her shoulders.

Sherry and I never tell anyone we are related. Different mothers give us enough of a difference in our looks, as her mother is Jamaican white, and mine is Jamaican Black. We share our dark-skinned dad's defined jawline, and there is spiciness and wit in our speech and mannerisms that are inherently woven deep into our bloodline. I came to LA much earlier in life than my sister, so she teasingly gives me a bad time because I have lost some of my island voice.

Through the slightly ajar door leading to the outer office area, I can hear banter from the front desk where Sherry and Cassandra carry on a conversation.

"Ms. Sherry, thank you for the tour of the inner workings of the facility. This map and patient bio on each resident will help me. It is nice to know I will be able to find my way around to all three floors as well as the basement. Might I add that you are so funny and sweet. I know I'm gonna love working with you." Cassandra grinned, "Not to mention, any woman who has a mini poster on her desk of all the men from *The Best Man* movie is my kind of woman, friend, and co-worker. You definitely have good taste in men."

"Yes, my dear Cassandra, I love chocolate assortments, but you never know for sure what is in the middle," my sister says, letting out a devious bit of laughter.

I can't help but grin on my side of the door. My sister's laugh is my dad's laugh, and I love it as I hear both women laughing quite hard now.

"Ms. Sherry, Mr. Rivers is a handsome man - some women would even be willing to say he's gorgeous. I say that respectfully in the sense of admiring.

Sherry, please tell me more about Mr. Rivers. Don't worry, I won't hit on him, but maybe I'll set him up with a girlfriend." Intrigue drips from each syllable of Cassandra's words. She chuckles.

"We have a little time before we need to go. Here...hold some of these charts and take a look at them. Mr. Rivers' reputation is well-known."

"Well, I will respect his personal life as it is his, but I have to share his bio with my girls. I'll never hear the end of it if I don't...I'm kidding." Cassandra laughs, and my sister lightly chuckles.

Sherry has told my bio more than a few times; it still makes me smile when I hear her recite the story that she is proud to work with me while never letting on that we are related.

I hear my sister in her sing-song voice, "My dear Cassandra, everyone asks, so I'll tell you before we make some rounds. Blunile Rivers, also known by Blu, started here as a night orderly working through medical school. This place was a private hospital that was too old and outdated for the most part. It was used more as a recovery center for long-term care after surgery for those who needed to be in a hospital but did not need trauma treatment.

"Some orderlies worked mostly passing out pills and tucking patients in at night. But Blu, he was different. We all love a paycheck, but he took pride in making sure the patients were more than reasonably comfortable. He made it a priority to go the extra mile in making a personal connection with each patient. He learned their likes and dislikes. From room temperature to how many blankets one might want and to the character of their personalities – it all was important to him. He cared about people and wanted them to be more than names on a flip chart. To him, they were family.

"He often stayed hours after his shift ended, even asking to meet with management to throw around ideas and suggestions for improving the facility to maximize care. He was a real go-getter and thirsty to make a difference here. As time went on, his patients would request him, and only him, when other orderlies were assigned to them or if it were one of his days off."

"I love hearing this," Cassandra interjected.

One of the RNs calls Sherry on the desk phone, and they have a short chat.

"Where was I?" Sherry asked.

"You were describing how *our* boss quickly became in high demand here."

"Oh yeah…well, over the holidays years back, Mr. Rivers stayed here while he was scheduled to be off, and he used the time to study. He volunteered his time with residents to make them feel special and to ensure that they were not alone. During his round-the-clock stay, he also dedicated his time to writing a detailed proposal concerning saving the facility money while adding personal touches to the activities and services we offered. The dear man worked on it night and day for over a week, while in school to become a doctor.

"When management came back from their time off, a proposal was waiting for them on each of their desks, and he had also mailed a copy to each shareholder. It was a huge leap for an orderly and second year medical school student to take. That bold move could have resulted in him being fired, which would have been tragic for him because he was in med school and near the top of his class. But it turned out that the powers that be were impressed with his proposal, and within a few days, he was promoted to management and instructed to put his ideas into action immediately."

I hear Sherry's chuckle.

"No guts, no glory from fine a chocolate brain making a difference."

Sherry's extended laugh indicates that she has not heard that description before.

"Cassandra…girl, there's much more to Mr. Rivers. You will see, and I think it will be fun working with you. So here is the kicker to this all of this. The hospital was scheduled to close, and the land was headed to the market in a few months. He's a smart businessman to boot; that's what I call a real winner. Half of the shareholders wanted out and my… I mean, Mr. Rivers found an investor who loaned him the money to back his idea."

"Wow, what kind of brain does all that?"

"He will help you with your career and open up possibilities for you when the time is right, once you learn his systems of patient care and business with the right attention to detail."

"Yes, Ms. Sherry, I get it."

I hear the ring of keys off the hook. Sherry peeks in at me and smiles. She leaves to make her rounds with the new hire in tow.

"Hey, you, I know you heard your new hire."

"Yes, I heard; what's new?"

Sherry walks into my office and flops down in my chair. If she catches me standing, we still play like kids and take the seat we know the other wants. It's mid-shift for her, but I can see the weight of the day in her eyes; even in the humor she dishes out. She's my assistant, and her dedication to this place is the same as mine.

"Sherry, she is cute." A sly grin caresses my face, as I know that will get my sister's attention. It's much like when as kids we saw a Volkswagen Beetle, and we hit each other in the arm saying *slug-bug!* to piss off the other one.

"I'ma tell your mama you're looking at the females on staff."

"And I'm gonna tell *your* mother you're starting mess. I would never really *really* look...and you know it."

"Yeah, right, my dear brother!" Sherry presses her lips tight and makes them do a big circle motion and shakes her head.

"Okay, I do peek occasionally, *Lil Janet.*" Sherry knows that, yet she gives me a hard time. All the women in my family have something to say about my love life – or lack thereof. Sherry and I share a biological father, but we have different mothers who became best friends due to both of them having a hand in raising us. We still tattle on each other even though we're both grown. I am the baby, and I take full advantage of it.

My sister is the cuteness. One of the names we call her is Lil Janet, because her round, pretty brown face resembles a young Janet Jackson from the 70's TV show, *Good Times*.

"Blu, you know both of our mamas are going to be on my side. You need to stop seeing that woman DeJohnette, who has been playing with your time, and who has no time for you unless you are buying her an expensive dinner. You need to get you a good woo-man," Sherry's laugh comes deep from her belly, and she holds her belly when she laughs. "That woman you are seeing – on and off – well, more off than on, unless you are hiding something…"

I cut her off. "I'm not hiding anything."

"Well, find another younger lady different from this gal. A fling with a young thing is okay for a hot minute, but only for a minute." Sherry turns up the corner of her mouth as if she has spit out wisdom of the century.

"Why do you concern yourself with my love life? Silly woman…you might have too much free time on your hands. You need more work?"

Sherry rolls her eyes at me before continuing her sisterly chastising. "My dear brother, I'm not going to let you change the subject at hand like you always try to do. Soon you need to belong to a woman who will bring me some nephews and nieces. I need a sister-law to go shopping with - someone who truly cares about my brother. Yeah, hopefully, she can cook so you can stop raiding my cupboards and stealing my leftovers. And she needs to be willing to do whatever, within reason, to make you come home to her at night, right?"

"You are being a busy body, my dear sister, as usual."

"Oh, yes, my brother…she must have certain things to bring you home – like a healthy backside like an Island gurl," she says as the corners of her mouth turn upward again.

"Really, Sherry?" I make sure she can see me roll my eyes.

"Oh, I know you like them book smart, creative women. I know you love peeling the layers off that onion. For the life of me, why have you not dated that kind of woman? Blu, I know you need someone whose life doesn't revolve around microwave popcorn and social media. You need a woman who knows how to create memories that last a lifetime. Until you find what you are looking for, momentary gratification is okay, but you need a future life with a wife."

"My dear sister, you know I don't like talking about her, but I know you have not forgotten I *had* the one. I loved Karimah, and if life had loved me like I loved her, we would be having at least our 15th anniversary."

"Blunile Rivers, you listen to me ... again: I know losing her will always hurt, but she would want you to move forward in life."

"I have moved on, but I will never forget, and if I did forget it would seem to me I never loved."

"Brother, I believe you, and I know you can't forget. But I know you can move forward if the right woman ever comes your way. 9/11 hurt the soul of a nation and even more so for those like you who personally lost someone. Let us move past this conversation. Talking about you and Karimah as one is a deep ache for you and all who ever saw you two together. I know you will fight for the rest of your life to hold on to that piece of your past...maybe. Or you can move on, please."

"It is in the past, and just because I bring her name up does not mean I'm stuck. If that were true, you would not be attempting to chastise me over other women who have come in and out of my life, right?"

"You are right my brother, so now for this last woman... she doesn't like your music. She likes twerking, rump shakin', and rappers like that little man, whatever his name is called with all dem ugly tattoos on his face, and other hippity-hoppity folks. You like Ledisi, Bob Marley, Jill Scott, and Marvin Gaye. You two do not blend well. You love your classic car, and she thought last year's model of Benz should be traded in for a new one, regardless of whether it had ever been driven or not! She loves fine dining and you want home-cooked meals. She would put ketchup on Filet Mignon and call it meatloaf."

"It was not ketchup; she likes hot sauce on her steak."

We both laugh, and I need to laugh because my sister was making it crystal clear that I've been refusing to recognize I had become caught up in the wants of a woman who is wrong for me.

The woman I was going out with, we talk sometimes, and I can tell she is not into me. Sherry made it plain I am only a means - a wallet. This woman loved what I represented, but she didn't love me and couldn't love me. The truth hurts, and it hurts even more when delivered by my sister.

My relationship status is both humorous and hurtful, and I am tired of dwelling on it. I try to deflect, but my mind is going around in circles with not so happy balls bouncing around in my head. I decide to get back to work.

"I read the reports about the new patients coming in next week. One is a Mr. Oakland Dell. He was a commander in the Korean War and Vietnam war, but now has no living family. We will make his stay here as if he is the Commander in Chief." We want war vets to feel respected. The Veterans Administration tends to send us vets who have higher pensions; they want those soldiers placed where they can get a higher level of care.

"We need to find out if Mr. Dell has PTSD or anxiety in any way. His chart indicates that his wife of sixty years passed away about a month ago, and there is no family to take him in." Sherry's words were exhaled with a pain of sorrow.

"Yes, you're right. We'll have to gather some more info on him to know what to expect when he arrives, because there is nothing in the file to suggest one way or another.

"The other new patient coming is a Ms. Serene May," I say while flipping through her chart. "Wow...she comes to us with a living will, an attorney's report, and a personal doctor. From the background we have been given, it's apparent that she is rather wealthy. Her affluence is evident from the report, and it's clear she loved the finer things in life. We must make sure that her room is furnished with most of her belongings as if it was her home. I have no problem accommodating her, even with some of her more eccentric furnishing requests. Sometimes the possessions of the elderly can seem odd to younger generations, but they give life to the owner. We did a full room make-over for a patient in the past, and it went well; let's make sure we do the same for Ms. May."

"She has a caregiver who is retiring and moving out of state but who is currently still taking care of Ms. May. We can ask her caregiver for pictures of Ms.

May's residence and use those pictures to model the room in ways that will make her feel at home."

"Sherry, yeah, that's a good idea." I continue to flip through Ms. May's file, from her attorney's requests to the preliminary doctors' notes. A diagnosis at the bottom catches my eye.

"Sherry, did you read this? Looks like she may have about a year or slightly more to live because of a tumor growing on her brain. Her record indicates that the tumor may mimic some form of dementia, but she is still very well aware of all that goes on. Her doctors state that she has full mental clarity, but moments come where she is lost for speech and blankly stares as if she is daydreaming. Her chart notes say that she does talk but is often quiet, even when she is lucid. She likes to watch old movies and loves Black music classics by greats such as Nat King Cole and Sam Cooke, Miles Davis and Dinah Washington."

"How are those two teenagers of yours doing?"

"Mister, your nephew, is sixteen and starting to grow a mustache, and your niece is eighteen, going on twenty-eight. It took some persuasion to get her to finally make up her mind, but she decided to go to college instead of joining the Air Force. She'll be living in a co-ed dorm. I am not so happy about that. As you know, she has a good head on her shoulder, but ain't no telling who or what she will be exposed to or influenced by."

"She's a pretty girl, so some young man at that college is waiting for the chance to corrupt her. But Uncle Blu will be on the case…you tell her that."

"Alright, alright. Uncle Blu, you have some talking to do with my children." Sherry raises an eyebrow as she looks me dead in the eyes, "I have to always remind you to spend more time with them to help them control what they do and don't do."

"Yeah, well, it's not hard to understand teenage hormones. I know it's been a while, but just think about what you were doing at the same age. If that doesn't scare you, nothing will." I grab my stomach. I'm laughing knowing my sister was wild back in the day.

"You think that's funny? Keep on laughing. It won't be so funny if you mess around with that young plaything of yours, and one night you swear you can feel your condom in action, but somehow, she comes up pregnant. Have you heard of condoms spontaneously having holes? Then she starts planning a baby shower. Knowing the good guy that you are, you will ask her to marry you. Next thing I know, I'm at a shotgun wedding. You have gone this far in life without misfortune." Sherry has always had a sharp, wicked sense of humor. Her eyebrows rise like our father's often did and with the same smart-ass smirk he had at times.

"Can we change the subject please? I told you, I'm not sleeping with DeJohnette. We are only going out occasionally as friends only. The truth is, I haven't slept with her in six months, and I may never sleep with her again. We basically just use each other as escorts for functions as needed. She is too young for me, I now know this from how she acts, and she's a control freak, which doesn't sit well with me."

"Well then, my brother I hit the nail right on the head about your differences. It must have been the sex was good, since you are in two different worlds when it comes to almost everything else."

"I'd like to think I'm a bit of an old soul in general and have been labeled as a bit of a romantic. DeJohnette doesn't understand me or my love language. Sometimes, when she talks to me, I feel like she speaks with a foreign tongue."

"You keep agreeing with me and you seem not to know it my dear brother."

"I do get what you are saying. Okay let's move on...again. I'll contact Ms. May's attorney or her caretaker to see if we can get a look at her residence or at least get some pictures of her current home."

"Okay, I'll let you off the hook for now, but find another girlfriend or companion or whatever you want to call it. I'll look into how we can make the commander's life as enjoyable as possible. I'll get on that, but please make sure you pencil in some time to get on your job as an uncle. I think your niece needs to hear from the mouth of a man what boys will say and do to try to get what they want. I know she has heard it all from me a thousand times or more, but I'm her mother, so what I say will only hold so much water. But she loves the ground you walk on. What you say and do go a long way in her mind. She is still telling everyone about how you let her prom date drive the Thunderbird with the top down for prom night."

"Yeah, I couldn't pee that whole night until my car was back in my garage." I chuckle while shaking my head. "The things we do for family and those we love."

"Yeah, you're a real softy. And one more time, let me tell you, think about parking that young girlfriend of yours for good...stop seeing her and talking to her. You can lead a woman on without knowing you are doing that by making her think there is hope or a ring at the end of your, *'Let's just be friends'* booty call. She is a roadblock to you meeting the one you are supposed to be with. If you don't cut her off, I'll tell your mama and mine and let them double team you."

Sherry removes herself from her chair after lecturing me to no end, as usual. She looks over her shoulder, smirking as she leaves my office. I sit and turn toward the huge bay window that overlooks the ponds and gardens. The genial morning sun shines on me from the east, casting brightness on the statue of Venus, the Goddess of Love.

I pick up my phone and turn the recorder on, letting the sights before me be an aide as I dictate words. It's easier for me to freely recite my thoughts in this manner. Later, I'll replay the recording and enter those thoughts on my computer. My phone is backlogged with hundreds of poems anxiously awaiting their turn for me to transform them from spoken to written word.

*As the sun high in the morning sky heats my back, I'm alone but guided in
love*

I feel the serenity of the thought of the perfect woman for me

Her mirage is by my side as we brown in the morning sun

Yet, I'm alone

I am safe from harm, as my head, not my heart,

has confined me

Yet, I want to be wild in love

As Venus, the Goddess of Love stands,

I wish to love in the garden of love

I stare into the sun

I want to feel the heat, the warmth, the desire

I feel it...

that love that's not here, but, as if,

she was letting me penetrate her mind, body,

and her soul with kisses of everlasting embraces of

...love

*I slowly spin in place - a slow dance with a vision of our naked souls in
relentless passion*

Her eyes looking into me is music to conduct our hearts to us

never missing a beat

together

She is revolutions with dreams that include loving me

I am in discovery of love, to love her forever

TWO

I almost don't recognize the room. The transformation is phenomenal. One by one, I hold pictures in Serene May's former residence to eye level as I compare her former living quarters with her now private room at our facility. The resemblance is spot-on with respect to the aura of her style. Our staff did an excellent job.

The first thing to catch my eye, as I step fully into Ms. May's room, are the elegant white sheer curtains hanging effortlessly over the bay windows that overlook the pond. A white, European wooden chaise lounge and a pair of regal matching chairs flank each window. Atop a small French coffee table, snuggled between the chairs, sits a Tiffany Cherry Blossom table lamp with a mahogany bronze base, giving the space the perfect ambience for the view in front of it. I can't help myself; something about the high-backed end of the chaise sloping seductively down to the reclining bench begs me to experience its luxurious opulence for myself.

Slowly, I lower myself to the chaise. I recline as my eyes linger on the manicured lawn, the perfectly sculptured hedges, and the rich red rose garden surrounding the pond straight ahead in my picture-perfect view.

"Instant peace and serenity," I whisper out loud as I hear two voices enter the room.

"I think you're going to be quite comfortable here, Ms. May. We have made sure that all of your favorite things are here. Everything is just the way you like it."

An elderly but stately woman grasps her attorney's arm with an air of dignity, as if she is being led onto a ballroom dance floor. She seems oblivious to where she is, and even more unaware of his words. A smile comes across her face as her heels begin to sink into the plushness of the room-size Persian rug beneath her. Her eyes look down and scan.

"It's the same rug that was in your estate."

Her approval, though not spoken, is evident in her smile.

"We thought you would like that special touch. I remember when you had the rug shipped from India and the joy you had when it was unrolled. You and my father had a glass of wine while standing in the middle, daring each other to spill a drop, which he almost did while laughing." Pierce, her attorney, pats Serene May's arm, and he smiles along with her in approval.

Pierce Witherspoon has been Serene's family attorney since his father, her previous attorney and close friend, died. Pierce and Serene have a history embedded between them of both trust and mutual respect. My Google search of him revealed he is wise in his business dealings and loyal. The information I received from her caretaker stated that Serene treats Pierce more like the son she never had than her attorney. Ms. May trusts him.

Slowly, they move further into the spacious elegant room. Pierce is careful to let her movements set the pace. Watching them in motion as they move about the room is reminiscent of a loving side-by-side waltz.

"Look what we have here, Ms. May...a bed fit for a queen. We know how much you love your poster bed."

A European Cortinella bed with cherry veneers, a sheer canopy, and silk drapes that matched the window dressing sat in the middle of the room. Pierce brought Serene closer to the bed so that she could feel the engraved bedpost. The entire room gave an ambience of a royal chamber and not a room in a nursing home.

Serene May didn't utter a word, but the smile on her face grew wider.

"Have a seat. Everything you could ever need is right here at your fingertips." Pierce says to her as he helps her to the bed. Then he proceeds to give her a mini tour as he points to all that is in the room.

"Now, this little thing right here will become your best friend. It controls all of your in-house entertainment needs," he says as he pushes a button, and from behind a vintage Motorola stereo console a flat screen lifts, and it instantly turns on. "We know it's a bit new-fangled for your everyday taste, but you love your classic movies, so we had it custom made for you. "I believe there are some of your favorite albums on the inside storage; you can listen to your treasured music whenever you so desire."

Mr. Witherspoon pushes another button and the melodic voice of Jackie Wilson singing, "A Woman, a Lover, a Friend," fills the room. He had the album preset to play, and Ms. May sways a little, side to side, while sitting at the edge of the bed. Cassandra enters the room and smiles at me and walks toward Ms. May. Pierce looks in my direction as I stand by the window and he nods at me as we both sense her comfort.

Cassandra speaks to Serene as we are leaving the room. I look back and listen, "And over here, you have your personal items." Cassandra's back is now to Serene while she points out other items in the room. I see Serene's attention go toward a large wall unit; it's a vintage hand-carved wooden armoire with an attached bookshelf. She tries to lift herself off the edge of the bed, and I run to her aid. We make eye contact for the first time since she entered the room. Serene traces the back of her hand along my face before allowing me to help her up.

Once we make it to the armoire, Serene stands and stares as if she is somewhere else. I open the doors of the large wardrobe cabinet, and she walks forward. Her hand reaches out slowly and gently runs down the front of her garments that hang regally inside. I watch as she lifts a few of them to her nose and inhales, as if trying to recapture the scents from the time in which they were worn.

As she takes a few steps to the left, Serene seems mesmerized by her own jewelry and trinkets arranged tastefully on the bookshelf. She reaches for a leatherbound book and pulls it gently from a shelf. It's easy to see that a memory or two have taken Ms. May's mind to a place far away from the one she is currently in. Almost instinctively, she closes her eyes and rubs her fingers across what appears to be soft suede and leather. I can see the paper inside is thick and has a very light tannish tone with a goldish shade of color, like a Bible might have. Her hand stays on top of the book as if she is swearing in before taking the witness stand. I give her a moment alone with her thoughts before Cassandra breaks the silence.

"Ms. May?"

With one hand now underneath and one on top, in the same manner that a priest would transfer a Bible, Ms. May hands me the book. She looks directly into my eyes but does not say a word. Her eyes speak for her to let me know the book is important to her. I simply nod while giving her hand a little squeeze as reassurance that I understand its importance, even though I don't.

Cassandra's voice draws our attention. "Ms. May, it's time for your medication. Why don't we take it over here so that you can look outside and relax?" Cassandra helps Serene over to one of the chairs by the bay windows, and she fluffs the pillows around her to make her feel cozy. "There now, doesn't that feel comfortable? I'll get your medicine and a cup of tea. How does that sound?" Her question is rhetorical in nature since Serene hasn't spoken a word since walking in the room.

Pierce looks in my direction and motions for me to join him in the hall, as we had started to do before. I walk over to the nightstand beside the bed and place the book in the drawer.

Out in the hallway, Pierce and I talk.

"I think she'll be fine," Pierce starts. "She likes it here."

I assume he and I are near the same age, but Pierce has an air of authority about him, as if he is far superior to everyday stuff. I would not call him arrogant, but he has a sense of order. On the phone he made a point to let me know his firm had hired people to inspect us from top to bottom, and they were extremely pleased with their findings. I took no offense. I have a sense of order as well.

"How can you tell what Ms. May likes? She hasn't said a word."

"Oh, by the way, she loves her name, so calling her by her first name, Serene, is okay. You'll get to know her over time. She may not say much, but you can always tell when she is pleased; right now, she is pleased. Give it some time, she will talk."

"Okay, I'll take my time getting to know her. I know how to handle her medical needs, but any advice you can give me concerning her emotional needs would be appreciated."

"Don't worry, Mr. Rivers. She touched you and handed you something. She will let you know if she needs anything more than what you and your staff have already provided. You did well in setting up her living space. She is far from difficult."

"Thanks for letting her come to our care."

We shake hands, and as I start to re-enter the room, I hear Cassandra talking to Ms. May. Instead of following through with interrupting them, I eavesdrop just a little.

"Ms. May, I think you are going to like it here; everyone is excited about having you here and making sure you are comfortable," Cassandra says as she stirs Serene's tea for her. "Ms. May, in time I will find out the special events you like to participate in and make sure you have all you need."

I hear Ms. May's voice for the first time, as she utters in a low tone, "Nobody sings anymore. Songs tell stories."

"Oh, is it music you want to hear? I will arrange that for you."

I enter the room.

"Well, look who's here, Ms. May; it is Mr. Rivers. Please don't be jealous of our girl time together, Mr. Rivers. Far be it for me to stop the intentions of a male admirer. I'm going to leave the two of you alone so you can get better acquainted." Cassandra gives me a long wink before gathering up Ms. May's medicine and leaving the room.

I sit down across from Serene and mentally prepare myself for the first step of my introduction. She stares straight ahead at the pond in front of her with her lips closed. Her cheeks rise, and she smiles. I turn to enjoy the same view.

I rise and go over to the stereo console and put on the first LP from the record storage. I watch the record drop and the tonearm touch down. A little pop and click enhances a time from long ago – Roberta Flack's voice crescendos in, "The First Time Ever I Saw Your Face." Serene lifts her chin, displaying her profile as if she is posing. She is a striking beauty at any age. A calm exudes from her, and I'm captured by her aura.

Mr. Witherspoon was right; Serene does seem pleased with her new environment. I let my eyes follow hers as we sit in silence, listening and admiring the view. I wanted to show her that we could connect even without words being said.

As the song ends, I turn in my chair so that I am facing Serene. Her facial features leave me wanting to know about her life. Serene is near ninety years of age, and I'm convinced that she is the most exquisite creature on the face of the planet. I am in pure awe. Her face is a smooth cocoa with cream with fine lines that, instead of marring her beauty, somehow enhance it – each one whispering of femininity and wisdom. Above her lip and on the left side is a faint mole; it is perfectly placed by nature and reminiscent of the beauty marks that 1930's bombshell models purposely applied with makeup.

Salt and pepper finger waves cover the top of her head, and the back is pinned up neatly in a bun. From the texture and fullness of her hair, it must be at least shoulder length when released to its full glory. She is slightly taller than average height for a woman, and her frame, arms, and legs show no fragility. I assume she was active all her life. She carries herself well with her shoulders straight as if she had old-school posture training. She is definitely a woman of style and grace. Without saying a word, Serene's persona has spoken volumes of her inner beauty as well.

I lean toward the table between us to pour her some more tea. As I move closer, my phone vibrates in my jacket pocket, as it had a few times since she arrived. I place the phone on the table and pour Serene's tea. Then I turn the phone in my direction to read the screen. I have a text from DeJohnette. Engulfed in Serene's presence, I am not sure if I want to read the message. My mind briefly weighs the differences between the personas of the two women. I fumble picking the phone up and end up knocking it on the floor. Then, as I reach for it with my foot, I kick it further under the table. In doing so, I accidentally hit the play button on the recorder of the phone. The last part of the poem I recited earlier begins to fill our space.

> Her eyes looking into me is music to conduct our hearts to us
> never missing a beat
> together
> She is revolutions with dreams that include loving me
> I am in discovery of love, to love her forever

Slightly embarrassed, I get on my knees and fumble even more while reaching for the phone again. Suddenly, I feel a gentle touch on top of my arm, pulling me. The playing of my recording continues, then starts over. I look up into Serene's face. Her glamorous copper-colored eyes meet mine. I can hear that she is whispering but clearly speaking to me, so I move in closer to her.

I hear her say, "Journey to love."

Her touch, voice, and words have my mind racing to add all this up to meaning – what? Her hand on my arm seems to move a connection – a presence. Serene's lips widen with a smile.

I finally stand with my phone in hand as the recording ends. I feel hot. *Is it the room or the circumstance?* The answer is unclear. I check the room's thermostat. It is fine. I lead Serene to her bed where she manages to lay down and stare at the canopy. I turn the record over and let her listen to music as I leave her alone to rest. Roberta Flack serenading "Our Ages or Our Hearts" floats throughout the room.

I daydreamed all the way to my car without remembering passing anyone or anything. Once inside, I decided I needed a nap.

CHAPTER

THREE

O ur husky voices rose above the rather loud music flowing from my car stereo.

"So, this old lady is a bit bizarre?"

"I said 'dissimilar' to the kind of person we meet under any circumstance, making her unique," I replied.

"Semantics. Anyway, you Googled Serene May, and she has quite the story, huh? It's nice you can google anybody...but man, she has your mind twisted if you go and look up an old lady who doesn't say much."

A big truck sped by going the other way, whipping my face with ocean mist. I am driving along the coast with my brother-in-law, LaFebra. I hit the power window buttons to let them rise so we could talk with the top down. I had to wait a bit before I could respond.

"It's odd, I know...but man, when she sits in her chair and she looks out that window, listening to classic soul music...it is really rare to see a woman that beautiful at any age. She is something extraordinary, and the whole setup of her furniture and how she dresses for everyday life...I guess you have to see it for yourself to understand and appreciate it. It's as if she has inner peace in waiting for her time to end. I've watched her for a whole week, and I talk to her every day. Although she doesn't say much, she will speak some. Sometimes she talks to me out of nowhere, suddenly, with profound trains of thought I can feel deep at my core. Maybe she's talking to me, or maybe she is off in some distant place. Either way, it captures me."

"Interesting, so what does Google say about her?"

"Let me pull over and let's grab a beer and something to eat."

LaFebra is not married to my sister. His brother, Samuel, was, but they are divorced. I do wish Sherry had chosen LaFebra instead of Samuel, because he hurt my sister, by being unfaithful. LaFebra, on the other hand, is a solid dude. I have known both men since we were kids on the Island. If I had it my way, LaFebra would have been the father of my niece and nephew instead of his brother.

Lately, LaFebra has been on a soul-searching journey to find the ideal woman of stereotypical perfection. A series of heartbreaks has left his mind and heart in clouds of doubt. For him, an ideal woman to love is *Leave It to Beaver*'s mom, June Cleaver. She looks, cooks, and dresses and is so sweet that her soul is sugar cane, and she is forever forgiving. In some way, he thinks this is the path to avoid the chance of another broken heart.

LaFebra hasn't always been like that. For some, one bad breakup and they drown. He has not drowned, but he as a long way to go to get back into sailing.

I don't have many close male friends, and LaFebra and I are two peas in a pod on many things and sounding boards for each other in many situations in life. A childhood friend can be closer than family. In this case, LaFebra is family *and* a best friend. He's scrolling through my playlist on my thumb drive adaptor that connects to my old car radio through a modern connection. I don't let anyone mess with my music, except someone who knows real music. He hits my Billy Ocean playlist, and we enjoy the view of the coast on the drive back from Pepperdine University.

I always have the top down whenever I can. The sky is clear and baby blue with sun-spiked sparse clouds in pink hues. "Zoom" by The Commodores flows out of my car speakers and rises to the seabirds. They fly over us as if dancing to the music. I think they are enjoying it just as much as we are. Today we traveled to Pepperdine to visit our niece who lives on campus. We treated her to lunch and talked to her about boys to men. It went well.

We double-teamed her to make sure she was on the right path when it comes to dating and focusing on school. We don't want our niece to go overboard with freedom and young men early into her college life and get off track. We want her hip to the fact of what is sweet, or the foul things young men may say, think, or do. All that glistens is not gold; and we want her to be able to distinguish the BS when it comes to men.

I pull over at a seaside sports bar and lounge so that we can watch the San Francisco Giants play baseball on TV. Now all the clouds are almost gone, and the sky is beginning to heat up. Opting to enjoy the fresh air instead of the game, we sit out on the deck overlooking the ocean. The sound of the waves hitting the rocks is music that I enjoy, but the salt in the air makes me want to cover myself with baby oil to protect my skin. For sure, I'll need to wash the aftermath of sea salt off my car.

In rapid fire, LaFebra shoots questions at me before we order our beers. "So, dude, back to the lovely old lady in your nursing home. What did Google tell you about this lady?"

"Man, I'm not joking about her beauty. I'm telling you...her age is timeless. If you didn't know her age and she walked in here right now, your head would snap."

"Dude, maybe we need to put you or her in a time machine so the two of you can be together."

"Man, please get serious. I don't look at her in that way. Although she is our grandmother's age, she looks as if she headlined the Cotton Club days and Lena Horne was her backup. Her name came up on Wikipedia, and ah...she does have a storied history. She has lived a life the rest of us would love to claim."

"Did you say 'Wikipedia?'" LaFebra's eyebrows raise as he asks for clarification.

"Wikipedia among other sites. There were other pieces of internet info that I pieced together. In doing so, it all makes sense. She was born into Black Renaissance wealth. Her father was dean of a Black college in 1915, and her mother was the daughter of an African king. Her mother was educated in France and England and was a scholar of African history long before it was a thing and before white historians rewrote successful Blacks out of history. You know in Africa, there was civilization and universities when Europe was in the dark ages and their queens and kings were interbreeding.

"Serene was born into a high-intellect household when both of her parents were long past the average birthing age. I think her mother and father were in their mid-fifties when she was born. As a child, Serene spent time in Africa and Europe because of her royal heritage. Even though she was a king's grandchild, her parents were Americanized. She was a child prodigy when it came to intellect. She finished high school by thirteen years of age and was teaching in a private school for what they called gifted Colored children."

"Now that's impressive! But now you say Serene's life quality is compromised with a tumor squeezing away fragments of her memory and life? That's sad."

"True, but even in the state she is in, her aura and her presence are both still alluring. I mean...everything she does, from how she holds her teacup to how she holds her head up...if I were an old man, I would love to be the man who holds her hand at every sunset."

"Wow, man."

"Yeah, I know."

"Well, you have to make sure she has the best life possible for what life she has left; the way we would want for any of our elder women in our families."

"I understand. It makes me want to be a distinguished gentleman just to walk her through a Paris garden, as if I were Sidney Poitier. In the info I found about her adult life as a professor of ancient civilizations, it seems she wrote mystery books based on the fictional experiences of the ancients. I had to order a used copy from a rare book dealer. The book was banned at one time here in the States. It was deemed too erotic for the times. It was known at one time that passion books by Black authors were suppressed from American readers and labeled jungle love books."

"When you get done, let me read it." LaFebra rubbed his hands together. "I have to find love somewhere, even if it is between pages of a book."

"It might be too much for your greedy, lustful mind. Anyhow, Serene became a lecturer at some of the best universities and she led expeditions throughout the world, but it looks like it might have interfered with her love life."

"Yeah, being in love is hard enough, especially when love lives afar." LaFebra had a love affair that lasted only two weeks because they lived too far apart - across the street.

"Dude, stop! You and she were rabbits in heat working different time schedules."

"True that. What about children?"

"Whew, ah-huh, it was tragic. Serene had a daughter and lost her daughter and son-in-law in a car crash in the late '70s. Her daughter was a writer of books herself – like her mother, Serene.

"Well, if it has wild sex in them, let me read her daughter's books too."

Cocking my head to the side, "I have not found any of her daughter's books yet; but I read a review in an old *Jet Magazine* online file, and it said her writing is sensuous and beautiful."

Our food came as I told LaFebra more about Ms. Serene May, but I could tell he was now bored. "When we get back to the car, I'll let you read her work on the way home."

Within a mile, I noticed LaFebra was deep into the read while I drove. I set him up to read a story titled - *Ruby & Diamond of the Blue Nile*. The book wasn't raunchy; but it was passionate and fantastically sexy for those times. It was published in the 1950's. It was a small book about two Ethiopian Hebrews of the Kingdom of Aksum. Ruby and Diamond fall in love despite enormous struggles.

Ruby had an evil slave owner who wanted to sell her to be a breeder. Diamond had freed himself and worked as a slave foreman. The slave owner promised to free Ruby if Diamond oversaw the slaves in the fields and helped build the great structures. The slave owner broke his promise when he saw how much gold he could have by selling Ruby. Diamond and Ruby found a way to overthrow the slave owners by upsetting the balance of power by undermining the slave owners. They became a king and queen, and they freed the slaves. Then they paid all the former slaves with land and wages and treated them well.

From Ruby & Diamond of the Blue Nile:

Ruby's master, the minor king of the Shalar Province, went away to see what price he could fetch for Ruby. By far, her astonishing visual attractiveness made her the queen of slaves. Her Ethiopian Hebrew beauty outshined all the Roman queens. Those queens wanted the slave girl put to death because her breasts enticed the great sculptors to frequently request her as their model. Ruby's hips flowed like slow curving rivers, and the minor king's friends all want to pay him to be allowed to drink her juices from between. Her posture and curvaceous body allowed her to run like an antelope fast and far. Her feminine arms possessed the physical strength to carry silver platters overladen with foods to serve six kings, all balanced in the palms of each hand.

Her face was without a ripple, as smooth as still pond waters, with an overlay of bronze-colored silk. Ruby's eyes smiled with the contentment of a black panther suckling her cubs. The prettiest slave girl lay on the master's bed covered in blankets of gold threads. Courtyard light glowed through windows in the shape of chess pieces. Each chess piece had a porthole, and the moonlight shone through like a hundred candles. She waited for the love of the only man who could set her body ablaze. In the shadows, Diamond's body was as hot as irons in a fire, and as hard as the unyielding handles of a guardsman's sword. He waited until he knew beyond doubt the master had traveled an overnight stay in Pathos – a two-day horse ride away.

As the master's foreman, Diamond ordered the house cleared. Only his most trusted were allowed near, and they had to wear blindfolds. It was not unusual that a mix of eunuchs and female warriors held and waved great palm leaves to cool Ruby's silken skin as she lay. The master loved his living art, and he wanted Ruby protected.

From behind red velvet drapes, Diamond watched Ruby slide grapes into her canal of womanly honey. She tasted herself on each grape and devoured them as her tongue traveled the length of her fingers, tracing and savoring the mix of juices. She knew Diamond watched. It was their sensual chess game for him to capture his queen and her to feel her knight fill her inner castle.

Behind her eyelids, she saw the full ferocity of his lust penetrating her, and her naked breasts rose to the ceiling painted with celestial bodies of sunrise, to sunset, to moons. She knew the sight of her writhing made his heart pound like a drum calling for her, and the excitement made her feel a small portion of pleasure in anticipation of his fullness making her body tremble. Her legs spread as eagle's wings, and her scent drifted to Diamond and intensified his arousal to unconfined heights, like a falcon in flight. Her allure pulled Diamond from behind the curtains to stand firm and erect before her. Mountain and hills were his calves, thighs, back, arms, and shoulders. His hands could crush bushels of cane into grains of sweetness, but soft they were from hours of tenderly massaging her with hot oil, as if he were rubbing her soul. His dark skin rippled as he crept to her beckoning.

His tongue met the arch of her foot, and he bit with no force. His lips kissed each toe, going back and forth to both feet. He placed her feet on his chest as he made his way to her to entice a cry of love. He rubbed her legs in hot oil, maneuvered his hands over her torso, and made her sing a song in words only he understood. His hand endlessly caressed her breasts, and her songs changed with each stroke as his touch whispered, *I aspire to be one with you.*

He moved his hips to hover over hers. A warm breeze met him, and he leaned down to kiss Ruby's eyes, nose, chin, and each cheek. Diamond's tongue touched her with butterfly lightness as he wanted to feel her thoughts float up in-between his lips.

Her head and breasts lifted, forcing him backward until he had to sit between her legs. She placed her hands on his smooth head to help herself stand up above him, and cast her eyes down onto her lover's dome. She felt his tongue part her and kiss her. She held the back of his head forcefully, although none was needed. His tongue was flicking. She felt as though she was losing her lucidity as he reached around her, clamping her firmness as his tongue circled her pulsating pearl. Her song changed to sighs of no rhythm until she melted to sit over his hips. At the same time, she took in his hardened rage. He filled her deeply, almost painfully, but she grasped his love with tremors and lusting spasms.

As he now stared at the ceiling of painted lovers, her hips movement made him firmer, and they both sang songs. His hips propelled upwards into her. They rocketed to desired releases.

Out of the corner of my eye I catch LaFebra closing the book; he appears to be looking at the light clouds in the sky. "Man, I'm not giving you this book back anytime soon. I like this story, and I like the way she makes you see history and passion." I nodded, but I knew better than to leave the book with LaFebra; I might not get it back. I've learned, one should never loan a good book and expect to get it back. Thinking about LaFebra's assessment of what he read and seeing the ocean and listening to Bobby Womack sing "Fire and Rain," my wonder at Serene May was front of mind. Her being had an aura of intrigue that would draw in most anyone, I assumed.

CHAPTER

FOUR

M aking my morning rounds, I visit Serene last. She is sitting by the window, holding a cup of tea. All I see is royalty. She is dressed in a summer wool pants suit as if she were debarking from a plane in the 1950s. She wears burgundy oxfords with her mauve and white pants suit. We have on-staff personnel who specialize in hairdressing, and her salt and pepper hair is free with loose curls and crowned with silver and pearl head bands. I sit across from her. In my hands I hold the historical romance book she wrote. I want to see if her expression changes upon seeing it. She sips her tea as if I'm not in her view.

"Mr. Rivers," I hear her voice, like when I heard her say, *journey of love* with a slightly southern tone, or French...hell, I don't know maybe a bit British, but for sure as if she is singing a slow-slow ballad, she speaks my name, and I love her tone.

"Yes, Ms. May."

"Rubies are considerably rarer than diamonds; if a true deep red shade, that ruby is rarer. However, the most precious diamonds come from atoms under a high temperature and pressure. They bond together to start growing crystals of hard material. Rubies are made from the mineral treated to extreme heat and pressure formed under the Earth's surface. A ruby is the most beautiful of all stones, but only the diamond can protect the ruby. The diamond can multiply light bright enough to hide the ruby, and the ruby sends blood red through a diamond to give them both life."

"I guess that is what I read in the story of *Ruby & Diamond of the Blue Nile.* A compromise of two lovers."

"Mr. Rivers, a compromise is not about what you are willing to give up. A compromise is what you give freely - lovingly without the feeling of losing. A man and woman devote the giving of themselves not as a concession, but to bring harmony to each other to be baptized in smiles and contentment."

I had to lean in to hear her last few words.

"Ms. May, is that a song? I think I heard those words in a song." I look in her eyes, and my past experiences with many of my residents told me she was tired, or at least the speech center of her brain needed reset time.

Cassandra let me know Ms. May will carry on a conversation, but when she is tired, she will stop talking suddenly, but you could tell she is still very much still in tune to you. I nodded and Serene reaches for my hand. She holds it while she pats my skin.

"Ms. May would you like to take a short nap before lunch? I recognize you wake early and walk the grounds."

I stand to help her up, and she walks over to her stereo console. She reaches into the storage side and pulls out an LP by Fats Waller. I put the record on and help her lay down. Serene sits up after a few seconds. She reaches in her nightstand and pulls out an item. The soft leather-bound journal with a brass clasp, it is the one she handed to me before and I put it away for her in the nightstand. Serene holds the journal out for me to take, but I still point to myself and she nods.

I examine the outside, and the leather is old, but well cared for. The binding is tight, and the page edges have that old Bible gold tone while closed. I look in Serene's direction as I undo the clasp. I want to make sure I am supposed to open the journal. Her head nods three times with a smile, letting me know I am to open it. She lays down again and turns on her side. Her eyes close about the same time the Fats Waller record ends, as if she fell asleep instantly. I see what every man through time would love to open his eyes to find a dream come true. Serene May is the infinite and boundless retrospective of a beautiful woman.

Placing the journal on the table for a moment, I retrieve one of the comfortable chairs in the room and place the paisley velvet-covered chair in the corner next to the nightstand. Sitting down, I look across the room and out the window to the bluest sky, and I feel good. From the record player I hear Fats Waller singing, "I'm gonna sit right down and write myself a letter."

I thumb through and see small, but lovely, handwriting. Most of the writing is in blue ink; a few pages are written in green, and some pages have pencil lettering. I put the journal down and step out in the hall and pour myself a cup of coffee from the cart. Well, I thought, I have time on my hands…let me read for a little while. If I'm lucky, what is written between these pages might be her unpublished writings, and I am privileged to be one to enjoy.

Glued inside on the first page is a weathered black-and-white photo of a handsome couple dressed in African robes from maybe the twenties. I look at Serene to see if there is a resemblance. Maybe the couple was Serene's mother and father. Turning the page, there is a large letter "Y" taking up the whole page with an apostrophe and the little letter "s."

September 10th, 1940. I was 15 years of age.

My mother ran her fingers through my hair as both of us were at my father's bedside. He could not see us with his cloudy eyes. Next to him on the bed, even then, were old reader glasses and an even older book. After many years of reading the fine print in articles and leatherbound books, the constant reading had contributed to vision loss for the once voracious reader. At one time, the books had been too heavy for me to lift. It amazed me how my father could carry on a conversation while engaged in what he was reading. I imagined how many pages my father had turned before I was born.

I was born into my parents' lifecycle long after many parents had stopped having children. My mother was 59, and my father was 69. Now 15 years later, I'm losing my father, but I have achieved a great deal, as I am close to turning 16 and have completed my college degree. I'm headed to higher studies just as I'm losing one of my mentors in life. As an only child, I often lived in a world treated like a princess, adored as a chosen one.

Since I can remember, from my first steps, my father educated me to look in every direction. He made it clear if I look up and down and behind me, I will see what is in front of me more clearly, which will help me make decisions to protect myself and others. I learned sounds were always valuable, whether they be words, whispers, sighs, or notes. My mother taught me to sing in key, and instilled that touch was to help me bring out the good in others and overcome bad times and events. My parents constantly spoke to me as if I were an adult, even at five years of age. My father mentored me to be uncompromising, to never suppress thoughts and emotions, and to consciously define a person's level of commitment to express love. My father made me feel I had alchemy without it being a fantasy. He helped me understand I have a mystical mental strength to give, lead, aid, teach, and see into what others need to lift them. And, in return, I soak up what others have to offer to enhance my life.

Somewhat isolated from the stock market crash and depression by my mother and father's wealth, I never assumed I was better than others; if anything, I'm more giving. Rumors of another world war loomed and people were generally depressed with the lack of civil rights, so I taught grade school kids in the afternoon for free to encourage and uplift my people.

I learned early on that life presents Ys in the road. Some things puzzled me on which way to go when those Ys presented themselves, but I placed each foot forward as if I were on a journey to find truth and give it certainty.

One of those Ys in the road came when I overheard my grandmother whispering to my mother one day, "She should know."

Know what? I did not understand what I was supposed to have knowledge of, but my intruding ears led to hearing that my father should let us meet. I assumed, since I had never met my father's mother, that maybe a meeting with her was what the secret conversation implied.

As I watched my father, laboring to breathe on his deathbed, knowing he was about to leave this Earth, I could feel his urgency in wanting to know I would be alright. My father harbored heartbreaking guilt about what had happened to me, his daughter. It was not his fault, but I sensed he felt condemned. I was injured in ways that hurt his family line and legacy. Father always told me he was sorry for what had happened a hundred times more than the breaths he had left. "Evil men scorch the Earth and leave deceptions to burn down the silence in the forest. I need you, my dear daughter, to be the voice in the silence."

I never blamed my parents for the evil of strangers who took them and me by shock and horror. For sure, I wanted my father to feel he had no reason to feel guilt. Knowing my father would not be here much longer, I laid my heart out to him and let him know I would try to make him proud long after he was gone. Neither of my parents were in good health; that caused me to grow up and move fast to another passageway of life. I was born and blessed with high intellect to compartmentalize existence and death. I felt my mother's fingers still nervously coursing through my hair as if holding me up with each stroke – trying to support me through what the world would present to me.

"I will always be strong," I said.

My father took his last breath.

My mother lived another year. A portion of the inheritance she left behind for me was a letter written on her deathbed:

My dearest daughter, I want you to know your father and I loved you. We know you knew this, but we were not perfect as no man or woman can or will be. I loved your father with my whole soul. I harbor no ill will toward him for fathering another child. You have a sister.

Your father and I, our life story reminds us of Sarah and Abraham's account in the Bible. Abraham, in his old age, fathered a child with a woman who was not his wife. Sarah allowed, and maybe encouraged, the situation because she did not believe she could give him a child due to her age. A wife's sacrifice often takes many forms for the man she loves. Your father and I had tried for many years to have a child, but we bore no fruit. A time came.

Your father went in another direction with a much younger woman; the indiscretion hurt me, but I understood. Then a miracle happened. Close to twenty years later, after years of trying, my old womb finally bore fruit. You came along, and at the same time as you were born, your father's other child was born.

The mother of the other child felt hurt for reasons only a mother can hold in various ways. Women recognize that children are not pawns, but we still harbor feelings about any move not made in advancement of our child, and our child alone. Your father and I did the best we could to locate his other child, but we could not find her. It is my hope, at some point in time, you will find your sister. Her people have not been forthcoming; but maybe with the way you make everyone feel worthy and happy, you can turn a heart or mind around so that it reveals where she is. Your father and I set aside a significant sum to help her life in any way she has chosen or chooses. Please find her; this is our language of love for you to live by, please. It's our legacy; you must continue to make contributions to future generations to love and grow through knowledge. Your father and I hope you share, teach, and empower. That is the living legacy we have wanted to leave to you and your sister.

I must share. Although I have loved your father, I knew he had lives outside me no matter his choices. He was candid and forthright; yet, I never agreed or condoned his other life. What I want for you is to set your heart and mind standards so that you never bend to anyone else's constraints. It is well to have desires and be desired, as long as both work within your world.

Be mindful, the world is steadily changing and you are entitled to change your ways or path. When it comes to love, I feel it is best never to live anyone else's design. Be the person you chose to be and let only the judgments, conclusions and decrees come from you for you.

Always see and hear, feel and know them as,

They only wanted you

They only wanted the best for you

They did for you everything they could to protect you

Within that, they found themselves to be themselves to do the things that gave them the most pleasure in life

And that is they only wanted to be with you

For as long as you need

Then they support you to transform your being to stay or go and be blessed with the grace to return as it is best for you.

Be with someone you look forward to making decisions with. Be joyful when you make decisions with someone to become one through the toughest or best times. Think, if this world were yours and you wanted everyone to have a voice.

At every turn in life, I have decided my life's creed will encompass Mother's words to make them a part of my soul.

Closing the journal, I look over at a sleeping Serene. The near high-noon sun coming through is casting items in the room into shadow makers, including a shadow over her. Reading her journal entry, I assume it is her original writing about her life. I rub a hand over the soft leather as if it were a genie lamp with magic inside. Reading what I have, gave me a feeling of knowing there was more that could only enhance my life.

CHAPTER

FIVE

T
t has been over two weeks, and everything seems to be going well with our new residents. Our Korean and Vietnam War vet, Mr. Oakland Dell, is fully immersed and has found other residents who play chess. As of now, it appears nobody can beat him, and he is teaching others to play. With Serene, we became aware she loves to visit churches and cherish the solitude of sitting alone in the pews with only a few others nearby. Maybe it was a personal moment for her to have relationship time with God.

The excellence of Cassandra's skills and desires to help make our facility thrive is glowing. I already have high praise for her thinking and creating. She set up the church visits for Serene and finds chess players for our vet. She has the residents playing games and has set up field trips to many different events. She has even partnered with elders who live in the community to expand the social circles of our residents.

I have not read more of Serene's journal, but I want to dive in to read more and will do so soon. I want to let her see other people within our facility and to know them. Mr. Boston is an elder gentleman who lived here with his wife; he stayed on after she passed away a few years ago. On a weekly basis, he gave his wife flowers. Now that she is gone, he picks daisies and shrubs and puts them in coffee cups so that he can give them to all the women residents. It's his way of making women smile; a gesture that hasn't left him even though his wife is not here to receive flowers of her own. Mr. Boston can barely get around with his walker, but he finds a way. I noticed he gives Serene many more daisies than some of the other women. Next week I plan to spend more time with Serene, as she has asked, "Is Mr. Rivers busy?"

Right now, I'm on my way to a blind date. I have a friend, Cynthia, who constantly attempts to set me up, and sometimes an awkward situation comes about. I'm laughing as I drive down the highway. I see people looking at me as if I have lost it as I plant my hand over my face, trying to hold in my laugh. I manage to look between my fingers at the road, with thoughts of my previous experiences. My sounds are up high to combat the wind noise while cruising and laughing my butt off. I wonder… *do people end up happily ever after from a blind date?*

The woman I'm meeting kinda turned funky on the phone. Or I read her wrong. She lives in the suburbs near the rural area of San Diego. I suggested meeting during daytime hours not far from where she lives. We agreed on a winery. She wanted to meet for dinner and hit a club afterward, but I felt that was too much for a blind date. I sensed some attitude as she said something like, "I won't spend all your money, and I might make it worth your time." Her comment didn't sit well with me, but maybe I have misread her.

I try to keep my judgmental thoughts in check, but I'd like to think that once an adult has lived past thirty, they have lived long enough to have had some experiences that fall into patterns.

I thought she would exchange photos once she asked me to text pictures of myself, and I did, but she did not share. I decided not to ask, and I'll have an open mind; at least I'm trying.

No matter what, this is a scenic drive from LA almost to San Diego, rolling down the highway passing housing estate compounds in the sparse vegetation of the foothills and a few mini-shopping malls and wine country.

Pulling in, I can hear a smooth jazz band playing from the outdoor venue. Many of the parked cars are classics and high-end. I see men dressed in slacks, polo shirts, and sports coats; my attire is on point. The women walking with men, or in groups of other women, are wearing sundresses and "Southern Belle" colorful wide-brimmed hats inspired by the Kentucky Derby headdress – decorated with flowers, feathers, bows, and ribbons.

A woman in jeans cut into daisy dukes, brown Roman sandals, and a pink t-shirt approaches me.

"Hello, are you Sylvanna?"

"Yes, and you are Blunile?"

"Good to meet you in person," I say. On the phone, we had a conversation about the lovely way people tend to dress when they come to Jazz in Vineyard. She came dressed far less in keeping with that image than I thought she would. I hear my father in my ear, "Son, never conclude your thinking based on what your eyes tell you. Let your ears be a part of your eyes to see the complete image."

We chit-chat about the drive here and our friend Cynthia who has set us up to meet. The conversation is light as we wait to be seated. Escorted to our table, I pull her chair out, and she looks at me kind of strangely like I've done something wrong. On this hot day, I'm glad that they have these little canopies over us. A little light spray mist kisses our skin and quickly evaporates. We order our wines. She likes a light white sweet wine, and I order a red blend.

"Well, Mr. Rivers, our friend Cynthia said you are pretty well-off, running your old folks' home."

"Ah, we don't call my facility an old folks' home. We feel our work is an investment into life. What goes on behind the walls and on the grounds is a place for rest and care for an older clientele; we want it to be more than a nursing home. Although many are older, they are generally not sick and helpless. Most do not have a connected family to be with them in their mature years. What we do is, we provide family."

She is giving me a nonchalant expression, and clearly, she wants me to see her face. Now she is shrugging her shoulders and chuckling. "Old people, they do die in your old folks' home ... right?"

I don't respond.

The foothills in the distance surrounding the winery are jagged and sharp like her eyes as she viewed me. I mentally put her attitude in my hip pocket, and I'll wash these pants and not check my pockets. I want to ask her, *why throw negativity?*

After an extended silence, I respond. "Sure, there are some who may not have a long life in front of them, but still, they deserve love and as much of a full life as they desire."

"Hmm, I would think you could have more time for yourself and keep more money in your pocket if you ran your place like a normal nursing home."

I try to hide my thoughts, but I'm sure my facial expressions give off a look of, *what is your problem?*

"If I were your woman, I would have to get you straight on how much money we could make and have for ourselves. Sometimes a woman must help a man see his potential. Or are you one of those brothers who has a problem with a strong woman?"

"There are different trains of thought on how to run a business, and this is what works for me. I sleep well at night knowing I'm making life at my place that brings joy to the living." I tried to make sure my voice had a lightness to it so as not to sound confrontational.

At that point, I decided to let her dominate the conversation and sit in wonderment about my friend who set me up on this blind date. I had a couple of inner laughs as this is more than a personality difference. I played devil's advocate and tried not to put it all on my blind date for her wanting me to be someone else, but I couldn't wait for the date to be over so I could be back on the road for the three-hour drive to my life's work.

I walk her to her car. I wasn't into hugging her; I shook her hand instead. We find out we are parked a few cars apart. She watches me put the convertible top up on my classic, and she shouts to where others can hear, "Hey, you do have some money, huh?"

I wave goodbye.

On the way back, I call my brother-in-law, LaFebra. "Man, tell our friend Cynthia she is fired for the blind date she sent me on."

"What? You were on a blind date!? What's that about, dude? Since when do you need help in the dating department? Get out of here! You're lying, right?"

I decide to change the subject. "Anyway, did you watch the Dodgers play the Padres? Who pitched?"

I hear LaFebra busting up laughing as he mocks me a bit. "Hmm yeah, I'm gonna let you change the subject until we sit down and have a beer. But wait, a blind date! Maybe I'm the one who should call Cynthia and tell her to hook me up. I'm in more of a need than you are."

"I wasn't looking…I was doing Cynthia a favor."

"Okay, Cinderella, make sure you get home before midnight." LaFebra mocks me and hangs up. I had the same laugh I had when I was driving to my blind date.

CHAPTER

SIX

The fire department cleared the last of their men after our fire drill. It is always stressful whenever we do any type of exercise of this nature. The stress is on everyone here. We want to get it right and keep our residents calm. The Fire Department scores us to ensure that each doorway is clear, exits are marked, and the emergency lighting is working. Thanks to our maintenance crew, we were on point.

All systems were proper, and everyone onboard knew their assignments to move efficiently. Most of the residents can move about on their own without any aid. We have a few people who are in wheelchairs, a few more use walkers from time to time, and we have a couple of residents in mobile beds with wheels.

Each department coordinator will receive my thanks and some extra comp time for doing their job well. It was a bit disconcerting as one of our residents seemed to have gotten lost. Our new guy – the war veteran – locked himself in a closet in a room that was not his. One never knows if someone has post-traumatic stress disorder – PTSD – and how it manifests itself. We found him in less than five minutes because we had an accurate accounting of where everyone was when we evacuated. The Fire Department said we did a great job, and it was good practice for us to find a lost resident. They were also impressed with how quickly we were able to locate him.

Coming out of my office, my sister and I want to make the rounds to thank each resident for helping us be successful with the fire drill. Having a little coffee first, I sit out in the hallway to try to decompress. Hell, I want a nap or breather. A fire drill is practice for a real emergency. I know most may not take it seriously, but I own this and run this. I love Blue Haven and I want to protect each person and save the building if possible, in the event of a fire, or earthquake, or whatever. I get stressed over this as this is home for everyone here.

I welcome the relief and try to connect with all the residents; all is fine. I ordered food for the breakroom, providing sweets and sandwiches for the staff. I'm walking through the halls of Blue Haven, and I love the robin's egg blue walls and the well-manicured wood floors in grey-wood tones. For our lighting, we kept the original 3-light inverted Tiffany pendant ceiling lights. The somewhat Art Deco refinish always captures the eyes of visitors. The tall windows and skylights send the sun through from morning, noon, and sunset. I never grow tired of admiring our facility, and I know why I always want to protect this place.

I take a seat across the hall from Serene's room. I'm going to spend some time with her. After sending a text, I look up from my phone. Before I know it, my sister is sitting down next to me.

"Dear brother, if I hear you are going on another blind date, I'm gonna take your car keys and hide them because you have a problem. You are too well-refined as a man to let friends try to set you up."

"LaFebra told on me, huh?"

"You know...and he's in big trouble with me if he doesn't tell me."

"It wasn't like that. I was only meeting a woman for wine."

"Yes, it was really like that if you went. You've got to do better."

"What are you saying? I'm not out here trying a woman out as if I'm in a dressing room trying on a new suit." I am a little annoyed with my sister, but her mouth is always coiled to be sarcastic with her truth. Sherry is always on my butt, being bossy, but I love my sister.

"I'm going to go see Ms. May. I haven't seen her in a while other than to say hello, and I'm checking on you. Now, please don't ruin my mood. I'm just now winding down from the fire drill."

"Oh, you think you can butter your sister up like a biscuit and pour syrup all over me. I'll let it go for now. But I'm going to tell your mama, and you know you don't want her to whack you upside your head."

"Alright," I laugh.

"Have a good visit."

I walk into Ms. May's room, and there she is, sitting in the window just as beautiful as ever with the sun against one side of her face. She drinks tea with a book in her other hand. At her gesture, I sit down across the table.

"Ms. May."

"Please call me Serene, Mr. Rivers."

"Alright, and you can call me Blu."

"No, but I can refer to you by your name, Blunile, if that is fine with you?

"Yes, ma'am."

Serene laughs. I had not heard her laugh before, and it is a little giggle like a feather touching your skin to make you smile.

"What are you reading?"

She holds the book for me to see, *Alexandria Cornet – A Collection of Stories, Poems & Essays.*

"Oh, is that a good book?"

"The book is expressive as a good book should be."

I hear the alarm for the blue light warning system going off out in the hall. It is not loud enough to put anyone into a panic, but it is to bring help to a room. There is a light over the door to each room to indicate which room has asked for assistance. We don't use the system for a medical emergency, but more to be in tune with psychological-emotional support for someone in need. I don't tend to become involved; we have trained staff to react. I see my sister scurry by.

"Serene, excuse me, I'll be right back." She placed her hand on my arm as she has done several times. I pat her hand. "It's okay." I think she reaches out to give support to let me know everything is okay. As I turned the corner from her room, I see her rising from her chair from my side vision. Maybe after the day's events with the fire drill, a nap is calling her to lay down.

Two doors down, I enter and see Mr. Oakland Dell, our commander from the Korean War. He is pacing and rocking and giving a sense of not wanting anyone to come near him. Our orderly, Terfel, has moved objects away, and my sister is calm and welcoming toward Mr. Dell. I will let them de-escalate whatever is going on with our veteran, who may be experiencing an extended response from the fire drill earlier.

Damn, I didn't see Serene walk in behind me; she is almost to the window in Mr. Dell's room. She sits down at his table, gazing at his marbled chessboard with brass and silver pieces. We don't move; we observe. Mr. Dell has stopped pacing. Serene lifts a bit out of the seat to reach and pull the cord to close the window shade. The room darkens. Sherry turns off the overhead light. Serene pushes the switch for a little piano light to illuminate the chessboard. She makes an opening move. The Queen's Gambit moves the white queen's pawn two spaces forward - d4 d5.

Mr. Dell, from across the room, holds his head up, lifting his chin in almost defiance. He walks over and sits across from Serene and places his elbow on the table holding his chin, rubbing his skin – in the thinking man position. I must believe he is weighing his move options.

In the darkened room, with the right light and silence, masterminds play a war game to bring peace to an unsettled mind. In whatever Serene has known and knows, she understands how to be a liberating queen, a must to bring peace to a troubled soul who once was a knight in shining armor.

CHAPTER

SEVEN

Sherry and I left the room while Terfel, the orderly, stayed inside. He is sitting in the corner, relaxing from a tense situation. Mr. Oakland Dell is past his anxiety attack from the fire drill, but I want Terfel in the area for now, so I brought him lunch and tea and a charger for his phone.

Serene brought Mr. Dell to his safe place with a chess game. Terfel said they had played in the courtyard with a painted chessboard and three-foot-tall chess pieces which are easy for even frail people to maneuver.

I'm going for a drive to refresh. Between the fire drill and Mr. Dell's reset, I need to get away.

I love pulling into my parking space at Blue Haven with my name on the sign that reads, *Reserved for Blunile Rivers*. With my stomach full and my mind at ease from a short nap while at the park, I go in and check on Mr. Dell. He is asleep in his darkened room.

I walk into Serene's room, and she is watching TV. An old black and white show, *The Twilight Zone*, is on. Rod Sterling is talking, but the closed captioning is on instead of the sound. I recognize the episode even with the sound off.

Serene smiles at me from her bed full of pillows that surround her and prop her up. I can't help but feel the connection that she and I have in common – fantasy, science fiction, suspense, black comedy, psychological thrillers – in watching *The Twilight Zone*.

I sit in the corner next to the nightstand; we watch the episode until it is over, and then Serene uses the remote to turn the TV off.

The last of sunset burned through the sheer drapes. I captured slightly different portraits of light kissing Serene like a camera shutter taking time-lapsed photographs of illumination of shadows. She moves her pillows and relaxes on her side facing me. Her hands are in prayer placement under her face and on her pillow. I lean forward to reach inside her nightstand drawer, and I pull out the leather-bound journal.

"Ms. May, may I read?"

She whispers, "Serene."

"Oh, I'm sorry, *Serene*. Do you mind if I read?"

She smiles. "Would you please turn on some music?"

I stroll through flashes of sundown reddish light shining on the polished oak furniture. My shadow changes in sundial time measurements as I move near the console. I hold up an album, and Serene's smile tells me I am on cue as the horns of Miles Davis and John Coltrane proclaim the birth of cool jazz. The volume is low, and I feel a pull to close my eyes and rest.

Another record drops. I think this is the fourth one, if not more. Nancy Wilson is singing, "Saving My Love for You." I see that Serene has fallen asleep, and I release myself from the comfy chair. I place blankets over Serene. I don't think I'll make the drive home tonight. I'll pull out my office sleeper and rest.

CHAPTER

EIGHT

We show our pride in providing a living experience by renovating the closed down wings of this old hospital. Now all rooms have been converted to double rooms by removing walls and adding two large window bays, a dining area, a sitting area, and a standard-sized bathroom.

Sadly, we lost a longtime resident, Mr. Bobby Roberts, who passed away after a long life. Mr. Roberts led a life of historical survival. He was born in Mississippi in the '30s. His mother and father were white, or so he thought, until his teen years when his skin began to darken at an age when facial features exposed something was different. He was teased by classmates that he had coon in him – a way of calling him a Negro or worse. He endured the same name-calling and threats that Negros bore, but a bit less loud. He told his mother what was happening, but not his father. He did not want his father to hurt anybody over what he thought was children being childish.

Mr. Roberts told me his whole story one day while on a field trip to a baseball game. Right before he told me his story, he pointed to the pitcher on the mound and said he was about to throw a pitch that would be a home run. He was right.

The Story as told by Mr. Roberts:

"My mother had the most beautiful auburn hair with traces of curls that other women seem to envy. She was curvaceous and proper in her ways. The boys gawked at my mother as the prettiest woman in town. Mother was a physically strong woman who helped my father build one of the nicer houses around. She could sing and often lead the church choir until the choir director told her to stop singing like a Negro. I remember this upset my mother because she was friendly with the Negros in town.

"In our town, we had a park with a small lake where both Negros and whites were friendly as they fished. Some of the whites would even sit with Negros when they cast their poles. The white and Negro kids played baseball together, but a Negro man knew not to walk in the same path as a white woman. Negros had store hours they could come in, but not at the same time as the whites. We had odd rules of engagement, but we got along for the most part.

"Early on, I showed a lot of promise when it came to baseball. I would play non-stop with white kids and Negros. One day, I was pitching a no-hitter against a high school team called the Rebels. I had hit a home run the inning before, and now with two innings to go, the coach came out to the mound and took the ball.

"He said, 'I'm sorry, son, but you're done. I think they know.' Of course, that was a time a child never spoke up to an authority figure, but I did ask, 'Coach, they know what?'

"My coach stared at me, and I did not understand. I looked around, and a lot of people leaned against the fence in silence. The sun was hot, and the hotdog stand where they sold sodas and iced tea, no one was standing there; they were all – staring at me.

"As I walked off the mound, I heard, 'You better not let that coon throw another ball at our kids.' My father was sitting in the car waiting for me. We drove home with not one word spoken. When we walked in the door through the kitchen, my mother was cooking and was cheerful until she saw our faces. I stood next to my father. I was taller, and my shoulders were broader than his at fifteen years of age.

"Mother sat down.

"My father asked, 'They call him a coon. Is he my son?'

"'Yes, he is your son.'

"I stood scared in the eeriness of confusion because of the question my father asked.

"My mother broke the silence. 'A white man raped my Negro mother when she was fourteen. I am her Negro and white daughter. My mother is a lighter skin Negro. I am what people say...passing. When I moved to this town seventeen years ago, I left my family behind. I wanted a better life than the one most Negros lived because whites treat anyone dark badly. Our son has Negro blood, and I was trying to protect him.'

"The yellow walls of the kitchen sweated from the heat, and as if I could see each drop of sweat, I felt my body become wet. I was peeing on myself, and it puddled on the black and white checkerboard floor. My father looked at me.

"'Go outside,' he told me.

"Ten minutes later, my mother was putting both hers and my clothes in the trunk of our car. Soon, the car was full of possessions. We drove away. We traveled until we were in Kansas City and pulled into a driveway. An older lighter skin Negro woman came out of her house, and it was my grandmother, a Negro woman. My grandmother accepted her daughter and me into her home.

"The following week, I pitched against some Negro baseball players, and I was signed to play Negro League pro baseball. I played until 1957, and I struck out Jackie Robinson more often than he got hits off of me."

I'm going to miss Mr. Bobby Roberts. Blue Haven had an All-Star as far as I am concerned. He left all his possession to us as he had no family, and we are placing a display case in the front foyer to honor his life. Mr. Roberts coached in the minor leagues for both the San Diego Padres and the Los Angeles Dodgers, and they celebrated his Negro League years and his coaching days by placing him here at Blue Haven and paying for his care.

I haven't spent a lot of time with Serene, but I watch TV or listen to music with her from time to time. I love our short conversations, as I learn from her.

I walk past her room when I want to go in and stop time so she and I can enjoy each moment she is alive. I went to a used record store and I brought her every LP they had of Phyllis Hyman. When I played the songs, "The Answer is You" and "Meet Me on the Moon," Serene mentioned a man she loved who played the piano for her and sang, "I Don't Want to Lose You."

Mr. Witherspoon, Serene's lawyer, phoned and told me she needed to go to the Bay Area because of a funeral and memorial service. He wants me to arrange for someone from Blue Haven to escort her, but he would prefer that it be me. She would trust me and feel safe, she has told him.

I agreed to take her on a trip by train. I will love escorting her and protecting her, and I will make sure she's okay. Mr. Witherspoon will cover the expenses including the train, hotel. A town car will drive us from the train to the hotel and take us to the service.

CHAPTER

NINE

I helped Serene up the stairs as she gracefully boarded the train. I assume she has ridden more than a few trains or buses in her life, which is a mainstay of traveling in other countries. I'm glad to be her medical care provider to assess if she needs attention. I want to be available for Serene; I love how she makes me feel about life.

We made ourselves comfortable in the dining car. We admired the countryside through the large vestibule window of the train as we moved along the tracks. I have her journal as reading material accompanying us on the train, and I pull the journal from my travel bag.

Serene reached her hand out as if asking for the journal. She opens the book and flips pages as if searching for something. Her mind is still vibrant, and I know her brain tumor has slowed down the amount of time she speaks sometimes. She hands me back the journal as she turns her head to the window and the vision of the countryside.

The heading date of February 16th, 1947 is on the page.

I'm trotting and walking fast while carrying a suitcase and a large paisley fabric bag. The Greyhound bus is my escape from the South. I'm headed west. It's 1947, and the war has been over for a few years. Soldier boys came home, and it's like they never left. They are back to picking cotton and sharecropping with their families. They are drunk on Friday and Saturday nights at the juke joint, and fighting over women is what they do. Come Sunday, with some reeking of strong drink, they sit in the pews with sainted women they don't take to the juke joint.

I stood at a line of dirty bus depot shacks next to cotton fields along the roadside, reaffirming that I needed to leave my neglected existence. I had enough of being a woman whom men did not respect. I had enough of serving white people and receiving *or else* treatment.

I board the arriving bus and walk unhurriedly down the center of the aisle, looking at passengers' eyes that hold varying degrees of happiness, sadness, fear, and hope. I had no clue what emotion was escaping from my eyes. I was on a ride to freedom. I sit and look at my reflection, and it reveals tired and beaten down on the inside. I didn't exactly know where I was going, but I was going. Maybe to a big city, or a lovely seaside town. No matter where I settle, it will be far away from these cotton fields and these dusty dirt roads.

Soaked from rain, I felt damp sitting in my seat. As a slight chill crawled down my back, I felt cold but destined for the warmth of a better life. I had to get on this bus to release the ugliness of what people took from me; I try to convince myself as I'm quivering from the cold and some fear of the unknown.

I lived parts of my life in a nightmare when it came to choices. My daddy made me marry a man who was 38 when I was 18. Why – I was considered spoiled goods. See, I had a boyfriend before he said I was to have one. I was lying down with a boy when he and I were 16. I'm not ashamed. We had fun rubbing our nakedness together. We'd do it down by the river, in his folk's barn, out in the fields, and during evening church service down in the basement – we sinned and were delivered at the same time. We taught each other what the other wanted, and we pleased each other with no shame.

I had seen grown folks laying with each other before. The man got on top, and if she was lucky, he might suck on her titty a little bit before he humped for a while. He would say, "Oh mama, give it to me, baby," and she would say, "Oh daddy," too many damn times. The man would hump her faster, then grunt, and then he would be done, roll off her and fall asleep.

When my father found out I was no longer pure, he did all he could to put mountains and valleys between my boyfriend and me. I guessed when my daddy humped me, it was okay because he did not go inside me. He just spilled himself on my buttocks.

My daddy had my boyfriend arrested for trespassing, and the judge – whom my daddy worked for – told my boyfriend he had to join the service and never come back to town or he would put him on a chain gang just for breathing. That sentence and threat was the end of my juvenile love affair.

I think my daddy sold me in a way to an older man at his church to wed and impregnate me with his blessing. The man was twenty years my senior. Yeah, not a real older man, but he had broken his back and was limited; he could not do much as far as working his farm, but he had a little more money. He worked for the white man's bank in helping to take away Colored folk's land. Rumor had it, family members would sell their family's property from underneath them – stealing the land. In the end, they work on the same ground they used to own, as it was the only way to have a place to stay. Many elders could not read or write. They trusted their children when it came to deeds and trusts.

I knew why that older man wanted me; I was the prettiest girl in the county. Men always wanted to touch me and be with me. They would say things to me that they would never say to their wives and girlfriends. I was no loose gal, even with the things my daddy did to me.

I had only been with one boy, and it was my choice to be with him. I would have married him, but instead, a man who had no love for me bought me to be a maid and bedmate for his limited sex ability.

As I'm riding on this Greyhound bus, it seems every man on here has left his seat at one time or another and has walked back here toward the back of the bus – slowing down to look at me and smile.

My boyfriend - Sharpley Sparks, he and I had known each other since the first day of grade school. We were close even when we couldn't read a page. From first grade on, he and I were good students. We loved to learn, and we read every book and magazine we could get our hands on as we became older each school year. Sharpley was good in math and science, and I was the best in history and English. We would help each other learn whatever was needed, but that was not often. Both of us consistently scored the highest on school tests, no matter the subject.

When we graduated, we celebrated with milkshakes. We had learned we loved each other by that point, and we had it in mind that we would get married and have a couple of children. Our babies would be intelligent and go to college. That was our plan, our desire. Then the world spun in the direction of being adults, turning our lives upside down. I became pregnant. As is the case with other girls, you married the boy – the father of the child. Boys and girls to wed at the courthouse – never the church by their own free will. Babies made out of wedlock were labeled with unchristian-like names.

I had picked out my wedding day of June 19th, as some scholarly Negros called it, "Freedom Day." I was almost two months with a baby growing inside me, but no one knew except Sharpley. The man I loved asked my daddy could he marry me, and daddy told him if he showed his nappy head on his property again, he would have him arrested or he would shoot him.

Before I knew it, Sharpley was in jail. Then, within days, the love of my life was picked up by a group of Colored soldiers and was off to boot camp. I was sent to my mama's aunt's house a hundred miles away, and I grew with a baby inside me until the birth of a son.

Sometimes I see a child, and I claim that child as mine for a moment. I passed a woman on the bus as I walked to my seat. She held a baby. I look out the window now as I ride this Greyhound bus. The darkened window from the nighttime lets me see my baby as if I was in a movie house. It haunts my soul. My son - they took him from my arms two weeks after being born and sent him to an orphanage for Colored children. My great aunt cried with me and held me as I cried all night long. She did not want to be a part of what had happened, but she felt forced to oblige. My great aunt was where young girls came to have babies ceased. When my mama and daddy brought me to her, they wanted my baby pulled out of me. My great aunt said I was too far along, and it would kill me. So, mama and daddy left me there to have the baby, but I was to give the offspring up once it cried the breath of life.

Eight months later, I came back to town with no baby. I wanted to walk into the raging water and end my life, but it always came to mind that I had a child somewhere out there. I would never want that child to come looking for me one day and find out I killed myself.

Back at home, I hated picking cotton and cooking for white people and avoiding the advances of men – even the white men. One day at dinner time, a man was sitting across from me at the table. Lufer, slick as a bag of snakes, was smiling at me.

My daddy spoke to me, "Fae, Lufer here wants to marry you, and I think it's a good idea. So, after dinner, you and Lufer go for a walk. He promised me he would never hit you or have another woman but you. So, when you come back from your walk, I expect you to have a smile on your face, and then we go down to the courthouse, and Judge Rutt will pronounce you man and wife."

I looked toward my mama, and she bowed her head. My mama was a slave girl as far as I was concerned. My daddy owned her, and he treated her like a slave. All the women I knew were under the thump or belt of their husbands. I'm on this Greyhound, leaving it all behind.

I am determined to be my own woman and be equal to my man. I have no problem with him leading me, but leading is not controlling me.

On the walk, Lufer said all the right things. He owned a lovely house on prime land, he had nice things, and he sounded like he would be good provider, so I agreed to marry him at the courthouse the following week.

It did not take long before I knew I wanted nothing to do with my husband. I would lay under him and let him do whatever he did – which wasn't much. Closing my eyes, I just hoped he would finish soon. He was never romantic, and he never touched me in a manner that I might feel pleasure.

I had tasted mutual satisfaction and experienced a sensual loving touch that made me almost scream with joy. My lover, Sharpley, kissed me as if he wanted my last breath. My lover placed his tongue on my womanhood, and his tongue did the lindy-hop making my body jerk. My lover, Sharpley, had sucked the sweetness from me, making me rain more honey from between my thighs.

The man I was married to, his manhood was stiff, but he could do nothing with it as he lay inside me due to his broken back. I would have to get on top and ride him to make both of us get something out of sex.

I had to stay in that arrangement until I gathered enough papers of proof that Lufer was stealing from Colored folk's land to give the white man through forgeries. Once I had proof, I told him that I had documents in the hands of someone who would go before the church and announce to the whole town his wrongdoings. He knew the Colored folk would shoot him. He had a white man carpetbagger associate who stole from the poor whites just the same as Negros – they would lynch the Negro for being aligned. I had a nail in his coffin, and he knew it. I demanded money, a lot of money, and a divorce, and for him to give people back their property.

Lufer and I never had any babies. Thank God! I inserted sponges inside my womanhood soaked in lemon pulp acid from the rind to prevent pregnancy. My great auntie told me lemons kills a man's baby-making juice.

Now, as I'm on this Greyhound bus, I see a sign that reads I'm entering a new state. I'm not sure of the future, but I'm charting my next life.

Rubbing my temples, I put the journal down and look at Serene. Her eyes are closed, and her head is starting to lean. I know I need to get her to a reclining sleeper chair on the train. While helping her to the area, she held her hand up and said.

"Ladies' room."

I walked her in that direction. She stepped inside but turned to me before closing the door. "Journey to love," she said.

In a sleeper chair, Serene scanned the countryside for a while and then dozed off. I continued to read the journal of the story about the Greyhound bus.

The Greyhound bus pulled into depots. I would get off and purchase a sandwich and use the restroom with each stop. The bathrooms were separate for Colored folks and white people. I started to see less segregation the further west the bus traveled.

Up north, I heard folks lived in slums where they make Negroes all live on top of each other. I read the west had sunshine and ocean water and lovely places to live. I heard about boats, and big ships that come to ports. Until now, I have only been 100 miles from where I was born.

The Greyhound bus stopped in Albuquerque. We had a layover of a few hours, so I walked in the sun and stopped at a Navajo silversmith's stand. An elder lady tapped her earlobes and pointed to the jewelry on a table. I picked up a pair of earrings with round-like blue-green and brown spotted stones wrapped tightly with silver wire.

"Turquoise," the woman said.

"Pretty - I like."

"Turquoise helps to heal and bring inspired ways to move or remove barriers. It is a symbol of romantic love. Turquoise absorbs all that is Earth and the Gods to heal your soul."

I felt my heartbeat slow and steady. "My ears have never been pierced. Where I come from, they call a woman a jezebel if she has anything pierced." I lowered my eyes and chin.

"Look up, young woman, no one can paint shame on you unless you paint it on your soul all by yourself. You are not there, and something tells me you are destined for roads far away from where you came from."

The Navaho woman stood and held her finger up to have me wait. She walked away and came back shortly, holding a cup with chipped ice. She had me sit down, and I put trust in her and in what I thought she was about to do.

"Squeeze this."

She placed a necklace with silver and more turquoise stones and a centerpiece with a crescent-shaped pendant in my hand. I felt a slight burn of cold and then a prick, but it was not painful. She did it to both ears. A few moments later, she held up a mirror. The beautiful earrings highlight my brown skin. The Navaho woman removes the necklace I was squeezing in my hand, and she places it around my neck. I look in the mirror. I had not felt this beautiful since my young lover told me I was the most beautiful woman his eyes could ever see, and he kissed me like it was to be forever.

I wipe tears from my eyes as I reach into my bag to pay for the joy I feel. Not knowing the cost, I did not care. I have small bundles of dollar bills, each bundle is fives, tens, and twenties, and I hand her two twenties. I know forty might be weeks of boarding. I might be able to buy a car for maybe sixty to one hundred dollars. The Navajo woman hands me back a twenty and will not accept any more. She tells me how to keep my newly pierced ear clean and safe from problems. The silver, she said, is also pure, and that helps.

Starting to walk away, I turn back and point to rings of the same type of stone as the earrings now dangling from my ears. The Navaho woman places a rather large silver ring with an oval piece of turquoise stone on my finger. This time the woman does take thirty dollars from me. She said twenty for it, but I insisted she take more.

Closing the journal, I craned my head to look down at Serene, whose head was leaning on my shoulder as she slept. I closed my eyes and believed I had seen the jewelry in the story. I have an account of all her items, and I swear I saw those earrings and the necklace in Serene's possessions. I'm puzzled that it is not Serene's life, yet I think she does have the jewelry in the story. I spent a while watching the train change the background scenery. I opened the book to where I left off.

I walk back to the Greyhound bus depot and take a seat. Through the bus window, I notice a Negro man in a uniform standing by the phonebooths. I was no stranger to seeing soldiers who had come back from the war. They all seemed to be full of themselves with a bit of money in their pockets, but soon those same soldier boys end up picking cotton no differently than before the war

The bus pulls away and travels into the state of Arizona, and I fall asleep. When I wake early in the morning, I see that soldier from back in Albuquerque, and he is sitting across from me.

At the next bus stop, I get off to use the restroom. The soldier and I looked at each other while inside the bus depot. He smiles, and I return one of my own. He walks away with confidence beyond his soldier training, as if he knows a lot. He strides with his head held high. I feel my skin itch from the rising heat inside my clothes. With the richness of his chocolate skin coming out of that green coat and that tan shirt with a green tie, I want to put my hands on his cheeks and slide my finger in those deep dimples and pull out blackberry marmalade.

I feel a bit shameless with my thoughts, which feels good. I feel excited – a feeling I haven't experienced in quite a while. I watch white people move out of his way, and I think, what manner of man is this? I can't keep my eyes off him. We both enter the bus at the same time. I take my seat with some fried chicken they sold outside the depot.

The bus pulls into the city of Los Angeles at sunrise. Palm trees and rolling hills – sights unseen by my eyes before now – serve as a backdrop to so many cars with Negroes, Mexicans, and people from the orient as passengers, with many white people crossing streets and standing on corners. We had another layover and had to switch buses to keep heading North. At this stop, I stay in the bathroom, a little longer to refresh. It is a large bathroom, and women of all races clean themselves up with birdbaths and change their clothes. We each stare straight ahead at the mirrors in front of us to allow the other a bit of privacy in an un-private environment. No excuse to be uncleanly or un-Godly; no need to make the other person feel awkward in being obedient to the nature of God wanting our temple to be kept in order.

Feeling refreshed, I step on the new bus connection, and there was that man in his uniform again. I caught myself staring at him, and he saw me staring. Eye connection leads to recognition of, *here we are again.* He tips his hat with his fingers. I had seen older men tip their hats before, but not country boys. Boorish men with no manners do not impress me.

I want him to speak. *Should I talk first?*

His voice brings me to full attention. "Excuse me, ma'am, are you on a long journey, if you don't mind me asking?"

"No, I don't mind you asking. Honestly, I don't know where I'm going. I may go to the end of the line, wherever that is. I might turn around and stop somewhere along where we've already been. I'm on a journey of allowing life to take me where it takes me with no commitments yet."

"Oh," he said with a kind of chuckle and a wide handsome smile. "I understand; but if it doesn't seem too forward, may I sit next to you instead of us talking across the aisle?"

His smile melts any apprehension. I move my bag and the folding map of all the places I had already traveled and of places that might be next. Soldier man changed his seat, and his wide shoulder touches me. My body shivers just a little.

I get a whiff of refined masculinity as he gets comfortable in the seat next to me. The manly scent he omits is a comfort I have not inhaled in years, and I did not realize I missed breathing it in. I want to take another breath.

I'm watching his long eyelashes move in slow motion when speaking to me. They are hypnotizing.

"I'm headed to Seattle. I have done all that I can in the white man's service for my country. Now it is time for me to settle down. But first…I lost a friend in the war, and I'm taking a few of his items to his people. Then I'm settling in a city called Oakland. I bought a house there."

His voice is a voice one could listen to on a radio in a dark room; it made me feel safe.

"I've been around the world, and now it's time to settle down. I have what is called G.I. Bill money. I purchased a home, and I am opening an accounting service. I did accounting and ordering of supplies in the Army, so my business will be grounded in familiar territory."

"How long do you think you'll be in Seattle?" I asked.

"A couple of days. The Northwest has a lot Negros stationed after the war, so I might visit a few friends and stomp the ground in their jazz clubs."

The way he smiles, I can't help but get lost between his chocolate dimples and enticing lips. We keep talking to almost dawn as we enter into the state of Oregon. I have Seattle marked on my map. It was the farthest city on the West Coast.

We pulled into Portland and transferred to a bus heading to Seattle. Along the way, I see tall trees, raging rivers, and mountains that touch the heavens. The view is all new to me, and it made me think about how powerful God is.

We arrive in Seattle. I see the sun setting as the bus travels along the waterfront. Against blue water, the sky has light clouds and red streaks of sunlight poking through them.

The Greyhound parks, and we exit.

"Now that you've made it to Seattle, I suppose you may turn around and head back to one of the other cities to make a decision where you want to go?" he asks.

"To be honest with you, after talking to you and seeing all the beauty that we have both seen, I think I'm going to get a hotel room here for a few days. I want to explore this option a little more."

"Why don't you and I walk around for a while, and I'll help you find a place to stay. I know of several rooming houses here that are clean, and you'll be safe."

I trust him. I love how he talks to me. He places our suitcases in a locker, and he takes my hand and guides me. After a few blocks, I wrap my arm around his arm as we enter Woolworths. We have a meal with the best milkshakes. I felt compelled to tell him that I want to stay in Seattle as long as he does, and then catch the Greyhound back to someplace in California.

Was I too presumptuous as a woman to say those things? I'm no quick and easy floozy; yet, I'm free to do whatever I want. Why? Because I left from the entrapment of daddy and Lufer and small-town minds down South.

We are standing by a giant clock, and I look up at him. "I want a friend. I want someone I can trust. Can I trust you?" I'm looking up at him, but I drop my head and see the tip of my shoes touching his.

I feel his big strong chocolate fingers lift my chin.

"Can we stop and love like we used to? We are no longer 16. We are grown, and for sure, we need to learn from each other again. I would love to spend some time with you. Let me get you to a rooming house not too far away."

We went back to the Greyhound station and retrieved our luggage. Because of his military uniform, I guess a taxi had no problem picking us up. Or could it be that the west coast attitude is different toward us Negroes? We arrive at a rooming house with an elderly lady who owns the place. I tell her where I'm from, and she happened to be from the next county over.

"I got a nice room for you," she says, twisting her pearl necklace between her fingertips.

I went to sleep that night, and for the first time in a long time, I was happy. I had my teenage love - Sharpley Sparks sleeping nearby. He is all grown up, and so am I.

He had never left me at heart. He sent letters ever since the judge and my daddy ran him out of town. The problem, though, I did not have a chance to read those letters. My mother received them and hid them. She passed away three months ago, and as I was going through her things, daddy said, "Take it all away." He had found another piece of a woman already and was moving her in.

In a trunk, I found years of our life apart in letters written to me. Sharpley Sparks never gave up, even though I never wrote a single letter back to him. When I read his last correspondence, I wrote a letter to where he was stationed in Albuquerque, explaining why he never heard from me.

I asked him to write back to me at the school where I taught the first graders. He had never stopped loving me. He tried to move on, but his heart stayed attached to me.

The first letter he sent I carry with me. He wrote about how it felt to be with me, and he dreamed of resting his head on my breasts as he used to as he listened to my heartbeat.

Serene was tapping me on my arm. I was deep into the story and unaware of how long she had been tapping. I had kept reading on and off, making sure Serene was okay and taking short naps myself along our train ride. She needed to go to the ladies' room. I walked her to the restroom, and we returned to our seats. Both awake, we play two-handed Spades along with chess; she always beats me.

A town car meets us at the train station, and it takes us to the Hilton where we had a two-bedroom penthouse room waiting. It made me wonder how much money Serene had. I was given a credit card for any expenses from Serene's lawyer, and the Hilton and the town car were pre-rearranged.

We had dinner delivered, and soon Serene was asleep in her bed. I went to the large deck and sipped a glass of Merlot. I was waiting for a chance to continue reading, and I did as I viewed the city from the Hilton Hotel balcony.

I dreamed of being in the arms of the man. I relived, in my daydreams, our talks to open a school for higher education to help our people down South. But it was not to be. But what is it now? We had played a coy game pretending we didn't know each other, with both of us wondering if we would still be attracted to the other. I want him. He wants me.

I'm not a teenager anymore, and I don't look like one. I am a woman with a lot of cleavage, and my thighs and behind are hard to hide. I wonder if I am the kind of woman he would want to touch. I contemplate the known and the unknown. I know I loved how he talked to me. I also know I loved just looking at him.

I had told him I resented how my daddy had treated my mother, and how I did not want a man who could not save all his love for me. Sharpley stated that all he wanted was to have me again and be happy as one.

In the morning, there's a knock on the door, and the boardinghouse owner spoke through my door. "The young soldier fellow is downstairs and wants to take you to breakfast."

"Yes, ma'am. Please tell him I'll be down shortly."

"Okay. Outside your door is a bowl of hot water for you." The woman was motherly and mentoring. I opened the bedroom door, and the woman gave me the feeling of my grandmother, who cared about my well-being.

"Ma'am, would you please come back in a few minutes to inspect my dress and hair? And oh, thank you again for letting me take a bath last night in your tub."

"Why, of course, I'd be happy to come to help you in a few, and my bath is the least I could offer a young lady who has been on a bus from the South and traveled all the way here."

I put on a dress and did the best I could with my hair. Sharpley had seen me worn down from five days on a bus, and I did not feel beautiful during that ride, so I'm trying to look a little more attractive.

The woman enters my room.

"Do I look okay? Do I look pretty enough for a man?" I run my hands along my dress to remove any wrinkles.

"Honey, if I were your age, I would do anything to get a man that looks as good as him. You and that man waiting for you downstairs look as to be one."

"One?"

"Yes, one."

A smile comes across my face as we stroll several blocks to a restaurant on 12th and Jackson. Sharpley said this is where a lot of Negroes come to listen to jazz. I was with my man; he pulled my chair out, and he pushed it in when I sat down. They served us Red Snapper and grits. Down home, they serve catfish and grits. I like this even more. I saw plates of chicken and waffles, too, and it all smelled wonderful. A blind man was playing the piano.

After we ate, we walked, and Sharpley placed his arms around me as if he were protecting me. My soul exhaled. I couldn't help but wrap myself around him as I listened to him talk.

"I know you haven't known me long in the sense of what is going on in our lives now, but I would love to make dinner for you. I'm a good cook; all the guys in the service loved when I cooked on Sundays when we had the opportunity. If you let me, I'll prepare a meal for you; but first, I would love to take you to church if that's such a thing that you do."

With the thought of this man talking about taking me to church, I felt myself sweating. I wanted to kiss his mouth, and I want him to put his arms around me. I said, "Thank you, God," as I looked heavenward.

I put the journal down and attempted to get up and check on Serene. To my surprise, she was standing right behind me as if she were a silent assassin. I walked her back to her bed and tucked her in. I don't know why, but I instinctively kissed her forehead. In return, she squeezed my hand as I turned off the light. I needed some sleep as we had to get up early, but instead, I went to bed and kept reading.

Sharpley and I caught a cab to an address over by a baseball stadium called Sick's Stadium. I had never seen a baseball stadium up close. They played baseball in a field where I lived. Everybody would come out on a Saturday afternoon and watch a Negro named Satchel Paige whenever he came to town.

Sharpley asked me to wait in the cab, and he walked toward a house in his military uniform – pressed and clean and orderly as he approached the door. A man answered, and a woman joined him. Sharpley handed them a small box. The couple put their arms around Sharpley, and they all held each other tight for a long moment.

When he came back to the cab, he had a tearful face. He put his head on my shoulder and let it linger there. My arms provided comfort without the need for further explanation as to precisely what he was feeling. Love requires that some things be better left addressed in their own time.

The taxi took us back to the boardinghouse. We decided to leave in the morning and catch the Greyhound to Oakland. Sharpley felt drained from delivering his friend's items to his parents. During the bus ride, he told me the small box for his friend's parents held a ring, cufflinks, and pictures of the young man when he was a boy with his parents. Sharpley's friend had been killed during the war. Delivering the box was bittersweet. He knew its contents would bring joy to the family's suffering hearts, but it also made him remember his friend asking him to deliver it in the last moments before he died in his arms.

The bus broke down, and it is Sunday morning when we arrive in Oakland. I'm feeling nervous, and I don't know why. In longing for Sharply as a young woman, I still have all those emotions and desires. I love this man, even though I have not told him as much. He is a man in how he has treated me, and I want to feel that for the rest of my days.

We gathered our things and catch a cab and arrive at a church. We partake in Sunday service. I loved the singing and the sermon about asking for what you want in prayer, and you shall receive it. Right before service is over, the pastor called out to Sharpley.

"Bother Sharpley Sparks, the church – we thank you for handling our books and ledgers for us. Folks, Brother Sparks found monies we had sitting and invested those funds to expand our coffers and reallocated funds to increase our youth programs. To all the youth, let us stand and give praise with our hands."

I'm watching the whole church clap their hands for him; the youth were the loudest. I became conscious that people might be looking at me, seeing me sitting next to one of their favorite members. I know women in the church! I feel these women had their beady eyes casting spears at me.

Sharpley stood, "To the church, I'm thankful that God gave me an understanding of numbers and the ability to help the church. I want to introduce someone you all."

Sharpley extended his hand to me, and I took it and stood. Being put on the spot, I was glad he let me change into a charming little church dress at the bus depot and fix my hair.

"This here is the love of my life. I have loved her since we were both 16 years old. I have waited for this moment to introduce Stormy Brooks."

I heard deep sighs murmuring. I wanted to look around, but I was frozen in place and having a hot flash at the same time. Sharpley lowered to one knee, and while still holding my hand in his, he slid a sparkling ring on my finger, and he asked me to marry him. All I could do was nod my head. I could not stop shaking. I could not hear a thing, but I began to see people standing and clapping, and they had to be shouting. He stood, and the pastor gave a prayer before Sharply escorted me out of the church.

I stood outside, and he ran back inside to get out the luggage that was just inside the door. We walked in silence two blocks until we stopped in front of a house.

"Your home - this is ours."

The yard had green grass, and there are flowers on the side of the steps leading to a double door. Perfect white paint with blue trim around the windows had me looking up high; there were three stories of windows.

"You - want - me - here?"

"I want you here as my wife."

He lifted my hand to the sky with the ring gleaming in the sun.

I saw other Black people outside on their porch; all had welcoming doorsteps and manicured yards. This house has a driveway, and there is a car parked.

People next door wave as we go inside. There is not much in the house. He has a dining room table and chairs and no sofa or sitting room items. I ask if I can go to his outhouse, and he laughs at me. He says we have two indoor bathrooms, and both are for my disposal at any time. He places his hands on my hips and walks me into a bathroom—there is an indoor toilet, a sink, and a mirror. My eyes widen when I look at the oval-shaped porcelain tub with claw-like feet. There's a stained-glass window, church-like.

I was amazed by this Colored man. There are pots, pans, plates, and glass cups in the kitchen, and he served me ice-cold tea from his refrigerator. He even asked me if I would like some ice in my tea. I have seen all of this in well-to-do white homes down South, but not for Negros.

He removes his jacket and tie and unbuttons two buttons. He rolls his sleeves up. He starts to move about the kitchen as I stand in the doorway. He moves as if he did this for a living.

"Can I help?" I ask.

"Can you peel potatoes?"

"Boy, please."

I was leaning over the sink, peeling, when I felt his hands on my waist. Then his lips were on my neck. I turned, and we were lip-locked as if we were 16 again. I needed air from being excited; we both stood back and then kissed lightly.

Earlier, while in the bathroom, I had removed my bra. Having large breasts and having bra wires cutting into my skin since yesterday, I needed to freshen up my body. I had left my underwear in the bathroom and was only wearing my dress with nothing underneath. I know my body and what it wanted, and I knew what Sharpley wanted; I had felt the hardness growing from between his thighs. I'm reminded of his penetration inside me after all these years.

"Stormy, we need to finish cooking, so we can have dinner."

"Alright."

We acted like teenagers a little longer, and then we went back to cooking. I set the table, and we made our plates. There was a knock on the front door, Sharpley went to answer. I heard several voices, and Sharpley said, "Thank you for your help." Then he came back into the dining room. There was a boy behind him.

"Stormy, I know this will be a lot to deal with, but I have a son. Meet Lamon Sparks."

My eyes felt as though I could not stop blinking.

"Don't be upset, please, because my son is our son. Lamon, meet your birth mother. Stormy Brooks is the woman I have told you about."

I fell in my chair. I'm dizzy, and my stomach is churning. I knew right then and there that the child I birthed, who was taken away, was now standing a few feet from me. How is he here right now and with Sharpley? I'm mad but not enraged. It has been eight years since I last saw the boy's face, which looks so much like my face. I know Sharpley is not fooling with me; this is my child.

I wanted to scream at Sharpley, but I would never do that in front of a child, and for sure, my child must be confused at me. I stood to try to feel my legs under me. I kept a hand on the table as I made my way around. The child was shy and scared, his hand squeezing on his father's arm. It frightens me that my son is afraid of me. My child has his head lowered. That is something I do.

"Are you, my mother?"

I sucked in too much air and almost choked. "Yes, I believe I am. You have a birthmark I called cream in coffee on your chest. I named you Lamon."

"Let me fix a plate of food for Lamon, and we can talk, as I know you probably have a lot of questions." Sharpley turned and went into the kitchen. I slowly approached Lamon.

"May I see your chest please?"

Lamon undid a few buttons, and I saw the birthmark. At dinner I could not eat much as Sharpley told me a story.

"I came back to town after I finished boot camp. I had two weeks before I was to leave to fight in France. I felt your daddy, nor the judge, could not touch me because now I was a soldier. I had left boot camp with some rank because I was brighter than most southern boys who lacked any form of basic education. I came to your folk's house at noontime, hoping to take you away and let you have our baby in a safe place and put you up in a safe place until I came back from the war.

"Only your mother was home. She told me I had to leave before your daddy came home. I was somewhat disrespectful, and I told her she better tell me where you were. She told me they had sent you away to have the baby. She gave me the address of your aunt who lived too far for me to get to you. I could not be late in getting back for our departure heading overseas.

"Not knowing what was going on with you, I wrote to you every month...as you know. I did not hear back from you. When I came back from the war, I found out you were married. All that I'm saying is that I have told Lamon some of what has happened. I went to your aunt, and although she does things, I'm glad she did not do it to you.

"Your aunt took me to an orphanage a few towns past her, and she told me to look for the birthmark. That is how I found our son. Damnit...the orphanage was a working farm for young Colored boys. Lamon was picking cotton at four years old.

"The Colored people who so-called ran the orphanage/slave camp did not want to give up Lamon. I left and came back two weeks later with a bunch of my soldier buddies. We were in uniform and had guns; we removed all the boys who wanted to leave. Most left with others and went in another direction. The couple who ran the orphanage, we took them hostage and moved them 100 miles away with just the clothes they had on their backs. We left them in a Klan town, so they had other problems than holding onto modern-day child slaves.

"All of the boys now have families. You saw a few at church today. Lamon and I have moved around a lot because I was still in the service, but I am blessed to have found an extended family here in Oakland; so when I had to be somewhere else, he was safe, and Lamon has been in school and is doing excellent. Then I get a letter from you after all these years; I dreamed you would want to be with me and be with your son." Sharpley exhaled like his body had been holding onto the story for centuries.

"I am troubled but thankful for you being the man you are in wanting your child, and to have rescued him. I hurt over our child having gone through troubling times because of us. Yes, us first being young and putting our child's life at risk for creating him when we did. I look at you, Lamon, and I don't know if I make sense, but I have missed you since you took your first breath. Can you and I stand, and let me put my arms around you and hold you as I did when you were born?"

Before I could start to stand, Lamon was in my arms while I was sitting. He sat in my lap and squeezed me. I looked over to Sharpley; we were both crying. He reached out for my hand, and I grabbed his.

"Please tell me you'll have the both of us," Sharpley said to me.

"Yes, please let us be a family, but both of you are going to have to let me learn how to be a mother and a wife."

"We have to learn how to be a family, and we will."

After dinner, Lamon and I walked our neighborhood. Neighbors waved from their porches, and we stopped by a park where kids played baseball. I had a chance to push my son on the swings.

Later, the three of us were on our knees as we said prayers. "Dear God, thank you." I put my son to bed and tucked him in.

Although there is not much furniture in the house, there are bedroom sets in both rooms – that counts the most.

Sharpley and I are under the covers in his big poster bed, as we are creating man-to-woman friction. The moonlight comes through to make shadows on the walls. We join as one. His tongue is tasting all of me, and I am doing the same to him. He has not entered me yet because we are taking it slow, attempting to make up for the lost time of being the lovers we were meant to be. He turns me on my stomach and kisses my spine inch by inch until I lift my ample behind high and wide. I want him inside me.

"Please let me feel you inside me. I - I - I want you to make another baby inside. We must give our son a brother or sister, and it must be now. I feel myself being ready. Please, please, please."

I feel hardness going inside me, and it hurts and feels excitingly great at the same time. I push into his thrusts; it makes me want more, and I ache. We stay in the lusting drive. My man was on top from the back, and then we swapped, and I squatted over his girth while he lay on his back. The sounds he made drove me to ride him as if I needed him inside me to live.

We are sweating as we both groan and moan. I wanted to feel more of his driving hips over my full behind while on all fours; I buried my face in the pillow to muffle my uttered pleasures. I feel released pent-up life flowing inside me. We stay connected, and I support a relaxed weight on my back as his lips suck on my skin. I angle my body to keep his river of life inside me until I could not hold that position any longer. We curl into each other and sleep. We wake and live for the future as one, always making up for a lost time - forever.

I'm sitting on my bed. What I read became intense and left me with thoughts of confusion. I know it was not Serene's life, but it seems so true.

Reading in bed usually makes me sleepy, but I'm wound-up, even though I need sleep; but damn - a ninety-year-old woman wrote a story that has me wanting the feel of a woman, and I see it when I close my eyes.

I lack sleep as we enter the waiting town car. The night before, I had pulled out a dress for Serene from her luggage. Serene wears a flowing blue dress that did not come off the rack. Her hair is in a natural style as it usually is, but it is more on point this morning. White gloves cover her fingers up to her elbows. Silver and turquoise earrings adorn and frame her pretty face, and a necklace of the same help announced her presence. Cassandra must have packed them for the trip.

I dress in a suit in a lighter shade of blue than Serene's dress, but she has a silk-like shawl around her shoulder that is a close match to the blue I have on. I feel a sense of being a prince escorting the queen, but she does have royalty in her bloodline.

We arrive at a cemetery, and we walk toward a gathering of people. Serene places both her hands on my arm as we walk on soft ground, but she walks stably and seems focused.

Two caskets are above ground. A man approaches us and extends his hand in a very welcoming manner.

"Aunt Serene…you are here. Thank you so much. You are the light I need to see. Sir, you are Mr. Blunile Rivers?

"Yes, I am."

"I am Lamon Sparks. Over there, speaking to some church members, is my younger sister, Serene."

"You are Lamon Sparks, and that is your sister named Serene?" I ask, although he has already said he was.

"Yes, I'm not sure how much you know, Mr. Rivers."

"Call me, Blu, please." I'm talking to a man older than me, and I wanted to drop some of our formality. "I know some. My main reason for being here with Ms. May is to keep her safe."

"I understand. Well, if you don't know, my mother, Stormy Brooks-Sparks, passed two weeks ago. My father, Sharpley Sparks being broken-hearted, he joined my mother. They always wanted to be together as people decades ago tried to keep them apart, and I was a part of the reason."

Serene had both her hands on my arm. "The journey of love," she said to both of us.

"And Ms. May is your aunt?" I collect my beliefs from the first story I read in the journal that Serene had a sister she was supposed to find.

"A long story, but I'll make it as short as possible. My mother thought her parents were her biological mother and father, but they adopted her. My mother found out when Ms. Serene May came to our home one day. She told my mom that her father had fathered a child, not of his wife. Yes, Aunt Serene is my mother's sister of different mothers, but the same father.

"I've known my Aunt Serene since I was nine years old; and oddly enough, I had just met my mother the year before." Lamon lowered his head, "This is a story for another day, but my Aunt Serene had a daughter, my cousin Sabine. She has been deceased now for about forty years. We all traveled together as my Aunt Serene, mom, and dad were intellectuals and believed in us learning about the world."

Lamon's sister came to us and put her arms around Serene. Serene released her hands from my arms and let herself absorb their embrace. I saw a tear slowly roll down Serene's face. I know she wanted to talk, but I knew it was hard for her now.

"Hello," the woman said to me. "I am Serene, named after my aunt here. We are so happy you brought her. Today is a sad day, but it is a little more bearable with our Aunt Serene."

I nodded while I was trying to fight being weepy.

Serene's niece came face to face with her aunt. "Auntie Serene, this is so hard. I'm a 55-year-old woman, and I thought I would be ready when this time came, but my legs are on shaky ground."

Serene placed her hands on each side of her niece's face. "It is okay to fall because getting up is what you do as if taking another breath. Fly above turbulences in life as to be air streams of peace. You are now the rock the treacherous ocean slams against, but the rock is a barrier. We all wear down in fractions, but still, we stand like a rock to build a house upon."

I place my hand on Lamon's shoulder. "We need to find a seat for your Aunt Serene."

We walked to a seat that had Serene in the center. A double funeral proceeded. Afterward, Lamon and his sister walked us to the town car. They both held Serene. She pulled out of her purse a large oval piece of turquoise held tight by a silver band. Serene placed the ring in Lamon's hand. Then she tried to remove the necklace from around her neck. I understood what she was doing, and I helped her remove the necklace and earrings. Serene handed them to her niece.

"Your mother and father handed these to me when I found her; there was no exclusive reason, other than they wanted to gift me for searching and finding them, but they now belong to you." Serene's voice was at whisper level, and she cried.

On the train ride going back, Serene slept most of the way. Before she fell asleep, she said she wrote the story in her journal as told to her by her sister Stormy. What saddens me is, most likely, this is the last time her niece and nephew will see her alive. The lawyer asked me not to divulge Serene's progressing tumor in her head. I'm here to protect her first and foremost.

CHAPTER

TEN

The door to an emotional bond opened for Serene and me since we came back from her sister and brother-in-law's funeral. I feel like I am family. I become close with all my residents and enjoy spending individual time with each of them. Blue Haven is more than just a business; it is a home for people who need family in the later stages of their life.

After the train ride and growing closer to Serene, I had a conversation with her lawyer, Pierce Witherspoon. We sat in my office after hours and relaxed. I pulled beers out of my mini-fridge, and we talked for hours as I learned about his father's past relationship with Serene as her lawyer, and his current workings. He spoke of schools she started in different regions of Africa. Those governments paid her rather well and still pay her. She invested money in training centers to teach people to start small businesses by becoming vendors to supply big companies here in America. Corporations fund them, and, once again, Serene reaped the financial benefit and expanded her portfolio.

I was left with *oh wow*. Serene chose to be here as part of the Blue Haven family. Serene could be in her own home receiving all the help needed or wanted, but I get to see her each day and listen and learn from her.

Serene has landed inside my soul, and now I share with her what is going on in my world. There are days I'm talking away and telling her about things I have done or want to do. When I'm puzzled, a few times she has made me realize that I have the answers to my dilemmas. She leaves me laughing at myself at times.

I'm in her room now to share an ongoing mental kite that keeps diving to the ground in my life. "Serene, I seem so far removed from being with the right woman. I know I told you before about the woman who left me for another man because he needed her after 9/11. He was injured, and she went to be by his side right when I was about to ask her to marry me. What I didn't say is, strangely, she calls, and I take her call each time when I don't want to."

"You do want to take her calls. You feel connected to a past when you were happy; but each time, that kite you speak of drives hard to the ground, but you manage to put it back together to answer her call again.

"Blunile, tell your past lover, you will always love her, but please let you go, and that she needs to give all of her devotion to her husband. You insist on this by never taking another call from her again. Men who had been in my life, I am friends with their wife or woman, and I do not carry on a lively connection to the man. I cut them off but will always admire them."

We were sitting in the bay window in her room. It was windy outside, and the trees and shrubs danced out of time, but I felt a clock inside me say it was time.

I swallowed hard, and Serene leans in and touches my face. "Blunile, you should also tell the other young lady to leave you be."

"DeJohnette?" I had not said much to Serene about DeJohnette, but sometimes, as my father would say, *we don't realize how much we have revealed to give ourselves away to those who are observant.*

Serene nodded and removed her hand from the side of my face. "It is wrong to give a woman hope, when there is none. It is no different than the woman who calls you and breaks you each time you answer. You know the reasons you hold her at arms' length; that distance will not change, and you know this."

"Yes."

"Leave her be." Serene has an undemanding voice but with a conviction of what is right.

"I have thought about how to tell her. Do I meet with her and make it clear we need to stop talking, or do I email or text, or do it over the phone?"

"When it is over, no matter how you end the relationship, the agony and the blame will shift to how one became aware of the end more so than the anguish of the fact it is over. There is no right or good way. Just be honest in your message. Do not hurt a woman and place condemning guilt on her, leading her to think she is the problem. For another man will love her as she is if you cannot."

"Serene, you always make it make sense."

"You always know the answer before you ask when you reflect on right from wrong. Blunile, I have not heard you recite a poem in a while, would you please?"

"For you, I will. Let me think. Can it be a bit spicy?"

Serene chuckles, and a smile overtakes her face.

I look down to the courtyard and see our French couple living their life in wheelchairs, but their love is binding to be as one. I see their love for each other when they stare at each other; it inspires me.

"EYE TO EYE
Behind your eyes
Let me make love to you
No need to remove your clothes
No need to lay with me…yet
I see behind your eyes in my dreams
We see the same
We feel the same
And I'm going down inside you
Deep in your sweetness

I'm pulled into daydreaming about you with every tick-tock

To have smelled your scent in my dreams

To have tasted you from behind your eyes I know your taste is sweeter than butter pecan ice cream

I see behind your eyes in my dreams

Why, I was daydreaming ... walking and holding you up tight against my thighs and making love to you like the ocean washing ashore

I see behind your eyes in my dreams

Locked in one on one, you and I are in an intimate mental journey

No need to remove your clothes

No need to lay with me...yet

To be near to you...all in my mind, near you in need for the final solution

You are the answer

Your eyes smile and your lips part and your voice slips into my ear as I take a nap

You are my 3D dreams of you and sliding your tongue in my ear.

No need to remove your clothes

No need to lay with me

I see behind your eyes in my dreams

But when I do open my eyes and you are here

Let's pop each other's pimples and then...let me see you from head to toes

And make love to you eye to eye"

CHAPTER

ELEVEN

We are on a charter bus with twenty of our residents headed back from an overnight stay in Palm Springs. A group of our more physically fit residents golfed with celebrity host pros. The pros were former NBA and NFL players who are up in age, but who play the game rather well. They took the time to show our golf players from Blue Haven a few tricks of the game.

Those who didn't golf sat by the pool.

Serene went along on the trip. At times, it appears she is slowing down and gives me worry she might be doing too much. Some days, a burst of energy shines through, and she wants to move about as if her time is unlimited. That makes me feel good when anyone does that, but I am watchful of her.

On the golf course, I teamed up with Serene; she did the putting. I would drive the golf ball to each putting green, and she would then putt. She was pretty good. While we were in our golf cart waiting for others to hit, I ask about her past sporting life.

"When my daughter was six or so, I took her to Saudi Arabia where I had met a prince. He took my daughter and me to many sporting events all through

Europe. He was an avid marathon runner, and I applied myself and did half marathons over the years. That prince loved to golf, so my daughter and I received lessons. Of course, women were not allowed on the golf course at that time, so the prince had the golf course cleared, and he and I and my daughter played. I love the sport, and my daughter loved golf as well as tennis.

"Sabine might have been a great tennis player. My adorable friend, Althea Gibson, gave her a start by training her. You may have heard of Althea; if not, look her up on the Internet. Althea was great in tennis during difficult times for a Black woman. A Negro woman, as we were titled, was almost hidden from view in the 1950s unless you were a maid. Althea eventually turned into a pro golfer, and she and I spent many hours playing golf.

"Keep in mind that it was viewed as unladylike for women to compete with men on any level. I haven't had as many opportunities to golf over the years, but I did go to the putting range; I enjoy that part, as it is kind of like chess in a sense."

The heat and long days and the bus ride have most everyone sleeping. A few are watching TV on their electronic devices.

I brought Serene's journal with me to read, but last night I had fun playing poker with our celebrity host pros, the former NBA and NFL players. I went to bed at 2:00 a.m., maybe later, and was back up for brunch to help watch over our group. Cassandra put this event together, and I am proud of her and her dedication.

I'm sitting beside Serene, who has the aisle seat, so she can go to the bus bathroom if need be. Cassandra is asleep in front of me with her head moving around on the window. It is a good thing our charter bus had comfy wide seats.

I open Serene's journal, and I hold it out for her to maybe find a story she might want me to read. She turns a thick group of pages, and I see Egyptian-like art above the heading, Windy City Blues – July 5th, 1948. The art is a man and woman facing each other. I'm not sure, but I think the art is called hieroglyphics.

Tired. His eyes close for a moment, and not only did he hear the rain pelting the street, but it's almost as if he can see the rain trying to invade through an umbrella. The rain, in its constant ant-crawling drizzle down the window, annoyed him, but it also kept him going. On this chilly night, as usual, he answered the call of duty to his job. He was the best; he was desired. He was counted on to count. In the end he had no choice but to tango in the mist, even though the work hours were disagreeable to the nature of his body's clock. Closing the final book for the night, he cracked his neck and knuckles. The sound of escaping tension filled the air around him like echoing sighs. Tension always had a way of seeping deep into his bones and marking its territory; tonight was no different. The work-related ache claimed ownership over his body, and he rubbed his lower hip while pushing the chair he had been sitting in closer to the desk in front of him. The cure-all pill he received from Dr. Johnson's pharmacy, two blocks from his apartment, never seemed to deliver relief. He couldn't wait to feel the warmth of a hot water bottle and some Epson salts once he made it back to his side of town. Big Ma's remedy for relief never failed.

For now, the client came first, as always. The people on this side of town often gave the hours of sunlight to the business of lining their pockets and chose the cover of darkness to do the laundering of those pockets. The chiming of the hour clock meant nothing.

The hands of the clock in the hall in front of him point to the 9:00 p.m. position. An epiphany brings about a smile...*What's soiled during the day, often comes out in the wash,* and to his clients from the southernmost side of Chicago...he was the wash.

The large suite where he was providing his services had high ceilings and gorgeous chandeliers; but the overpowering artificial light was beginning to give him a headache. His client always provided grand accommodations for him to do his work; but grandeur is sometimes overrated when all you really want to do is get up from the underbelly of the shady business that you are doing.

Money can't buy peace of mind; but it can romance it for a while.

Ms. Tension, his high-anxiety mistress of a headache, nags at him once again; reminding him of her presence. Rubbing his temples brings only seconds of temporary relief. It had been a long night of checking the books, but he found comfort in that fact that this was the last time he would have to do it. He had been lured by this lifestyle for more than a decade; but now, the thought of finally being free of the slime, which seemed to drench him inside and out from being on that side of the law, was refreshing to his mindset.

Getting into the bookie business had been a necessity for Malveaux, at one time, to make ends meet. By most people's standards, the new job title had been a promotion. He had started off running numbers when he was in his teens. White mobsters were notorious in Chicago; but Colored gangsters weren't doing too shabby, and with a lot less attention paid to them by the authorities. Negro convictions made headlines at about a third of that of whites, so chasing them was not important until time for quotas.

During those tender teen years of his life, one of the most well-known of the Colored gangsters had welcomed Malveaux into the fold with open arms. Although he was young at the time, he wasn't naïve. He knew what being a part of *that* family and lifestyle meant; he also knew the cost of the alliance. But to him, the bottom line was financially easing some of the stress off of his parents. Family always mattered first to Malveaux, and grinding in the streets gave way to meat on the table, even if it meant he had to be someone other than who he was raised to be.

When he first entered the game, Malveaux was a streetwise stud; built mentally and physically. Just ripe for molding by his new bosses. They figured he could hold his own if someone tried to jump him, and his long legs would help him move quickly if he needed to get away from the police or his bosses' rivals. Luck was on Malveaux's side. His speed and agility were only tested once or twice. They had proven their worth each time. While initially getting the number running hustle had been easy for him, trying to get out of being an actual bookie when he was in his twenties had been quite the opposite. Easy turned to hard, and hard had turned into impossible...that is until today.

In a world where you trust no one and tests came often, the bosses always felt spotlights on them; but more so lately. He felt the men above him, who acted without a second thought to make you disappear, might have their sights on him as nearing elections put police on a mission to clean up the streets of Chicago. The heat coming down on his bosses pushed his understanding that he did not have long to be safe. He had to create a new world for himself if he wanted to avoid being in a prison cell, or being earthworm food, or even becoming a forgotten name.

There was never a day while in the game where one could relax. Malveaux had washed the books with an almost religious ceremony. He made the unclean clean. His extraordinary IQ managed to make gambled-away wages thrown in the gutter smell like spring flowers after the rain. All while also creating a reputable business career on the side in the process.

Tonight, he was going to elevate over the sidewalks with the metal grates and hot steam that made one slip and fall into a hell where killers and thieves roamed. This is his gamble to step out into a world free of his bonds to this illegal lifestyle. Hours in the tiny, but dignified hotel suite had been the last moments of dutiful service to the benefactors who had been his overseers for most of his young adult life. Tonight, he could shed the web of entanglement, and be no longer corrupt for others. When the new day comes, he will be on the other side – free and clean.

Walking backwards to exit the room, he turned off the lights to the chandeliers, deeply exhaled, and slowly closed the double doors behind him. Instinctively, he threw the hotel keys for his conference suite up into the air and caught them effortlessly when he began to walk down the long corridor. Cold elegance surrounded him on both sides as he passed hotel room after hotel room. As usual, he heard fake sultry, lustful sounds from slightly upscale hoes earning good money. The suits and ties had fetishes they could not acknowledge with their wives and girlfriends. They often sounded like wounded animals or could be heard taking hedonistic orders. The room across the hall from his room had two men who were always loud in the throes of sex; but one wore a dress, high heels, and a cheap wig, while both wore wedding rings. Chuckling in the moment, Malveaux found himself engaged in soulful whistling. Music is the soul's comforter. He wasn't much of a singer, so no words bore fruit, and there was no song dictating the rhythm of his lips; just a soul that was happy, free, and expressing itself musically.

The elevator door opened; this was probably the last time he would pass through it. His heart rejoiced. He welcomed a humble life, free of pretenses. His body relaxed against the cold glass mirror behind him as the bell announced floor after floor while he descended.

Reaching the bottom floor, he walked out of the elevator and into the Palmer House foyer. Shiny tiled floors, waxed to a high shine, massaged his journey with every step. The ceiling of the Palmer House held one of the most enchanting interiors in Chicago. It had twenty-one individual paintings on the ceilings, and Malveaux had studied and counted each one over the course of his numerous business assignments there. Upon his exit, he counted them once again, still amazed by their intricate details.

Giving the keys to the receptionist at the front desk, he smiled and walked out the front door. The heavy cross of his slavery of stealing and hiding away an empire of wealth had handcuffed him for a long time. Malveaux relinquished those chains and allowed them to exit his body. As he descended the stairs, he took a moment to stare back up at the top of the stairway to get one last glance at the Romeo and Juliet statues that had greeted the Palmer House guests since its opening. He was free.

"That's a love that has withstood the test of time," he murmured to himself as he continued to walk down the stairs to the valet area.

"Where to, sir?" the concierge asked as he picked up the courtesy phone to call for a cab.

"Home. I'm just trying to get home."

Stepping under the covered awning to wait for his cab, Malveaux's mind began to relax and wander. Although his body still ached from the tension of the night, his headache no longer had life. Dense drops of moisture were developing in the scattered clouds as they played hide and seek with the moon. Malveaux's mother had always told him not to fear the rain, but to welcome it instead. His head leaned back, and his eyes looked upward in appreciation of the heavenly connection. The angels were crying; he felt sorry for their sadness, but happy for the chance to bond with them through their wet expressions of love.

Off in the distance, he sees a young man waiving to a woman several feet ahead of him. At first glance, Malveaux senses they are out of their element. The well-to-do Colored population lives on this side of town; it is clear this young couple is far from their comfort level. The rain dances harder, and neither of them have an umbrella. Being naked of protection from the steady beating of rain does not seem to bother either of them. Anticipation of uniting in love serves as their shield against all enemies.

As the young woman's attention meets that of the young man's, she instantly runs toward him and jumps into his arms, wrapping her legs and the entire lower portion of her body around him. Mutual desire dries the space surrounding them momentarily. His tightly fitting jacket was too small for his frame and barely served its purpose amid the winter weather. The jacket could not keep bread warm if already in the oven. Her skirt was that of a much older woman; it was too large and hung sadly on her slender frame. She wore a wool sweater, and the rain had it sagging; for sure she would not want to hang it inside afterwards for the wet smell would permeate the air. Their physical appearance and clothing suggest that money is not a friend of theirs, but love seems to be their main source of day-to-day sustenance. With the young woman still attached to his upper torso, the young man carries her to a covered doorstep of a closed establishment across the street from the hotel. Rain no longer soaks them, but their passionate kisses continue to swaddle them like a blanket from everything outside of their embrace.

Envy devours Malveaux for a moment. He had no love. He had no family anymore, and family he desired. He wanted to be a man of the house, a father, a protector and provider. Unable to continue to view a future outside of his reach, pride makes him look away and focus on his cab, which has arrived.

"Where to, sir?" the cabby questioned as he enters.

"The south part of the Black Belt – the other end of South State Street. I'll point out the exact location once we get closer."

"You got it, sir."

The driver pushes the taxi meter to the on position and makes a U turn just as the rain begins to pour down harder. The Black Belt of Chicago is only about thirty blocks long up and down State Street, but it never ceased to amaze Malveaux what a difference a few blocks made in the social and economic status within those blocks. Four city streets pass by them before the cab comes to a complete stop at a red light. Staring out the window, Malveaux notices a woman standing at the corner ahead of them. A large black umbrella serves as defender of the trench coat within its belly. A blue satin knee-length dress peeks from the bottom hem of her coat. His cab ride has entered the middle-class section of the Black Belt now, and it's hard for him not to notice the air of moderate grace surrounding her person. Her legs are long and slender, catching his eye, and he can feel miniature waterfalls forming within his mouth. He had always been a leg man, and his eyes had often betrayed him when it came to inconspicuous admiration.

Every movement she makes, even if slight, garners his attention as she steps off the curb trying to hail a cab. Firm and unyielding calf muscles flirt with him from the distance between them, and he feels the need to save them from the storm. Leaning forward from the backseat, Malveaux asks the cab driver to pull over so he can share his ride with the mysterious woman standing in the rain.

"Pull over here. I can't leave her like that. It's going to be hard for her to get cab in this weather at this time of night. Pretty women shouldn't be damsels in distress. I'm in no hurry, and I will not have someone assume she is less than a lady and out here working the streets. Clearly, she is not, let's take her wherever she's going and then you can take me home after that."

"You got it, Boss. Your dime buys my time. The meter keeps running no matter if I got one passenger or two," he replies as the light turns green. He puts on his blinker and quickly pulls over to pick up the additional passenger.

She knew she should have left earlier. The weather was definitely slowing her down, and tiptoeing through puddles of wet misery was getting old real fast. She had spent hours picking out her dress and getting ready. The blue satin dress spoke to her above the others in her closet. It begged to be part of the gaiety of the evening. Tonight, was definitely her night; she could feel it in her soul; she just should have gotten her act together a bit more quickly before heading out the door. She had been walking in the rain for five minutes, but that was five minutes too long when you are wearing three-inch heels. When the cab pulled up in front of her, she was a taken off guard, as the medallion light was off on top of the cab. The driver either had a passenger already or was off duty. Nonetheless, the cab was stopping for her, and who was she to look a gift horse in the mouth when it came to a warm, dry ride through the rain.

The door opens, and a man looks out. "Excuse me, Miss. I apologize if I have startled you in any way, but I must offer my taxi to share."

"Share?"

"Yes, please...it was difficult for me to look out and see you in this rain. It appears you are trying to be someplace else, and I couldn't pass you by without at least offering to be a gentleman."

She slightly squats and peers inside to make sure there was, in fact, a cab driver behind the wheel.

"It's too nasty out there to be waiting on a cab. Hop in and allow me to share mine with you."

Deep base tones lower her guard even further. She had always been a sucker for a man with a deep voice. Normally, she wouldn't accept a ride from a stranger; especially a ride with two men in a car late at night...but the gentleness in his eyes and his warm welcoming smile put her at ease. Besides, her matching satin shoes begged her to take a chance on his offer so that they could resist destruction from the falling rain.

Looking around her, she notices that the streets are becoming empty; her chances for another cab coming along are bleak. Her mind weighed safety versus a gallant deed.

"I promise...my intentions are only to get you dry and out of the rain." Moving as far to the other side of the back seat as possible, he continues, "I will stay on this side of the cab until we get to your destination. I swear I will keep my hands to myself and you are safe with me. Just allow me to make sure you make it wherever you're going tonight."

She glances from the backseat up to the front seat and back again. Gallantry was the victor, and she prayed she had chosen wisely. Collapsing the big black umbrella, she places one satin shoe inside, and slowly brings her other foot inward to enter the cab.

"You two aren't some type of Jack the Ripper killing duo, are you?" She was half joking and half serious with her question.

"Don't look at me...I just drive this piece of shit. Oh, I'm sorry. Please excuse my manners. I'm speaking alley talk in front of a Miss, but I can assure you the man sitting next to you hasn't killed me or anyone else on my route since I picked him up," the cabby answers from the front seat with a witty smile.

"Well, ma'am, Jack the Ripper killed ladies of the night, which clearly you are not. Leaving you out in the cold and rain, hoping that you will get a cab...now *that* would be a true crime. My upbringing taught me better than that...my only deadly trait is a constant need to be chivalrous."

Unbuttoning and removing her coat once inside, she gets comfortable on the faux leather seat beneath her. As she folds it neatly next to her, she feels two sets of eyes fixated on her every move.

"Okay, I like your gentlemanly ways so far, but you cannot address me as 'ma'am' unless you plan on staying a gentleman." She gives him a playful bat of her eyes. "And I'm removing my coat because the cabby here has the heat on coal furnace hot. You two act like you've never seen a woman before. Don't get any ideas. I know how to handle myself."

"I bet you can," the driver whispers under his breath before turning around to face forward and wait for further instructions.

Between quick glances at her outer thigh, which has become exposed through the slit on the right side of her form-fitting dress, Malveaux tries to regain focus on his noble intent.

"Ma'am, something tells me you're one tough cookie. Maybe I am the one who should be worried about his safety…not the other way around."

"Maybe you're correct. One should never underestimate a woman."

They snicker slightly between them, and she gives him a wink while smoothing out her dress and relaxing deeper into the cushioned seat.

The driver loudly clears his throat, looks back at Malveaux in the rearview mirror, and points to the meter on his dashboard.

"I think he's trying to say we can't stay here all night. We better get going. Where are you headed?" he asks while moving his eyes away from her thighs to make eye contact.

"The east side of State Street; right at the junction of Garfield Avenue. Cabbie…5521 South State Street, please," she states loudly while tapping on the seat divider.

"That's the same area I'm going to. There has to be something special going on other than you grabbing a bite to eat at this time of night."

She rubs her hand behind the nape of her neck and then lightly brushes her fingers through her hair so that the edges rest comfortably and seductively behind her ears. The slight shimmer of her pearl drop earrings catches his eyes; majesty is revealed. He can't help but notice how beautiful she is even under the dim overhead light from the car's interior. Reveling in the sight before him, he is relieved that she can't detect his arousal from her view. This time his body is an ally; it remains calm instead of betraying him. The space between them on the backseat proves to be a much better idea than had been his intent when taking refuge within the distance.

"I'll take that as a compliment," she blushes and lowers her eyes. "I'm actually headed to the Club DeLisa. I'm sure you've heard of it."

Batting eyes accompany a bit of smugness in her statement...or maybe it was just her way of trying to impress him. Either way...Malveaux liked the bait she was throwing at him. The DeLisa Club was arguably one of the most prestigious venues in the city, falling in line behind the Regal Theater. Not only had he heard of it, but he had done a lot of business there for some of the patrons of the DeLisa brothers. He wasn't on their payroll, but the four brothers who owned the place often sent business his way.

"Yes, I've heard of it; anybody with a heartbeat has. I'm very familiar with the place. Are you going there for business or pleasure?"

"A little of both," she replies before folding her hands in front of her chest. "A girl has to have a few secrets; I'm more interested in you sharing yours than I am in revealing mine."

"Fair enough. We've got a bit of time on our hands 'til we get you to the club...so what do you want to know about me?"

"First off, it would be nice to know the name of the hero who rescued me from the storm," her eyes and body language court with him through each word. He welcomes the attention of both.

"Well, I don't know about the hero part, but for my family and friends I answer to the name Malveaux." From his side of the backseat, he takes her gloved left hand in his own and kisses the top of it. "Malveaux Adero...that's me."

"Malveaux, huh?" she mimics the actions of a southern bell and fans herself with her hand while leaning back against the window beside her. "Well, if that isn't a fitting name for such a gallant man, I don't know what is."

She makes a sound at the end of her statement, and to him it sounds like she is purring. He can't distinguish whether the sound is wishful thinking on his part, a product of his imagination, or if it is subliminal seduction on her part; but either way...the purr and that dress of hers are working him to the fullest.

"I guess I should introduce myself as well. My name is Serene...Serene May. But if you are saying the right things, I'll answer to almost anything respectful."

Malveaux couldn't help but smile. Everything about her so far demanded a recognition of her femineity as well as her ability to demand a certain level of recognition of who she was.

Changing positions in her seat, she leans in his direction with her legs crossed one on top of the other. In doing so, she shortens the distance between them on the backseat and places her other attributes within his view. The leg man now pays attention to ample perky breast begging for the same attention that had been given to their counterparts.

He knew his eyes were betraying him once again, but this time, he knew that betrayal was being solicited. He felt a little sweat under his collar, and he shifted his hips while moistening his bottom lip.

"Your name sounds like it originates from the Bayou. Men from the Bayou are intriguing to me. I met a man there when I was at a summit once, but I haven't been to the region for a very long time. When I was there, I experienced quite a few 'firsts' in my life. It was a time that I still hold dear.

"I'm not from the Bayou, but there has always been talk within my family about us being a mixed breed of French, African American, and Native ancestry. Maybe it's a flaw of mine, but my life has been more focused on looking forward then it has been on looking back. I've always been too busy making a living to dwell on the origin of my life. Maybe a time will come when I can step back and get the chance to enjoy researching all of that, but right now, I just do my best to live up to the strong-willed name I was given. I pray that I can make a name for myself based on the man that I am now. I have studied the stars, the moon, and Egyptian philosophy."

"I like that. We have to live for today and hope the strength of our ancestors will propel us in spite of ourselves and any flaws we may have as a result of our ignorance."

She looks out the window. This trip is one that she takes at least twice a month. Even with the darkness outside of her window, she knows there are about ten blocks remaining before they get to the club. Time is getting short, and she wants to know more about the handsome man she is sharing the ride with.

"Mr. Adero, you know where I am headed…what has you out on this cold ugly night?"

He can't help but notice she is rolling her lips to smooth her very red lipstick as she asks the question. Slowly, she rubs her hands along her legs, enjoying the feel of the satin dress against her fingertips. His instincts tell him to nibble on the bait she is dangling in front of him, but his mind steers him to stay in the gentleman role he displayed from the moment his cab pulled over to her side.

"This dreary night is actually the beginning of brighter days ahead for me. I'm headed home after my last day at my current job."

She looks him up and down again and he can see her mind is trying to answer the questions floating around inside of it.

"You look way too young to be retiring from anything, and yet, you don't seem unhappy about no longer being employed. Something tells me you weren't fired. From the calmness in your voice, I sense you are happy about separating from whatever it was you were doing. What exactly did you used to do, and why did you quit?"

Malveaux lowers his head slightly, shaking it side to side. She was proving herself to be just as tough as he thought she would be when she entered the cab. Brains and beauty – an intriguing combination in his mind. He had been a private man all of his life, but in that moment, his solitude met her honey and sugar. It wasn't his normal inclination to share his personal business with others, but something about tonight seemed different to him. The air in the cab felt different than any other ride – lighter, cleaner, more exhilarating. His mind felt different – willing to share a part of itself with someone outside his comfort zone. She was different – a breath of fresh air from the others he had met before her. His life was about to be different, and tonight was just the beginning. He felt that deep down inside of him, and surprisingly to him, he welcomed and accepted it. Before he could talk himself out of it, he began to do what he wasn't used to doing...he honestly shared the truth about his world.

He leans into her so that the cab driver cannot hear his confessions. "Are you sure you aren't some sort of femme fatale spy for a rival or the cops, because you are very good at quickly getting to the bottom of things. I can tell nothing gets by you easily. While I wouldn't say that that you are right that I 'quit' my last job, I will say that it was a mutual agreement that I won't be doing it anymore. To make a long story short, I'll just say I used to travel on the wrong side of the tracks and now I have crossed over to the other side. Tonight ends my street booking career. I'm on my way home after having severed the last ties with my old life. Tomorrow is a new day - one filled with legitimacy and the legacy of my name on the doors of my own accounting business."

As he talked, her eyes surveyed his total presence. His hair was perfectly trimmed without a strand out of place. His smooth caramel face was clean-shaven, and even though it was late in the evening, she could still smell a hint of manly oakmoss Aqua Velva aftershave as if it had recently been applied. The charcoal gray suit he had on fit him as if it had been tailored specifically for him. There was no doubt about it, he was well put together down to his highly shined black oxfords and the gold chain hanging from his pants. The chain disappeared into his trouser pocket, and she knew a pocket watch was attached on the other end. She was having an inner laugh thinking he would be a gorgeous man one day when he is old and walking with a cane. The watch was a distinguished touch in her eyes. She liked what she saw as she looked at him, but she liked his mindset most of all.

Respecting his need for discretion from the prying ears of the driver, she leans in to whisper her response. "Wow. I never would have taken you for someone skirting the law. I guess you can never tell what is in a man's mind. Money runner turned visionary, huh? That's very ambitious, I'll give you that, Malveaux. Ain't nothing wrong with a man having a vision."

The distance between them affords a whiff of each other. Animal attraction tells them they are approaching rituals not meant for their current circumstance. They realize they are closer than either of them intended, so they pull back from each other a bit.

"I never looked at it that way, but I guess you are right and I'm about to walk into my vision."

The city blocks outside of their window had transformed from spacious landscapes with sparse buildings to a crowded downtown area filled with skyscraper after skyscraper. Brighter lights illuminate the roads, and neon lights point to late night taverns, restaurants, and establishments of ill repute. They have reached the heartbeat of the Black Belt. One block separates their current location from the DeLisa club, and as the cab gets closer, she realizes she doesn't want their encounter to abruptly come to an end.

Being forward has never been an issue for her, so she takes the lead. "You asked if I was out tonight for business or pleasure. Given all you just told me, I think a celebration is in order. Why don't you escort me into the club and give me the pleasure of helping you celebrate your new business?"

The cab comes to a stop a few steps ahead of red carpet leading the way from the curb and under a large blue awning. Large bulbs spell out *Club DeLisa* above the awning for all to see. During the twenty-minute ride the rain has stopped, and a line of people has formed in front of a rather large doorman dressed in a tight black suit who is eyeballing all who enter. Malveaux looks at the line, the bright lights, and the beautiful woman on the seat beside him. A few seconds pass as he weighs her offer against the lonely one-bedroom apartment that is to be his destination. There's no comparison in his mind. She had threatened him with a good time, and her invitation sounded like a much better celebration than the hot water bottle and Epson salt he was initially looking forward to.

"If you can make me the same promise that I made to you when you entered this cab...then I would love to."

"And just what promise was that again?" she says as she sits back in the seat once again.

"That you will keep your hands to yourself," he says with a wink and a smile.

A sultry laugh escapes her lips. "Let it be known...I make it a point to never attack the unwilling. If you're unwilling concerning any of my advances, then consider yourself safe from me and my advances. I promise to keep my hands to myself for as long as you want me to; but I make no promises if you feel the need to become a willing party."

She winks back and reaches for the door handle to exit the cab. The slit in her skirt exposes her thigh again as she turns. Feeling the strength of his glance, she knows there is no way he will allow her to get out the cab alone. As predicted, a warm touch captures her arm mid-reach.

"Allow me to get that for you."

Gallantry precedes him as he quickly gets out and hastens to her side of the cab. The front passenger side window is down and he looks into the cab at the meter to learn the fare for their ride. In his mind, it's a paltry amount to pay for having had the opportunity to connect with the mysterious woman in the rain, so he adds a hefty tip to the amount owed and hands it to the driver. Instinctively, Malveaux straightens his suit jacket and then licks his fingers before running it through the slight cowlick in the front of his head. He had never been a vain man, but he wanted to make sure he matched the beautiful woman who was going to be on his arm. It was unclear to him whether she or he was the intended arm trophy for the night, but he wanted to make sure he looked the part either way.

Opening her door, he says, "After you," while reaching in for her coat. "Allow me to warp your coat around you."

"Why?" she responds. "Since it's no longer raining, all that will do is block the view. This dress is meant to be seen."

"That it is. That it is." He agrees while draping her coat over his arm and running a little to catch up to her as she sashays to the front of the line at the door. His eyes are glued to her backside; he appreciates watching her sultry poetry. The large bodyguard nods at her. It's clear he knows her, and she is working him just as hard as she is working the blue satin dress. With each sway of her hips,

Malveaux is intoxicated. *I'm in a dance and the music is getting faster; I'm not sure who's leading, but I'm enjoying the dance*, he thinks to himself as he matches the pace of her seductive stride inside the club.

Malveaux is no stranger to the inside of Club DeLisa. When he first became a bookie, he had worked the gambling tables in the basement and made up the *policy slips* for the Colored folks in the community who placed their bets there. However, back in those days, he mostly entered through the back doors and wasn't an actual patron of the main portion of the club. Seeing the club from this vantage point made him glad he had stepped out of his comfort zone and joined her for the evening.

As they approach a second bodyguard on the inside of the club, Serene comes to a halt. Placing her fingers to his lips, she says, "Hold on, I've got this. Watch me work."

Malveaux lets her handle her business. Up until this moment, she has been a woman in charge and he has enjoyed the ride; he had no reason to add any speed bumps to her flow now. As she talked to the bodyguard and pointed at available tables, Malveaux allowed his senses to devour the sights and sounds around him.

Club DeLisa was owned by the four DeLisa brothers, who were of Italian descent. It was a hot spot for the African American community. A sea of Black and tan patrons, dressed to the hilt as if they were royalty, filled the building in anticipation of the round-the-clock entertainment and vaudeville acts that took place there. Originally a speakeasy until the end of prohibition, Club DeLisa had some of the greatest comedians and dancers in the world. It had showcased performers like Frank Sinatra, Red Saunders, Count Basie, and Sun Ra who played there among other great jazz legends. Most nights consisted of a variety-show format, and full course meals were offered for breakfast, lunch, and dinner.

Malveaux's mouth began to water with the smell of oregano and spices from the Italian dishes, as well as the aroma of the crispy fried chicken; the two mixed together and attacked his nose. Oversized white sheer drapes, with burgundy and gold ropes holding them in place, hung around the stage as well as at the doors to the entrance of the kitchen. Autographed framed photos of local

Chicago artists as well as musical greats like Nat King Cole, the Ink Spots, and Sammy Davis, Jr. covered the walls. He watched as cocktail waitresses went from white linen table to white linen table taking orders, while the ten-piece house band with a baby grand piano in front of it belted out jazz, blues, and rhythm and soul music. His body began to sway in unison with the brass section that hit hard with their Count Basie big band sound. The trumpets, saxophones, and trombones struck chords in soulful harmony. They tilted their horns up and down simultaneously. The slight choreographed moves they pulled off while playing was mesmerizing. With a heavy bass line walking in between horn riffs, the grand piano played with the melody like a child had found a new toy and would fight anyone who tried to take it away.

Conked hair flip flops to each side of the male musician's head. Most women and men in the club had the same hairdo, although the men's hair moved around and the women's hair stayed in place.

Looking back over his shoulder, searching for the whereabouts of his date for the evening, Malveaux sees the conversation between her and the bodyguard come to an end as she kissed her fingers and touched the center of a five-dollar bill, and placed the money in his hand before they both walk in his direction. The bodyguard escorts them to a cozy table right in front of the band. Malveaux pulls out her chair for her, and as they take their seats, a single candle in the middle of the table is the only thing between them. Just as the waitress comes to their table to take their order, the MC for the night comes out and announces that it is amateur night.

A round of applause is heard as the MC details the different variety acts that will be performing in hopes of capturing the evening's monetary purse that will be given to the winner.

"Without further ado, our first act needs no introduction as she is not a stranger to any of you. She was last month's winner of this show and if you haven't heard her soulful voice before, you are in for a real treat. I now present to you Miss. May and her rendition of "Long John Blues."

Bright lights from the stage become dim and the spotlight changes its direction, focusing on their table. Shock engulfs Malveaux as he watches the MC hand the mic to his mystery lady. Sultry is the electric guitar melody that introduces the song and the songstress as she rises from her seat and begins to walk on stage. A gut-wrenching hum from the bottom of her belly fills the air before she seductively sings part of the chorus, "Long John, Long John," setting up the song while ascending the stairs. Once fully on stage, her back is turned toward the audience, giving them full view of her voluptuous behind as she begins to tell a story through song.

I've got a dentist who's over seven feet tall.

Yes, I've got a dentist who's over seven feet tall.

Long John they call him, and he answers every call.

A sway of her hips garners applause, cat calls, and whistles from the audience in the smoke-filled room. She feeds on their excitement. Working the room like a true professional vocalist, she turns around while belting out more of the dirty blues lyrics,

He took out his trusty drill. Told me to open wide. He said he wouldn't hurt me, but he filled my whole inside.

Watching her body gyrate, Malveaux is lost in lust. Dinah Washington had a distinctive voice and sexy style all her own; but he is amazed at how close his mystery woman comes to mimicking and impersonating that style and technique. If he closed his eyes, he was sure he could be fooled into thinking Dinah was actually on the stage in front of him, rather than the woman he met in the rain.

The waitress drops off their drinks. Engrossed in the performance, he finds himself leaning forward and grabbing for the dark-colored hooch in front of him. The room and his collar are getting hotter by the minute. He loosens his tie and needs the drink to calm himself down. The woman from the rain was becoming more mysterious as the night ticked away, and he is captivated by everything about her.

It is clear to everyone in the club that she is at home and in her element. She holds the audience captive with her version of the lewd lyrics. Like a pro, her voice paints a picture of the sexual allure and prowess of the dentist with the "golden touch." She delivers each stimulating metaphor using her body movements as her brush. The performance is racy, provocative, and sensuous – a stimulant for the passionate soul.

Her voice rises to a crescendo as she gets to the last line of the song. Delivering the final words, she looks Malveaux straight in the eyes as if they are the only two people in the room and she is speaking directly to him.

Long John, Long John...don't ever move away. See...I hope I keep on aching, so I can see you every day.

After singing her last note, the acoustic guitar ends the song with the same melody it started off with. She takes a bow, and the MC comes back on stage and escorts her back to her table. Malveaux takes her hand as he pulls out her chair for her to sit. His eyes are fixated on every inch of her as she eases down, but he lets her soak up the clapping of the crowd before he says a word.

"You really are full of surprises. Little did I know when I offered you a ride that I was picking up a famous celebrity. With a voice like yours, I should have known you were some sort of professional singer."

Blushing, she pats her pretty face and the sweat glistening on her neck and cleavage. He reaches into his suit coat front pocket and pulls out his monogrammed handkerchief.

She nods her head and uses his handkerchief to dab herself dry before replying, "I'm not a famous celebrity, nor am I a 'real' singer. This is just something I occasionally do to make extra money on the side. The way I see it...all Colored women can carry some sort of tune in a bucket; it's in our lineage. We're born knowing how to at least hum. Holding a tune is the easy part for us. It comes naturally. What's hard, and more impressive, is the presentation. It's all about giving the people something they can feel. Singing is not my passion; storytelling is. What you just saw on that stage was my attempt at good storytelling. I'm just lucky that sometimes I get it right and I'm able to tell a story in a manner that is good enough to compete in amateur shows like this so I can collect the money purse at the end of the night."

"Well, if you are that good at something you *aren't* passionate about, I can't wait to see how you perform at things you are passionate about."

"If you play your cards right, Malveaux, you just might get that chance."

Their conversation is interrupted by one of the club's bartenders coming up to their table. As he approaches, Malveaux smiles and stands.

"What's up, man? I thought that was you, so I had to come over and chop it up with you. I haven't seen you in here in a long time; especially not on this floor of the club. What have you been up to? It's good to see you relaxing instead of having your eyes cemented in the books for my cousin's retail store."

"It has been a long time, and you looking at the new me. All work and no play makes for a dull life. I'm trying new things now."

"I can see that," he says, eyeballing Malveaux's date. "You sure know how to pick 'em. I saw you staring at her the same way you stare at them numbers. I swear I didn't think anything could hold your attention unless it was number or money related."

I need this fool to move on. Standing here talking company business like this. He knows he should not be talking shop before, during, or after. But I'm stuck with his arrogance and ignorance. I give every man a fair shake. I give every man, woman, and child the best of me. I'm a patient person, but this is pushing boundaries. He does not know if I have business or pleasure going on with this one-of-a-kind woman. I don't know a lot about her, but I know she is not to be played with. Clearly, she is on the level of any man, and much better than most. How to handle this? I'll just have to let it play out.

"My man...you still in comedy? You should be up there on the stage right now like the man that is up there making people laugh. It is quite a feat to make people think about something they should not be thinking."

"Me? Who me...doing comedy, huh?"

I'm staring at him hoping he gets a clue, but he is clueless. "I'm grateful for the DeLisa brothers bringing me all of the business that they have over the years; your cousin included. It's actually been my bread and butter and has been the tool I needed to be able to finally open my own business on my own terms. Like I said...you looking at a new me, and I'd rather not talk about it right now if you know what I mean."

"Yeah, okay, I got ya'. Just know...success looks good on you, man. Well, I won't distract you from this beautiful woman any longer. Have a good night, and don't do anything I wouldn't do."

They both laugh before the bartender respectfully nods in Serene's direction before walking off on his way back behind the bar.

"Okay, Mister, is it true?" she asks him while taking a sip of her hooch.

"Is what true?"

"Is it true that numbers are the only things that you enjoy looking at?"

They both know her question is loaded. Malveaux takes a few seconds to look deeply in her eyes before responding.

"Actually it's numbers, hieroglyphics, and now...you."

"I like that answer," she replies with a wink.

They continue to watch the other acts for the evening, and finally the MC returns to the stage to announce the winner of amateur night. Malveaux hadn't seen any of the club's variety nights before, but he wasn't surprised when Serene May was awarded the $40 purse for her performance. He knew he was biased, but he thought she was the most talented of all of the acts that night. When the MC gives her the cash award, she counts the money, stuffs it in her cleavage, and takes another sip of her drink before turning toward him.

"Congratulations on the new you. The next round is on me."

The problem with being in a club that never closes is that time has a way of escaping. Before they know it, the wee morning hours are upon them. Laughter, smiles, and mutual attraction have chaperoned their evening together. Neither of them wants the night to end, but they both know that it must. They leave the club and Malveaux hails a cab. As luck would have it, they get the same cabby that brought them together. That seems odd to Malveaux, so he hesitates before opening the door for the two of them to get in. A small concern in his mind was that he and Ms. May had talked of business in the cab, and it might have been overheard. One never knows who to trust in the world he walked in but was now striding away from. The driver leans over to the passenger side of the cab and tells them that he usually hangs around the area trying to get the last-minute late-night fares before going home for the night. Malveaux wonders if the driver is speaking the truth or if he actually came back around and waited for them. *And, what reason would that be?*

Sensing Malveaux's hesitation, the driver tries to seal the deal. "Hey, it looks like you two had a good time tonight. Clubs can be loud and are not the best places to get to know each other. Before calling it quits for the night, why don't you let me take you over to Lake Shore Drive so you can take a walk together. You are my last fare for the night; I wasn't pulling your leg about that. I actually like seeing you two together, and I'm in no hurry to get home to the old ball and chain."

Serene likes the thought of spending more time with Malveaux, so she grabs his hand before he has any more time to rethink the ride.

"My first ride with you two was safe, I'm sure this one will be as well. I see the look on your face. Yes, I know what you're thinking, Malveaux. He's a cab driver for God's sake. Let him do his job and drive."

They get in the cab and the driver takes them to Lake Shore Drive. He goes to a spot that is secluded with easy access to the waterfront. Parking the cab, he tells them to take their time and enjoy the view; he'll wait. As Malveaux comes to her side of the cab to help her get out, she asks him to wait a minute so she can take off her shoes, opting to walk barefoot along the lakefront. Following her lead, Malveaux takes off his shoes as well, then taps the side of the cab, telling the driver that they will be right back.

"For your sake, I hope not. But I'll be right here when you get back," the driver replies as he turns off the light on the top of his cab, takes the baseball cap off his head, places it over his eyes, and reclines in his seat watching the couple walk off toward the shore.

A gust of wind blows off the rippling water and she wraps her arms around her shoulders to shelter herself from the breeze.

"Here...take my coat," he says, removing his suit jacket and placing it around her shoulders.

He loosens his tie and takes her hand in his; palm wrapped in palm. It's the first time that she actually had a chance to feel a part of his flesh against hers. The strength of his grip makes her feel protected. A full white moon stretches across the horizon. Water ripples glisten in front of them as the sound of waves hitting rocks serenades their moonlit stroll.

He squeezes her hand. "I must admit, I knew today was going to be a great day for me, but I had no idea how great it would be. Thanks to you, I actually feel like I had something to celebrate. Something about you has me wanting to know more."

"What do you want to know? Now that I know you aren't some sort of serial killer, I guess it's safe for me to be more open with you."

Her guard is down and he welcomes the chance to learn more about the woman who has taken his mind off of work; something most women haven't been able to do.

"The woman in the rain, the woman in the cab, and the woman on that stage all were very intriguing; now I'd like to see the woman behind all of them. Who is she? That's the woman I want to get to know."

She had heard many lines in her nearly three decades of life, and she had run a few lines herself; but his words seemed genuine. She wasn't sure if it was the way he carried himself, the exhilaration of performing, the hooch, or the hypnotic effect of the shore...but whatever it was, it led her to remove the wall she usually put up.

"I'm an old soul – I feel that if we can learn from the past, we can direct the future. Currently I am a substitute History teacher at the high school, but my real desire is to get accepted as a professor at the university and eventually become part of the faculty for the History Literacy Exchange Program. It teaches and lectures locally, nationally, and abroad. Getting to that goal takes small steps over time, as I bide my time.

"The substitute teacher pay is not very good, so when my girlfriend told me about the variety shows at Club DeLisa, I decided to enter their shows whenever money gets tight. There aren't many legal ways for a woman to get money on the side...well, you know what I mean. As I told you before, God gave me a half-decent singing voice, and I used to sing in church all the time. It's not a passion of mine, but I decided to use what momma and God gave me. I let the voice and a tight dress help me when money is tight. I can cover all my bills with the sub pay, but getting a purse from the club sometimes means the difference between a decent meal for dinner and an open-faced sandwich to save on meat and bread. I'm a party of one. I like it that way. I like not having to worry about anyone else's comfort or security other than my own. As long as there's a roof over my head for shelter, everything else is optional as I press toward my goal."

He feels her hand tremble in his; he is unable to distinguish if the chill of the night is the cause, or the vulnerability within her words. He knew she was sharing a side of herself with him that she was uncomfortable sharing; he felt special knowing that she undressed her emotions in front of him.

"A wise woman once told me there is nothing wrong with a man who has a vision; I think the same can be said about a woman as well."

He wanted to kiss her, but he felt like a hug was needed more than intimacy. Pulling her close to him, he held her tightly and kissed the top of her forehead. The scent of vanilla and gardenias emanated from her hair, encapsulating him. Gentlemanly manners confined any other feelings he had. Her inner beauty, struggle, and strength all needed his acceptance and comfort; there was no way he could allow himself to do anything to belittle or cheapen that need.

Their embrace seemed to last a lifetime. Neither one of them wanted to let go of the other. What had started off as a rainy night in the Windy City with two people going in different directions ended up with the blues leaving its note on souls uniting. There was more than an intellectual attraction going on between them; there was the oldest kind of chemistry swirling in their blood when they held each other. They both cherished the moment enough to know that all things were best enjoyed in their own time.

They make their way back to the cab to find the driver asleep behind the wheel in the same spot where they left him. Malveaux says, "It's really getting late; or should I say it's really early since it's practically morning now. I need to get you home. Let me wake this dude up; he can drop you off first, and then I will have him take me back to my place on the south side of town. I'm sure he won't object to the bonus fare."

She agrees and they wake the driver in order to bring the evening to an end. As the ride starts, she lays across the backseat with her head in his lap and her feet on the ledge of the back window – allowing the wind to dance through her toes. As he rubs his fingers through her hair, Malveaux chuckles within at her free spirit. He has never met a woman like her before and he enjoys the uniqueness of who she is. A woman like her was not meant to be tamed; it was the beauty of who she was. With each stroke he bestowed on her head, he thanked God for the night, the rain, and the opportunity to breath the same air that she did.

As they pull up to the address she had given the cab driver, Malveaux felt a bit of uneasiness surround him. They come to a complete stop and he tells the cabby to wait while he walks her to her door.

"You got it, Boss," the cabby says, leaning back and pretending not to watch the events unfold in front of him.

Malveaux walks her to her doorstep. Holding both of her hands in his, he says, "I had a great time. Let's do this again."

"Ain't no time like the present. Why don't you come in? I want to show you something."

Reading her face, he ponders whether her desire to continue their connection is really as strong as his. It's unclear if her statement to show him something can be taken on face value or not, but he's cool with where she is going in whatever capacity the statement allows.

"Just a minute." He runs back to the cab and unrolls several bills from his wallet. He knows he is overpaying the driver handsomely for his time.

A smile crosses the driver's face as he holds the bills up counting them. "Boss, something tells me she has more in mind than you bargained for tonight when rescuing her from the rain. I think the heavens have smiled on you. Run with that."

"Well, my man, the flip side of that is I guess I can't be your excuse for not going home now. Enjoy the rest of your evening, albeit morning now."

Malveaux taps the side of the cab for the last time. Jogging back to Serene's doorstep, he places his palm into the small of her back and follows her inside.

Upon walking into the tiny apartment, he is struck by the uniqueness of her living quarters. Much like the woman herself, her livingroom is eclectic and unparalleled. From ceiling to floor, distinctive artifacts give life to intellectual thinking. Stretched across the entire length of the main wall of the room is a mahogany bookcase that houses more books than he can guestimate at first glance. Harbored between the sofa and oversized sitting chairs, a large ocean-blue swiveling world globe sits on an oakwood tripod. A cozy windowsill reading nook splendidly shares the world outside her window, and it is garnished with large plush throw pillows on one end, and stacks of notepads on the other end. With all of the handwritten notes on the pads, and all of the books on the floor in front of the nook, he can tell it is her favorite spot for working as well as relaxing.

She tosses her keys onto a tray next to the door, kicks off her shoes, and hangs her coat on a wooden coat rack next to the door.

"Make yourself at home. I'll go find what I wanted to show you."

His eyes become glued on her as she heads toward the bookcase. He unbuttons his suit coat and sits down on the curved-back crushed velvet couch in the center of the room. Once directly in front of the bookcase, she steps up on a small stepping stool. He stands up, as he is still not comfortable. Removing his suit coat, he lays it across the arm of the couch. After pacing the room for a bit, he takes a seat on the couch. He glances at the length of her legs again as she raises her leg behind her in an effort to reach the top of the bookcase. Envy toward the dress's fabric for being lucky enough to caress her behind takes up residency in his mind.

"I know it is here somewhere," she says out loud as she reaches further for the top shelf.

His eyes are still glued to her behind. He tries to turn away so that she doesn't witness him staring, but he has already been caught in the deed.

She gives him a sly grin, knowing and enjoying his undivided attention. Finding the particular book she is looking for, she steps down off the stool. Curiosity is killing Malveaux as he watches her walk toward him carrying a massive book with leather binding. She plops down next to him, sitting on top of one leg while the other hangs over the side of the couch. Moving her hair out of her face, she places it behind her ear and scoots closer to him. The shortened distance is welcomed.

"I know you probably think I wasn't listening when you mentioned it, and that I was just busy soaking up the compliment being given at the time...but back at the club, you mentioned your interest in hieroglyphics. In that moment I connected with you and you didn't even realize it was happening. I've never known anyone who had a fascination with hieroglyphics, but I did have to take a class on the subject as part of my undergrad study. That was an interesting semester. I learned a lot about the historical significance of that writing system."

"Studying hieroglyphics is a side passion of mine. I don't share that with anybody, but I shared it with you."

"Exactly," she says, excited and moving closer. "Given that this topic is right up your alley, I'm sure you have seen everything in this book; but in case you haven't, I thought you might like to have this."

She hands him the colossal book and scampers off into the kitchen.

"I'm going to grab us something to drink and to coat our stomachs," she tosses over her shoulder. "Take a look at the book. It's yours if you want it."

He flips through the pages in amazement. Surprisingly enough, the book is not one that is a part of his personal collection. It is composed of the origin and history of hieroglyphic Bibles.

"Definitely not light-reading material," he says partially out loud, yet in a tone slightly above a whisper. *Leave it to a History teacher to use a book like this as foreplay*, he thinks to himself.

"I have used hieroglyphics in my books when recording money coming and going, and the names and places of where things transpired."

She speaks to him in a loud voice from the kitchen. "I had a thought you might have done as much. With your high IQ, I imagine you have a treasure trove of uncanny ways to use knowledge to not just survive, but to thrive. I'm sure there's much we can teach each other. Just so you know, I meant what I said about not attacking the willing; so don't think I am trying to get you drunk and have my way with you." He can hear her laughing to herself from a room away. "But I do want you to feel comfortable. I only have one beer, but I have some wine that I have been saving for a special occasion. I hope you agree with me that tonight is a special enough occasion for me to let it breathe."

"The wine is fine. Thank you," he says, distracted and fascinated by page after page of syllabic and alphabetic elements. A part of him, being the daydreamer he is, wants to add more hieroglyphics to his life no matter what he is doing. He feels a kinship to times of long ago when Negro queens and kings sailed over to the new world long before America's history book will ever acknowledge.

"Good! I was hoping you would say that," she says, appearing out of nowhere and placing a tray of fruit and crackers, as well as two half-filled glasses of wine on the table in front of them.

She reaches for large green grapes. Watching her place them in her mouth is a diversion from his book perusal. The attraction of the book takes a backseat to his attraction toward her.

She asks if he likes the book, and small talk ensues between them about their mutual love for history even in abstract forms. A citadel of love was being created between them in the tiny room. Fruit and wine served as their nourishment. If her living room walls could speak, they would cheer on the intimate uniting of their souls.

Over a few more glasses of wine between them, and while flipping through the book that brought him to her home, the couple grows closer mentally as well as in the proximity of their bodies. The spark of a flame ignites into a fire. He has been staring at her body all night long, but he stayed in the lane that made her feel comfortable enough to let him sample her world. As her pretty mind rambled out her intellect, he enjoyed the physical connection; yet he longed to move beyond the roles established.

In the midst of jam-packing knowledge and moments in history for him to digest, and while illustrating the commonality between them, her mind was racing to find ways to taste him. She recognizes that for most of the evening, she had been forward...*why change now?* Something inside her told her that the time was right. Seduction had not been her intent when inviting him to her apartment, but she could feel in the vibes she was getting from him that the moment was right to establish a new intent. Putting down a half empty glass, she takes his glass out of his hand, closes the book between them, and kisses him.

"You bookworms move much too slow. Action speaks louder than symbols and numbers," she says as she kisses him again.

He welcomes her kisses with more passionate ones of his own. He had been waiting for this moment all night. The knight in shining armor routine was cool in the beginning, but he wanted nothing more than to show her a side of him that carried more than just chivalry and manners. He wanted to give her the moon, the stars, and love in a way that only a man can deliver.

"In hieroglyphics, symbols speak volumes and demand action. I always act when prompted to, and as I told you...three things have gotten my attention lately; let's focus on the most recent one and the one that is intriguing me the most...you. Many hieroglyphics are based in love, sex, and marriage in ancient Egypt. In a way, as you sit next to me, it could be we are an example of a sexual hieroglyphic."

Malveaux stood and stared down on the woman's face. His heart beat to a rhythm his body had never danced to before. Never had a woman filled him completely, especially in such short amount of time. He smiled as his mind said he could be with this woman forever; yet he didn't know nearly enough about who she was. What he did know, as he stood over her and she gazed up at him, was that she was a woman to love as she needed.

Serene took in his long leopard-built body. She focused on the obvious hardness in his trousers, and she knew he wanted her to see his girth. It made her eyes widen. He was living caramel-covered hieroglyphics.

He leaned over, and, at the same time, she pulled his shirt collar hard and forcefully. Their tongues tangled, and she stops him briefly – releasing his shirt to ask a question.

"I told you that I don't attack the unwilling...is it safe to assume you have moved into the land of the willing now?"

He leaned in closer and spread his thick lips on her neck. Sucking the fold between her ear and her shoulder, he kisses her and whispers in her ear, "I'm ready, willing, and able."

His manly hands couple her face, and he kisses her passionately while crawling forward on the couch. Her body slowly falls back into the cushions until it is covered by his. She reaches down to his trousers and unbuckles his belt. A mountain of lusts awaits her as she slides his pants down in the front and over his behind in the back. He moves with her willingly; sheer elation seizes her as she feels every inch of his body harden at her touch.

Malveaux's hands hug her from under her torso, and his fingers find the zipper going down her back. A simple downward stroke brings the semi-hard on that he has had all night to notable heights. The shaft between his thighs grows in anticipation of reward.

As they each own their part in seducing the other, the area surrounding the floor of her couch becomes cluttered with her clothes and his as they each aid the other in making flesh on flesh a reality. Her breathing becomes rapid as his hands outline her breasts; her nipples sing glory at the pressure and attention they receive. Their bodies pressed together bear deliciously wet fruit that they both can no longer resist tasting. Malveaux stops mid-grind and stares deeply into her eyes. For a few seconds, they allow the moment to speak for itself.

True love asks for nothing, yet it gives way to everything.

Handling her warmly, his initial insertion brings forth an exhilarating sigh. The tightness and warmth of being inside her, although previously unknown, feels comfortable and as familiar as being at home.

She tightens her arms around his neck in a desire for his body to melt into hers with every thrust. Their bodies dance a dance of life-long lovers united in thought, mutual satisfaction, and deed. If her living room walls could talk, they would now tell a tale of lust relinquishing itself to climax.

As Malveaux pioneered the two of them through peaks and valleys of ecstasy, the words from Dinah Washington's song played simultaneously through both of their minds.

"Long John, Long John...don't ever move away. See...I hope I keep on aching, so I can see you every day."

The impromptu meeting and the naked tango that happened the night they met was long from being only a one-night stand. They wanted and desired more of each segment of who they were to be shared with the other. Being in each other's presence was a daily essential. They met often for long walks; enjoying the sights and sounds of Chicago. They visited museums and enjoyed listening to street musicians while eating Chicago Style hot dogs made with Vienna Beef and infamous deep-dish Chicago pizza. They became a team in many ways, even going back to the club of their first night, but now both of them would go up on stage together, performing a comedy routine of teasing and mocking each other – and each time they did it, they won. Resembling two teenagers in love, they often made out in movie theaters just for the hell of it, before going back to her apartment for a night of full passion.

Malveaux's business had begun to take off, and he was making a name for himself in the Colored community – a name that no longer had attachments to the wrong side of the tracks. His clientele was respected business owners, and word-of-mouth advertising had grown his business by leaps and bounds. He was living life comfortably as had been the case before; but this time the money was clean and based on the content of his talent and character and not that of his gangster friends.

Her career was picking up in its own right as well. No longer a substitute teacher at the high school, she had landed an adjunct professor job at the university like she wanted to. She was also on the list for consideration as future faculty for the History Literacy Exchange Program. Although that gig would be a long time coming, at least her ultimate goal was closer to within her reach.

Teaching at the university was a lot different than teaching at the high school. Paying for an education brought about two kinds of students: the ones who skipped class, and the ones who were eager to sop up every bit of knowledge.

This fateful day started out like any other. As the students arrived, she began writing notes on the board about key points for the lecture of the day. As chalk met board, she burped and the foul taste of vomit covered every inch of the inside of her mouth. Placing her hand over her mouth, she could feel the acid traveling upward from her stomach.

She tried not to let her students see the urgency she was feeling; but soon, quick strides gave way to a full fledge run as she made her way to the nearest restroom. Raising the seat to the commode, she regurgitated things she didn't even remember consuming. Steadying herself, she wipes her mouth and then runs her hands across her breasts to remove the sting of soreness that resided there. Exhaling long and hard, she flushes the toilet and walks to the sink outside of the stall. Running water never seemed so enticing as it did to her at the moment. Cupping her hands under the faucet, she gargles with the water in the basin, then places both her hands on the sides of the sink to calm herself. Within seconds, she finds herself staring at her reflection in the mirror. Her face is clammy and pale; going from cream colored to pasty white. She hasn't had this type of sickness before. Her mind scrambles for understanding. When other women displayed this sickness, it was...*but no it can't be that*, she reasoned.

"But can it be? It has to be something else," her words rise into the empty restroom without anyone to affirm or deny.

Dr. Johnson, was going to have a visitor first thing in the morning.

Several days go by and Malveaux doesn't hear from Serene. This is foreign territory for them and unlike how their relationship has been over the last year. They had keys to each other's apartments but respected each other's privacy. He normally called her nightly, and she always eagerly answered his calls. But now things were different. He imagined her phone ringing and her being unable to answer because something had happened to her. Concerned for her safety, he goes to her apartment. Laying on the doorbell for what seems like hours, he is relieved when she finally answers the door and reluctantly lets him in.

Once inside, she heads toward the bedroom as he begins questioning her from the living room as to why he hasn't heard from her. Their relationship had never been about control or insecurity. As far as he was concerned, they gave each other the right amount of space, love, and sex that they needed, so the conversation at hand was going to be uncomfortable. He had no clue as to why she was acting so strange. *Had she taken a new lover? Did she view their relationship differently than he did?* These questions were bombarding him inwardly as he asked others outwardly.

As he sits down on the couch, he sees a large manila envelope on the table with an official looking letter sitting on top. He pulls the letter fully out of the envelope and reads it. Although it doesn't officially start for another year, she has been accepted into the position of her dreams. In one year, she will be a part of faculty for the History Literacy Exchange Program.

As he places the letter back into the envelope, she emerges from the bedroom. Her eyes meet his and the envelope in his hands.

"Is this why I have not heard from you? This is good news for you, right? Baby, this is what you have been dreaming of." He pulls her close to him and hugs her tightly. "I KNEW you could do it. They would have been fools if they didn't make you a part of this. I know you have to be happy about this!" His grip is tight around her and he lifts her off of her feet, swinging her around in a circle. "Is this the reason why we haven't talked in a while? What??? Are you having some sort of nervous attack and need time alone to absorb it all? I can't blame you; but you really should have shared this with me and let me celebrate it with you."

He lowers her to the ground, not realizing that her arms are behind her back and she has something in her hands.

She stares at the man she loves. She is aware that he is saying something, and that it is probably the right something, but his words sound like garble to her ears; he might as well be speaking a foreign language because her mind can't decipher anything but the object in her hands.

"Malveaux, just stop. That's not the only letter I have not shared with you." She brings her hand in front of her and shows him a letter from her doctor.

"The rabbit died," she says as she begins to cry.

"Rabbit? What rabbit?"

"The. RABBIT. Died!" She gives him a serious look..."THAT rabbit," she says while rolling her eyes.

"Ohhh." Clarity sinks in for him.

She walks over to the couch and sits down. Tears begin to fall, and she hangs her head. Malveaux walks over to her and kneels by her side.

"I can't pretend to know how you are feeling right now, or what you are thinking; but I hope you know that I'm with you no matter what. I know we didn't plan this, but the selfish side of me wants this child. Your sadness is apparent; I can't change that. But I need you to know that you can count on me to be a worthy father."

He leans his head forward so that it is touching hers. The confusion of her future has been weighing heavily in her mind for days. She has been alone with her thoughts and knows it is time to share them with the father of her child.

Cupping her hands around his face, she tilts his head upwards toward her so that there is direct eye contact between them as she says the words she has been toying with for days.

"You have to understand that being a mother was never in my life's equation. I've got ambitions, goals, and dreams; birthing babies, chasing after them, and being stagnant in one place was never part of the plan. If I was ever going to have a child, I would want you to be the father. You are a wonderful man, Malveaux. You deserve a child. Any kid lucky enough for you to be their father would be one blessed child, that's for damn sure!

"As a teenager, my parents and I went on long travels. While in French Sudan, I was accosted by several Frenchmen. They did things to me that white men down South did to Negro women, and often there is no justice. I had internal bleeding after the attack; it turned into an infection of my womb.

"It was said I would never have a child. I enjoyed our freedom to be open for us to make love with no reservation of the threat of having a child. I'm an intelligent woman, and I would not be gambling with chance. I spent time with doctors for years to see if I could have a child, and they all said no. From day one, you and I have been free to be as we have been. I am honest with you; I had only one other before you...long before you. Your intellect was a drug to my desires, and I had to have you in the way we did. Then we fell in love. I do love you. The meaning to all of this to me is, it was meant to be. Except..."

He smiles from her statement and wipes the tears that are flowing from her eyes, and then from his eyes.

"...the problem is not you, Malveaux. The problem is me. I'm sad for any child who comes from my womb. I am just not mother material. I had to adjust my thinking that no child would come from me; and maybe what some woman thinks of as maternal instincts...well, mine are not strong. That is what saddens me. I always envisioned that the footprint I would leave in the sands of time for eternity would be the offspring of educating both myself and those who seek higher learning. I always wanted to give the gift of life through knowledge; I never wanted to give the gift of life in the literal sense of the word."

Malveaux wants to attack her thought process in order to comfort her, but he shies away from doing so in order to allow her to empty the boulders which are weighing down her soul.

"You can only image the joy I felt in getting the letter of acceptance for the faculty position for the Literacy Exchange Program. It is a dream come true for me. But it came at the same time as finding out about the baby. How can I possibly do both? It's just not possible. The program will entail a lot of traveling and lecturing and sleeping in hotels for days at a time. That is not the life for a child. A child needs structure and stability. A child needs to stay put in order to grow. Everything I will need to do to give the life growing inside me the security it needs means that I will have to kill the person I have been striving all my life to become. I'm not sad about the baby; I am sad about who God chose to be its mother. I hate the fact that my heart is being torn in a selfish direction."

Rubbing the top of her head, Malveaux kisses her gingerly. "I love you Serene."

"You love me? How can you possibly love a narcissist like me? I'm not worthy of this baby; and I'm certainly not worthy of your love."

He gets up off his knees and sits on the couch beside her. Pulling her in close, he tells her everything is going to be alright. "You are not a narcissist. Giving love comes in many forms. Your need to teach and enlighten others is a very unselfish act. You just have to remember that things don't have to be black or white; one way or the other. It truly is possible to do both...to give the love of teaching while loving *our* child enough to let it be in the capable hands of its father."

She raises her head and allows herself to truly listen to what he is saying.

"From the moment I saw you standing in the rain, I knew there was a strength about you unlike any woman before and I'm sure if ever after...as time has passed, I also know that you love me as much as you can possibly love any man. You are a butterfly. Butterflies are designed to spread their wings and fly; pollenating everything they touch along the way. I never fooled myself into thinking that we would be an old married couple one day. You were always meant to be free. I only wanted to share being a part of the same sky that you fly in."

Her tears flowed, and her nose ran, and her dry mouth could not swallow because her nauseousness was creeping.

"You can't buy trust; but it's safe for you to put stock in me. When you stumble, I'll hold you up. When you fall, I'll catch you. In short, pretty lady...we can get through this together."

"That all sounds easier said than done. Are you really looking at the whole picture? I have spent the last few days reflecting. I'll never be the kind of mother that our mothers were to us. I can and will love my child, but I don't feel I can be what many are in the traditional sense in order for me to be the best *person* I can be. If I stop being me to raise a child, I won't be able to complete the life I have set forth because my life will have travel demands as I teach abroad or do any of the other things I want to do in life. It wouldn't be fair to me or to our child."

"This is all new to me too, and I don't have all the answers. But I do know this...if you didn't pursue all of the things that you have yearned to do, you wouldn't be the woman I love. Continue to chase your dreams; as a matter of fact, catch them! Let all those tears create a new ocean for you to sail across and make a new way, and I will always be at the dock waiting for you.

"We all only get one life to live, and we should live it in the way that gives us satisfaction and peace. I have caught my dreams, so raising our child is just icing on the cake in my book. You continue to do the things you love, and I will raise our child. You can raise her from afar, yet on your own terms. I won't interfere in your role, and you can have peace in knowing that I'm holding things up on my end as well. We don't have to all be in the same place in order to show each other love, and you will always have a place to come back to as we raise our child together."

Between tears, she manages to reply, "I have to have peace of mind, or I have nothing."

Day gives way to night. As they discuss and marinate on how an arrangement could work with her following her dream while he takes care of their child, a sense of calm surrounds them. The more they talk, the more the vison takes shape. The meeting of their minds reminds them of how they connected on a physical level that led to their child's creation. Weary of allowing logic and plans to engulf them any longer, the lovers decided to do what lover's do...they laid back and let nature take its course.

A growing belly brought on a closeness beyond what they already shared. Months passed as they enjoyed intimate conversations between stomach rubs and hands strategically placed in order to feel the kicking flutters of the life they created. Daydreaming of the future, they were giddy while discussing moments when their child would come home from school eager to share his or her excitement about the A they got for their hieroglyphs display which was presented as a part of Show and Tell, and how Malveaux would be the one to show support and love in that moment. Equally discussed was the type of personality their child would have. Be it a girl or a boy, they both were excited about the possibility and likelihood that the child would have her individuality, creativity, and zest for life. They agreed that a child with her personality and free spirit, coupled with his intellect and sensibility, would have no choice but to go far in life. As their child baked in the oven of her womb, both parents found refuge in the plan they had laid out on how to raise their child.

"Malveaux, remember when I told you how intriguing your name was to me?"

"I do."

"Remember when I told you I thought there was strength behind your name?"

"I do."

"Well, I did some research on it. We both know research is my thing, so I couldn't resist. What I found is quite on point. The origin of your name suggests that you can carry on for others with joy. It says that you have a receptive nature and often bear the burdens for others. You are bold, independent, inquisitive, and interested in research. You know what you want and why you want it; but above everything else, you like home and security."

He listens, nodding his head at all the things she is stating about him that he believes to be true.

"In case I forget to say it later, at a time when it needs to be said, thanks for being you, and thanks for being a present parent in our child's life."

Months later, unto them a beautiful baby girl is born. True to form and expectation, the parents live up to the plans they put in place while cultivating her. The day their child took her first step, Serene made travel plans and she was teaching in another country a month later. Every other month, Serene would come home and find her child could talk, then write, then sing, then dance. Their daughter was flourishing under her father's watchful eye, just as he said she would. The joys and pains of being a single father encompass the daily life of Malveaux as he raises his daughter in a stable environment that he provides. In comparison, the child's mother is an active parent, albeit mostly from a distance, in molding and shaping their daughter's world. Day-to-day caring is given by Malveaux and he puts the phone to his daughter's tiny ear so that she can enjoy her mother's voice when she is out of town. Her mother spends as much time in Chicago as possible, and when given the luxury to be in the vicinity of her daughter, Serene stays in Malveaux's home when she is in town. He enjoys watching Serene rock their daughter to sleep in a rocking chair in the nursery. He sees Serene does have nurturing ways that come from her soul, but it is all her own and not in the usual ways of others. On most occasions, she ends the evening by starting off reading to her daughter from a book of fairy tales that Serene has written and concludes their mommy/daughter regimen by telling her daughter stories of her mother's real-life travels and adventures.

A family unit takes many forms; theirs may not have begun in the traditional sense that they both were raised under, but their mutual agreement to jointly raise their child amid their unconditional love worked perfectly for them.

At the end of the day, *true love asks for nothing, yet gives way to everything.*

What I read spoke volumes of Serene and her wisdom, and her views on relationships from a woman's perspective.

If comprehended correctly, she must have asked the father of her child his side of the story and wrote his feelings. I know it is not true, but I feel I'm receiving a Ph.D. from a source of knowledge no one else has.

I'm sure men would love to tap into her deep well of living to become better men. Yet, she not only gives me a woman's train of thought, but she also wrote, "*love is love,*" and is not a comparison of one way is the only way.

Along the way, our charter bus was in standstill traffic, often times not moving. I was traveling with her word in a black and white movie; the film was rolling. I noticed while I was reading, she seemed to be reading right along with me. I wonder, was she reliving the moments she met this man and her child was born?

I feel strange, knowing her personal life and the pain she felt that may still swell up in deep suffering.

When I first met Serene, I read in her bio on the Internet that she had lost her child tragically. Here she was reading right along with me, falling in love with this man and having a child with him. The courageous decisions both parents put forward to do what is best for their child and what was most suited for each other transcended society and individual ego. I wanted to be her child.

TWELVE

The music that Serene plays in her room the most is Sam Cooke. Her album collection is full of his music. I knew about his hit songs, but not a lot of his other music. I've now become a fan of his style of soul, which sounds like a mix of gospel and sensual blues.

I went to a conference, and when I came back I went to see Serene. Sam Cooke albums lay spread across her bed, and Serene is positioned between the LPs.

"Serene, please tell me, what is it about Sam Cooke?"

"He is that man, with a suave manner and handsome looks, and he was beyond average in how he dressed in satin, silk, or wool. When he spoke, you listened, and when he laughed or smiled, you wanted more. Sam Cooke made a woman feel desire. Only a few men made me taste inside my soul the aura of a magnetic personality the way Sam Cooke did."

Serene lowers her head and tears slowly trail down her cheeks. She wipes her tears away, and she asks, "Can we go out in the courtyard? It's a nice day out there. I want to sit in the sun."

I nod, but first I gather her albums from the bed and place them in the record bin. We walk out the front doors to take the walkway around.

In the bright blue sky to the north, a full moon is out in the early daytime. It doesn't appear so far away, and even during the AM, I can see the craters, like small oceans amid the whitish surface of the full moon.

"Blunile, you are that kind of man."

"Me? That kind of man...like a Sam Cooke? I don't sing, but women say I am a good slow dancer, and I know I am." I'm chuckling.

"Maybe one day I will test your skills," she giggles. "Confidence makes a man. When a man is confident and does not let ego or arrogance become negative, he commands a woman's attention and keeps her loyalty because he will make her feel as if she is the queen of the world and that she can trust whatever and whenever. Confidence makes a man gorgeous, handsome, and desirable, to the point a woman will almost do anything for that man."

Serene and I sit in the garden under a large umbrella to keep the sun off. I thought she might be nodding off, but...

"Blunile, please recite a poem for me, your voice is soothing, and your words are inspiring."

"Let me think." I thought for a couple of minutes thinking of a poem I could recite.

Full moon effects are in

Her body is talking in secret codes

Some secrets are exposed, like the scent of a wildflower

Sending up smoke signals smoldering in alluring scent

The gravitational pull of sexiness rains down

Lusting dopamine reflects in moon shadows

Inner cravings hot, as if the moon burns like the sun

Legs quivering, like the earth is spinning

Breasting sensitivity moon effects in universal protrusions

The full moon effects, like shinning a light on the visuals of a man doing her desires

Lasting into the day and beyond

Moon craters are deep

Wanting a rocket to land

Penetration of the surface is wanted

It's damp, and the full moon sends swells

While lying prone, the full moon finds its way into her being

The full moon is moving in and affects throbbing

Aching in moon echoes between

The dark side of the moon feels heady, doggie, and free to be

Midnight calls,

The moon is riding high at midnight while morning lusting is reaching out to be lifted and laid

Daydreams clouds can't hide full moon passions

She moans, and her eyes roll; she arches her back and points her breasts to the stars as she feels the sweetest pain

The full effects keep coming

Prepare for a landing

The full moon affects a kitten's purr

I can't wait for the next full moon

So, I can howl at her full moon

THIRTEEN

The nurse told me they'll be back in an hour. Serene is having an EKG and another short test. The tests will show if the tumor is squeezing away even more of her mental awareness and life. She still talks, but it is less often. After our train ride to the Bay area for the memorial service, she seemed okay. But it is now about sixty days later; I've become concerned with her lack of interaction at times. Serene will talk more at length and in-depth with me, but less often. We went to Palm Springs a few weeks ago, and I thought maybe the trip wore her out. I let her legal guardian – her lawyer – know how I felt. I thought it a good idea to do a check-up, and he agreed.

I realize there's nothing I or any doctor can do when it comes time for Serene to leave this Earth.

I went to a café here in the hospital for breakfast and now, back in the waiting room, I'm sipping coffee. I pull out Serene's journal to read. It has been awhile.

A-Train Kiss. July 7, 1963

My lover's face is dark brown with chiseled cheeks and beautiful eyes with long eyelashes; he is a handsome man.

He is a Pullman porter on the train I was riding from Washington DC on my way to the Big Apple to teach at NYU. I taught there during the week and went home to DC on Friday evenings. I didn't mind paying extra to ride in the luxurious Pullman sleeper car so I could put my feet up and relax before and after a long week. Each time I saw him on the train, he treated me well as a passenger. I recognized he was a man about town or what some call a playboy. I am a woman who has traveled the world and come and go as I please to be with whomever is my choice. In his white Pullman coat and black slacks, this fine man had his pick of the litter in life.

I knew he wasn't a man who bedded the first heels-up tramp; he presented an aura of seeking class, intrigue, and a woman with uniqueness. Mr. Pullman porter made every woman dream of being his lover.

After I exited the train, we met in Penn Station, and he was on his last stop. Like him, I have confidence. When I dress, my figure pulls in and pushes out a coke bottle shape with a little more up top and a little more at the bottom. My legs match Wilma Rudolph's stride for stride.

I loved hearing my heels click-clacking on the train station floor with people moving about like ants and the clocks and reader boards that play for all to see. I heard his voice. I knew it was him from the politeness and professional times he spoke to me on the train.

"Excuses me, Miss, hello from the trade winds of my mind. Can I have a minute of your time? I want to dance with you in conversation and let the twist and turns of time be the music that moves us. If you will, like a summer breeze at your back, I'll guide you to where you would love to go. I'm here to open doors that maybe have been closed. Please greet me with your soul, and I will respect you with a genuine, honest soul in return."

"Oh, you can recite alluring verses."

"If I may, let us look at what's in front of us, and I will have your back. Can you dig that?"

He held out his large, manicured hands as if he was holding something. "Here, hold this hot cup of soul between us. Don't spill, as I'm clear as water for you to see to the bottom. There are moons and stars, and then there are galaxies."

"Where do you want to travel to?" I said to Mister.

The overhead speaker in the train station kept repeating a theme of, "Last call. And now boarding and arriving."

He and I could be swept up by a time machine and transported to before or after any event in time. Someone's luggage behind me brushed against me, and it nudges me into his chest. He reaches out to support me with his hands on my upper arms, and his voice is closer to my ears.

"To a place we create as our own; I have no use for the same air others breathe. I want space and time we invent, that we craft and originate. I'll let you name our path if you let me get to know you."

I turned my face to give him the same treatment of talking into his ear. Our cheeks touched like feathers floating in the air. "Will you let me know you from under your skin where your heart beats and through the rhythm of your soul? I won't put stipulations on you or constraints."

I look up into his eyes, and his lips move, and I hang on each word he releases. "Life is sweet when living in the moment, and you don't fret about seeing what's ahead. Drop the baggage in the backseat of what if. Ride with me and feel the trade winds as we kiss the sky."

I handed him my luggage, and off we went.

Amadore Booker wined and dined me and talked with me until the break of dawn. We finally fell asleep leaning on each other on a bench in Central Park. A Negro policeman woke us and said a beautiful couple like us should head over to the Hotel Theresa on 125th Street if we needed a place to stay.

During the week, I live at the Hotel Theresa as part of my perks of being a Professor at NYU. They outbid Harvard several ways to get me on their faculty, including these lodgings. As part of negotiations, I had wanted Harvard to give twenty full scholarships to Negro students each year. After all, they had their earliest beginnings making money through the slave trade; reparations are in order. They countered with an offer of 20 scholarships one time only – not each year. I said no and went to teach at NYU. I will write a book about Harvard and the stealing of Negros lives for the higher education of White America. In the summertime I offer my knowledge for free, and I teach between Howard University and Morehouse University. I'm proud to dedicate my time to my people's advancement.

In the coming weeks, Amadore and I were together each day, except when I had to go back to DC. I always came back early if there was a chance for us to be together. We had not had sex. We had not even kissed. We did lay with each other held close as if our skin melted into one. Amadore said when the time comes, we will know, but he considered me his woman.

I had not encountered such a man. Amadore Booker walks with confidence, but he is not arrogant or conceited. With me, he is loving, affectionate, and classy. We walk down 9th Avenue and women do double-takes. No matter their race or economic status, they admire Amadore.

New York City trains and subways move us about from Brooklyn to Manhattan, to the Bronx and Staten Island. While on the A Train, we're squeezed tight on a crowded subway car and holding the pole. Amadore recited in my ears,

"Downtown love affairs
High rent Manhattan romances
Long Island end of the line lustful tales
Harlem kings venture underground to love queens in Queens
Brooklyn to Brownville strolls from afternoons till it's too dark to return
Packed tight on this train
Riding with lost and found
A-train of musical scales to Spanish Harlem
Above ground from uptown to cool jazz
Short on change, jump turnstiles and catch the last train home

Bebop flows on the platforms

Strangers lean on strangers

Beggars, thankful for a dime

Our eyes plead for change

You're never alone in New City with me

What's more important in my life?

Wanting to feel you in the romance of New York City

I must kiss you

That's my state of mind as we stand here on a subway in the middle of New York City"

My man, Amadore Booker, placed his hand under my chin, and as if we were not on a crowded train, he kissed me for the first time since we first stopped and talked to each other in Penn Station three weeks ago.

A mist of warmth spreads through my body as he kissed my lips. I want more. Our wet, sweet kisses are making parts of me shimmer. I open my eyes, and I see smiles and even some blushes as I scan the crowd. I'm center stage, like I'm in a theatrical production. I see women smile and nod their heads, wishing it was them. I reclose my eyes and I feel his tongue tangling and twisting, locking and unlocking with mine, I cannot resist. I hold onto the pole on the train, trying not to be weak.

My man is every kiss, every touch, and every moment I had wished for in my life. The way he is kissing me, it is a once-upon-a-time dream. His lips against mine overshadow every fantasy I have had. The stimulation is like a warm tropic rain to make love in as he kisses my eyelids and I see dreams. He kissed my cheeks on each side of my prettiness, and then he's back to my open mouth, and the taste is rich and sweet.

On the A Train, I don't know if the crowded train is hiding him lightly brushing, stroking my thighs and other cheeks, but I don't give a damn. Along with his tongue dancing between my lips, I know I want all of him. I know I want him to let his soft baby hairs mate with mine under the sun, moon, and stars. His lips let me know he will bring lightning to my body. I want him as he parts my body to bring a tear of joy and pain of pleasure.

He didn't stop kissing me until the train doors opened to deposit us in Harlem. He could have kissed me for the rest of my life. An elderly woman, almost last to exit along with us said, "Does he have a grandfather living? If so, I want to meet him now. If he's not living, I want to visit his gravesite." She put her hand on my arm in a loving way. "Honey, that kind of man you have there, is hard to find."

Under the Apollo Theater marquee, a freelance photographer takes pictures of us. On the marquee, the name of the great Sam Cooke shines brightly. We are holding hands tighter, and I squeeze the arm of *my man.*

Amadore knew many well-known people from his travels as a porter on the train. One of the most notable is Sam Cooke, and Sam gave Amadore backstage passes.

Showtime and we are backstage. The group the Moonglows are performing. The Valentinos have already opened the show, and a talented young man from the group with the sly look of a womanizer came strutting over to me while Amadore was in the restroom. He said his name was Bobby Womack and he was the lead singer of the group. He wanted my number or address, but I turned him down.

About the same time he walked away, Amadore was walking back in my direction with none other than Sam Cooke. They were slapping each other on the back, laughing it up.

"Ms. Serene May, Amadore has told me you are one the prettiest women on this Earth and also one of the smartest." Amadore has told Sam Cooke my name, and I'm trying to breathe because he is so damn handsome. I'm in front of two gorgeous men.

"Hello, Mr. Cooke."

"Call me Sam, and you and Amadore come on back to my dressing room and have a drink while I get ready for the show."

I had a vivid imagination, but I had to force back my thoughts; I can't even let my mind say it, although I see in my visions the two men holding me tightly. *Serene stop, I can't have these thoughts.* I giggle to myself as I walk between them on my way to Sam Cooke's dressing room.

We hardly had time to share a drink when Sam's tour manager burst through the door telling Sam he would be going on early as the performer Little Willie John hadn't showed up.

"That son-of-a-bitch, I loaned him some money, and now he's not here. Excuse my language Ms. Serene; it's just some men are blinded by wine and women. Some men tend to choose a woman who enhances their life. My friend here, Amadore, you and he enhance each other."

Sam went behind a room divider and changed into a grey silk shirt tailored to a mauve-colored cashmere sport coat and grey silk slacks. He slipped into snakeskin loafers, the color of his sport coat. His collar was open, showing his light-bronze chest.

The tour manager came back into the room, and Sam spoke to him before the manager could get a word out. "Here, take this camera and take a picture of my friend and me and his beautiful woman. The three of us sat on a velvet couch, and Amadore and Sam Cook put their arms behind me with their legs crossed. I smiled more expansively than I would usually. I was a happy woman.

Sam rushed out of the room, and we followed. Sam stood center stage and said, "1, 2, 3..." and the band and Sam opened with, "Having A Party." We could see from behind the curtains the Apollo Theater erupted in song and dance. After the first verse, Sam waved to all who were backstage to join him on stage, and we all danced behind him. It was the first time I had danced with my man, and we pirouetted and bopped together as if we had danced together all our lives.

The song ended, and we all went backstage as Sam sang "Nothing Can Change This Love." I had heard the song on the radio, but it was slower and more passionate performed live. Amadore and I slow danced backstage, as did several other couples. We danced slower than the song, but it felt right. The band segued into another slow song, and Sam Cooke started humming like old-time gospel preachers used to do, but it was sensual and lustful, almost impious. We heard women screaming when he sang the opening words, "So many days since you went away." The song was "Troubled Blues." The screaming made me peek out, and women were falling to the floor. Amadore and I started doing a dance called, *The Stroll*, and a few more couples joined in with us while backstage.

Amadore rubbed his hands up and down my sides and spine; I felt his large hands through my dress. He might as well have been caressing my bare skin or my womanhood. I had to squeeze my thighs tight to keep my juices from soaking my panties. I had been teasing and pleasuring myself nightly in my bed or shower, thinking about him.

Sam Cooke's voice enslaved the crowd, his looks and persona ooze confidence; his was overpowering sensuality. Amadore's grace in movement made our eyes lock, and it seemed to block out the sounds and the people near us.

Amadore takes my hand and leads me in different directions as if he is looking for something or somewhere. We end up by a door, and he turns the knob, and the door leads to stairs going down a narrow path. We are under the stage. Small windows are along the wall. Amadore slowly peeks, and he can see the audience having a good time as we hear Sam singing and the band playing, but the sound is a bit muffled. We walk a little further, and we are in a storage area with the instruments. We see how a grand piano is stored, and we look up and see the stage floor hatch.

Amadore picks me up and sits me on the large white grand piano. He and I are kissing like we were on the A-Train, but our hands are reaching, touching, and unbuttoning. I stand up on the piano and pull down my laced panties. I run them across his nose, and he turns animalistic. He kisses and licks my legs and reaches up and squeezes my ass. I feel weak; he takes off his sport coat and has me sit on it. I lay back and feel his tongue coming near my womanhood, and I know he is inhaling my scent. I almost scream when his tongue tastes me inside and out. He is licking my lips down there and then starts sucking on my pearl. At the same time, he is licking and parting my hot chocolate and devouring me as if he needed to so he could live. I can't control my movements as we hear the sexy rhythm in cadence, meter, and measure above us.

I wanted to touch his hardness, and lick the shaft, and stroke him to give him pleasure. I sit up and put my hand on the side of his face. I look at his wet lips that have me all over. I point to his pants. He unzips and steps out of his trousers. I feel daring knowing on the other side of the wall women are going crazy wanting Sam, and here I had a fine man in my hands.

I come down and sit on the piano stool as my man stands at full erection in front of me, and his length is above his belly button, with plenty of girth. I look up at his face as I stroke him. He is seeping much slippery wetness. I taste him and I want more. I love the look on his face as he has given in to me complete control, and it shows in his expressions.

We hear Sam telling a joke, and the band starts to play "Twisting the Night Away." I need my man inside me; I lay on the piano spread wide on my stomach. I feel him edging close to going inside me. My mouth parts anticipating, and when his manhood touches at my opening, I bite my lip. He starts parting me, and I grab the edge of the piano to help me lift my ass. The sensation of him fills me up with ecstasy as he lightly strokes in and out and a little bit deeper each time he pushed forward. I feel him almost to the bottom of me, but it turns into a sweet feeling mixed with agony I was not ready for or used to. It had been way too long since I'd had a man like him inside me. He must have sensed my state and lay still inside me. Then he kissed me on the side of my face.

He leans over and sucks lightly on my collarbone. It relaxes me, and I start to move my hips. I'm ready for his jazz to make me hit some high notes. He begins to stroke in and out. His fingers tremble on my marble of bliss. My ass protrudes. As hard as the piano top is, I am on my knees, taking all I can take because it feels like nothing I had ever felt - the moment - the place - the danger - with the right man. I have waited, and I am enjoying this to its fullest.

I call his name, and I hear the crowd call Sam's name, and they are clapping their hands. I'm calling out, "Amadore, Amadore."

We had been going at it for what seemed like ten songs. We changed positions with me now on top of Amadore, and he is on his back. I was squatting over his hardness with my heels on and with my hands on his chest. He called my name in a long exhale of breath. "Serene." And he and I felt each other taking in and giving our love as we are trembling, shaking, and releasing. We are panting as the sensation of each other keeps throbbing as he is inside me and I lay on his chest.

We hear Sam Cooke say, "This is the last song, and I hope we can do this again," as he starts to sing, "Darling You Send Me."

I sit back in a chair, waiting for Serene to come back from her tests. The journal entry was erotic. I'm feeling a bit embarrassed – turned on reading about the sex life of a near ninety-year-old woman.

Serene walks around the corner with a beautiful helper. After reading the story, I admit I wanted to have a woman who had Serene's mindset, who could ease my lonely sensations in many different ways.

The woman escorting Serene, I thought maybe I should try to get to know this woman. She looks at me with more than polite interest, I tell myself. I almost make inroads to getting to know her. I had Serene with me, though, and she looked a bit tired. I thanked the woman for her help, and I drove away with Serene without asking the woman's name or even introducing myself. So much for a confident man.

FOURTEEN

S aturday mornings are always ushered in with me standing outside of her door inhaling. It's delivery day for Serene and the rest of the residents. When they receive blessings in the form of gifts and special treats that fit with their previous lifestyle, we try to fulfill them in earnest. Our staff lives vicariously through the indulgence. We ask ourselves how we would like to be treated and gifted if we were in their shoes, and we accommodate them accordingly. Of course, our residents have the means to afford their extraordinary living.

Our facility is home to several couples who live here due to their medical needs and limited family support. Those are limitations for them, but income restrictions are not an issue. One of our more popular couples is Mr. and Mrs. Beamly. Originally from France, they've lived in LA since 1970. Their one and only child, a son, moved back to France several years ago. The Beamly's both use wheelchairs to get around, but they are a lively couple who go out whenever they choose, and they don't let anything cramp their eccentric lifestyle.

When age and ailments had begun to creep into their ability to perform normal day-to-day functions, they offered their son a handsome salary to take care of them, but he declined. He preferred being a playboy, chasing after the lifestyle of a male model who lives off his well-paid female counterparts. Mrs. Beamly has told me his looks will fade, and in the meantime, they are spending his inheritance.

"We are not leaving him a penny! You can't take your money with you when you die, and we damn sure ain't leaving it behind for him. Might as well enjoy it while we can."

The Beamly's, have season tickets to the Lakers, the Dodgers, the LA Rams football team, and the Sparks women's pro basketball team. Their money also buys jerseys for lower-income soccer teams for inner-city kids.

Their Saturday treat at our facility usually comes in the form of a special hand-prepared French bistro breakfast of fresh fruit, French croissants, and sweet pastries, or Mr. Beamly's personal favorites of green eggs and ham crêpes, or an omelet with pressed caviar. We were able to find a chef who prepares the items in a manner they both say reminds them of home.

From amazingly exotic to simple and unpretentious, Serene receives fresh flowers once a week as her treat. This extravagance began the moment Sherry looked at photos of Serene's home before her arrival. One thing remained constant throughout her photos – Serene always had bouquets of fresh flowers surrounding her as part of the things that brought her comfort. Sherry made it a point to ensure that the simple indulgence displayed in Serene's home would be duplicated weekly as part of her stay in our facility. Sherry's attention to detail is one of the things that makes us a good team. Kinship aside, her softer side makes up for my lack thereof.

I often stood outside of Serene's door on Saturdays for a moment of solo indulgence in the beauty of all living things. Some would say it is downright disrespectful to ignore flowers in bloom. We believe in giving people flowers while they are still here to enjoy them. Hearing Sam Cooke's voice crooning from Serene's stereo and knowing she has her flowers gives me satisfaction. The delivery for this day is sunflowers. Bright and overpowering with inner sunshine that dares to be denied, these new hybrids have a warm honey fragrance. Outside Room 307, the aroma is earthy and pleasing. While I appreciate the smell, it is apparent our staff enjoys the Saturday delivery for reasons other than mine.

It seems Casandra and the other female staffers had a bit of a crush on one of the men who made deliveries. He was leaving as I was coming, and I watched as the ladies follow his every move with shameless eyes. The blue uniform pants beneath the white starched shirt and the matching blue hat could not take a step without going noticed. As I stood outside Serene's room, I couldn't help but lower my head and smile to spare my eyes from the visual undressing the young man was getting from my staff.

Although I'm down the hall, I can still hear. "I'm a sucker for a man in a uniform, even if it is just a flower delivery man," Cassandra said, biting her lip while watching him. "And did you see those thighs? He looks delicious and deadly!"

Sherry doesn't take her eyes off of the chart she is reading. "Chile, trying to devour that man every time he comes here will get you nowhere. He's here to do a job. He is not stuttin' you."

"Maybe not yet."

"Well, you gon' have to find another time to make your move on him; 'cause just like he got a job to do, we got 'tings to do right now too. We got rounds to tend to; no time for your matchmakin'!"

The other nurses laugh, and I inhale, entering Serene's room and closing the door behind me. I notice the flowers on the table near her bay window. Serene lays on her side, facing the flowers, and the light coming through the windows highlights her ankle-length, velvet caftan dress. It's royal blue and green paisley and trimmed with gold lace around the neck, cuffs, and hem. As I approach her, she sits up on the bed and reaches both of her hands out toward me, beckoning me to come to her. My mind gets joy out of the fact she is always so happy to see me. I am always pleased to see her as well.

"Good morning, sunshine," I say as I take her hands in mine.

Smiling, she does not say a word, but lowers her head in a regal manner she has done many times before. I kiss the backside of both of her hands. She squeezes my hands as I do so. It's the gesture of a queen, and I feel honored to be in her presence.

"Looks like the Gods smiled on you while you were sleeping."

She nods and stares toward the flowers. No words are needed for me to understand what she wants. I walk to the sunflowers and remove one from the clear crystal vase. It seems as if the sun gives it a kiss of approval as I remove it. For a moment, I sniff it with my back to her. When I turn around, the smile on her face assures me that I understood.

"You know, there is a history behind the sunflower," I say as I make my way back to the side of her bed. "It symbolizes different things in different cultures, but they all agree that it epitomizes truth and light."

The words roll off my tongue as if I am telling her something that she does not know. The book she published decades ago of ancient history, and her degrees in anthropology, would exceed all I know tenfold. Her eyes smile along with her lips. She reaches out her hands again to welcome the flower. She takes it from me and inhales deeply.

I watch as a sense of peace permeates through her. She places the sunflower behind her ear, allowing its face to share its radiance with hers. The world seems softer and more tranquil. Then she lays back on her pillow, but not before reaching for the leather journal by the side of her bed. She then turns to a portion, and I take the journal as she rests her head comfortably on her pillow and closes her eyes. I see this entry is written in pencil. All the other entries are in blue ink.

San Francisco has made a name for itself as the city that knows how to give brotherly love; keywords being, "how to give." Its rolling hills, comfortable summers, and laid-back multi-cultured acceptance of outsiders made it the perfect place to cop a squat for a while. Especially now – in 1967 for counterculture hippies like Sunbeam and Magenta – the names the two self-proclaimed flower children had taken on when denouncing their government names. They both refused to allow the restraints of anything but peace and love to define them.

The green station wagon they were traveling in had seen better days, but it was a gift from the last compound they stayed at, so they weren't going to turn it down; especially when they needed wheels to get to San Francisco. The wingtips on the back, and woodgrain paneling on the sides, made it a moving work of art, but it's a beauty with mismatched whitewall tires and deoxidized paint on the hood. Several suitcases and duffle bags were tied down to the top with rope, weighing the wagon down and making each of the passengers feel every bump and pothole along their journey. The number of occupants over-filled the capacity intended by the Ford manufacture as they took turns as to who got to sit in the rear-facing seat in the back.

One of the men pulled out a guitar and began strumming. Soon the chorus of the Mamas and the Papas song was sung by everyone in the wagon. They were all brothers and sisters as far as they were concerned, and the unison of their voices was colorblind in harmony. In the travelers' minds, "California Dreaming" epitomized their desire to live a simple way of life.

Magenta had chosen her name because, in her words, that color was a mixture of reds, pinks, and blues, bold yet loving, the colors that represented her heart. Her free-spirited ways had always been a problem for her snotty parents. Throughout her upper-middle-class childhood, they struggled to tame their daughter and keep her in the lane of white affluence with the attitude that we are better than those who are different. She had lived this life of arrogance. It wasn't until she went off to college and was away from parental control that she learned other people – different people - were no less than she. Liberal – free thinking was the term used to describe the people she met and admired, and the label was one that Magenta wanted to own. During her first year in college, she felt that she was finally becoming the person she wanted to be. She no longer wanted to be the typical cliché of a well-off white woman; she wanted to be one with the world.

One day, her parents came for a visit, and they began to tell her about a boy they wanted her to meet. He came from a respectable family; they approved of his pedigree. As their lips spoke of how good of a couple their daughter and the young man could be, Magenta felt sick to her stomach. The images running in her mind of what they wanted for her began to suffocate her. She couldn't breathe. The life they were trying to create for her was not the life she wanted to live. That night, after they left, she packed everything dear to her, which in material things was not much and fit into one suitcase. She left the college grounds and the commercialized world behind. That day, Kathrine Marie Wellington became Magenta. One name. One existence with the vibrant being she had longed all her life to be.

Sunbeam stared at her friend. She had agreed with the name her friend had chosen for herself and with the assessment as to why – both concerning the color magenta itself and concerning her best friend whose pale skin was the only thing lacking color about her. Sunbeam had chosen her name because it signified vitality and warmth, characteristics she exuded, and the mantra of her *live and let live* personality.

In her own right, she was on a rebellious journey. Maybe it was her way of being like her mother. Mother dear was a world traveler who constantly sought adventure and knowledge. For the most part, her single father raised Sunbeam spiritually. Nine months out of the year, her father led her life, and then she ventured with her mother to faraway places, big cities with great art, museums, or jazz joints. Mother and daughter often spent time in the Middle East. However, dad wanted his daughter to stay away from anything "worldly" until she was older.

Sunbeam's world teeter-tottered between a stricter lifestyle and a more open world with diverse ideologies and positions worldwide. Her mother was moral, but she believed the world was to be seen, tasted, and experienced. Her dad and mom loved each other and never disagreed on what the other put before their daughter; they only did as they wanted when their daughter was in each other's care. That is until she went to high school.

During the school year with dad, Sunbeam dressed differently. The other kid's clothes had character and were cool, but her clothes blended in the background. When with her mom, she dressed high class, or in the Mediterranean garb. Along with her beautiful mother, Sunbeam dressed as if on a beach with Sophia Loren in rare two-piece bathing suits.

Everyone in school talked differently than her; she had a higher IQ than those around her. The American kids spoke of early rock and roll bands and singers they listened to on the radio. Sunbeam heard jazz in her household and even met a few known jazz greats. Her mother introduced her to royalty and sports stars. Born in the fifties, she was a teenager in the sixties who watched segregation, marches, and she saw firehoses turned on kids when she watched TV. She grew with the complex emotional impact of seeing a president murdered and the somber feelings of a nation mourning. Yet, most of the kids in her school spoke of parties and wanted to find an adult to buy them beer. She felt like an outsider. She felt abnormal. Even though she lived in the same world that they did, she couldn't relate to anything around her.

In her senior year, two boys pinned her up against the lockers as she walked down the hall. One patted his hand on the top of her afro, then touched the side of her cheek. He told her she was too pretty to be such a geek.

"Don't you know you are missing out on a lot of stuff when the only places you hang out is home and to play tennis on a team where you are the only Negro? Nobody cares that you are better than all the other players. You should live a little sometimes."

"Yeah, what a waste," the other said as he looked her up and down before walking off and motioning for his friend to come along.

That night, she stared at her image in the mirror. The reflection was of smooth chocolate skin with perky breasts and a flat stomach. Her rear-end received too much attention as if something was wrong because it was fuller than most other girls. She hadn't compared herself to other girls because doing so was vain, and vanity was a failing inside one's soul. Her parents told her as much, but she couldn't help but be vain at that moment. The image staring back at her was bold, Black, and beautiful. Even her naive mind could see that. She thought about the words from the boys from earlier in the day.

"But how can I miss something I have never experienced," she said to the mirror.

"That's the problem," her mind heard the image say, "you haven't experienced anything on your own. Sunbeam had lived her father's conservative life, and she had lived her mom's adventurous life, but it was under the watchful eye of her mother's guidance."

The mirror told her that she craved to experience things in life on her own. She desired memories, not just scriptures. She wanted to judge life and the people in it and be part of the world – the good, the bad, and the ugly of it. She aspired to have accomplishments and make mistakes to grow and seize an opportunity to shine her guiding light. Sunbeam wanted to know and experience it all, and she knew she could not do that living the life of either of her parents, but she did favor being freer like her mother.

Graduation came shortly. Sunbeam's parents had their moment of pride and rejoiced they had shielded her from danger and the evils of the world up to that point. Two days later, Sabine Rose Adero left her father's home in the middle of the night, and Sunbeam stuck out her thumb on the highway as she began a journey to find herself.

The two young women had met while hitchhiking. Magenta's pearly white skin was strikingly juxtaposed to Sunbeam's dark chocolate tone. Their reflections enhanced one another in furtherance of universal beauty and unity shared by the women. They seemed to enjoy each other's vibe from the first word spoken in the backseat of a Chevy that took them across the state line. United in their determination to let life take them to whatever destination it chose, they also found safety in the fact that they had each other's back each time they hopped into a car with a stranger. They believed in peace and love, but they weren't oblivious to the fact that there was safety in numbers when seeking it out. The more they talked about their desire to find solace among their fellow man, often ignoring the people who were giving them a ride in the process, the more they connected on a level that even blood sisters don't share. Soon, they became inseparable and a bond formed between them along their journey.

The heels of their dirty feet were exposed as they sat Indian style in the wagon. It was their turn to enjoy the extra room provided by being in the back seat. Matching peace sign rings adorned their toes; they had purchased them at a truck stop as a symbol of their bond. With the rear window of the wagon down, they swung their feet out the window and into the wind as they admired their toe rings.

They had done each other's hair and loved how Magenta's blond hair seemed to accentuate Sunbeam's dark brown kinky crown when they stood side by side. Their braids blew in the wind and out the window as they sang about California weather while making beaded bracelets and waist belts to be sold once they reached their destination. Rumor had it that Haight-Ashbury was an excellent marketplace for travelers to sell their wares. It was a relaxed, friendly space and an eclectic beacon for exchanging physical, emotional, and spiritual values. Young but not that naive, they knew about selling drugs or panhandling, but Sunbeam and Magenta had always paid their way with no intention of crossing certain lines when it came to selling drugs or sex. Their beaded jewelry always brought in money.

"I see you keep staring at that dude on the guitar. You sweet on him or something?"

Magenta puts the thread in her mouth to moisten it before putting it through the needle. "He is the most beautiful man ever. He touches my soul each time he picks up that guitar."

"Looks to me like you want him to touch more than just your soul."

The women laugh as a joint is passed their way. Each woman takes a toke, and Magenta exhales a perfect ring of circular smoke into the air. Sunbeam tries to mimic the French inhale her friend does but immediately starts coughing and pounding on her chest wildly, almost hitting her braless nipples instead of the center space between them. She was a lightweight when it came to drugs. Magenta takes another puff and holds it in just as the guitar dude leans over the backseat and whispers something in her ear. She giggles and exhales as his hand brushes across her breasts as he walks away.

"Touches your soul, my ass!"

"He said we're almost to the camp. He asked me to go with him to get a water pipe in town once we get there. He has a gig lined up for later tonight. I dig him; I do. I want to be a part of his flow. You can dig that, can't you?"

"So, you're just going to leave me hanging once we get to the Bay?"

"Mellow out. It's just for today. You sell more of our beads than I do anyway. Pretty people like you get advantages in life that normal-looking people like me don't get. Use what your momma gave you. We'll be a team again tomorrow. Today, I want to fly solo. Butterflies have to spread their wings."

Sunbeam wanted to be angry at her friend but doing so went against the free love philosophy that they lived by – people should be free to love whomever, wherever, and whenever they wanted. There was no loyalty to your girlfriend when free love and sex were in the vicinity.

"Let your freak flag fly. I'll cover sales for today, but that means you will replenish our stash by yourself."

Their station wagon pulls into a clearing on the undulating hillside of Hippie Hill. It will be home for the travelers for as little or as long as the wind tells them to stay put. The campsite has about seven other cars and buses with trailers in tow parked on the sloping hill of coyote bushes. The sandy soil and low-to-the-ground shrubs told them not to park on the edge and be extra careful of where they walked. The trees were windswept, and shaped by high winds, often hidden in thick fog before noon.

The two young women felt strongly about a new generation born freer than their parents who lived with white picket fences, utopias, and daddies who went to work in a suit and tie, and mommas who wore aprons all day with pearls and perfect hair. Well, Sunbeam knew that was not her mother, but all her friends lived under that shadow. They laughed at the thought of how they had seen parents on the television sleeping in twin beds and how it had made them wonder how they were conceived since their parents never spoke of sex. Yet in their new world - they made love freely, calling it sex and hiding very little in the process.

Music of peace and love fills the air around them. The smell of reefer passes between the lips of everyone on the compound as they kiss and touch each other's bodies and souls. Puffing and passing the joint is as normal as drinking water. A contact high, one could not escape; it took extra effort to avoid.

After the long ride, taking those first steps on the compound felt good as she felt grass and sandy dirt under her toes. Sunbeam stretches her hands to the sky and allows the warmth of the sun to luxuriate her. The multi-colored crocheted halter top she wears scantily covers her breasts. They are perky and welcome the sun's rays. The sunflower that Magenta had painted around her navel the day before enhances low rider bell-bottoms. Her belly button is pierced and is eye-catching when she moves. Each arm has seven or eight of the beaded bracelets that she and Magenta had made. The rest, along with the beaded waist belts, are in a pouch around her waist.

Walking over to the portable shower area of the campground, she notices a sign that reads, *Why be rude when you could be nude?* Her fellow brothers and sisters aren't shy about sharing glances at one another and more than that because several people are making love in the shower area. She steps halfway under a showerhead and pulls the string, allowing a short burst of lukewarm water to drench her scalp. Running her hands through her long bohemian-style French braids gives them life again. After untangling her braids, she puts a headband of flowers around her hairline and heads up the slope of Hippie Hill to walk the short distance to Haight-Ashbury.

A waft of competing smells engulfs her nostrils the closer she gets to her destination. Hunger pains remind her that she hasn't eaten for at least a day, so her nose, head, and appetite all had inner discussions. She had noticed the smell of canned spam grilling at the camp as she left, but it did not agree with her stomach. The smell of fresh-baked bread at the hilltop edge led her in the direction of a small bakery. Once inside, she reaches into her pouch and counts the money that she made the last time she could sell beads at a rest stop. $4.75. Not much, but enough to buy some sourdough bread to eat now and still have some to share with Magenta later on when she returns. Her mouth began to water.

Purchasing a few slices of bread, she exits the bakery, nibbling on the bread and feeling satisfied.

The sights around her overwhelm her senses. She had never seen a place filled with so much creativity and radiating with so much love. Large Victorian homes lined one side of the street, while burgeoning trinket stores sat almost on top of one another on the other side. Neither tried to compete with the other, yet both seemed to welcome the other, and both seemed to belong. Street musicians had taken ownership of every corner, and their songs often overlapped each other both in lyrics and in sound. She watched as people stopped in their tracks to dance along to the guitar fast-strumming folk music. Some pulled out tambourines and considered themselves part of the bands, even if only for a moment. Every few feet were street vendors panhandling. She knew that soon she would have to do the same, but she just wanted to take it all in for a moment. It was the Summer of Love. The beatnik spirit was alive and well in Haight-Ashbury, and Sunbeam felt at home among everyone on the street.

Her attention becomes focused on a man standing on a platform speaking with a bullhorn. A small group has formed around him, and she walks in the direction of the powerful voice. Many of the crowd's faces are like her own – brown hues from dark as nighttime to golden Egyptian sand, but they were much like the white hippies. Standing among the hippies are people dressed differently than she has ever seen in person - only on TV in the news and from Ebony and Jet magazine. Their camouflaged pants, black t-shirts, and black berets seem to speak to her in a manner that only colorful garments had spoken to her before. There was something beautiful in its simplicity.

Intrigued by the crowd and the cheers for the man's words, she sits on the curb well back of the gathering and finishes her bread during the final moment of his speech.

"Black Panthers and hippies are two sides of the same coin. We are allies. However, let's always tell the truth! Many of you come from white middle-class homes, and you have grown conscious to understand the man is trying to hold *all* of us down. The difference for us, as Black people, is that we do not have the undeniable luxury you have of being able to 'drop out' if the going gets too rough and, at some point, have the opportunity to go back home to a middle-class environment. With that said, we need to know...are you down with us with your soul to help bring us all up and not leave us to fend for ourselves when the billy clubs come a swinging. Look at us, your Black and Chicano brothers and sisters. We are glad you share your good smoke with us, but are you going to leave us holding the bag when the cops come? Will you walk away when we need you the most? Understand the struggle is for all, not just for some, or we all fall subject to the man holding us down.

"I'll leave you with the words of one of my Panther brothers. He said, 'We've got to face the fact that some people say you fight fire best with fire, but we say you put the fire out best with water.' We say to you; we can't fight racism and prejudice with disregard for everyone's rights, especially legal rights. Both Black and white cannot live with preconceived judgments or opinions based on ignorance or old ideas passed around the dinner table. Changing the world will take us leaning on each other and forming a bond of truth. We're gonna fight racism with solidarity. I want you to search your souls. If you see that by not fixing the problem, you become the problem, then I ask you to help us fix what ails us as people."

He stepped down from the podium, and she watched as people walked toward him to grab the pamphlets he was passing out. The crowd became loud as some clapped and whistled, and others chanted, "Right on, brother; right on." "Power to the people," and "Let's take it to the man."

The crowd slowly disperses, and Sunbeam stands from her seated position on the curb. She is never a slave to time and does not own a watch but can tell by the sun's positioning that she's running out of time to peddle her wares. It's time to get her hustle on. She brushes off her bellbottoms and turns to walk down the rest of the block in search of a good place to go to work.

Out of the corner of his eye, he sees her making her move to leave. The drumbeat of his ancestors echoes inside of him. It's the same pounding he felt when he saw her walk out of the bakery moments before – an undulating rhythm from inside of him urging him to pay attention to her. He felt it as she walked, almost in slow motion, in his direction as he was speaking. He never gave much thought to the notion of love at first sight, but his first glance at her made him yearn for another and then another. The sway in her hips as she joined the crowd in front of him and made it hard to concentrate on the message he was delivering, but somehow, he had managed. Now the beating from within told him, once again, to put his focus on her.

"Where are you running off to? What's your hurry, sister?"

Before even turning around, the deep baritone sound of the voice gives her a chill. It's the voice that drove her to the curb in the first place. He might as well have called her name. She had wanted to run to him when she heard it for the first time, but she could not make it too easy for him.

"I don't run anywhere. It's more like frolicking."

"Well, pretty lady, where are you 'frolicking' off to? I noticed you listening to my message, but I also surmised that I must not have done enough since I did not stir you to action."

He had on dark sunglasses, but they could not shield the rich, smooth chocolate skin behind them. Sunbeam's eyes remained focus on his pearly white teeth as he spoke. She had lived the last few months of her journey with only a few Black hippies in tow, and even fewer of them were Black men. Sunbeam had almost forgotten how sexy a well-put-together Black man could be. Her father, a retired numbers runner and book fixer turned legitimate moral businessman for over twenty years, was a strong dark-skinned assertive man who made her feel like a queen. Heavily spiritual in the study of ancient times, her father also studied Egyptian hieroglyphs. He considered Egyptian hieroglyphs to be holy writings, and he taught Sunbeam how to write in a language that made her feel as though he held his daughter to a higher standard than any woman.

"Some of us have to do our part of promoting love and peace by other means. Some of us have to work to survive. And now it's time for me to go to work. My beads won't sell themselves." She gives a swirl to both of her wrists so that he can see her beads.

"Power to the people. How about this, let me empower your hustle, and you empower mine. I will buy all of what you planned on selling today in exchange for you allowing me to enlighten you."

"And WHY would you want to do that? There were a lot of people here today hanging on your every word. Why does it matter if I drape from that same curtain rod, man?"

"I don't want you to be the one that got away. Oh, and I'm a man, but everyone calls me Parker. And you are…"

"If you are serious about buying all of my beads, then I am honored, but you can call me Sunbeam."

"Well, Sunbeam, name your price and allow me to spend the rest of the day showing you how the Bay Area gives brotherly love."

Parker gives her the value of her beaded items plus some. Then he asks her if she is ready for the second half of the agreement. She tries to hide her excitement of being in his presence, but he sees right through it. It mimics his own. She had caught his attention from the moment she walked out of the bakery. Whimsical were her movements as she nibbled on the treats she had purchased. He couldn't help but admire how oblivious she was to how cruel the world could be. The way she dressed made it obvious that she was a beatnik; her aura screamed of a uniqueness he had not experienced before. With each step she had taken toward where he was, her outer beauty became more relevant. The liveliness in her prancing steps, and the way her breasts bounced, screamed for him to relax and let his world attention slide for the moment. A small headband of sunflowers held back coal-black braids that came to rest at her shoulders where they caressed skin that was flawless and looked to be softer than the clouds in the sky. That kind of beauty is hard to ignore. As she walked toward him, he couldn't take his eyes off of her.

"I can tell you are new around here. I assume you are staying on Hippie Hill. Allow me to give you a tour of Haight-Ashbury and the power it possesses, and I'll have you home by nightfall."

"Are you sure you'll have me back where I should be?"

"Well, I live over in Oakland across the Bay Bridge, and as a Black man, I should not be in certain places unless I absolutely need to be where I happened to be at," he says as he walks in no particular direction. Sunbeam follows while absorbing everything around her.

"I don't need to be out too long, and you need to be safe."

"I do have my cousin's crib where I can lay my head down and catch some dreams of a woman like you if I need to. It's not far from here in a section of the city called Daly City, or I also have an aunt who lives down Hunters Point, but I prefer to go home at night to check on my mother."

"Oh, a man who loves his mama," she smiles while walking backward in a teasing childlike manner.

"Yes, she is a queen, much like you. Women give men power, and when a Black man comes into a place like Haight-Ashbury with that power, a capability arises to uplift others."

"Power? What kind of power can a place have?"

"It gives power to the people who dare to be different yet treat each other all the same. To those who dare to believe in peace and unity. To those who understand the strength in making peace, not war."

"It seems like you are speaking my love language. Let's go."

Parker begins delivering the central message he wants her to embrace by taking her past several different hand-painted street murals in the neighborhood.

"In any other area, people look upon the murals as graffiti, but the messages in each one makes them beautiful works of art that promote peace and unity. Look at this one on the side of the building, the words of Jimi Hendrix are written in large letters in all the colors of the rainbow, 'When the power of love overcomes the love of power, the world will know peace' I wanted you to see this one because it is self-explanatory yet forces you to think."

Sunbeam doesn't speak. A comfortable silence surrounds them as she stares at each word.

After a while, he shows her around the corner another message painted in the middle of the street. It is a large picture of a white woman with both of her hands over her eyes. Written on the back of each hand is the phrase, "Close your eyes and open your mind."

As she absorbs the message, Parker comes up behind her and places his hands over her eyes.

"Open your mind, Sunbeam. Let your mind lead to an open heart."

They turn another corner, and Sunbeam notices that the street vendors have changed. This area has more people in it who look and dress like Parker. Their trinkets all seem to have a closed fist theme, and the colors of the shirts for sale don't have the same vibrant colors as a few streets over. Instead of tie-dyed patterns, the shirts for sale in this area all have influential Black figures on them. Parker takes her to one last mural painted on the wall in a community garden. Sunbeam admires the planted vegetables and the sweet, fresh, but pungent smell emanating from the small area before looking at the mural. It is a picture done in sepia colors of a Black woman with a large afro and her fist in the air. Written next to her fist are the words, "I am no longer accepting the things I cannot change. I am changing the things I cannot accept."

He reads the message aloud as they both stare at the image. Feeling that he has accomplished the tour's mission, Parker sums up each mural that he has shown her and tells her the significance of each painting and the importance of its placement.

"God's love is selfless; we should emulate His love in the way we love each other," Parker adds as they leave the garden.

"That's deep. I like that."

"I can't take credit for the saying. It's not my words, but I do take them to heart."

"Are you always like this?"

"Like what?" he responds, somewhat confused.

"So focused. So ah…goal-oriented."

"I guess the answer to that would be that when we lose focus, it's harder to reach our goals. I've just learned how to stay focused on more than one thing at a time, but I never lose focus."

Up to that point, Sunbeam had been walking by Parker's side, mostly absorbing what he was laying down. He grabs her hand and stops in front of an older man sitting outside of a small restaurant on the stoop. He is the sole musician on this corner, and his congo drum echoes throughout the air. As a sign of respect, Parker points in his direction and says, "I see you, brother. Speak to our souls."

He continues walking and sits down on a bench across the street from the man, then pats the seat beside him, motioning for Sunbeam to join him as he listens to the silence that engulfs everyone within ear's shot. The congo player raises both hands into the air, then breaks the silence by banging both hands vigorously on the two drums in front of him. The music he makes is deep in tone, and the sound is intoxicating. It pulsates down to their core. Intense and faster the man beats the drums, the more Parker's head bops along with the congo player's hands. It is as if he is in a trance, and his ancestors are speaking to him once again.

Sunbeam is enjoying the music as well, as much as she enjoys seeing a side of Parker that is relaxed and free. She begins swaying on their bench, allowing the rhythm to move her. He had been watching her watch him, and he enjoyed the subtle connection they were making. Their souls were bonding, and it felt good. Inspired by Parker's head-bopping, Sunbeam stands up to dance. His eyes follow her as she begins to do a belly dance around him in a circle. His eyes lock on her hips. Drumbeats pulsate along with her femineity, and she can see a smile forming on his face.

"Ha. It seems like someone lost their focus for a minute; didn't they?"

"That would be true, but for the fact that you don't know what I focused on, Sunbeam. Remember, I said that I always focus on more than one thing at a time."

"You focused on sharing a message with me for the last few hours; what else have you been focusing on? What did I miss?"

Parker removes his sunglasses, "My second focus was to stir your soul."

He begins walking toward a parking lot. "Continue frolicking yourself in this direction. The next place I want to take you is a little too far to walk."

He heads straight to a black late-model Chevy Impala and unlocks the passenger side door. It was clean inside and out, not a single piece of paper lying around or a crumb in sight. Sunbeam couldn't remember the last time she was inside a real car without more than six or seven people crammed inside, and it was a bit dirty – sometimes a lot filthy.

"So, do you care to elaborate on your last statement, Parker?"

"Not just yet," he says as he starts the engine. I have a stop to make before our final destination."

He pulls out the lot and drives about a block, stopping in front of a two-story building. He kills the engine to the Chevy.

He moves closer to her, and their bodies touch for the first time. She feels a heat generated between them in that brief moment and wonders if he can feel it as well. She captured a sly grin on his face, and she has the answer to her question. Parker points out of the window on her side of the car and begins to speak. She misses the first few words because of the intoxication of his scent. All she knew, it sounded like, "Hendrix."

"Okay...roll back the tape. Are you talking about Jimi Hendrix? THAT Hendrix?"

"Yes, he has an apartment up there on the second floor. It's not much to look at, but he stays here when he is in the area. Okay, now hold tight, I'll be right back." He slides back over to his side of the car and opens the door.

Sunbeam begins reaching for her door and starts yelling, "If you think you are going in to chat with Jimi without me, you are sadly mistaken, sir."

Parker laughs. "Slow your roll, woman. Who said anything about chatting with Jimi? I don't know him like that. I told you I was going to the store on the first floor and that Jimi lived on the second floor of this building. But I guess you missed that first part."

He continues laughing as he walks to the door of the small business. Temporarily embarrassed about being starstruck, Sunbeam can't help but laugh at herself. The sun is starting its descent, and she ponders where their final destination will be. Parker returns with two large bags, and he places them in his trunk. He gets behind the wheel and fumbles with his 8-tracks. He is searching for a certain tune because he fast-forwards through several songs before finding the one he wants to play.

The lyrics ask a simple question:

But will you love me tomorrow?

They drive the short distance with their lips silenced and the song lyrics hovering in each of their minds. As the car slows to a crawl, Sunbeam is in awe at the scenery around her. The Bay Area changed vision within a block from the Victorian houses and the painted schemes to the colorful people, to buildings reaching the clouds on top of already tall hills. The trollies were not just for show and tourists; they were a way of life for old ladies carrying bags of groceries and business suited, briefcase toting men jumping on and off the trollies. Sunbeam loved all things concerning nature, but the Frisco Bay inner city was tranquil and stirring at the same time. The sights before her were the most beautiful she had ever laid eyes upon.

Parker leaned over in her direction as he whipped up to the curb to park. She loved the fact that he seemed to be in control of everything around him. Sunbeam gained her independence after leaving her parents' home, but she also loved the feeling of being protected and felt that from Parker. Once the car came to a stop, she pulled the door handle to get out of the car before he could open her door for her. Being a part of the hippie lifestyle had made her forget that regular men had gentlemanly ways. Her individuality had jumped ahead of him being the type of man she liked and preferred. Her father had always opened the door for her and every woman he encountered, and she had to laugh inwardly to remind herself to relax and just let a man be a man.

Removing her sandals, she began twirling around in a circle with her hands in the air. Her free spirit felt at home. Parker leaned on the Chevy trunk with his hands crossed in front of him and enjoyed the view. The pounding inside him from his ancestors began again. Everything about her was ravishing and satisfying to him. He watched her do this thing of pushing her lip to one side. He pondered whether she was deep in thought or if maybe she was impressed with him.

"Hey, pretty lady, you may want to refrain from doing a Gypsy-like dance around a campfire light without your sandals. Some of the plants up here have needles."

"Would you pull the needles from my feet and wash them and then kiss away the pain?"

"I think before I let something happen to you, I'd rather pick you up and carry you."

"Hmm, yeah, please keep me from getting hurt, please."

Parker felt she had a double meaning in her statement. He walked over to her and lightly kissed her forehead. "Put your sandals on for a little longer, and I'll rub your feet once we settle. Oh, and yes, I promise not to hurt you."

She hugged him briefly but with her whole body immersed inside his space. "What is this place you have brought me to?"

He begins unpacking the trunk while answering her. "Outsiders call it Grand View Park, but those of us that live in the area call it Turtle Hill. It's the best place to look at the Golden Gate Bridge during sunset. The view is spectacular from here."

"What's all this stuff for?" she asks once he closes the trunk and proceeds to walk out of the parking area.

"Just a few things for us to be comfortable while we enjoy the view."

"I know you got some of this when you stopped at the store under Jimi's place, but you put these other things in your car for..."

Parker cut her off, as he assumed he knew the question she was about to ask. He thought she wondered, as any woman would, if he comes to this spot often and with other women.

"I inherited this car from my dad last year. Ever since I was a little boy, we went to parks and beaches together and ball games to see Willie Mays play. So, these things were always here, and I honor Dad by having them in here now that he is gone. Today, I get to share my past with you by finally taking these things out of this trunk and having a reason to use them with a woman I want to spend some time with."

"I'm sorry for your loss; sounds like your dad was good, man."

"He was better than good. He supported my life so that I could be what I wanted to be."

"And what is it you are or want to be?"

"Let's go over here and get set up, and I'll answer your question and any other question you may have."

They walk to the area he intended. He had chosen the location, as his mom and dad would often go there and play spades until the sun was gone and the stars and city lights were their playing partners. Methodically, he began setting things up. He unrolled a large quilted blanket and laid it on the grass. Then he pulled out two plastic cups, a bottle of wine, fresh salami, cheese, and fruit that he had purchased at the store. Sunbeam plopped down on the blanket Indian style and smiled as she watched him pull out a pocketknife to cut the meat and cheese.

"You promised to elaborate on your statement earlier about being focused. Can I get that promise fulfilled?" Sunbeam lays back on the blanket, nibbling on a piece of fruit, waiting for an answer

Her navel had been talking to him all day, but he did not address it until now. He takes a sip of wine for courage and as a lubricant. With his lips wet from the wine, he kisses her navel. Something he had been dying to do all day. Sunbeam welcomes his advances, and her body relaxes further on the blanket.

"Yes. I will elaborate on my focus. But first, let me tell you a little story. In Greek mythology, Apollo and Clytie's story ties into the body paint you have. Your sunflower triggered something when I first saw it."

He continues caressing her flower and running his fingers over her navel piercing.

"As the story goes, Clytie was a nymph – a spirit of nature who often appeared in the form of a young woman – and she adored Apollo. In the beginning, Apollo loved Clytie as well, but soon, he lost interest in her and fell in love with Leucothoe. Filled with anger and jealousy, Clytie told Leucothoe's father about his daughter's relationship with Apollo. She thought the reward she would receive would be the father ending the relationship between her beloved Apollo and Leucothoe; instead, he punished his daughter by burying her alive. When Apollo found out what she had done, he turned Clytie into a flower out of anger. Her punishments did not change her love for Apollo; she spent her days watching him as he moved the sun across the sky in his chariot, in the same manner a sunflower's face moves to follow the sun. At least that is how one story goes."

"Interesting story. I had not heard that before, although my mother and father are well educated, and Mom teaches as a professor of Archaeological Anthropology."

"I used to study some of the variations in Greek mythology, and while this story is not one strongly held, it does have a following. When I saw your body art, it brought to mind the myth because of Clytie and Apollo and the sunflower as a symbol of adoration and loyalty."

They both nibbled on the snacks in their spread and had another glass of wine. Soon, the sun began to dip below the land. Bright yellows and baby blues began to turn into oranges and purples. Parker laid on his back, staring to the sky, as Sunbeam gazed with him.

"Now to elaborate on my 'focus' comment from earlier. I have always been a focused man. Until about a year ago, I was in college at Berkley. I was doing well, but I began to feel suffocated by institutionalized learning. I wanted to be the change that I wanted to see in the world. I dropped out of school and joined a group of hippies. Their thinking was more in line with mine than college had been. One day, much like how today has been for you, I stumbled upon a Black Panther rally. I found a lot of their party line thinking was on the same beliefs of peace, love, and anti-war, the difference being that they were putting action behind the message and pushing for solidarity for all. The hippies preached about love and peace, but there was no means of changing anything. So, I joined the Black Panther movement, which has been my main focus since that time. My father followed Malcolm X, so he encouraged my direction and supported my goal to change the way the man controls us and makes us fight other nations over money and race when we should be caring for our people."

Sitting up slightly on her elbows, Sunbeam turns to face him. "So, if that has been your main focus, now elaborate on your multi-focusing goals."

"I have been content being a lone wolf. I knew when the stars, the moon, and the universe felt the timing was right, they would send me a goddess of my own. They gave me that gift when you walked out of that bakery. My soul stirred, and from that point, I knew I had to make yours stir as well. The perfect combination in a relationship is one where love, peace, and soul all reside as one."

His words gave validity to what she had been feeling all day as well. As if on cue, the day turned to night. The view in front of them lit up with lights from the Golden Gate Bridge. The colorful illumination of the bridge seemed to reach endlessly into the dusk. The view was just as spectacular as he had promised it would be. Her body felt warm and tingly. She couldn't determine whether the wine or Parker was causing her condition, but it didn't matter because she welcomed the feeling. She had always been a good judge of character, and she felt sure of his truth, even if it had been only a day.

Watching her eyes widen with excitement at the lights off in the distance, Parker felt the need to heed the drumbeat inside him and take action. He took the wine and poured it over her belly, and let his tongue chase every drop as it ran near her waistband.

"These are just in the way, and I would hate for them to get ruined," she said, standing to her feet and removing her bellbottoms. She stood before him in canary yellow, low riding panties, and he couldn't help but admire how good they looked against her dark chocolate skin. Her wide hips give her frame and her legs a longer look than her pants portrayed. He wondered how those legs would feel wrapped around him.

With her hands on her hips, she added, "Are you going to force me to make you more comfortable, or do you Black Panthers make love with all your clothes on?"

Smiling, he replied, "I do nothing by force; everything I engage in is coming in time."

He removed his hat first, followed by his shirt. Sunbeam's heart jumped out of time when she saw his chiseled chest muscles. Her temperature began to rise at the thought of tasting his skin. Sitting down on the blanket with her legs crossed in front of her, she put her finger in her mouth, acting innocent as he began to unbutton his pants.

"Go slow. Much like the view across the river, I want to savor the sight in front of me as well."

As camouflage pants met the ground beneath them, she nodded her approval. The juices between her thighs began to flow, signaling their approval as well. It had been a long time since she had admired a man's body, and she couldn't take her eyes off of the V-shaped muscular grooves where his belt resided when he was fully clothed. He was tight in all the right places and thick where he needed to be. She made no pretense about staring at the noticeable bulge in his underwear. On sight, it made her yearn for that *'hurt so good'* feeling.

Bending his knees, he slowly joined her on the blanket. The spot he chose, the thick grass padded the hard ground. He crawled over her, kissing and licking his way upward. He loved the salty taste of her skin as he began nibbling on her neck. She felt him inhale her and her back arched, accepting his seduction.

She ran her hands up his arms, and she felt a raised burn mark high on his left upper arm. Consumed at the moment, she assumed it was the mark from his fraternity days, and she reminded herself to ask him about it later, but not at the moment. Her hands continued up to his neck and the top of his head. She ran her fingers through his low-cut afro and pulled his head deeper into her neck so he could continue the attention he was giving it.

As he made love to her ear, breathing deeply into it and nibbling on her lobe, she knew she needed more. She wanted to feel him, all of him. She needed to taste his mouth and the passion that resided inside it. She initiated their first kiss, but it was the green light he had been waiting for all day.

Parker took control. He sat up off of her and removed her canary panties. Then his arms cradled her neck, untying her crocheted halter top and exposing her full plump breasts that he had been fantasizing about all day. For a moment, he just stared and admired them, and she let him. The silence between them somehow connected them. He rolled her over on her stomach and extended her hands above her head. Slowly, he began massaging her from her extended fingertips down to her toes. Her skin felt soft to his touch, and he let soft kisses linger down her back and her buttocks – his tongue paid close attention to her inner thighs and the wetness that was already accumulating between them.

Her body rose and fell like an incoming tidal wave. Making sure the lover man covered every inch of her backside, Parker rolled her on her back and placed his face between her thighs. At first, he made no movements with his head cradled at the mouth of her womanhood. He inhaled her scent deeply and exhaled satisfaction with her aroma of impending sex. Sunbeam had several lovers since becoming a hippie because free love was part of the lifestyle, but she had not experienced such sensuality and passion as with Parker. Unlike the others who only seemed to care about chasing an orgasm, he seemed to want to relish devouring her very essence. He didn't want just a piece of her; he wanted a part of her to become one with him. He lingered on her navel area – almost obsessed with it. As he lay there, she ran her fingers through his hair again before giving his head a slight nudge to continue with the mission at hand.

The night sky began to get darker, and soon the stars above them were almost as bright as the lights from the bridge. Parker allowed the moonlight to guide his fingers as he ran them up and down the opening to her womanhood. Spreading her thighs further apart and following the path his fingers had made for him, Parker began to use his mouth to sample the nectar of her flower.

Lips had never tasted anything so sweet. Famished souls had never felt so complete.

Parker was not the only one feeling gratified. Sunbeam's body lengthens as electrifying bolts of pleasure shoot through it. She could feel the ground shaking underneath her, but she realized her body was producing the tremors. As he took in every bit of her, she could feel his manhood rising. That brought her joy because she was dying to feel him inside of her.

Almost abruptly, Parker sat up and asked a simple question. "The stars, the moon, and the universe seem to have all lined up, indicating the timing is right for me to have a goddess of my own. Will you allow me to accept their gift?"

She stared at the taut body above her and saw that his hardness pointed to the stars. Her eyes took in his girth, and they widen like the moon above them. His thighs looked to break passages in mountainsides, and all she wanted to do was help them along with that plight.

She pulled him back on top of her, spread her legs wide, and whispered, "If you don't accept their gift, you will disappoint us all."

With the Golden Gate Bridge as the backdrop behind them, they made love, not war, on a steamy night during the Summer of Love.

CHAPTER

FIFTEEN

I am with my brother-in-law, LaFebra, headed to a lounge in Long Beach for happy hour. He has determined this is the hottest place to go for women in our age range. I have the convertible top down on the Thunderbird letting the sun ride along and the tunes flow. When you look, LA is beautiful and stylish; it is sundress season year-round. The both of us wear Kangol hats matching what we are wearing on this late Friday afternoon as the sun radiates. I'll admit, I'm feeling good. Life is good. I'm doing my thing in life. I have made transcendent business decisions, and I'm not missing anything I need. I can focus on wants whenever I desire.

Anthony Hamilton blasts through my speakers as the song "Sista Big Bones" draws attention at the stoplight. My car sits lower than the midnight blue Cadillac SRX luxury SUV to my left.

"Where are you two brothers headed to on this sunshiny Friday? Where is the place to be?" I hear a sweet, flirtatious voice coming from a tinted window rolling down. I see oversized sunglasses and red apple-colored, pretty soup-cooler lips smiling as I look up.

"We're heading to the Long Beach River Tap and Pup. Maybe you need to head that way." LaFebra speaks loudly over me, literally, as I am about to open my mouth. I look over at him wide-eyed. Then I look at the woman and the driver who is peaking over too; the driver is attractive as well.

"You over there playing my song; so, you really into Sista Big Bones as if you want to be with her. Or are you like most men who like her at nighttime but not during the daytime?"

I'm caught off guard with the driver's question. I see both ladies are what we call *thick*. I know LaFebra prefers thicker women, so the two are right up his alley.

"Me, I'm attracted to who is attracted to me and whether we have life desires in common, whatever they may be. No matter what, the Long Beach River Tap and Pup happy hour awaits us. They have a great outdoor patio, and at sunset, it's the place to be. Your choice whether to meet and greet."

"We might head that way, and if not, you two fine brothers have a good weekend." The pretty woman with the pretty soup-cooler red apple lips smiles as they pull away when the light changes to green.

"Man, LaFebra, don't be in my car hollering at women, making me look tacky."

"I ain't messing up your game. The sister saw us in your sweet convertible chariot, and they saw money. This is LA, home of the stars. They think we co-stars in the next *Best Man* movie."

"Yeah, right...more like the security guards at the gate of the set. Man, be quiet; you're messing with the jams." I turn the volume up to drown him out, merge onto the freeway, and get back to my happy mode. We hit the 710 and head to Long Beach.

Nowadays, when we go out, we run into a much younger crowd. Sometimes it feels like we are old guys at the hot spot. The young ladies we engaged with at the stoplight were maybe in their 30s; LaFebra and I are 44 and 45. I don't want to put myself into the same situation I was in with DeJohnette.

She was super attractive, but age differences can block compatibility. Age was not our only problem.

Driving over the Gerald Desmond Bridge, I overlook downtown Long Beach, and the view is romantic. The sunset sends rays of prism light off the hood ornament of my '61 Thunderbird. It blinds me a little, but I can still see Catalina Island. I think to myself that I'm going to take Serene over on a boat to a jazz festival soon, as I enjoy the viewpoint of San Pedro from above.

My stereo playlist brings up Sly and the Family Stone's "Everybody is a Star," and it triggers thoughts about the story in the journal which I believe was about Serene's daughter. It was the one about her and the Black Panther and their sexual adventure while overlooking the Golden Gate Bridge. I found that story to be odd. Could it be fantasy? The intimate details were so passionate.

My brother-in-law wants to know all the sex details, and I won't share them with him. I tease him a little bit as we go inside the lounge.

"Serene's daughter is hot...very hot, man."

"What?! Tell me...what did she do?"

"Nah, man, you're not grown enough; you would lose your mind."

"Man, forget you."

The music is soulful and smooth-flowing as we find a seat. The beautiful people are out, and a spirit of "Thank God It's Friday" has smiles on faces while drinks lift and toasts are made. A guitar, keyboard player, a drummer, and a singer have fingers popping. They know a lot of songs and they take requests. I see beautiful women all around us. I think I'm in the right place as they seem to be in our age range.

I know a few people, male and female, in here. We greet and have short conversations, then keep it moving. I'm enjoying the smiles and laugh along, engaging in small talk while sitting outside on the patio as the fans blow a gentle wind around us.

I request the band to play, "What You Won't Do for Love." They play a funky version that has people bopping their heads.

A woman sits down in an empty seat at our table. LaFebra has gone to the restroom. "Hello, I saw you pull up. That is a beautiful and rare car that you have. Is that like a '61 or '62 Ford Thunderbird?"

"Yes. It is a '61; and oh…I see you know your cars," I give her half a grin. She is a pretty woman.

"Yes, my dad is a car collector and I learned a thing or two from him. I think he had the same car, but it wasn't a convertible. Yours looks well cared for, and you looked nice pulling up in that classic. A man's car says a lot about him."

"Thank you. I appreciate the acknowledgment." The woman leans in, and she appears even prettier up close and personal. I didn't see any harm in chatting it up with her, so I lean forward and smile. I'm hoping she likes my cologne.

"You requested that song?" she asks.

"I did, yes…it's one of my favorites. It has a lot of meaning."

"What does it mean to you?" her lips have me gazing at her mouth, staring as she parts her lips. I'll admit, I love when a woman is a bit creative and assertive in her approach.

The music is getting louder, or the conversation around us is more resonant now. It feels as if we are alone even among many. I lean in closer. Maybe I'm drawn in.

"Sometimes you have to go the extra mile for what you want. Let me introduce myself, my name is Blunile Rivers, but you can call me Blu."

"I don't want to tell you my name yet."

"May I ask why?" I ask, playing along with her coyness.

"Hmm, let's leave it like that for now until we dispense with…."

She places her left hand on the table. She is wearing a sizable ring on her wedding finger - the diamond sits high above her finger. Until this moment, I hadn't noticed anything about her other than she was drop-dead gorgeous and tall with natural hair and pretty-almond eyes, with deep milk chocolate skin. I guess I had been lost in her looks and did not see the whole picture.

"Let me get to the point...my husband and I, we keep different schedules - different lives."

"Oh, interesting. You are a married woman, and you want to get straight to the point about whether that is going to be a problem for me?" I laugh, feeling like one of us, or both us, are on a cliff and the other wants to know whether to jump, and if the fall will be alright.

She nods, and I think about Serene and what she told me, "*Another man will love her as she is, if you cannot.*" I know I can't love a woman and she has another – a husband - no matter she says is going on.

"I need to let you be. I'm not the one for you." I want my tone to let her know that I'm insulted that she thinks I would be content with being someone on the side, but I also want her to know I am flattered and amused simultaneously.

She nods and then says, "I approached you because a brother that drives that kind of car and carries himself as you do, comes across as a man with a lot of confidence; but maybe you saying no, you're not interested, is more of a sign of your confidence." Her face showed she was sizing me up and pondering the wisdom of her own words.

Her recognition did not change my stance, "Miss, you have a good evening," were the last words I uttered her way.

My brother-in-law passes her as she leaves the table. I try to relax for about another hour, letting the sounds from the band calm me. I didn't have a drink, and I wanted one; but I couldn't let that woman put a damper on the thought of chilling, and I don't drink and drive. I stay in my zone and begin spending time talking with people I know again and let LaFebra have a good time. I'm happy to see that he may have finally met someone he is comfortable with. Those two ladies from the car ride came over to Happy Hour, and he had them both at a table laughing it up. The driver, she and LaFebra, are in each other's personal space. They seem to have connected as far as I can tell. I hope he has good intentions. I can see she is happy talking to him. After an hour, he lets me know the three of them are going to another place with a DJ so they can do a bit of dancing. More power to them.

Bobby Womack's, "If You Think You're Lonely Now" flows through my speakers on my way home. I have hit repeat twice.

CHAPTER

SIXTEEN

I walked around the facility, checking to ensure all is in place and saying hi to a few employees I had not seen in a while. I'm not usually in on Sunday mornings, but I felt like being around my workplace to tidy up some office work and check in on each resident.

It is well before breakfast time, which comes at 8:00 a.m., so I was headed back to my office to make myself a peanut butter and jelly sandwich to hold myself over, but on the way, I hear music coming from Serene's room: Mahalia Jackson's "Trouble of the World" from the movie *Imitation of Life*. I decide to watch the end with Serene before grabbing a sandwich. I come into the room, and Serene had on a Sunday church hat I used to see when growing up. Many Black women wore those big hats when they went to church. As if a model on a runway, she's styling a white dress that hems at her knees; it has a lengthwise broad blue stripe. Serene stood tall in one-inch heels. Using a finger clad in white elbow-length gloves, she pointed to her Bible on her nightstand.

I wasn't sure if she was scheduled to go to church, but she looks ready. "Serene, do you want to go to church?" She picked up her Bible and started in my direction. "Wait, I need to change, please give me fifteen minutes, and I'll be ready to go."

I had a suit in my office, but I'm walking down the hall, not quite sure what church or where to go. I tried to be quick and look at her file, hoping to find church affiliation. While reading her journal, I read she has a spiritual base. Since she has been here, we know she loves to sit in empty churches, and we arranged for that to happen, but I see no church membership info.

We are in my car, and I'm driving on a beautiful sunny day in Southern California. I had the convertible top up; I didn't want her hat to blow away. I asked Google where a Baptist church was. Google told me of several, including First Baptist Churches and Second Baptist Churches. First Baptist Churches tend to be white congregations, and I had no problem going there, but a Second Baptist Church showed up that I knew of and had forgotten.

As I pulled into the parking lot, I see mostly Black people and a few Hispanics and whites walking and dressed beautifully. The visual of beautiful sisters walking together with well-dressed men looking sharp made me feel blessed about my decision to come to church. Some men and women wore more relaxed shirts and slacks. On my arm I had the elderly, but stunning at any age, Serene May, as I walk her into the church. Several women nod their heads or smile at me. I assume they are appreciative of me escorting an elder into the church. Maybe they believe I'm with my mother, I don't think they see her as my grandmother, as Serene does not look her age for sure, but her measured walk might speak for her.

Churches, the buildings of spiritual practices. I spent many days watching adults be one way in the buildings and act other ways when not in the church building. As a child, it frightened my young soul, which did not understand. I believe in God, and for sure, I have faith, but it was a challenge as a child. Sometimes church felt forced more so than a celebration. As I walk into the church building with Serene, I am thankful. I feel inspired to maybe look into going more often.

Most of the stories written in Serene's journal had some reference to faith or connection to God or Gods. Each story I read had me going places and

172

feeling her thoughts on love, sex, desires, travel, good people, and a few times, navigating around people without good hearts. Serene inspires me with triumphs over trials and tribulations.

The gospel choir and church band swung in rhythm and high volume of praise. It was emotional to watch Serene swing back and forth to the music. I observed her body language during the service as she closed her eyes. When the pastor was preaching and the congregation shouted Amen, she nodded her head firmer than usual.

After the service, I went up to a few people I knew and had not seen in a while, and we all encouraged each other to meet here more often. I chatted with a couple I had known since high school, reminiscing about the old days in school. I was happy to see they were still as one and going strong. I introduced Serene May as someone special from my care facility, and that is why I was here today. Serene nodded as each woman took her hand and said, "Glad to see you, ma'am; please make sure you make Blu come back." Serene nodded and smiled.

As we walk into the parking lot area, teens at a table hand out brown paper bags of fried chicken and a Styrofoam cup of baked beans and cornbread with napkins and plastic spoons and forks, as part of their youth activities. I was more than glad to give them two twenty dollars bills. Serene opened her clutch and pulled out a hundred-dollar bill. The youth pastor said, "Oh no, ma'am, we thank you, but that is a lot." Serene handed the hundred-dollar bill to me, and I said, "Please take the money. It will please her."

When we get to the car, Serene points to the roof.

"You want the top down?"

She nods, and I put the top down. She removes her hat, and we are traveling with the wind in her hair. Serene looks like a movie star with her chin held high. I pull into a park that had a water fountain with children playing in the water. We stroll over to a park bench and have our fried chicken dinners. It is a beautiful day, and as I'm enjoying the moment, Serene places her hands together and opens them like a book is open.

"The journey to love," she says into her hands.

I only had to walk 50 feet to the car, and I came back with the journal, and I started reading a story.

Peachtree Street. August 29, 1967

We traveled from Memphis with every window down to try to stay cool in the sweltering heat. Earland drove his new 1965 Pontiac convertible at the speed limit and drove the highway with other Black drivers when they were present. To be careful during these times, we had to use the Green Book to tell us where we could eat and stay. We kept the top up; it could be a thumbing of the nose by uppity Negros to travel with the top down.

Martin Luther King had invited Earland to come to Atlanta. My man was a well-known civil rights lawyer from Detroit and currently worked in Memphis with the sanitation workers' union. The union is locked into a long battle with the city over the Black worker's treatment when they picked up trash in the white neighborhoods, and they wanted better pay. It would be a war over a long-haul of legal challenges against a white justice system. Martin Luther King admired Earland for his dedicated work. He told Earland, one day, he will come to Memphis to help.

While we drove, Earland always held my hand as we went along our journey, and sometimes I placed my hand on his thigh and squeezed while we traveled. A few times when we were on road trips, we pulled over and found a private spot and used the bathroom, as we could not use white restrooms. Sometimes we ended up making love in a wooded area. It was dangerous, but that made the sex more intense.

I had it on my mind I had to call my daughter at a designated time because she is on the west coast. We found a payphone at a Negro service station. I had received a message from her father that our daughter had news to share, and she'll be at a certain phone number on this day during a certain time range. I needed to call during that time.

174

After the call, I walked to the car feeling a little numb with what my daughter told me, but she can make decisions for her life separate from what I might want for her. I made my path in life all based on what I thought was best for me.

We got into Atlanta late, and we checked into the Howard Johnson on Peachtree Street. It was just a few years ago we could not stay in a place like this in Atlanta. Good people like my man Earland and Martin Luther King, Andrew Young, and a young man named John Lewis, and many others, worked with their life's blood to make change come.

As I look down on the traffic from my room, I think of Margaret Munnerlyn Mitchell, the novelist and journalist who wrote *Gone with the Wind* - her only novel to get published during her lifetime. She was crossing Peachtree Street in 1949, and a speeding car hit her and she died. Although Margaret Munnerlyn Mitchell was white, I think of the hundreds, if not thousands, of Black people killed because of their skin color since the time portrayed in *Gone with the Wind*. I feel a sense of royalty to be a Black woman in a fine hotel while south of the Mason-Dixon Line.

A growing number of us were starting to use the term *Black* as opposed to being called *Negro*. It felt like the name was from a place of power to title ourselves, instead of being labeled by the white race.

I saw Martin Luther King on TV, and Earland had several meetings with him. My man shared Dr. King's dreams, and we spoke of those aspirations often when we lay in bed late on Saturday mornings drinking coffee. I felt I had an insider's view of the world ahead for Black people. I knew of people doing the behind-the-scenes work for Dr. King and the work out front for all to see. However, I wanted to have my opportunity to sit in church and hear the man. I listened to his voice on the phone once when he called.

"Hello."

"Hello, may I speak to Earland Du Bois? Tell him it's Martin King."

"Mr. King, hold on a second. Earland is just coming in."

"Is this Miss Serene? Earland has told me great things about you. He says you are the smartest and most beautiful woman on this Earth, and the sound of your voice leads me to believe he is right." I was not sure if he was flirting or being charming.

"Oh, Mr. King, I'm sure you know plenty of beautiful women. I have seen pictures of Mrs. King in magazines, and she is what I would call a queen."

"Oh, my dear, please call me Martin; and if there is anything you may need, please let me know, and if it is within my power, I will accommodate."

"Oh, okay...here is Earland."

I know many people heard his voice on records and TV from speeches and sermons and marches. I know Martin gives a lot of himself, so I could never ask anything from someone giving so much to his people.

The morning after our long road trip, we were in the hotel lobby with several other Black people, some notable including my old friend Vivian Dandridge, Dorothy's sister. I miss Dorothy since she died. Vivian and I sit down and have the continental breakfast. She invited Earland and me to ride in her town car to the church, but we had plans to go sightseeing after church.

I wanted to be at the church early, as there might be a line to get in. We were sitting in the middle of a packed, tight church. It was hot! I pulled up the little fan stored on the back of the pew in front of me and looked at the picture of white Jesus with all-white disciples at the Last Supper. I believe one should know correct history, as I have written books of fantasy about Egypt, North Africa, Israel, and all the areas near Mecca, and all who lived in the Holy Land. What the people look like was never fiction. Those people were not European in appearance.

I started fanning myself as the choir was doing a marvelous job making me feel the spirit. I'm glad I wore loose-fitting silk chiffon over lightweight cotton to help keep cool.

Speaking of hot...oh my goodness, my man, he was in a blue pinstripe suit; he was striking. His dark-dark chocolate skin and clean-shaven head drew attention as usual. An older man might have been naturally bald, but not someone of Earland's age. He had played football in college and said it was always easier to keep a shaved head inside his helmet. He continued shaving his head after college. My man is not as tall as some men who would grab the attention of women. He is built strong, fierce, and handsome in every feature. He looks like he could walk through a brick building and save me from a raging fire and come out unscathed. Earland had me fearful when driving down through the South, worried one of those racist cops would pull him over. I know my man to be sweet to me, but he is the total opposite if anyone tries to cross him or disrespect him. He would use the knowledge of the law first, but if a person did not heed to his intellectual persuasion, then he would be at Earland's mercy: *by any means necessary.* As much as he believed in the non-violent ways of Martin Luther King, he had lost a great friend, el-Hajj Malik el-Shabazz. Most people knew him as Malcolm X. Malcolm came from the school of thought, *I will not be a problem, but I can become a problem when presented with someone wrongdoing my people.*

Dr. King came out, and he was a very sharp-looking man. The moment he opened his mouth, he expanded our souls and pushed our thinking forward. Without hesitation, he preached to enlighten us.

"It is our time to rise!" he shouted, and people rose from their seats. "Look to your neighbors and tell them it is time to rise." People started shaking hands and patted each other on the back throughout the church.

When the church retook their seats, Martin Luther King preached of hope. "We will march, and we will overcome all obstacles. God has us in his sights not to be beneath anyone, and we are not trying to be above anyone as we are all God's children no matter our race, creed, or color."

I was mesmerized by the delivery and power in his words.

"With all that was going on in America, it is challenging times still. As we looked back some years ago, and we fought through the courts, *Brown versus the Board of Education.* We know the courts and laws can't change hearts, but laws can give inroads to better living while hardened hearts may find they need healing."

Dr. King talked of the future in store for our people and better days ahead for the United States.

"The war in Vietnam needs to end because our young brothers come from troubled times by way of generations of not so long-ago slaves. Then, it's not Godly to go off and fight against other suppressed peoples in other lands. Yet, our young Negro men are not free to the same education and the same jobs and the same homes as their white brethren. However, nearly all our people desire to live and raise their children free from violence and unjust laws.

"When we read our Bibles, we read about the sickly woman who was not allowed to be around the townspeople. That woman who had been shamed and mistreated for so long set out to touch the hem of Jesus's garment. She wanted what all others wanted. She had the faith of better days ahead if only she could feel Jesus's clothing. Her life changed; the moment the woman sensed her healing. Like all people, she needed a chance for her life to be like everyone's life. Jesus did not tell her not to touch him, don't live here, or don't eat here, get away from here, or don't shop here, or come in the back door and leave out the back door. God did not send His son to come down to die on the cross for our sins, but we mistreat God's children."

Dr. King finished the sermon and received a standing ovation leading into a rousing chorus of, "We Shall Overcome." It felt as if every very voice lifted the church to shake. Tears flowed down my face as my man put his arms around me and pulled me in close. I was thankful for this day.

I met Dr. King for a short visit as he had many people to meet. Earland and I knew a few of the people invited to come to town as we were. We joined them for dinner right after service at a beautiful Black restaurant. Afterward, we decided to walk Peachtree Street. By 2:00 p.m., it was already 100 plus degrees. We changed our mind and decided to go for a ride.

Earland removed his suit coat, and his shirt was wide open. I changed into some cotton pants and penny loafers and a cotton blouse. As we were driving around Atlanta, we knew where not to venture. Along the drive, we saw Confederate statues. I watched my man's jawbone cinch tight. "We will take them down one day," he said. I rubbed his arm and kissed him on his firm chocolate cheek, and reminded him that he and I are together, and nothing was better than the time we spend together. He pulled over and kissed my face and then my lips and onto my forehead. I loved his forehead kisses. We were near a small park and believed we might be safe; the few cars we passed in the area showed other Black people driving by. We heard soul music coming from their car radios, and we saw smiles on their faces.

We were near a wooded area. We got out to walk and made our way through a bushy area; we came upon another Confederate monument of a dead Confederate soldier.

"Hey, babe, you have to forgive me, I have to pee, and I'm going to pee on the back of this monument," he laughed.

"Go right ahead; if my man needs to urinate, let it be on a dead Confederate soldier's grave." I'm giggling like a little girl. "Do you need me to aim for you?"

He is laughing hard. "Next time, speak up before I let loose."

Earland came back around and put his jacket over the plaque in the front. He gives me a look, as he had not buttoned up his trousers. I unbutton my blouse and remove all I have on except my panties.

"Hey babe," he says as he pulls me and my naked breast to his bare chest. "Why don't we take advantage of this private space and time, and dishonor this Confederate whoever he is."

It didn't take us long to get busy. Pants and shirts and underwear now cover the ground. I'm sitting on top of my man's stomach, and I know he can feel my wet heat. He caresses my breast, making my nipples hard as he flicks them. I lean over and let him suck me vigorously. We were touching and rubbing on each other and kissing. I stand up over him and reach down to squeeze his hardness. He is so tall and stiff, I stroke him, and he drips. I pull my panties to the side and slowly squat on his hard-on. It always took a while, but I ride him like a spring – up and down. He felt fantastic, and he was moaning and calling my name.

"Serene, Serene, oh shit, it feels so good."

I enjoyed him, and we just stayed there, me riding him until we moved around to other positions and kept on pleasuring each other. We took our time tasting and sucking until both of us release our juices with deep groans. We laid close together and almost fell into a nap.

"Earland, let's not get caught with our clothes off out here amongst who knows."

"Yeah, I don't think my law degree can explain this away."

We laugh and get dressed and walk out of the little wooded area.

"Wait a minute," I say. Now it's my turn to urinate on the monument. I walked behind the cement ode to a failed Confederate soldier, and I squat and pee. Earland is cheering me on.

We walk back to our car, and we pass a white couple walking and pushing a baby in a stroller, and they stopped and looked at us in amazement or shock.

"Do you know where you're at?"

"Yes, we were fertilizing the ground over by a dead Confederate soldier." In the same breath, Earland gave him a stare that said, "*What are you going to do about it?*" The white couple walked away fast.

We put the top down on the Pontiac convertible and laughed to the point of me holding my stomach as we drove away. We were acting like uppity Negroes and proud of the fact that we didn't give a damn. "A Change Is Gonna Come," the song, came on the radio, and we turned the volume up as loud as the radio would play. We took our time going back to Peachtree street to have glasses of ice-cold peach tea.

CHAPTER

SEVENTEEN

"I had a lengthy conversation with Pierce Witherspoon, Serene's lawyer."

"Oh, you never call your patients by just their first names, but you no longer refer to her as Ms. May. Hmm, my brother, she must be extraordinary to you."

My sister is teasing me. "As I was saying...Mr. Witherspoon and I had a conversation, and he let me know Serene loves fine dining. Although we have been making her food as she likes, he proposed we take her out to various restaurants for a bit of a change. He is hoping that either I or maybe someone here at the facility might take her out. He did say that she does prefer to be on the arm of a man, so I guess I am taking Serene – Ms. May out for some fine dining.

"Okay, have a good time when you do. When are you taking her?"

"Can we schedule a hair appointment for her tomorrow morning, and I'll take her out in the evening. Please let Cassandra know so she will help her pick out the clothes she might want to wear and maybe have someone help her dress; if she needs any help."

"I will do, my brother. It sounds like you need to pull out that suit your mama bought you that you have never worn. You know that suit she was hoping you would wear at your wedding someday."

I wanted to call my little sister some of the names we called each other as children, but we are in the hallway, and there are too many people walking by. We are standing near the TV room where people gather to watch movies and play cards and board games. It's human nature for people to want to know what our conversation might be. Prying eyes and ears, I can see they were trying to eavesdrop. People see the same folks day in and out, and seeking gossip would be the main activity even if it snowed in LA.

I slyly walked up to my sister, whom so few knew is related, and I quickly removed an almost full can of iced tea out of her hand. I gulped it down as I walked away, much like I did when we were children.

"You come back here, mister. Better yet, meet me in the office; I do need to talk to you." I could tell by Sherry's tone it was something more serious.

In my office, Sherry sits at my desk, and I'm standing looking at her. "What's going on, my sister?"

"You see the grounds are not as kept as they should be?"

"Ah yes, I was going to ask about it; for sure, it is not up to par, and I have not seen workers on the grounds for a few days. What is going on?"

"I fired that company."

I'm looking at Sherry. She has the authority to make any significant decision if need be. I trust my sister, but she usually talks to me right away if she makes an impactful decision, such as this.

"I fired them because I have spoken to the owner more than a few times about the young men who work for the company. They make flirtatious, disrespectful, sexual comments to the women who work here. One of the young men followed Cassandra and Missy, a young woman I hired to work in the laundry; well...he followed them to a Happy Hour bar. He tried to act as if he just happened to be in the same place, but after a few drinks, the man confessed he came there just to get to know them better. The ladies are a bit scared that he might be stalking them. So, I fired the company."

I feel dry air going down my throat; my mouth must have been dropped open, and I caught myself not breathing and then took a deep breath. "Sherry, I wish you had let me know. But I know you...I know you did what needed to be done, so I wouldn't have to. I thank you, and I love you for you and for being on top of this."

"A new landscaping company starts in the morning. I knew you would be mad and might go hurt someone's feelings. I know how you are about fools making foolish mistakes. You are like your fawdur'; a great guy, but you have another side when people cross lines."

I handed her the can of iced tea I had taken from her earlier, although it was near empty.

"Blu, you are an ass, and if we were not at work, I would whup you."

"Oh, look who has a temper." I walked out of the office laughing, and I heard a few more choice names my sister called me.

I keep my classic car clean, but I felt a bit more sense of pride in wanting to have it cleaner than tidy as I'm taking Serene to a 5-star restaurant. As if she is the First Lady of the world, she is wearing a dress to greet millions of followers. Her head is held high like royalty. Because of Serene, I had read about the Egyptian goddesses. The most powerful of all goddesses was Isis. Isis was known in Egyptian mythology to be a ruler of the moon and a protector of women and children. She had the power to heal the soul.

A gold-toned dress flows down to Serene's ankles; it appears to be silk. There are white pearls laced throughout the gown. She wears a white shawl around her shoulders that has gold threads woven throughout. On her lap lays a white pearl clutch matching her heels. Serene is elegant in her heels. I would think she might not be able to handle a three-inch heel at her age, but she walked to the car with no hint of struggle. White pearls cover her natural salt and pepper hair with thin threads like a fishnet from Tiffany's finest collection of jewelry.

Serene, at almost 90 and sporting light pink lip-gloss, looks ready to be the next model to walk a Paris runway. I sense she feels good about herself. On the drive, she and I share small talk; when energized, Serene will join in or create conversation. As it fades below the horizon, the setting sun sends a flare of light down the middle of Sunset Boulevard. I watch her head turn slowly and stare at Roscoe's Chicken & Waffles. She pointed, but more like she held her finger up; I did not know why. Maybe she had dined there before.

The 101 turns into I-10, and we are about ten minutes away from our destination.

"Blunile," I reached to my stereo and turned down Jerry Butler singing *For Your Precious Love,* "One must seek the same rhythm with another soul, two must always meet in the middle to transform wants into giving. Seek to have love come from a woman's dreams fulfilled, and she will awake to the realities of who you are and what you need for your dreams to be completed."

"Ms. May, that is profound. I will take all you said and apply it to my future."

"She may not be perfect enough in her mind. If you be her dreams fulfilled, she will be perfect in trying to love you in the ways that make you love her. A man is born with faults and sins...he is not perfect outside his control, but he can be perfect within his soul in how he feels and what he does for a woman. A woman's soul is too narrow and too wide in wanting and accepting her own emotions, but a spiritual woman will make it all right. The reason being, she gives the understanding to learn and overcome. Her softness should be high, but that can lead to her being confused when a man can leave her lost. Always know, when she is perfect, she is at her weakest point."

Serene's voice trailed off as she had said a lot, and I know it tired her mind to speak as much as she had. I had nothing to ask or any more to understand from what Serene put in front of me with her soft, perfect diction. All she said was sustenance to my soul. I will place her words in front of my eyes and ears, when I speak to a woman I want to love in the future.

I drove along Wilshire Boulevard in Santa Monica and pulled in front of one of America's most expensive restaurants. The place has the plushest stately dining rooms. The thick white tablecloths could keep one warm in the winter cold. The meals are impeccable dishes, and the *carte blanche* menu is not for the of faint wallet. The wine list contains bottles one might need to take out a small loan on before it comes out of the cellar. I felt slightly strange that I would not be paying for the evening as a man, but Serene's lawyer insisted that the restaurant bill the lawyer directly. It was a regular treat for Serene to dine out before she came to Blue Haven.

It had not turned to full night yet, but dark blue sky greeted Serene's exit from the car, as a valet opened her door, and I helped her out. I dropped car keys in the other valet's hand; he was very kind and respectful in saying that she was a beautiful woman to be in such a beautiful car. I said, "Yes. Thank you." She and I walked between brass pillars on a red carpet, and a door greeter opened the door for us to enter a foyer. The bar was to the left, and I stepped in that direction to peek at the people inside. I saw refined suites and designer dresses holding drinks and chatting. I turned toward the dining area with Serene. The maître d', a short, dark-complected man with a French accent, made me a bit desirous of his tailored blue suit as he greeted us. His voice is rich in charm. He knew Serene and greeted her.

"Ms. May, I have not seen you in quite some time; welcome back. I have the right table for you. And you, sir, thank you for escorting such a beautiful woman into our establishment; we will make sure that you enjoy yourselves. Follow me, please."

The maître d' sat Serene and helped remove her shawl. He placed it over his arm as a waiter approached. Inside the dining area, we are in the indoor garden atrium with large green shrubs and Bonsai trees and flowering plants. The atrium's clear dome ceiling and architectural trellis structure allow for a framework of climbing and hanging plants interwoven between each table or booth. It is a royal garden ambience. The white tablecloth has beautiful crystal and shining silverware in perfect placement.

The waiter poured water and asked if there was a wine we would like or if we preferred cocktails from the bar. I am not an expert on the subject; even though my ex-girlfriend drank wine, I only paid attention to the price, which seemed to excite her each time. The last time I paid $100 for a bottle, and I thought that was exorbitant. LaFebra, told me I was not winning her over; I was buying her, and I would always have to do that once I started.

I guess I'm not a baller, as my younger-than-me ex-girlfriend did say, supposedly jokingly but I knew she meant what she said. By paying attention to the price, I think that puts me at a certain level as a man in the minds of women who want a man who flaunts his status. Yes, I have money; but I made my money by not being excessive.

Serene held her head high, as she does, and addressed the waiter in French. The server nodded and said, "Yes, Ma'am." He looked at me, and I ordered a rare dark beer they had on tap.

Serene scanned about her and smiled at me. It made me feel she was happy to be there, and I was more than grateful for the opportunity to escort her to such fine dining.

An hour later, with Serene telling me of some the best dining she has experienced in her life, we had finished our meals; it was wonderful, the best steak I have had. I had devoured my steak and Serene had adored her seafood fettuccine with perhaps every type of seafood one could imagine. Out of nowhere, she let it be known that, still, her favorite meal of all time was in Brazil and is called *Cachorro Quente*, aka, a Brazilian Hot Dog. Serene reveled in telling me, as if she was hungering for one now. She said the best ones are laid out on French roll and covered with seasoned beef and toppings of ketchup, mustard, mayonnaise, corn, mashed potatoes, lettuce, bacon bits, parsley, vinaigrette, plus Catupiry cheese and shredded mozzarella cheese and lots of cumin cooked in! She said it becomes quite messy, but after an evening of partying at the carnival, it was the best meal ever.

I asked her if she wanted to order dessert, and I watch Serene's eye divert upward as she nodded. Someone tapped me on my shoulder. DeJohnette, my ex-girlfriend. We talked a few times after our breakup, but she kept on flirting assertively. So, taking Serene's advice, I cut her off altogether. It's been a few months now since I made it clear, and she was not happy about the outcome.

I could not imagine DeJohnette being here. This place, as far as I know, is beyond her money; yet she is standing over me. I'm nervous. I don't know how to handle this intrusion into what has been a fine evening. She has a look on her face that lets me know she's been drinking.

A redness came to the surface of DeJohnette's light brown skin, matching her red dress. Her unfocused eyes told of her condition. I was hoping that she would say hi and keep it moving, but she said my name with such venom I felt fangs biting deep enough to feel for the rest of my life.

"Blu...well looky here. Of all the juke joints in town, you're here with another woman where you've been here with me several times. I saw you when you poked your head into the bar. Did you not see me? Couldn't you think of any other place to go? You bring another woman here as if it's okay to share a place where you and I have had a good time."

As she is talking, I'm ashamed of myself concerning forever letting her in my life. I can blame her for this event, but I should have done better in who I let in my life period.

"I get it, Blu. I've been dismissed. You have no feelings for how I might feel if you come here with another woman. She ain't no spring chicken either. But Ms....excuse me, you're a beautiful woman, but you look like he could probably be your son. And..."

I stand in front of DeJohnette, trying to cut off her verbal onslaught in having the nerve to address Serene. "DeJohnette, you need to go away! There's no reason for you to be at my table. You are rude, and you don't even know what's going on."

"I don't need to know what's going on; you're here, and I'm here. You won't even return my phone calls. You won't return my emails. The last time you spoke to me, you said you didn't want to see me anymore ... but why would you come here? You know I like it here."

Tears were seeping into the corners of her lips, and her voice had lost some of its hostility, but she is still belligerent. "What in the hell are you thinking to come to a place where you and I used to enjoy ourselves when we came here, and now you come to the same joint with this old biddy. I guess I was too young for you, so you've gone in the other direction."

I knew I had to stop this classless situation. I'm with Serene, who is supposed to be in my care, and who should never see this kind of behavior. I'm her protector, and here I have my past bad decision of who I shared time and space with making a public display. DeJohnette's voice wasn't low, and out of the corners of my eyes, I can see people staring. I moved to block DeJohnette's vision of Serene altogether.

The dark skin well-dressed maître d' approached, "I can help; please let me help. Let me remove Ms. May. Can I do that for you, sir, please?"

"Absolutely, please."

The maître d' extends his hand to Serene, and she takes it. He leads her away.

I tried to escort DeJohnette by lightly putting my hand in the small of her back to lead her, but she jerked. She said, "Get your hands off of me." I'm not the kind of man to put my hands on a woman in hostility; I was trying to be classy about ending this situation. I planned to order an Uber ride home for her, figuring if she brought a car, she should not drive.

I walk toward the foyer of the restaurant, hoping DeJohnette's would follow me, and she did. I came to the front at the maître d' stand, covered in a white tablecloth with the restaurant's initials embroidered.

In the slightly isolated area between the bar and the dining area, a man in a fronting-like posture moved in my way. My head came to the bottom of his jaw, and I'm 6'2." I had to look up as he stood in front of me, and I didn't quite understand, as DeJohnette walked around me and stood behind the tall man. This man stared down at me as if I were dog shit under his shoe. Every man in this exquisite restaurant has a suit on; he doesn't. He wore a simple shirt with an open collar. He had on slacks and what some people might call tennis shoes, which is a no-no wherever there are tablecloths. I recognize him. He played for the Lakers, or I should say he was on the team, but when he was on the team, he rarely got in a game. He's one of those players who made it to the league full of the promise of greatness, but he didn't work hard after the first big contract.

His voice came with a bit of spittle. "Hey chump, why is my woman crying after she comes back from saying hello to you? I let her come say hello, and she comes back crying. Did you talk to my woman crazy because she doesn't want your sorry ass?"

"Excuse me, if she is your woman, talk to your woman. You might want to check your woman; she approached my table when I had company. She was rude. So, I guess you are the latest fool to pay for her way of foolish behavior."

DeJohnette moved to the side of him and dropped her head.

"We should be able to act like men and just let it be so we can finish our evenings." I stare at him and hope he gets the message.

The dude poked his finger in my chest. "Don't talk bad about my woman. I will stomp your ass!"

I'm in a tight place; this is embarrassing. As some people say, I don't roll like this, and I don't. I don't do this crazy-laced antagonism. I don't do public ignorance.

"Please don't put your hands on me, and I will not speak to her ever again. I'm not here to have a beef with you or her. I'm here with a lady trying to show her a good time, which is not a part of any of this."

DeJohnette, let out a wounded yelp and buried her face in her hands. The dude poked me in my chest again, but much more firmly. Before his hand came back to him, I grabbed his finger and violently bent it back at the same time, and I lifted his elbow with my other hand. I heard the bone crack, and he barked a weird sound. His knees buckled, and I reached behind his head and smashed his head down into the maître-d' stand. He dropped to the floor with blood gushing. The white tablecloth on the stand now had a blotch of blood.

I stepped outside in case he was coming for more. I'm going to finish this here. Little did this fool know, I've trained in martial arts since I began to walk as a child. I don't brag about it, but DeJohnette, she knew, so why did she put this dude in that situation? Or maybe that was her intention in the first place. When a person drinks too much, as these two have, they make miscalculations into situations. Drinking hurts people, and they don't realize their impact on lives and how they cause others pain mentally and physically. And as often as they do, they blame others for what is caused by them.

A moment later, a couple of men who look like one of the chef's helpers and one of the waiters have their arms around the man while his arms wrap around their shoulders. The dude does look my way but is in too much pain to give off any more attitude. They walk him to a taxi stand near the end of the parking lot. He slowly eases himself into a taxi, and it drives off, and here comes DeJohnette. I walk past her as she leans against one of the brass pillars. I don't say a word to her bowed head. Inside, the maître d' is walking Serene back to our table and helps her sit. I sit down and reach across with both hands. I am trying to humble myself for what has happened.

"I apologize, Ms. May. Although this situation was beyond my control, it still happened in your presence, and for that, I ask your forgiveness."

She takes my hands and rubs them. "A protector must do what the time presents for them to do. You honored me; that is what you did."

"I should take you back to the residence. Is that okay?"

She nodded; there was no anger in her face. She smiled at me and patted the top of my hands. "Men have dealt with other men throughout time, and sometimes because of women, wars and battles come about. No matter where or when in life, always protect the woman. You did that. You protected me, and you also helped her even if she is unaware as of it yet."

I helped Serena stand to leave. The maître-d' brought her shawl, and he draped it over her shoulders. I took Serene's hand, and I escorted her out. Outside, we walked past DeJohnette's distraught face. The valet brought my car, and I helped Serena into the car. I started to get inside the car, and Serene stopped me.

"Take her home," her voice was soft yet insistent.

I stood in my car doorway, and I observed such sadness leaning against the brass pole. I walked over to DeJohnette, and I said very firmly, "Please, get in the back seat of my car. I'm taking you home. Don't say a word, just do it...please."

She followed me, and I opened my car door and pulled my seat in position so she could climb in the back.

I made it to the freeway, and my stereo played Kool and the Gang's "Summer Madness." The volume is low, and I'm hoping DeJohnette does not say one word. Serene opened her clutch and pulled out an embroidered handkerchief. She then turned slowly, reaching toward DeJohnette. I watch the exchange in my rearview mirror.

"You are a young woman, and you may not understand now, but you have a world of blessings if only you learn to give and lay aside self-destruction. A wise man and wise men once walked this Earth, and they spoke of, 'whoever shall be great must serve the least.' You must serve others to overcome selfish wants and desires. Be on guard so that your heart will not be weighted down with indulgence and drunkenness.

"The soul under the influence will make life complicated for you and for others and then you are serving no one. This day is hurtful, not because of rejection you do not accept, but because you have not accepted yourself. From this day on, you need to make a legacy for the least to love yourself. Are you understanding me?"

I watched in the rearview mirror DeJohnette's head nodding nonstop. Serene's words were like the laying of hands of a preacher healing the wounded.

I walked DeJohnette to her door, and she told me she would be a better person and grow from all this. She asked me to tell the lady in the car she was sorry, and she would take her words to heed.

Once I got Serene back to her room, I had one of the female night staff help her retire for the night. I sit in my office chair, feeling myself falling asleep as I'm too mentally drained to go home. But, at my home away home, I feel myself drifting in thoughts of how much worse this evening might have been; and I'm thankful, but also sorrowful.

CHAPTER

EIGHTEEN

Not knowing what I could've done better, I still feel awful about having Serene out for an evening, something that she cherishes, and failing to keep her safe from people's ignorance. My past life decisions on who I let in my life caught up to me. Still though, I don't understand how a relationship turned into what happened tonight.

As a man, it is on me to set the bar for the kind of people I want in my life. It is on each one to decide whether to be a part of or anywhere near drama in their life - I don't want this in my life. Tonight makes me consider the thought of whether I should ever be in a relationship. I wonder how many untold stories there are of the bad break-ups and ex-lovers gone bad. TV *Lifetime* movies we all wait to see are made from people's lives.

I come to Serene's room, and she is watching an old Betty Davis movie. I sit in the corner. I know I don't need too, but I feel like I must watch over her. I'm here, so I pull out her journal and turn to where I have not read. I see pencil writing and a picture of a young couple. The man is a tall dark bearded fellow with a muscular build. The young lady has Serene's face, but she is fuller than Serene, at least at whatever age she is in the picture. There is no doubt, it is Serene's daughter.

Endless Love - 1975

Ageless, spellbinding notes float effortlessly into their window. The music comes from a ney flute from the street below. The enchanting sound, majestic like the pyramids within view of their balcony, awakens him. Pitch-perfect cords stir his soul, soothing it as slumber gives way to reality. Smiling, he flashes back to when he first witnessed the instrument in action. A musician in a long tunic had played the simple, end-blown hollow cane at the airport upon their arrival. So far, Cairo had been a breath of fresh air and renewed comfort and sensibility to him in many ways.

Stretching his body beyond the position it rests in, he lavishes in the luxurious feel of real Egyptian sheets against his skin. The Mena House, set at the base of the pyramids, has been a home away from home for many dignitaries and famous people, including Frank Sinatra. It was a bit pricier than other resort hotels in the area, because of the security they offered it is worth every penny.

Parker felt a slight breeze stir the sheets that covered their bodies. It brought him to fully awake and do what he loved to do, and that is to move his feet to touch hers. Like children, they let their toes caress each other's arch and on down to each toe. Instinctively, it was their nightly ritual as well their first touch in the morning - his feet rubbed up and down her calves feeling her soft skin to pacify him.

He spoons into her, pressing his chest into her shoulder blades, wanting her to feel his heart joining the blood flowing through her body. Everything they had done as lovers had brought joy to their future. His hand spread wide over her belly, and he gently pulled her into his hips tighter to let her know he was the right soul protector of their future. A smile ensues as he remembers that her navel had been home to a hand-painted sunflower when he first met her. He reminisces on having drunk wine from it and how the taste of her slightly salty skin quenched his thirst. The warmth of her flesh reassures him that he will never be thirsty again if she is part of his life. She is his oasis. Their love is his haven. Snuggling his face into the nape of her neck, he inhales her—a delicacy of indulgence he routinely enjoys.

Warm affection from strong, comforting arms engulfs her. His flesh pressed against her flesh summons her senses to awaken. *Mornings were made to start off in this manner,* she thinks, as she rubs the side of her face against his. As her eyelids part to meet the morning sun peeking through the open window, she is reminded of where she is. They both lie together in silence, except for the sweet sound coming from the ancient flute that is flooding their room.

Parker squeezes her tighter. His hands are on top of hers. "How is my wife doing this morning?"

Light kisses on her neck cause her to release a long exhale as she looks down at their intertwined fingers. The matching bands on their left hands are gratifying to her. Simple gold had solidified their unity, but it all still seemed like a pleasant dream. If it was a dream, she prayed she would never wake.

"You calling me that will never get old."

"Remember that the next time I do something stupid as husbands do."

Snickering, she responds, "I will. Consider it an IOU for the next time you are in the doghouse."

"Well...wife of mine, I have a few more plans to build up IOUs for the future, but let's start with breakfast first. Are you hungry?"

She sits up on the bed and stares him directly in the eyes. "Hungry is not the word; starvin' is more like it."

"Somehow, I figured you would say that. Let's order room service and then get dressed. I need you to have a full stomach for today's adventure."

"Adventure? It's our seventh-year anniversary; when did it turn into an adventure?"

"We have been married for seven years, wow."

"Yes, 1967 until now. I can still hear my mother's voice on the other end of the phone asking me am I sure, and yes, I am still sure."

"If we do this married thing right, every day should be an adventure where we make memories."

Kissing her on each side of her collarbone, he gets out of bed and begins reading the room service menu before calling and placing an order. Enamored eyes follow his every move. She looks at her husband's naked body and smiles. It's been seven years since they first met, yet his body is still a chiseled work of art unblemished by time. Gazing at the back of his thighs, she is reminded of the many nights, back in the states, when the strength of his thighs served as the foundation for him to deliver ecstasy and many orgasms. Last night, his sexual prowess traveled across the globe to new heights inspired by the nights over Egypt. She swore the spirits in the nearby tombs released their energy to his manhood as an anniversary gift to them.

Their meal is delivered, and Parker places the tray on the white wicker table for two on the balcony. A single red rose garnishes the table. He took the suggestion given to him when placing the order, and they are going to have the Beid Bel Basturma, an authentic breakfast favorite of the people in the area. A slightly spicy aroma escapes from under the lid and attacks her nose. It reminds her of soul food dishes, just slightly different. She detects a whiff of cumin, garlic, and paprika seasoning on the beef that is topped with eggs. Hesitating at first, before taking a bite, she is pleasantly surprised once she does. The rich flavor is the Egyptian version of the traditional American breakfast of bacon and eggs. As his wife picks up the pace of constantly moving the fork from her plate to her mouth, he nibbles on some of the fresh fruit on the plate between them. His eyes move from the breathtaking backdrop of palm trees meeting the base of a sand-kissed pyramid less than a mile away, back to the most exquisite sight his eyes had ever seen – his wife sitting across from him in a short, form-fitting, silk flowered camisole with her breast partially exposed from the low-cut V-neck collar. Both sights are ambrosia to his eyes.

"Why are you staring at me like that?" she asks, blushing between chews.

"Like what?"

"Like you just committed the crime of the century and got away with it."

"Because I feel like I did. Your father told me as much at our wedding. He said I stole his most precious prize."

"Really now. Did daddy say that? What else did he say?"

"He said he remembered the day he woke up to an empty house because you had left without saying goodbye. He told me there was a hole in his heart for many years from the space where you used to reside. He said your mother relieved some of his worries when he spoke to her about your absence. She told him that you were showing the world the greatness that was inside you and that you were ready to share that greatness with the world. She reminded him that being free to spread your wings was in your blood, her contribution to your make-up, and that you were walking in her footsteps. He went on to say that once you contacted him again and began to talk about me being in your life, hearing your happiness began to fill that hole. He made me promise to always make you happy and keep you smiling. I gave him my word that I would. I also told him about this trip and how it would reconnect you with him once again. I sense, after the pain of that separation, he still feels afraid to get too close to you."

"How is you taking me halfway around the world and away from him going to connect me to him?"

"Patience, my love. All will be answered in time. When I first met you, you wanted all the news at once. You have not changed at all in that regard. I love that about you, and I would love for you to let me, in the end, tell you in my time. Allowing me to do that is when I feel trusted. We've got the rest of the day to make the magic happen. I'm going to go take a shower now so we can begin our adventure. I'll make sure not to use up all the hot water."

She finishes her breakfast and stands along the balcony edge alone, sipping the final bit of orange juice in her glass. Her eyes are full of wonder from the view, and her mind is satiated with life as she is living it.

"How did I get so lucky?" she whispers to the sky. Her question is answered in the form of memories of her childhood, her hippie days, meeting Parker, and the whirlwind relationship that evolved; and finally, the simple exchange of their wedding vows in the community garden that he had taken her to the first day they met, all play over in her mind. Then it hits her; she isn't lucky. She *is* blessed.

After a quick shower, she changes into a loose-fitting khaki-colored sundress and sandals with long strings that tie upwards toward her knees. She liked those sandals because they reminded her of the exact place she was waking up in – Egypt. Smoothing out the wrinkles in her dress from it being in her suitcase, she prays that her choice is appropriate for his plans for the day since she had relinquished her will to her husband's desire to surprise her for the first full day of their adventure. Her destiny for the day is unknown to her, but if she is with the man she loves, she feels confident all the rest of her days will be filled with enchantment, happiness, and love.

Hand in hand, the couple walk the long majestic halls of the hotel, through the lobby, and up to the front door. Staring at the high cathedral-like ceilings, she is awestruck by the grandeur of the old hotel and the history oozing from its walls. Looking around, she notices sand-colored walls are trimmed in deep royal blue, burgundy, and gold. She is almost afraid to touch the furniture, as some of it has hints of nobility, while other pieces seem like they should be in a museum. Passing different rooms, she takes in the different motifs, which include stuffed figures of sacred animals such as cow and the heads of lions and hippopotamuses. Some of the furniture has hand carvings of flowers, animals, and birds. She can't believe her eyes seeing the high-backed chairs with legs in the shape of lion's paws, gazelle legs, or crocodile feet. Gold sheathing, ivory inlays, intricate marquetry, inset jewels, and fine stones are included in most of the tabletops. No matter which direction she turns in, she feels as if she has stepped back in time and has become part of the royal court of Egyptian kings and queens.

Parker asks the bellhop to get them a taxi, then he puts his arm around his wife's shoulder, pulling her so close to him that her breath becomes his own. A passionate kiss unites them further. An older white couple, in matching white short sets, stops and blushes.

"I remember when you used to kiss me like that," the older woman says, looking up at her husband.

"And I remember when you used to look at me like I was your knight in shining armor the way she is looking at him," the husband replies.

"You're still my knight. Your armor is just a little rusty nowadays." She pats him on the behind as they head out the front door.

"Will you be that frisky with me when we are old and gray?" Parker says, staring deep into Sabine's eyes, which still have the same sparkle as when she went by the name Sunbeam.

"I'll never be old and gray, but I promise to always be frisky." She twists her upper body seductively in a flirtatious manner before grabbing her husband's behind with both hands in a slightly more aggressive way than the elderly woman had done to her husband.

Parker jumps a little from her squeezing his behind, then he notices that their taxi has arrived. "Your chariot awaits, my lady," he says in a bad English accent while tipping the straw-woven hat on his head and pointing toward the door of the hotel and the awaiting taxi. Once inside the taxi, he instructs the driver to take them to the Museum of Cairo. The driver nods. The ride is short but spectacular. Sights only read about come to life as the couple passes the Sphinx of Giza. The traffic is slow and congested, allowing them to get a long look at the famous landmark. King Khafre's face, on the body of a lion, seems larger than life through their windows.

A short distance later, the museum comes into focus. Sabine's eyes grow larger than the sockets that try to restrain them. Her father had spoken of this wonderful place and the history it held. She can't believe that she will soon walk among preserved kings and queens and get a chance to experience the legacy of Egyptian royalty. Cupping her hands around her husband's face, she stares into Parker's eyes deeply before kissing him long and hard. She then takes his hand and runs her index finger up and down the inside of his palm – their personal, intimate gesture that signaled love and affection for the other.

He smiles, "Did I do good? I take it this surprise makes you happy?"

"Yes, it does, and you definitely kept your promise to my father. I can't wait to get inside." She lays her head on his chest as the taxi comes to a stop.

Helping his bride out of the taxi, the driver pulls away leaving his two passengers standing together, holding hands, and staring at the outside of the building as if they are staring at the gates of heaven.

"We can't stand out here forever. Let's go inside. This is just the first stop on today's adventure, but it's the one that I promised would connect you to your father."

She squeezes his hand tightly and with her other hand she held firmly to the handrail as they slowly ascended the three steps to the front door. The building is stately with the rich and detailed décor of neoclassical architecture from the turn of the last century, it's dark coral brick startling in this sand-colored city. As she gets to the large wooden doors with vertical gold handles, she exhales before pulling the doors toward her to open them. Once inside, she takes two steps before stopping in her tracks. By the time Parker catches up with her, he finds his wife frozen in place. He senses that her brain is in overload – pleasantly so. Her eyes roam from ceiling to floor, and her mouth transforms from open gasps to being covered with her hands while containing a scream of excitement. He chuckles inwardly at the way his wife looks like a child who has stepped into an amusement park. Grabbing a map and brochure of the museum, he turns to her.

"I did some research, and I really want you to see the ancient hieroglyphs exhibit, but let's start at the Pharaonic antiques."

"I don't know how you pulled this whole trip off, but I am very happy that you did. Always remember this, wherever you lead, I will follow."

Hand in hand, they begin to explore the museum. The dynasties of Egypt are represented here, and tombs of Pharaohs are on display. To the right is a statue of King Tutankhamun, made of cedarwood and covered with gold. To the left are coffins and a mummy artifact of a child in a glass casement. Egyptians believed that possessions could still be used in the afterlife, so some of the exhibits included items of furniture which had been buried with the dead in sealed tombs. The ground floor has a collection of papyri, coins, stones, and ancient belongings. Gold masks cover most of the walls, while busts of several

Pharaohs line the hallways. Each glance leaves her feeling satiated with rich historical knowledge of ancient Egypt.

"Time is getting away from us. I want you to see what I think you will consider the cream of the crop here. Right, this way." He points to a set of glass doors leading to the section of the museum dedicated to the pictographic script of ancient Egyptians.

What once lined only the walls of temples and other holy structures is now enclosed within these walls. The sacred carved signs of the writing system are inscribed here. Standing in amazement, she feels proud that she can read the majority of what is written. As she absorbs all that is around her, she begins to remember nights sitting at her father's feet soaking up his wisdom and digesting his love for a language deeply rooted in religious descent.

Parker watches his wife standing in the middle of surroundings that bring her pleasure. Every few seconds, her lips move in outward silence as she reads the symbols on the walls. He smiles...her delight is his delight. He can tell she is pleased, and it makes him feel good knowing he has given her a pleasure she has longed for. He takes pictures of his beautiful wife with the great wonder of the world, framing her womanly body. He must keep changing the 35mm film to take hundreds of pictures. They even ask strangers to hold his camera to take pictures of them for the photos. Sunbeam had struggled with taking the pill, and each time she was on it, it made her body fuller, and the curves had filled her body out. He adored the thickening of her breast and the widening of her hips. He thought when the time came for her to have a child, it might be easier for her to do so knowing her hips were spreading. She teased him by telling him that by having thicker hips, she could have a bunch of babies for him. Parker loved the thought of the future. Noticing time elapsing, he allows her a few more moments to indulge before gesturing to her that they must leave. Sabine takes one last look at the exhibit, allowing her memory banks to fill with contentment.

"This is the best gift you could have ever given me. Thank you for this."

Warm kisses meet his waiting lips. He had hoped she would be pleased, but her reactions have been better than he expected and are priceless.

"Seeing you smile the way you did is something I will remember forever. I didn't expect the Tutankhamun exhibit to take four hours, but I am glad you enjoyed it and the rest of the museum. We have been here since sun-up, and evening is fast approaching. But I'm not through with you just yet. Let's go make some more memories."

They leave the museum and get in one of the taxis waiting outside for a fare. It's late afternoon now, and as the sun is beginning its descent, so too is the patience of the drivers on the road. Everyone seems to be in a rush going nowhere. Their driver tells them not to be concerned as they watch cars drive quickly in and out of slow-moving traffic. One car after another cuts their driver off, all while laying on their horns and with him returning the favor. There is a mutual disregard from everyone on the road for lane discipline, and pedestrians are treated as a nuisance. The couple gets a little anxious witnessing common road courtesy being replaced with aggressiveness and aggravation. The entire ride is in stark contrast to the calm and serene ride they had taken earlier in the day to get to the museum.

As they come to a busy intersection close to their destination, a police officer, using a whistle and waving white-gloved hands, frantically signals which cars have the right of way. Taking liberty when it is his turn to proceed, their driver makes an abrupt right turn, speeding around a corner and hitting a pothole before coming to a stop at a restaurant situated on a busy corner in the middle of Camel Market. Parker and Sabine almost jump out of the taxi when it comes to a full stop. While they had heard from other tourists how bad drivers were in Cairo, they didn't expect to witness it on such densely populated streets. Paying the fare, Parker added a tip even though he felt one was not deserved. He didn't want to be lumped into the category of being a stingy tourist.

Putting his arm around his wife's waist, he guided her into the restaurant. The bellhop at the hotel had suggested the place, indicating that it made the best Koshary in the city. Parker wasn't too fond of the thought of rice, lentils, and chickpeas over pasta as a meal, but he thought his wife would enjoy the authentic cuisine. As promised, the restaurant was located at a fork in the road with a beautiful view of the cruise port on one side and the marketplace on the other. It was the perfect location to do a little people watching of tourists in the market and for viewing the boarding of ships for day tours of the Nile and the Red Sea. Several large boats slept under the clear blue sky, waiting for patrons dressed in tourist attire as well as locals who were dressed in colorful tunics and hijabs. From their viewpoint, the Camel Market seemed to be a shopper's paradise. Vendors were set up every few feet selling spices, perfumes, gold, ceramics, and fabrics. Sabine vowed to visit one of the clothing vendors to buy a piece of sexy Egyptian lingerie – headdress included – once they finished dinner.

The couple opted to sit outside on the patio. People bustling by on the narrow sidewalk between their table and the curb nearly brush them as they sit at their table for two. Parker drinks beer while Sabine sips on water with lemon. Their intertwined fingers tango across the white linen tablecloth with a single red rose on top. An atmosphere of smiles and laughter surround them as they wait on their meal. Sabine has to resist her urge to point when noticing the Christians and Muslims walking the streets in order to trace their ancestry and their influence on Egyptian evolution, yet bawdy female street dancers known as ghawāzī performed their rural dances every few feet along the path of their journey. The mixture of religious people intermingling with urban residents was fascinating to her. A group of belly dancers walks past their table on their way to perform in the marketplace, and Sabine turns Parker's hand over and rubs her index finger up and down the inside of his palm again while winking at him. Her message is clear to him; they both are instantly reminded of the belly dance she did for him the day they met.

The locking of their eyes during their trip down memory lane is interrupted by the waiter bringing Syrian bread to tide them over until their entrée is ready. Sabine is famished from all the walking they did at the museum, and she tears into the vanilla-scented bread with her fingers before Parker can say a word. He leans back in his chair, smiles, and allows his wife to enjoy the appetizer. Today is all about her in his mind, and he is determined to make every indulgence count and be centered on his wife.

As she takes a bite of the last piece of the bread, the waiter returns to their table carrying their meals. She looks up at the waiter as the sound of sirens can be heard getting closer and closer. Trying to block out the noise that is getting louder and focusing on his customers, the waiter places their plates in front of them and asks if he can get them anything else. Blaring sirens get louder and louder, making it hard for Parker to answer the waiter. The sound is so loud that he gets up from the table to look down the street in the direction of the sound. Before he knows what's happening, he sees a car barreling down the street in front of them with several police cars in pursuit. Parker watches, as if in slow motion, as the car hits a pothole – the same one their taxi hit almost an hour before.

The car's speed, the pothole, and the tight corner conspire to make the driver lose control of the car. He can't believe his eyes, but Parker knows they are in danger. Instinctively, he rushes to his wife's side of the table, pushing the waiter to the side as he tries to help Sabine up from the table. Chaos takes over in the restaurant. Screams and fear fill the air. Tables are frantically turned over. Food, plates, and glass fly all around them. Other patrons on the patio attempt to run for cover, as it is evident the car is going to collide with the restaurant and those outside of it. Some are successful. Some are not. Parker manages to get Sabine up from the table, but only in enough time to push her violently to the side before the car strikes several tables on the curbside patio.

Gallant actions from a gallant man.

Her eyelids partially part before closing again. She can hear the beeping of some sort of monitor, but it is being drowned out by the pain pulsating through her entire body. It feels as if a fire is flowing through her veins instead of blood. The beeping sound in her ear is weak and burning pain in her chest feels like thunder sounds. She tries to move, only to feel manly arms holding her in place.

"Please don't try to move, ma'am. You have been injured very badly, and we need you to relax." His accent is thick, but she can understand his English well.

She wants to sit up and look at his face, but her brain can't force her body to comply.

Moving her head side to side, trying to shake off the ringing sensation pulsating through her head, she asks, "Where is Parker? I want to see Parker!"

"Just relax, ma'am. We need you to calm down."

"I don't want to calm down! I want my husband! Where is he?!"

Unable to move, she senses someone scurrying around her. The soft hint of lilac tells her that the movements are being made by a woman. Delicate hands place a cold compress against her forehead, and for the first time, she realizes that she is feverish. The fire is within and on the outside of her body. Sabine tries to open her eyes again but can only do so for a few seconds. Long enough to see that she is in a hospital room, and there are more people watching her than she thought. Looking at her arms, she sees several tubes attached to them and that they are attached to the machines that are erratically beeping. She raises her torso slightly and sees that she is bleeding from different parts of her body. The vision is that of a bad horror movie, with her in the role of the slaughtered victim. Her legs have no feeling, and the bed beneath her is filled with blood. Struggling again, she hears the beeping sound get louder and louder with each twist she makes. Frustrated, she flops back down. Surrender comes to mind, but she pushes it back and begins to flail about again.

"Mrs., please calm down. We are trying to help you here, but we can't do that if you continue to fight against us like this."

"I'll calm down as soon as you tell me where my husband is."

The doctor looks side to side at the other people in the room. The nurse beside him shakes her head before lowering her eyes. He knows the news will agitate her further, but she deserves to know the truth.

"I'm not sure how much you remember about what happened, ma'am...but your husband didn't make it."

"Didn't make it! What the hell is that supposed to mean? Are you trying to tell me that Parker is dead?! That can't be possible! We were supposed to be together forever." She begins to struggle in the bed more. Low beeping sounds get louder, more urgent in tone.

"Ma'am, we need you to calm down, or we won't be able to take care of you. You have lost a lot of blood, and you are hemorrhaging inside and out. If you don't relax, we can't control this, and you are going to bleed to death."

"Parker is dead? PARKER IS DEAD!"

Sabine continues to twist on the bed. Loud beeps get louder, and there is more scurrying about from the people in the room.

She feels herself drifting. The light above her head gets brighter, and her soul tells her to stop struggling. Peace and love, that's all she wants to feel. She knew she couldn't have either without Parker.

"My life is nothing without Parker, but life needs to continue to go on."

Exhaling her last breath, she says, "Nefertiti."

The nurse and doctor do not understand why that is her last word. "Was it something that she saw earlier?" they whisper amongst themselves as the beeping sounds become that of a flatline.

I close the journal and lay it in my lap. I almost slap my face as I take two hands and cover my face, as if I could not see what I read. I wanted to hide from the story I read. To know they died was knowledge I had, but now to know how they died…my stomach churns.

Serene has fallen asleep. I had covered her up and turned the TV off some time ago. I go down the hall to my office and I sit with a small light on my desk and I write a poem for Serene.

I come back to Serene's room and sit and read what I wrote for the third time before I place the poem in Serene's journal and dim the lamp on her nightstand.

"Blunile," I hear Serene's soft voice.

"Yes, ma'am."

"My days are numbered, so if you have written to me, please let me hear your voice. Read to me."

I cover my face with one hand and speak from behind my hand. I'm fighting back emotions and I'm trying to mask them from behind my hand. Serene has said her time is coming. I know this, but...

I read the letter.

Let God Give to You

I have lived to love and live through a lifetime of experiences

I encountered a loss of a child

One can never fully recover and never forget

Yet I lived on to love and help others because a living spirit is in me

I am grown, I am mature, I have lived several lifetimes, but at times it feels as if I am still a young girl, not a woman yet, when I close my eyes and ask the Lord, to have my soul to keep.

My soul still feels the loss of my mother while still young woman, I lost my father and I pray his soul is settled for what he could not help

My soul triggered responses

It is human nature to hide I choose to live with positives, joys and pleasures

My life became my normal

I expressed humanity from the many things not to define one's soul to others, but to love with no labels and judgements, to see the beauty inside and out each soul

Our living experiences can beg borrow and steal from us, as tomorrow is not promised. We must tend to our souls no matter the hurts and disappointments in life as our heart only beats for so long, so I have learned to feel the excitement of living despite it all. In a world that uncovers so much, we have little understandings of, we see what we want to see when we are seeking to heal.

This is when we must seek to see God in our directions. Often, we are blinded with no direction, but when we seek God, He will fill us with wisdom.

The Bible says,

What has been will be again, what has been done will be done again; there is nothing new under the sun.

I lived the life of a woman who falls in love with life

The how, when, and who, often help produce new life and relations we are then responsible for and as in many women we are forced to become Superwomen to provide, protect and raise God's blessings

Through it all, God's grace, and mercy, He kept me alive and taught me how to live and love through any loss

I have gained understanding from tryin' times

My vision has now become comfort

Through eyes that cried in the dark and in the rain, my tears have soaked my soul, and even when the sun shined I cried, and I fought, I worked hard and gained understanding that it was going to be alright.

Through open eyes focused to love for one's self

A broken heart is not the end of the world"

When life hurts the most, we must grow stronger to face our responsibilities

I'll never walk alone

I was never walking alone

My trials and tribulations was my gift in teaching and understanding to be with you whenever and no matter shall hold me down

I fold the letter and place it in her journal.

Her soft voice is weaker than any time before. "My living was not in vain, thank you for letting me know. Goodnight Blunile, I love you."

"Goodnight Serene May, I love you."

CHAPTER

NINETEEN

W alking the halls of Blue Haven this morning on my way to Serene's
room, I can't help but think how much colder it has been there.
Stagnant air has been hovering around her for a few weeks. I know the
cause. There is nothing wrong with the physical structure of her suite. The change
in temperature is due to the fading sparkle and spirit of its lifeline. Our residence
is more than just a building providing care; the heart of this place pulsates when
our guests are happy and content. As of late, Serene May has had less of a sparkle
in her eyes. She is more distant, and her aloofness has caused a stiffness of the air
around her.

Serene's medical condition has not changed much lately. Her disorder is
not the source behind the dimming of her outward shine. Medically speaking, she
has leveled to a plateau in her condition. No changes are expected in her
prognosis. Fear of her affliction getting worse is not the cause of Serene's mood
change, but I'm not sure.

A crucial part of treating the body involves healing the soul. Throughout her stay here, Serene has often drifted off into a world of her own. Those moments of reminiscent daydreaming never last for very long. Lately, she seems to linger in her quiet place much longer. Reliving past memories seems to give her peace inwardly, but they are starting to manifest themselves in a manner of constant withdrawal from the here and now. Her life has always been filled with adventure, and I find myself pondering ways to bring back more spice to her life in order to return her outward shine.

While making my rounds through the facility, thoughts of Serene float through my mind as I browse the charts affixed to the walls outside of each resident's room. As I get to the end of the hall, I can hear the radio from Terfel's desk in the corner. It is not loud, but softly echoes down the bare hall. A smooth jazz station is usually the selection of our orderly, and today is no different. As I approach Terfel's desk, I can hear a commercial break on the broadcast. A music festival on Catalina Island is detailed by the announcer. In my mind, the event is a perfect step forward in bringing fresh air back to Blue Haven by invigorating the sparkle that is Serene.

I enter her room to find Serene gazing out of the window. Her eyes are fixated on a flock of birds mid-flight. Her head moves up and down in conjunction with their movements. I sense she is silently soaring along with them. I interrupt her fantasy dance with the birds.

"Let's make today special," I say, easing closer to her.

She turns her head in my direction but does not say a word.

"I was thinking that you and I could get a bit of fresh air and treat ourselves to some live music. Would you like that?"

She does not say a word, but heads to the mahogany armoire in the corner and begins selecting her wardrobe for the day. That's all the affirmation I need to begin my mission of lifting the spirit of Blue Haven's lifeline.

The village of Two Harbors is beautiful. A sea of mixed cultures and nationalities surrounds us once we depart the boat. Colorful outfits and personalities appease our eyes. Street vendors and food tents for all tastes are endless as far as our eyes can see. Amidst the hustle and bustle of the festival's attendees, Serene and I seem to forge an unobscured path in front of us as we make our way between exhibits and portioned off spots on the grounds for bands to play. Her arm is wrapped around mine tightly; both as an anchor for leverage, and as a sign of being escorted by a gentleman. There is dignity in her steps, and everyone around us shows her respect by giving time and space for her to enjoy. The venue is loud, but even without her saying it, I know the event is pleasing to her. She smiles often, moving her head along with the music and closing her eyes in the process so that she can make the moment her own.

Sensing Serene's need to rest, I lead her to one of the food stands. I sit her down at an unoccupied covered picnic table while I order a bit to eat. A local band is playing slightly off to our left, and while standing in line to order, I watch as she hums along to their rendition of the classic song, "Bye, Bye, Blackbird." Her shoulders sway in rhythm with the saxophone solo. At that moment, she and the sax are one in the world. By the time I return with a small serving of calamari to tide her over until we get back to the facility, recognition sets in that the festival has helped me accomplish my mission for the day.

Serene takes a sip from the clear plastic cup of wine that I have purchased for her and whispers, "Thank you" before biting into her island-inspired, bite-sized appetizer.

I allow her as much time as she needs to enjoy her food and inhale the sights and sounds around her. Her contentment is vivid. I pat myself on the back for giving her a moment of serenity. My watch says it is time to head back to the boat for our ride back to Long Beach. I dispose of our trash, and we say goodbye to the covered sanctuary that has been benevolent to us for over an hour. Reaching for my arm, she lets me know she needs my strength to support her. The sea of people begins to part again on our departure from the event in the same manner it did upon our arrival. This time, there is a bit of a pep in Serene's steps.

The sun begins to set. Hues of orange and yellow suffocate the sky in a manner that is pleasing to the eye. As we board the boat, I can hear Serene exhale, glancing upward to the darkening sky. The heat, mixed with the water beneath us, makes the air humid. A gentle breeze provides relief. She wore a shawl today that has been wrapped around her arms. I gently pull it up over her shoulders. Her head rests on my shoulder as the boat's engine engages. Unconsciously, my head tilts toward hers as we both give appreciation to the sky and the skyline.

From the corner of my eye, I notice birds flocking over the Pacific Ocean. I admire their beauty. I wonder if Serene feels the same peace she had viewing the birds outside of her window at our facility earlier today. Looking downward at her, trying to weigh her emotions, I see that Serene is watching the birds, but she seems more captivated by what is beyond them. In the distance, a hot-air balloon glides gracefully through the sky. The harmonious beauty of the birds in flight is surpassed by her view of a captivating balloon.

My words to her inquiring whether she enjoyed the trip are muted from her awareness. She does not respond to my questions. She merely stares at the sky and the balloon in flight. Floating high in the sky, it brings another level of tranquility to her. Instead of continuing to try and elicit conversation from her, I allow her to be in the moment in the manner that brings her the most joy.

Once back at Blue Haven, I escort Serene back to her room.

"Let me get Terfel or Cassandra to help you get dressed in your night clothes."

She reaches her hand out to me; stopping me as I try to leave the room.

"Read to me, Blu." Her words are slightly above a whisper.

Her hands reach to the nightstand. She retrieves the journal of her adventures. She finds the entry she wants us to share as the culmination of a perfect day.

Turning down the covers on her bed, I help Serene get comfortable. I take a seat on the edge of the bed beside her, and the space between us is appropriate and comfortable. Her head rests on her pillow while we both allow the blue ink on the pages to take us back in time on one of her cherished adventures.

A grieving heart has no respect for time. The loss of our daughter brought me back to Chicago, hoping that being with Malveaux might provide comfort for each of us in our mutual time of grief. We attempted to start a new life together in the same manner that we had back in 1948; yet here we are, thirty years later, and while we have love for each other and share the same pain, our loss is not enough to ignite passion from long ago. We love each other, but we are not in love any longer. We share the same roof, but not sexual intimacies. We console each other's broken heart, but even half a century of wisdom can't fix the problems in our souls. Agonized hearts often block healing; no matter how hard we try to pretend it isn't so.

Malveaux is much better at what we wish we both were. He had and has maternal instincts, so he may seem to care more than me. My heart cares, but I am simply not like him. He is patient and giving. I feel lost and guilty for not responding as he has and does. I am thankful for him being who he is. However, when we look into each other's eyes, he is a constant reminder of what was lost with Sabine's death. When I see Sabine's face in any form, young or older, I'm no good to myself or to the needs of others. The woman I am, I have not mastered to be better than I ever have been when it came to being a nurture.

Malveaux, without one word of mutual discussion, became master of a plan to us moving forward. That is who he is, in the same manner he did thirty years before. That quality about him is something I will forever love about that man. He allows me to be free and live the life I am meant to live. There came a time I could not be near him and all he has set out to do in life.

Xavier University of Louisiana offered me a teaching position; I gladly accepted. Doing what I love most was rewarding, but I still hadn't found a way to shake the void left by my child's death. My mind flashed back to when I told Malveaux I was not mother material upon learning of Sabine's impending birth. It's ironic how the mouth often tells false tales. I may not have been a mother in proximity, but I certainly mothered my child from birth to death with the same love and devotion that all mothers have – the kind of love that only severs when one of them becomes dust. The fact that Sabine met her untimely end before me has been hard for me to accept. No child should perish before her parent. That agony plants roots deep and does not weaken with time.

In a daze, I went through the routine of finding a home, starting a new job, and attempting to make friends. I was intent on creating a new version of me. To others, I was succeeding at it, even though all I felt was constant failure. René was among the first of the tenured professors to whom I was introduced. She quickly became a friend, and she helped me acclimate myself to my new job. She showed me the ropes and gave me tips on living in the area near the university.

Still saturated in grief, I haven't managed to let my guard down long enough to become more than a shell of who I once was. Depression is real and takes on many forms. I know that I am functioning as expected, but I also know that I have become numb. I have shut myself off from feeling anything. The source of my problem is that I harbor extreme guilt. Guilt from not presenting more of a physical presence in my daughter's life. Guilt from outliving her. Guilt from leaving Malveaux alone, once again, to sweep up the pieces of our legacy. Guilt from feeling selfish in wanting to run toward the life I want to live.

I beat myself up with guilt daily. That personal torture is my cross to bear.

René knows my history; well…she knows it as much as I am willing to divulge to anyone besides Malveaux. Unsuccessful at trying to lift my spirits, she suggests I attend a conference being held here in New Orleans.

"Allow them to further your knowledge while they open doors to let New Orleans lift you out of this rut you are in. The conference is during Mardi Gras. If that isn't the best place to shake the dust off your shoulders, I don't know what is. Hell...go there and earn some damn beads if nothing else. Nobody knows you there. You can be whoever you want, or even reinvent a new you if you want to."

René had a way of making me look at things a differently. She was right. It was time for me to rise from the sadness surrounding me. What better way to do that than while alone and at someone else's expense?

"Serene, the only way to get out of the funk you are in is to do one thing every day that scares you. You have to get out of this sad comfort zone you are in. Your daughter loved your fearlessness. Return to that place within you. Do what is uncomfortable, yet enjoyable. That is how you will regain the old you."

Her words spoke to me on a level I had not reached in a long time. I registered for the conference and prepared myself for solo Fat Tuesday celebrations in New Orleans. I was determined to take René's advice and make it my goal to do something to scare myself every day.

At the end of the first day of the seminar, I decide to check out the festivities, so I go home and immediately change out of my work clothes, putting on a brightly-colored sundress with a beaded strap that ties around my neck. As I stare at myself in the mirror, I can feel a transformation taking place inside me. During the short drive back, I feel another layer of inhibition dropping to my feet. Slowly, I am shedding the depression and guilt that has clothed me for the past few years.

Stopping at a Cajun bar and restaurant along Bourbon Street, I go in and order the house specialty; the bartender adds extra umbrellas and fruit to the drink to give it the flare tourists expect. The sight helps put me in a festive mood. I embrace the concoction and the exhilaration it fills me with. After a few sips, I am dancing out the front door, joining others who are watching the entertainment happening on the city's main street.

Leaning up against a streetlight pole for support, I continue to sip on my drink as bands march, torch bearers perform, and people in colorful costumes hand out gold, purple, and green glass beads to everyone within reach.

Swaying of my hips accompanies the drumbeat as a band passes by with street dancers trailing behind. Some dancers are acrobatic in nature, doing summersaults and choreographed moves. Bringing up the end are several solo dancers. I connect eyes with one in particular as the band stops in front of me. Something about him is mesmerizing. I can't tell if it is him or the drink that is causing me to be intoxicated, but I welcome the feeling either way. His hips draw every bit of me to him. His skin is pitch black smooth coal. My eyes and mind survey him. This young handsome monarch has sex appeal dripping off of him with each movement. My lips take in more of my drink while my eyes continue to devour him.

With the band paused in place, I feel his eyes connecting with mine. I want to stop staring at him, but my eyes do not allow escape. Others converge in the middle of the street as the music and carnival lead many to be unabashed – unashamed. Free of inhibition, the young man grabs my hand and tries to entice me to dance with him. I am struck by the sweat dripping down his wet abdominal muscles, which have made his stomach hard without an ounce of fat. His lean body is enticing to me and has me in a trance.

Persistent in his desire to dance with me, he hovers over me with only air and possibility between us. The totality of his taut frame forces me to look up as sweat from his face drops onto my lips. They roll, catching his sweat, and I savor the salty taste.

His face bears a large scar from the top of his head to the bottom of his chin. Others might consider the marking to be unsightly, but I think it enhances otherwise handsome features.

He places his arms around my waist tightly and forces me to grind with him to the band's hypnotic beat. I'm in a tailspin. Never have I been such a willing participant to public enticement before. As he presses his body closer to mine, I am alerted that a hard body like his usually comes with a tender age. As we continue to dance, our conversation solidifies my assumption.

"Une si jolie dame. D'où viens-tu?" He speaks to me in French – his native tongue. A language I speak as well. Loosely translated, I knew he said, "Such a pretty lady. Where are you from?"

"Un peu partout; mais nulle part en particulier," I reply fluidly. "A little bit of everywhere; but nowhere in particular."

He smiles and steps back, sizing me up. "Oh, I see you speak the language of romance." He seductively nods his head in approval.

The music slows in tempo and our street grinding follows suit.

"I'm not from here; but you, young man, have probably stumbled into a forest much denser and much more cultivated than you anticipated."

He brushes a loose strand of hair out of my face before responding. "The best fruit comes from cultivated trees. Besides…I'm not that young of a man. I'm wise beyond the years that you see."

"And just how wise in years are you?" I ask, knowing that I might regret the answer.

"I'm well past the age of consent, but I'm not quite thirty yet. Don't let age be a barrier in allowing us to connect. The people around here have the ability of sensing the needs of others. I can sense that you need to let your hair down and be true to you. You have baggage that weighs you down. Surrender it. Surrender, madam. Allow me to help you release all which has captured you."

I give him a suspicious look. He is twenty years younger than me, and my dance moves slow down as I contemplate running instead of walking in the opposite direction.

Pulling me in closer, he forces me to continue the dance. He senses my apprehension and wants to combat it head on. Being this close to him allows me to see his heartbeat, and I feel a dampness swelling between my thighs.

He looks deep into my eyes. "Madam, please continue to dance with me. Help me be the expression of our imagination within this Haitian liberation dance. It will free you from bad and make you feel good. The tenacity of love is always near, and it will beat inside you once again. Dance with me, and your memories of the past will not leave you; instead, they will encourage you to live for what is not here in this world, but what is held in harmonious dimensions. Our union within this dance will bring balanced connections to your soul. Please...I ask you to tangle in dance with me and let the rhythms of your essences, in spite of your challenges, help you to find joy."

In his movement and his words, I find freedom.

The carnival moves further along its route. I am surprised when the young man stays behind; his attention focused on me.

"You probably need to catch up with the others."

"I have everything I need right here. These festivities happen all the time here. There will be another. If my spirit chooses to join that one, like I did this one...I will. It's leisure and enjoyment for me, and I have found both in you. I have made you smile; please allow me to help it remain there."

"And just how do you plan on doing that?"

"I'd like to show you a way to look at things differently. Follow me."

"Follow you where?"

"Somewhere a little less crowded."

"What's wrong with crowds? I'm enjoying this one. I'm having a good time...besides, real danger avoids groups."

"I promise, you risk nothing by coming with me, but you will gain what your soul has been searching for."

He takes my hand in his; we walk to a destination unknown. Along the way, he reveals his life in Haiti and the cruelty inflicted upon him that resulted in his scar. I feel a connection to his pain, his strength, and his fears. His disclosures allow me to release my own. I confess my motives for being at Mardi Gras and tell him that the only reason I agreed to follow him was due to René's insistence that I do something every day that scares me. I tell him about Sabine and how my life has been since I lost her. I surrender my emotions to someone I know can sympathize with my pain.

"Among everyone at carnival, I was drawn to you. Your story, I did not know; but I knew I wanted to help ease what might be perceived as guilt, shame, or regret."

I know I'm in a region where people believe in Voodoo. *Can he read me?*

We approach an open lot with large oval-shaped pieces of nylon on the ground. Near them are big wicker-woven baskets varying in width, and several metal tanks. A white shed is off to the side and he pulls me to it, but I step back several feet...twice I do.

"What is all of this, and what are we doing here?" I say, warily watching him unlock the padlock on the shed.

"I told you I wanted to give you a different view of things. This is how I am going to do it. At carnival, you saw a street dancer; now you see another side of me. I am a hot-air balloon instructor, and I'm going to show you new heights by taking you on a private hot-air balloon ride."

The enthusiastic smile on his face begs me to share his excitement. I don't. I have traveled a lot in my lifetime; but in over a half a century, I have never flown in a contraption without doors and wings.

"Is this how you usually seduce women?...by scaring them into liking you?"

"I'm not in the business of scaring anyone. Fear is an emotion that we all need to overcome. I like to give people comfort and peace; sometimes viewing the world from the sky can aide in doing that. Besides...didn't you just tell me on the walk over here that your friend advised you to do something that scares you every day?"

"*Touché.* But is this thing safe?"

"Trust me, you are in good hands. You are safe with me. Allow me to take you closer to the heavens. From there, you can reach out to people in heaven...if only for a moment in your lifetime. That is the peace I want to give to you."

I don't reply. How could I? He does not look like he has many possessions in life, yet he offers a gift that is priceless.

I watch as he prepares the lighter-than-air aircraft for flight. His biceps glisten with sweat as he puts in work. I listen as he explains the physics behind heated air making a balloon buoyant, allowing it to rise from the ground. Studying his actions, I notice him placing large containers inside the basket. It's leverage for weight while in flight, as I have been told. With precision, he turns the burner on. I can feel heat surround me as the hot air enters the bright yellow balloon, filling it rather quickly.

An outstretched hand invites me onboard the prepared aircraft. I allow him to cradle my body and lift me over. Uncertainty leaves me when I look at his welcoming smile. His trustworthy eyes speak safety to my heart. I'm willing to follow him, even if a gigantic picnic basket in the sky is our vessel to get where we are going.

Take off is surreal. Earth, Wind, and Fire caress me from all angles. It's like I am in a dream, and the gentle floating sensation is soothing as we are teased further and further from the ground.

The sight of trees, water, and land becoming smaller and smaller brings comfort. I feel as if I am observing the problems of the world through God's eyes. What we see as massive mountains that are difficult to climb, God sees as ant hills easily stepped over. A few birds share the same altitude that we do. I take note that their flight is just as graceful no matter how high or low they fly. Life should be the same way. Neither situations nor perspectives should change our flight.

"Beautiful isn't it?" His words are accompanied by his arms wrapping around me from behind as I lean forward against the ledge of the balloon.

"Not just beautiful...breathtaking."

"Does the height please you?"

"What do you mean? You are not trying to go higher are you?" I was starting to be comfortable and had shed my initial fear of heights.

"I'm not referring to the altitude of the balloon. I'm referring to how close you are to the heavens. I promised to give you that feeling of closeness of all who have gone on before you. You can talk to your ancestors and all who are looking down on you, and one day you will be among them and look down on others who loved you. Go over there in that corner and look out and up and meditate. When you are done, please come back over here to me."

I follow his instructions and go over to the corner of the basket. I pray and have conversations with my maker and the heavens. I feel myself releasing and receiving.

After a few minutes, I return to his side. Once again, he slides behind me hugging me warmly and tightly. He nuzzles his nose into the back of my neck, inhaling deeply.

"*Peux tu le sentir?* (Can you feel it?)"

"*Je peux. Je peux vraiment, merci.* (I can. I truly can. Thank you.)"

We float on for an hour. I see bridges and water tributaries of the great river – the Mississippi. Chills begin to form on my arms as I lay my head backwards into his chest.

I take a break from reading this story to Serene, she is still with me, but I can tell she is winding down. I guess when she was writing this journal entry, her pen must have run out of ink. The writing is now in pencil. I look over at Serene and she nods, and I continue to read to her.

I feel his hands beginning to explore my body while he kisses the back of my neck and ears. My body and soul surrender to agile fingertips fishing at the hem of my sundress, easing it upward so he can caress my bare skin.

Tilting my head upwards and backwards, he positions me so that our tongues can tango. The same fire used to inflate the balloon is contained in our kiss. Placing my hand over his, I guide his fingers up and down my inner thigh, showing him the pressure that gives me pleasure the most. As a voyeur, I watch the rising and falling of my own chest while moans escape me with each touch delivered to the right spot.

My backside welcomes his stiffness which I feel growing behind me as we grind together fully clothed. The virile girth brings about a desire within me to become one with it. He moves his other hand from holding my face in place for the kiss, to a giving it a mission of its own. The hug from behind becomes a full circle as one hand fondles my breasts through the top of my sundress, while the other fondles my thighs and the wetness contained between them.

We enjoy each other in this manner until the sun meets the shore. The sky is awash in a suffusion of pink and orange. A single formation of birds passes us by. Artistically, they seem to celebrate our union so close to heaven. The beauty of the sky around us and the land below us gives oxygen to our passion.

He turns me around so that we are facing each other. Staring directly into my eyes, he says, *"Faites chaque jour quelque chose qui vous fait peur. Aujourd'hui, fais-moi l'amour.* (Do something every day that scares you. Today, make love to me.)"

"Je le ferai tant que vous voudrez faire de même. (I will as long as you are willing to do the same.)"

No more words are spoken. His actions are his final response. Laying a blanket down in the bed of the balloon's basket, he moves over to the vent that controls the airflow of the balloon. With a slight twist, he slowly begins to let air out of the balloon and it begins to descend. Gracefully, the balloon glides downward, like the path taken by my young Haitian lover's hands over my body. Our descent will take a good amount of time he whispers behind my ear. He says he will be equally generous in the amount of time he takes in making love to me before bringing the hot-air balloon, and me, in for a smooth landing.

I close the journal and I look to Serene who is now very much asleep. It has been a long day for her. The boat ride over to Catalina Island and then the jazz festival may have taken a toll on her.

Was her mind challenged? Did she go back to a time of soul searching and recovery?

Whatever that time meant to her, she can look back to a moment of finding comfortability enough to let her hair down, to feeling wanted and desired, and to remember that the right person allowed her to define a place for her soul to rest its grief and turmoil.

I look away from Serene toward the window, and it is dark outside, but this time of the year being near the Pacific Ocean, the sky is blue instead of black and stark. Stars twinkle. I imagine Serene's view in the sky in a hot-air balloon as she looked to the heavens. In her remaining days, she deserves all the peace her soul can have because she has been through a long life of many changes. I assume going back to her daughter's father, she might have wished for a traditional family, but that wasn't her life.

I'm tired, and tomorrow I'm gonna do something different. I'm going to get in my car and make a few stops...get out and about. I'm making amends with a friend who's been trying to get in contact with me. I'll come into Blue Haven in the morning, but after that, I'll probably take a couple of days off just for myself.

TWENTY

"My dear brother, that woman, DeJohnette, has called you a few times, and it has been a while since she was calling you. If she is trying to reach you here, I'm sure she has called your cell phone."

"I have talked to her if you are referring to the last couple of days."

"Are you and her seeing each other again?"

I'm having my coffee out in the courtyard watching Mr. Oakland Dell play chess against himself on the walk-around chessboard. He moves the white three-foot piece and then goes over to the other side to the black pieces and makes a counter move. Some residents watch as he plays against himself often. They pick sides and lightly cheer when they think he has made a good move against himself. It is amusing.

"DeJohnette called and talked about the grief she had caused at the restaurant, and to let me know she is in counseling to help improve her outlook on life."

"But you and she are not going to go out or try to be together again, right?"

"Don't worry, we are good and have an understanding; so no, we are not going down the wrong path. I had to own up to my behavior to her also. As a man, I failed her when it came to being committed in a relationship. I knew, as you let me know too many times, she was not the woman for me, but I let her...well, I gave her hope when there was none.

"Serene's words from that night inspired her to make a change. She did her best to remember the words Serene spoke that night and she wrote down those words. She had them printed and sent me a copy; she looks at them every day.

"She wants to give Serene a gift and give me back my gold pearl handle razor. She knows it was my father's and I cherished it."

"What? Wait...you left our daddy's razor and did not retrieve it. Blu, I'm going to tell your mama to whup you."

"If I get in trouble, that means you gonna get it too. DeJohnette loved to watch me shave in the morning, but I slipped up and left the razor by accident because I got distracted when she asked me to shave her down there one morning."

"Stop, I don't want to hear the nasty things you did to a woman. Yuck!"

I'm laughing loudly. I disturb the chess game, and a few residents look over at me to hush me.

"I'm going to meet her later at a coffee house near her place by the Venice Canals to exchange a few things we have of each other's."

"You make sure you exchange items and not fleshly things." My sister lightly pops me in the back of my head.

Leaving from meeting with DeJohnette, I'm feeling accomplished. She and I had a great conversation that cleared the air, and we both apologized to each other for the way things turned out without blaming each other. I was happy to get my father's razor and she had custom-made embroidered handkerchiefs for me to give to Serene. It was a sign of respect for the gift of that horrid night when Serene gave her a personal, embroidered cloth.

The embroidered handkerchief had the words, *"Whoever shall be great must serve the least."*

I have no plans for the day, so I head over by Griffith Park. I want to park over by the LA River and pull my folding ten-speed bike out of the trunk to get a ride in for some exercise.

Traffic is a little thick, and although I love driving with my top-down, the sun can beat me up some days, so I must keep a hat on my head. One of the added aftermarket items I had installed in my car is air-conditioning. I have it up high, and my music is up too. The two sounds help drown out traffic noise.

At a light, one can be waiting for some time. I'm almost where I want to be, but the stoplight is long. A woman is in the lane next to me. She nods, and I nod to her; she points to the front of me, signaling she wants to get in front of me so she can get out of the turn lane. I wave for her to go. The light changes, she goes, and I follow.

I hear a loud horn.

I see sky.

I feel my body tumbling hard over the ground – I can't...

I have the sensation of water going up my nose.

I...

"Sir...sir, let us help you."

"I don't think he can hear us, but we have to drag him up higher out of the water."

"Look at all these people looking, I hope the fire department gets here."

"Let's hope one of them onlookers has called 911."

"Okay, sir, tell me what you think happened."

"Officer, my truck lost brakes, and I did all I could. I tried to downshift, but I was already going too fast. My truck hit the car broadside at about 50 miles an hour, maybe faster. From there, I felt my body jar, but my truck blasted through, and it looks like I lifted the car before it rolled on what would be the top. Out of the corner of my eye, I saw a body fly in the air. Then I felt the pain of my steering wheel, almost feeling like it was lodged in my chest. I hurt something bad."

"Sir, you're hurt. We will get someone to check you out, but over there is a man they are carting out of the LA River. His body might have flown 50 feet in the air and then down from 50 feet."

"Officer, is he going to be alright?"

"Well, his body landed on a homeless couple's tent and bedding which covered the soft sand of the embankment, before his body slid into the river. The couple pulled him out before he drowned. He's breathing, and it appears he has no external bleeding, but he could have internal bleeding.

"The way the car rolled over may have been lucky for him because he does not have that heavy car on top of him on this street surface.

"You hit his car hard enough to have ripped the old-style seat belt out of the vehicle. The seat belt failing might have saved his life if that car had flipped on top of him."

"Where is my brother?" an out-of-breath Sherry said. She held up her finger either to say she needed a moment, or a *you better tell me what I want to know* type of signal.

"Who is your brother?"

"Her brother is Blunile Rivers," Cassandra responded, sounding under more control than Sherry. Sherry placed her hand on Cassandra's arm, letting her know she appreciated her being there with her. Cassandra drove.

Sherry's face held dried tears; all vanity was gone.

"He is having an MRI."

"When can we see him?"

The ladies looked around at their surroundings in almost panic. They work in an associated environment, but instead of what they offered, the hospital feels cold and distinctly separated from what they worked hard at giving and living in providing loving care as a home to their residents.

"Can you tell us anything?"

"I see the ER doctor coming; hold on. He can tell you a lot more than I can."

"Hi, I am Dr. Ferrnet. I'm sorry we meet like this." Dr. Ferrnet caught Cassandra's eye even during the moment it was. He has the soap opera, gorgeous and polished appearance. His voice sounded like a midnight call she could wait a lifetime to receive.

"Mr. Rivers has a concussion and bruised ribs but no broken ribs. He has no internal bleeding, but he has a slight bruising of his kidney area. Mr. Rivers will heal, but he will be sore in a day or two. The man is tough to have survived the accident as described to me. You people must be some praying people. I will have him here for a few days or more for observation."

"Can I see my brother now?"

"He is on a heavy dose of pain medication to help him rest, but at the same time, we have him on a monitor to wake him every ten minutes because of the concussion; we don't want him sleeping long periods. You can go in to see him, but please don't touch him because even he doesn't know where it all hurts right now."

Sherry went into the room, and although the doctor told her not to touch Blu, she slid her hand under her brother's hand. He lightly gripped her hand; they had done that for each other when they were children and one got in trouble. It was their way of showing they were there to comfort the other.

Cassandra had told Sherry to go in by herself to be with her brother. Dr. Ferrnet and Cassandra walked down the hall in light conversation.

CHAPTER

TWENTY ONE

I look at the off-white walls and the windows that let in a view of another building. The best sight is my sister sitting in the corner asleep. I know she and I talked a bit late last night, but I had to be on some strong meds because the room was moving. But here in the morning, I feel stable. Shit hurts! Damn, even my baby toe hurts - I mean, it really hurts and so does my ass. These scrapes, I'm going to have scabs for weeks, but at least I am alive. *Damn...I'm alive!* Thank God I'm living. I need to pee. Sherry walked me to the bathroom last night, but I can do it by myself now.

"Don't you dare get out of that bed without my help."

I welcome my sister's voice; it's familiar and soothing, but it also urges me into a state of vulnerability that I am not yet willing to accept.

"Let me help you," she states in a loving manner, meaning well with each word.

"Sherry, please let me do this on my own. I know you mean well, but I feel stable. The pain is not crazy right now. It's nothing like last night. I love you for caring so much, but I'm not about to let you escort me to the toilet. I got this, and I'm going to take a shower too while I'm in there. Please, let me handle all of this by myself. If the devil didn't break me, that's a sign that God has kept my life intact enough to help myself."

"I'm not some pretty girl you're trying to impress. I'm your sister, and I called your mother and she said you have to do what I say to do."

I stare at Sherry. She is going to make me much sicker having to deal with her controlling mother hen worrying and ways.

"Well, you just tell my mother then. Do whatever you feel you have to do in that regard; but I'm okay, and I'm going to the bathroom by myself."

Sherry senses my urgent need to handle certain things on my own. She watches as I slowly make my way to the bathroom; my determination leading the way. Once inside, I lean against the bathroom door, relieved at my accomplishment of making it there on my own. Squatting is a little tenser than I expected, but I do what I have to do. I make it to the shower, and the hot water over my body feels so damn good. The mirror shows my face has one minor scratch near my hairline. Unconsciously, I rub my finger across the paper-thin follicles along the top of my head which gave life to the thick rope-like strands which formed a lion's mane. My hair had been a symbol of courage and power in my heritage; but now, looking at the scratch, all I could think about was the fact that my hair may have cushioned the blow to my head.

As I come out of the bathroom, I notice that Sherry had someone change my sheets. Food awaits, and I eat some oatmeal, dry toast, and grapes; a gourmet meal to someone in my condition.

"I suppose my car is totaled?"

"Yes, it looks like a tuna can. You are lucky to live." Her voice cuts at me at the wrong time with her disdain-laced scorn. She's upset and mad that this happened. I understand her concern, but she is coming at me all wrong.

"Sherry, stop! Please stop. I know you care about me, but you have you stop, at least for right now. You are doing as you always do but, my sister, I lived through this. I'm up and walking. They didn't have to cut into me or cut anything off me. I had an accident even though I did nothing wrong. It happened because I was kind and let someone cut in front of me in traffic, and that put me at the right time and place for that 18-wheeler to hit me. Someone else might not have been as fortunate. I could have witnessed the end of someone else's life in my rearview mirror or in front of me. I'm alive. No one died. I could have landed on the homeless couple; but no...instead of killing them, they pulled me out of the river and saved my life. I know you mean well, Sherry, but instead of focusing on how bad this could have been, I choose to be thankful for the sparing of my life."

I see tears. Dammit...now I have hurt her feelings and that was not my intent.

"Sherry, yesterday I felt your hand slide under mine in the same manner we did as kids. I know you care about me, and I truly feel you must take care of me in certain ways; but ... let's just celebrate this one. Instead of focusing on how bad this could have been, I feel I need to look on the bright side of this. It could have been a lot worst. I'm grateful it wasn't, and I want to focus on that."

My sister nods, and we sit in silence for a while. "Ms. May...I had Cassandra tell her you were in an accident. She sensed something was wrong. You normally tell her if you are going to be gone and won't have a chance to say goodnight to her. When you didn't contact her, she kept calling the front desk asking for you. I gave Cassandra permission to be honest with Ms. May. I felt it necessary to address her concern."

"That is fine; that is good. Serene does have an aura about her that lets her know when something is shading the light."

"She is insisting that she be allowed to visit you."

"I don't know, Sherry... is that a good idea, is it appropriate?"

"She is more than a resident at Blue Haven, and you two mean the world to each other. You have been a guiding light for her journey. We know soon her journey will be over, so you need to let her come to see you; if not for you, then for her. I will go back to Blue Haven and bring her later this evening. So, let me go and get out of your hair and stop bugging you so that you can rest."

"My dear sister, before you go, would you please unwrap my dreads from their bun and massage my scalp. The pressure from the bun is starting to bother me, and feeling fingertips on my scalp would sooth me a bit."

"I would love to; thank you."

I open my eyes and capture the limited vision from my room's windows. It is almost dark. It must be near 10:00 p.m. Turning my head away from the window, I see Serene standing at my bedside. She is wearing a flowing Egyptian-style robe in a burgundy coloring with gold lace. A headband holds her hair in a crown. I know she is 90 years old, but she looks to be even less than middle age. I got hit on the head which may have my mind a bit hazy, but it's almost as if she has a low glow about her. She has an elegance about her that's rare, but am I dreaming?

"Hello Serene, thank you for coming to visit me."

Serene lifts a finger to her lips to hush me. I feel her hands on my arm, and she holds me firmly. I want to close my eyes and dream as I feel my body is turning warm and warmer but not hot.

Am I floating? In an isolation tank of warm salt water?

I feel weightless. I hear her speak lightly.

"Please watch over him, and guide him, protect him."

The morning light comes from the window where my view is of another building. It awakens me. I feel good. The doctor said I'd be sore and feeling a lot of pain for a while. I feel a little achy, but nowhere near how I felt yesterday. Although I'm somewhat dizzy with a little blurred vision, my headache is gone. I now see without any issues. I swing my feet out of the bed with ease, and I stand

JOURNEY TO LOVE

without hesitation. I'm moving my shoulders, and I stretch with hardly any discomfort. Maybe it's the good meds, or perhaps the doctor got it wrong and I wasn't as injured as maybe he thought.

I'm thinking of asking the doctor to let me go home. I'll wait for my sister Sherry to arrive and then I will talk with her about that possibility. I know she will have something to say about me overdoing it, and I know there is a need for me to be cautious so soon after the accident. It is a good thing I landed on some soft ground, before almost sliding into the LA River. I know I need to pay attention to make sure I am actually well enough to leave the hospital.

LaFebra enters my room; behind him are Cassandra and Dr. Ferrnel. The sight of them is peace for a weary soul. I'm happy to see them. Standing in the window of no view, I'm hoping I'll be released.

"Hey doctor, you see me standing, and I am feeling good. I'm hoping you're here to let me know I can go. My friends here can take me away if you release me."

"My Rivers, it is not uncommon to feel as you do. In some ways, you may be feeling an adrenaline rush. For some people who have lived through something traumatic like you have been through, the adrenaline reacts as a positive output; in a sense, it's a pain reliever. Lack of pain is a good thing, but I need to take your vitals to make sure you are okay, and we need you to stay at least one more day. I can't, in good conscious, let you leave so soon. Let me listen to your heart and your lungs, and move your joints around a little bit. Please relax and stay here for one more day before we discuss letting you go. Give me a few minutes to check you out right now, and I'll get out of your hair so you can visit with your friends."

"Alright, but you think I can leave by tomorrow, right?"

"Mr. Rivers, barring any complications, I do believe, by what I see in you being up and moving...I think tomorrow is a strong possibility."

"Let the doctor check you out and stop trying to play Superman."

"LaFebra, don't you start sounding like my sister, please."

We laugh and joke around while the doctor takes a quick look at me. Cassandra answers her cellphone and steps out in the hall, and returns a moment later.

"Doctor Ferrnel, I would like to ask you a question, please...out here in the hall please. Doctor, I need to ask a question."

"Sure, I'm done with Mr. Rivers."

"Cassandra, is everything okay," I ask.

She doesn't respond, but leaves the room.

LaFebra and I talk about how bad my car is and my thoughts of wanting to get another classic. After discussing my options, I ask LaFebra if he wouldn't mind finding the homeless couple who helped me. I want to help them with housing, or jobs, or any other way that I might be of some assistance to them.

Cassandra comes back into the room. She stares with her mouth moving around as if she is trying to remove something stuck between her teeth.

"Cassandra, what's is going on?"

"Serene has taken ill. Her vital signs were indicating that her life was in crisis. Right now she is resting and is stable. She is at Blue Haven; she has refused to go to the hospital. Her lawyer said it is her choice because of her life expectancy, and there is nothing they can do for her now because of the tumor. She is probably looking at having more of these types of episodes until her end."

I felt for Cassandra as she spit out, as fast as she could, the troubling news that she knew would break my heart.

"Your sister is with her, and she is a little better. The doctor said something drained her energy, but he stabilized her with some meds and an IV. She is sitting up and watching TV. I asked Dr. Ferrnel his opinion about her situation, and he also said from what I told him, that she will have times like this and seem to recover."

Before I could say a word, LaFebra jumped in, "And no...you can't leave from here. Wait until tomorrow like your doctor said. We need to know you are on solid footing with your own health before we allow you to check on hers. Your body traveled in the air as if you were Supermen without a cape and landed a long way from where you were first hit. If I must hold you down, I will, because you're not Superman, just a lucky man. You wait until tomorrow; this is not even up for a discussion."

I wanted to be left alone. I got back in the bed and pulled the covers over me.

"I'm staying here," I hear LaFebra say.

Then I hear Cassandra say, "I will go trade places with Sherry so your sister can come to see you."

CHAPTER

TWENTY-TWO

"Sherry, you think you're so funny. This is a tank. Why couldn't you just come in your car?"

"My brother, if you're gonna leave the hospital after all you've been through, I figured I should at least protect you until I get you home."

My sister has shown up in a black Cadillac Escalade. "Sherry, I'ma let you be funny for a moment. I can't believe you spent all this money on a rental car just to pick me up."

"Yes, and I'm gonna take you home. I'ma make you something good to eat, and you're gonna rest for a while in your home and then you can come to Blue Haven. I know you want to see Serene, but I need for you to go home and get your sea legs underneath you. Serene is doing well, and I have told you several times she is. I would not hide the truth. I wanna see you walk around. I promise I won't fuss at you if you do this for me."

"Okay - okay, take me home. I'll relax for a little while."

I ease into this tank of a vehicle and takes a lot out of me in doing so. They made me come down from my room in a wheelchair, and because it was low, it felt uncomfortable lowering myself into it and climbing back out. I'm feeling good considering how much pain I could be in after what I've been through. Reality is, I should hardly be walking right now, and the stiffness is kicking my butt.

"Thank you, and now I can call your mother and tell her that you're doing well. She was about to fly out here. You know if I get on your nerves, you really don't want your mama to be here."

"My sister, no…please tell her to stay where she is. I know mama would be all over me and wouldn't let me even brush my teeth by myself."

"Oh – ah, you think it's only your mama that was coming; no Blunile, my mama was coming too. Yes, both of them were going to fly out here, so you ought to let me take care of you so I can report back that you're doing well."

"Whatever! Take me home so I can get out of these clothes. Thank you for bringing me something decent to put on, but I haven't worn these things in a long time. They don't fit me very well, and I'd like to take a shower in my own shower. Thank you."

While my sister is driving, I ask to go by the accident site. She is hesitant, and I understand why, so we head to my house.

I had a home-cooked meal and went right to sleep in my own bed. Sherry had to wake me to go to Blue Haven. It is near the end of sunset when we pull up. I'm nervous about seeing Serene. I want to be there for her, and it's killing me that I wasn't there for her when she fell ill.

I stand outside of her door. I have been standing here for at least fifteen minutes. I don't know why. Leaning against the wall with my eyes closed, I think I hear her voice from the other night saying, "Please watch over him, guiding him, protecting him." I open my eyes, and Serene is standing there looking at me.

"Are you going to come in and visit with me?" She looks the same; I'm not sure why she would look different.

"Serene, you should be in bed. Come, let's get you back in bed."

She walks back into her room and she seems to walk with no problem.

"Blunile, it is well that I see you walking and talking. What a blessing."

I sit and stare at her for a while. I'm happy, and if I had high blood pressure, it would be down from being near Serene.

"Blunile, I am sorry for what has happened to your car. It was a beautiful car, and I loved being a passenger in it. You took such good care of your rare bird. I could tell you were proud and cherished it. I am also sorry that you went through an extraordinarily frightening experience. Someone is looking down on you because it was not your time to go yet; and for that, I am thankful.

"Blunile, you have a lot of good work to do on this Earth. There are those who will be counting on you because of your moral code; people need to see the kind of goodness you possess. You have a legacy to put forth and to maintain.

"In the most persuasive sense, I also believe that there is a mate for you to help change the world for the better. I know, for a fact, there is someone who needs you as you need her. Although your car is no more, you are still here to be a blessing to someone. As I see you sitting here, I feel blessed. Let us enjoy this evening."

"How about we watch the movie, *The Spook Who Sat by the Door*, about a Black man in a fictional CIA, and Ivan Dixon directed the movie. The same Ivan Dixon we watched in an early *Twilight Zone*, TV episode. I read about him, and he was quite remarkable."

Serene and I watched the movie, and even stopped the film for her to give social commentary on the climate of the times. Her worldwide knowledge helped me understand the environment during each era to put in perspective the changing times.

In her lifetime, Serene has lived through times of economic depressions and recessions, and she's lived through several wars, one being a World War. She has watched young men go off to war and not come home. Cars, truck trains, and airplanes have changed over time. Housing changed from moving from the city to the suburbs, to the rural, and back again. Serene has felt fear of a nation from assassinations of key historical figures and world leaders, Black and white. She saw the country turn ugly with drugs and guns and ghettos, prisons, and corruption manifested in American dreams. She saw the horrors of Jim Crow and segregation, and decades later, she witnessed the election of the first Black president. Then shortly after the election, Jim Crow segregationist attitudes and proposed voting rights laws attempted to discredit the Black president just as easy as when there were no laws to protect Black men and women.

Serene can laugh at the early times with monkeys going up in spaceships, and then eventually a man landing on the moon. Through decades of social change, Serene has seen Black people fight and die to march and vote as fire hoses peeled skin. She told me of many Trayvon Martins in a history of young Black men who died at the hands of evilness.

She's also been around to see the glory and triumph of Black women in politics and owning businesses much like hers, as I've come to find out. She told me I was a Black star of Black excellence for how I run my business.

She shared her hurt when they booted Nat King Cole off his TV show because White America was not ready to see him sing with Judy Garland. And she shared her father was best friends Marcus Garvey, and how it hurt him when they falsely convicted Garvey for trying to help his people.

I'm watching movies with her, and she always takes time to explain how the social climate was at the time of each film to give me a perspective. I feel blessed and know I am receiving the best education one could have.

Then we watched, *In the Heat of the Night,* the Academy Award-winning movie from 1967 about a Black detective, starring Sidney Poitier. Serene loves the scene where Sidney and the woman he was about to sleep with fold back the covers on the bed while looking coy.

We are coming to the end of the movie, *Nothing but a Man*, a 1964 film starring Ivan Dixon and Abbey Lincoln. About a month ago, when I was playing Phyllis Hyman in Serene's room, she pulled out a record by Abbey Lincoln, singing,

"Softly, as in a Morning Sunrise." I had a sense Phyllis might have taken some Abbey Lincoln into her stylings. To see Abbey as a great actor was enlightening.

It's now 2:00 in the morning, and Serene wants to hear Sam Cooke sing, "Nothing Can Change this Love." Then we play Aretha Franklin singing, "Skylark." It brings a smile to Serene's face during the whole song.

"Blunile, I know you are still pretty sore from your accident, but will you slow dance with me, please?"

Without hesitation, I stand and turn the light down low. Serene is standing before I have a chance to help her out of bed. I take her hand, and we dance to the song, "Somewhere in my Lifetime," by Phyllis Hyman.

"Thank you, Blunile," she says as the song ends. "You are a wonderful man."

"Serene, it is time to get some sleep. I will see you in the morning. Goodnight."

She smiles and returns to her bed. As she pulls the cover over her, I turn out the light and leave the room.

Cassandra, Sherry, and I are all up and out in the halls early in the morning. I'm feeling better than yesterday. My sister says it's a miracle. Terfel steps out of room 307 and stares down the hall at us. He keeps staring.

I start to run, but my body is not ready to run yet. I get to the room in pain, and I know...

Serene has passed. She lays on her back, and her face seems to have a smile like when I last saw her when I turned her light off last night. There is peace in her forever sleep. She is at rest. Her life...her life...her life on Earth has ended.

I am the last man to slow dance with her.

I am the last man she taught.

I am the last man to say goodnight to her.

I am the last man to tell her I loved her.

CHAPTER

TWENTY THREE

We did something different today when removing Serene. We created a new ritual with the staff to follow in the future. The funeral home came and directed the wheeling of Serene's body in a processional through our courtyard. Many of the residents came and stood among the flowers and the water fountain to honor a fallen resident.

The overcast sky was burning off, and the white clouds decorated the sky above her last passing through the garden. Her body lay in repose by the water fountain for twenty minutes. Most walked by and said their goodbyes.

The Beamlys wheeled up in their wheelchairs and prayed. Mr. Dell, our war vet, placed a black queen chess piece on Serene and stood and held a salute the whole time until the mortuary personnel took her away.

My sister went out and brought some food, and we picked over it in my office. My body was aching, and I had a slight, persistent headache as I did the necessary paperwork and called Mr. Witherspoon, Serene's lawyer. He and I spoke at length as he guided me through a few details concerning affairs connected to Blue Haven. I needed a nap. I used to take my naps in my old car, but I couldn't do that anymore.

I hinted to my sister to let me alone for a while to have the office to myself. She closed the door, and I lay on the couch. I dozed off, mentally tired for sure.

My brother-in-law came by a few hours later, and we hugged it out. He knows how I feel about Serene.

Inside me, stored up, is a new understanding of love. I understand the love of a parent. I comprehend the feeling of love and desire for a woman and heartbreak when torn from that soul. I appreciate falling in love and the possibility of spending the rest of your life with that love.

I appreciate the love of people you care about with some rain, some pain, and that the sunshine of love can ebb and flow.

I learned to love Serene. I loved her. It didn't have a hint of sensual or sexual or anything of that nature, but it was man to woman and woman to man for sure. Me loving her was about protecting her to the fullest. Some might say this is the same type of love that one may have for a child and a child may have for you. I learned a special kind of love having Serene in my life, through her words, thoughts, and kind guidance.

I'm still hurting from the accident, probably more mentally than physically, but my body has aches. LaFebra decided the best thing was to take me out to look at cars. We went to a few places downtown to look at classic cars. I was already dead set that I was going to buy another classic car for my daily driver. That is who I am. I didn't know what I was looking for, but I figured it would hit me right when I saw and drove the right car.

We went back to Blue Haven and had a drink in my office. Then LaFebra left and said we will look again tomorrow.

At sunset, I enter Serene's room. I see a made bed and a clean room. That old clock with a cat face and the eyes and the tail moving back and forth told me it is 9:00 p.m. I close the door behind me. I sit by the window across from where Serene would sit. I get up and sit in her chair. I want to read the last entry in her

journal. I wish reading about her, and her thoughts and feelings would never end. I see blue ink.

A Tear to a Smile - 1999

Jamison and I sat in his Aston Martin classic sports car, what he called his Black James Bond car. The LA scene could care less nowadays when a Ferrari or a Corvette were parked or drove by, as they had become commonplace. My man's 1964 Aston Martin DB5 convertible turned heads from car enthusiasts and non-car people. Behind the tinted windows of the car, our breathing is on the edge of hyperventilating with the top up. In the parking garage, Jamison had complex contemplations going on in his soul, and I was having a talk with God about how I could help the man I loved. The air conditioning was on to help; still, I had occasional hot flashes after seven decades of life. Jamison had gone through significant trouble having air conditioning installed in a vintage sports car. The LA morning air was not fresh in the underground parking garage, so we didn't crack the windows open. Music was his life and a refuge for us; the increased volume did little to submerge his fears and lift hopes like the bright LA sun.

That morning, the skylight in our bedroom had highlighted my tender touch to make love to my man's lips and down to the soles of his feet. I wanted our hearts to race in sensual desires and deflect the worries crashing inside our current life.

Time arose to exit the car; an answer awaited. We are in the last phase.

We walked in a different direction than the previous times. The sun was bright in LA, but it's cold outside with the wind blustering against his face; maybe he wanted to walk this way to feel alive. We could have taken the elevator inside the parking garage, but instead, I followed Jamison to wherever he led me.

As a couple, the one sure way to show we love each other, we gave the "Ws." We always asked each other, "What can I do for you? What do you need of me? What can I do more of?" Then, we try to complete that need or want or request while avoiding asking, "Why," so we don't make the other feel their asking is not needed. We think of each other first, as this is our way to make love; it's all-embracing of each other to forever grow our passion for one another.

Jamison wrote a song a few years ago that became a hit. He said our love inspired a verse in the song.

Lover's Concession

A compromise is not about what you are willing to give up.

A compromise is what you give freely - lovingly without the feeling of losing.

A man and a woman devote the giving of themselves, not as a concession, but to bring harmony to each other to be baptized in smiles and contentment.

He licked his lips, and I handed him some Chapstick. I enjoyed watching his full heart-shaped lips when he drew them in and out as if he were kissing me. My arm was around his arm, and I held tight. I wanted him to know he was not alone. From the corners of my eyes, I glanced at his worried face. Waterworks tempted his eyelids, maybe a byproduct of the chilly wind or the iceberg of worries growing below the surface in his soul.

Tall double glass doors slid open. Cold marbled walls, frosted glass divides, and paintings of flowers in gold frames fake elegance. Inside an emotionally barren building, we approached a help desk of name badges and mouths moving on autopilot. We stood in line to check in. The phone was answered at the same time Jamison gave his name. The attention given to the caller stole the moment, and we received a finger pointing us in the direction of the elevators; then the name badge flicked five fingers signaling our destination.

The elevator lifted and delivered us to a waiting room. An attractive brown skin woman walked out with a male nurse from the back area. The woman in a stylish pants suit with almond eyes angled high on the outside corners. I admired her cat eye glasses that matched her eyes. The woman's face was sad, and the nurse held an expression of, *I'm sorry,* as the woman's beautiful eyes seemed to turn dark, and she slowly walked away. I watched her body almost lurch forward two steps and stop, and her finger stabbed the elevated button.

I sit next to a plastic plant and I catch my head shaking in disgust at the dust from the sunlight coming through windows landing on a fake plant. The window is showing other tall buildings blocking any view of hope shining through. I try to see the beauty in paintings of nature and flowers, reproduced copies I'm sure, sent by the thousands to offices everywhere. The sterile-looking furnishings make me think of a mortuary where one goes to make arrangements to pick flowers and decide whether to go with the blue casket or the black.

"Serene, in the midst of all of this, I am blessed to see your smile." Jamison touched my face with a finger as if he were signing his name on me. "I know what you are thinking...'Why do they try to make life tranquil in a place where people often wish to be tranquilized?' And that smell...actually it's not an odor one can identify. It was neither wrong nor right; it's clean, but almost without air any of us want to breathe."

Jamison reached for the small stack of magazines; two women's interests and one a sports car aficionado magazine were in the stack. He picked the car magazine.

"How do you know I didn't want that one for myself?" I asked while lightly pinching him.

"We always share, right?"

"Always baby, always." I smiled at him. About the only thing we disagreed about was that he likes sugar and butter in his grits, and I like salt and pepper.

A couple came into the sitting area. Ring fingers made me assume they were husband and wife. The husband's face was pale. He was a Black man of a darker hue, but his skin was pale and his face slightly gaunt. The wife appeared older than her age. I knew the wife was younger than what was shown on her worry-lined face; those lines stole her rightful image and painted it with stress.

I was leaning back in the chair, almost hiding behind the love of my life's shoulder; maybe trying to suppress feelings. In his unspoken ways I knew he felt my fear as I felt his as it jumped from his heart, and bounced off the cold walls that we sat between. I watched pulsation at his temples beating like a drum major keeping time. We hoped for the opposite of what we saw in the couple across from us. *Will that be he and I?* We prayed before we left the house that morning. I'm praying now.

The couple's eyes were on us. We nodded, acknowledging where we all were assembled, and it is all very far from laying in a field of flowers in a calming, peaceful lover's enchantment.

The couple pushed their foreheads together tightly as if they could pass through each other's cerebral stream. We watched the couple over the top of the magazine with pictures of cars that in twenty years will drive by themselves using battery power.

The wife kissed her husband's face; she could not hide her love and her pain. Her hands cupped his face and she pressed her lips to his as if they were magnetized. Tears slipped past her lips and his cheek. His and her souls melted in an embrace of time and space and hope. The one window in the waiting room allowed the sun to hit their hopes for brighter days. Her body turned away in a sudden moment as if she was trying to hide. She stood and left the room swiftly, enough so to pull air in behind her as she left, pain dripping with each hurried step.

I witnessed love.

We watched the husband take a breath so deep it made the man sit up straight to allow his chest to expand. The husband's head turned toward us.

"My wife has been my rock...my rock; she has been the lily in my field. Every once in a while, she struggles with my illness, and it flows out in one way or another. Neither one of us has any control of those moments, nor...well, she needed some air."

Jamison leaned forward. "My brother, you have love; you have someone by your side. I know what that means." Jamison looks at me and turns back to the man. "If your wife needs some air sometimes, well, she'll bring back air to you," Jamison said, and stood and walked over and shook the man's hand; both men nodded.

Jamison and I fight a war with the future, but my man is there for someone else. That is who he is, and it made loving him easy. He would give his eyes away if it gave sight to someone else. I know love; his name is Jamison Blaize.

A young lady in pink scrubs entered the room. "Mr. Blaize, please follow me."

He looked at me. "Please come with me, Serene. Don't ask me if I'm sure." He held out his hand, and I went with my man to find out what our world will be like.

She led us to a room. "The doctor will be in."

We were in a sterile space, small, and that smell of not bad but not good was more substantial. Pale green walls, chrome carts, movable lights, and an examination table with roll-on sanitary paper all caught our eyes. We sat in two of the three chairs in the room.

The door opened, and Doctor Tall and Slender walked in, "Mr. Blaize, how are you feeling?"

"Okay." Jamison's answer came with a shortness that said, *Let's not play the bedside courtesy thing. Get to the reason why I'm here.*

I do love that my man was direct. I pressed my lips tight, knowing sometimes he makes me quickly turn my head toward him to send a message of, *I'm your woman who loves you.*

"Okay, your results. The biopsy..."

"And?"

"Mr. Blaize..."

My man had been quiet ever since we left the doctor's office. I know he was processing, and I gave him peace and just stayed by his side as his woman. I will always be his safe place. We were standing in the window overlooking the valley from our home, with all bright lights flickering below. Jamison held a glass of wine; my drink was more potent as we tried to let the day turn into nighttime calm.

It was a beautiful evening. The day warmed, and it had not cooled. Windows were open, and the curtains danced in the breeze. We were invited by many to celebrate New Year's Eve 1999, leading into the next year which will be the start of a new decade and a new century. The FM radio engaged us in what people called *smooth jazz* and played a version of the Prince song, "1999" and it finally brought a laugh out from Jamison.

I laughed, thinking about the artist formally known as Prince, and the word is, he was going back to his name Prince. Although being older, I enjoyed his music, but I would never be in a club dancing to his music. I thought.

People would pack Times Square in New York to celebrate, and I wasn't sure which city I wanted to bring in the New Year with. Either city, no matter what, Jamison had to come back to Los Angeles to do what he needed to do. Los Angeles chose us, as we could have been at my place in New York City. We could have chosen to be in the Bahamas at his summerhouse, but here we were, overlooking Los Angeles.

Jamison produced and edited music to move without interruption from one piece of music or scene to another on music soundtracks for movies. I enjoyed his work, and I relished the actors, as many of them knew of my work as an author. I was a star to many of them, and they show me much respect. They asked me for life guidance, and I was blessed to offer my views and understandings as a lover of life.

I had on a sheer robe, and my man was in his boxer shorts. His body was still strong and lean despite all he had gone through as he approached 75. I was 70, and I still loved turning my man on. I did everything I possibly could in how I walked and I talked and how I touched him. I let him be free with me to the point that I loved feeling myself in front of him. I excited him as if we were young lovers of 30 years old, but we learned a slow hand is beautiful. We had relearned passion for our age as we learned that making love is mental and physical. If there was a time that he couldn't be that virile man of 30 or 40 years ago, he knew how to please me to bring out the best in me. I didn't miss a thing, and when he was ready to give me all of him, his desire for me made him the king of my world.

As if I were a young woman, he ran his hands through my hair and inhaled my scent. He pulled me tight in his arms before he went down on me to taste me and devour me as if he needed me in order to be alive. I loved when he was aggressive and pinned me against walls while sliding his tongue down my throat. I loved the way he grabbed my ass, showing me I was beautiful even as an older woman, while I felt his strength that rivaled a young man.

Days before, I stood here in the window enjoying the sunset with him at the baby grand piano and the sun silhouetting him while he played "The Answer is You" by Phyllis Hyman. Jamison had a rich chocolate-like voice, and he melted me. He would play a song from 50 years ago, like "Stormy Monday" but then he would play and sing a love ballad. My man sang a song that was so sexy, but I had to ask myself, *Am I too old for that song?* It was a song by Prince, saying, "Do Me Baby."

The song didn't have explicit lyrics, but it told me what the man wanted to do to me, because we were a couple in that big old empty room wanting each other now. It was a beautiful feeling. Jamison stood up from the piano and came over to me. I felt his chest on my back, his hips pushing into my ass, and we tangled together, going down to the floor. I can feel his lips on my neck and kissing me down my spine and over my ass. I turn over, and he's ready to go in me, and I was on the verge of having the rug utterly soaked. I took him inside of me and wrap my legs around him; slow dancing with his hardness conducting my screams of joy. We slept right there throughout the night, and I woke to sunrise. He was at the piano playing, and I had blankets over me.

We had not eaten much since leaving the doctor's office. The desire for food was on the back burner. We had eaten some fruit earlier, but hunger had set in, but neither of us wanted to go into the kitchen and cook. We thought about ordering Chinese and having it delivered, but it would be a hit and miss on how good it might be on New Year's Eve.

We were in Los Angeles, but we didn't want the fancy restaurants where everybody would try to have a great meal. We wanted something home-style delicious that we could put our hands on. We sought good food and didn't want to worry about proper etiquette.

Jamison said he knew the place to go, and we dressed in casual clothing and drove down out of the hills to Sunset Boulevard. As if we were supposed to be here, out front was a parking spot at Roscoe's Chicken and Waffles, and we park. I had planned to cook shrimp and grits in the morning, but now we will have breakfast for dinner.

As we're walking in, other friends of ours in the industry working on movie sets were there to eat. I watched Jamison's mood change, bringing him out of the quietness he had been about all day. Besides him knowing I wanted him to live, I can see it helped him see others who loved him and admired him as well; that brings life to all of us. For me, I long since had matured beyond thinking I should be enough. One should feel elation from every direction it can be sensed. It made me happy to see his smile and for him to roll those heart-shaped lips in. If he only knew how hot that made me.

We decided to order our food to go and eat Roscoe's Chicken and Waffles at home.

Once back to seeing the night lights and a few colorful fireworks going high into the sky, shedding entertainment over the valley, Jamison and I enjoyed our food with good conversation. He opened a bottle of wine, and we had a toast at midnight. We slow danced to no music, just feeling each other's breath on each other's skin as the music to our song, and we kissed.

We held our wine glasses out to the world and toasted.

"To a long life. My love, I was glad you were with me when the doctor told me my cancer is gone. I have been silent for the most part today, just giving thanks for you being the love I needed to overcome and heal, and now to live on for us to love."

As I have changed and lived through much, life has changed me. Jamison lived five more years before cancer came back. He chose to go back to the Bahamas to live out his life, and I stayed here in LA. He could not stand the thought of me watching him pass away. Our last kiss will remain fresh on my lips. I decided that I did not want to know the day he was laid to rest. He arranged his life so strangers will take care of him and never know much about him in the end. Only God was to know him. I'm blessed to have had Jamison as a man who loved me, and I love him, and there is no end.

I had lost people who meant the world to me. Now each day, I face losing another near and from afar. So, each New Year, I'm blessed each and every day.

I could look back at all the places I've been and look back at all the people I've known. I keep them in my mind's eyes, and I hear every voice and remember each touch in my heart.

I have been loved by great men who cherished me and allowed me to teach them, and learn from them. We shared days of a lifetime. Some no longer walk this Earth, but I cherish each moment they held me in love for us to make love while overcoming obstacles that others may have put in our way.

I have lost a daughter and a son-in-law, but their combined heartbeats live. I gathered and absorbed one very important life-lesson while I was a young woman, and that is to love as long you have a breath, and then your love will live on in someone's heart. I have been loved by the best, and I see them as one at times, but I always feel them each as unique in how we met and lived and learned. They all loved me for the time we had, and we loved with no regrets. I have no regrets, but I always hope for the journey to love to be one for all to have and adore the value of love.

Here I stand on a beach along Highway 101 on the California coastline. I went to visit my sister, her great man of a husband, and my nephew and niece. I spent New Year's with them to bring in the year 2010. We toasted having a Black man as President, and a beautiful Black First-Lady, and I am so inspired to see their Black family structure which is more prevalent than many might know. My study of history since the times before we crossed oceans bears the truth of kings and queens, and their family structure is one of wholeness.

I was hoping my special love, a one-of-a-kind who I made amends with, would join me for New Years, but he is doing God's work helping to heal people in foreign countries where doctors are needed with modern medicine. I discovered I must let my love be in places to do good to help one have a legacy and leave a legacy.

Before I left for the trip home, I shared with my sister and family the understanding of my days being numbered. I'll be on a medicine that will help limit the growth of a tumor in my head. The doctors tell me through all the tests and knowledge, they think they can maintain a quality of life for me for about five years; but there will come a time when I won't be as energetic, and there will come a time I won't speak as much. Then there will come a time my health will start to forsake me, and one day, I will be no more.

I would have withheld such news of my coming years and last days with that someone special I love, so in retrospect, I am in a way relieved we could not get together for New Years. For both our sakes I need the mission of legacy to be the focus, now and after I am gone. We will be together in a few weeks, and we will love as we have always loved when we are near, but I will still not tell my secret.

I'm hoping I leave a legacy of growth, understanding, knowledge, and wisdom to help anyone who knows of my life. I know days will be shorter, and the sun won't rise as fast for me; but if I awake, I'm going to love the best I can and lead one to the journey to love.

TWENTY FOUR

Today, my feelings run steep with pain in my soul. My heart beats hard with anxiety, as when I lost my father. Serene May had become a part of me and will be for the rest of my life. She has touched elements in my soul to go on a quest to satisfy passions to have my legacy. Her words and ways have sent me on my way to find a love like the love I would have had with Serene if I were born in the same time frame. Her wisdom has led me to see, hear, and feel on a higher level from reading her journal and our conversations.

Now she is being laid to rest, and I have lost an angel. Her journey has affected how the world turns as far as I'm concerned. Through her, I've come to understand what is hurtful or sad or unfortunate can be turned into a prevailing pride of overcoming.

Serene May helped me know with each heartbeat that life is a journey to love. I learned love is fluid and never-ending and should never be judgmental of what someone wants and gives.

From her enlightenment, I transformed into a better man with faith that all things can come in one way and leave restored, improved, and more valuable.

When my day comes, I know the journey to love will have found me and completed me. I come to bury Serene May, but I know she's alive inside me to help me achieve my journey.

Months before her passing, one of our residents, a retired professional photographer, took photos of our staff and residents in the garden. One of those pictures shows Serene standing in our garden, and the sunset painted a silhouette of her image. I had that picture enlarged and added a passage from her journal printed alongside her image. I framed the picture and put it on the wall in my office.

Be mindful the world is steadily changing, and you are entitled to change your ways or path. When it comes to love, I feel it is best never to live anyone else's design, but like the person you chose to be and let the only judgments, conclusions and decrees come from you for you.

Always see and hear, feel and know them as,

They only wanted you

They only wanted the best for you

They did for you everything they could to protect you

Within that, they found themselves to be themselves to do the things that gave them the most pleasure in life

And that is they only wanted to be with you

For as long as you need

Then they support you to transform your being to stay or go and be blessed with the grace to return as it is best for you.

The life and times of Ms. Serene May

1925 – 2015

The weather in LA is sunny and with a light breeze this morning. It will be hot, too hot in the afternoon. As of now, it is pleasant on a difficult day as we are heading to the gravesite. My sister is driving while holding my hand and occasionally she reaches over and wipes a tear from my face. She is well-aware of the impact Serene made on my life. There are times we at the facility arrange funeral details, but Serene's lawyer, Pierce Witherspoon, has taken care of all. As we exit the car, we walk toward three tall palm trees with their fronds touching at their peaks. Under the kissing palm trees is the location for the service. I see people walking across the cemetery lawn toward the sight. A hearse pulls ahead of my sister's car along with several other vehicles. I am amazed I see so many people. I thought this was going to be a low-key ceremony, but there are many people gathered. Coming in my direction in the distance, I noticed Serene's nephew and niece, whom I met when I took Serene to the memorial service for their parents.

From the other cars that pulled ahead of the hearse, exit older gentlemen dressed all the same in beautiful matching burgundy suits. They are talking as friends do while walking to the hearse. They are now carrying Serene's casket. The morning sun highlights seasoned warriors. They all look strong for their age while carrying Serene's burgundy casket adorned with wide silk ribbons of mauve-rose and white-colored kente cloth patterns. Those are Serene's favorite colors, and the men have the same kente cloth draped around their shoulders. The older gentlemen were all handsome and held their heads high with no trace of sadness.

People were talking in low, respectful voices while shaking hands and making introductions. I am meeting many Serene followers from her years of teaching; many here are past students who happened to live in the Southern California area. Some people flew into pay their respects. From all over the globe they flew in from places like Lagos and Benin Nigeria, Nairobi, Kenya, Palestine and Brooklyn and Egypt, Washington DC and New York.

We still had about one hour, so it seemed people came early to meet others and to share Serene's loving impact in their lives. I arranged to have few residents from our facility be in attendance to honor Serene. There's Mr. Oakland Dell, the war vet, who Serene played chess with. They would play for hours and never say a word; their games ended in stalemates. Also present, sitting in their wheelchairs were Mr. and Mrs. Beamly, the most giving couple, originally from France. Watching over the residents, Cassandra sat with them in a satin blue dress gifted to her by Serene months ago. Cassandra said Serene told her that the dress had connected her heart to that of another, and she hoped it would do the same for her.

I'm meeting lives touched either through Serene's books or through her years of being a teacher, going back from the time she taught high school and many different seminars worldwide. Pierce Witherspoon, her lawyer, sent notice of her memorial service around the world. He wanted to have the service next week, but it had been two weeks since her death, and most of the people who wanted to honor Serene could only come this week.

The gentlemen who carried the casket, I had quite a shock in meeting them, as they were once lovers of Serene. Some of the journal entries I read were of some of those men.

One of the men looked younger than the others, but still at least twenty years older than I was. He said he met Serene in New Orleans when he was a young man. He spoke of how she was not whole with herself when they met, as Serene was grieving a death.

"Her face was beautiful but pained when I noticed her on Bourbon Street during Mardi Gras back in 1978 When I saw her beauty, I was smitten and had to bring some joy to her life. I danced in front of her as the music and carnival led many to be unabashed. I was acting as freely when facing her, which would not have been the norm for me.

"You see this scar?" He ran a finger from the top of his head and slowly on down. "I was macheted from the top of my head and, as you see, all the way down to under my chin. In my native country of Haiti, I suffered abysmal child labor conditions. When 'Papa Doc' Duvalier took over Haiti in the late '50s with his reign of terror, it forced many into exile or to submit. By the1970s, thousands of us Haitians began to flee the poverty and repression in Haiti by boat in hopes of making it to America. 'Baby Doc' Duvalier succeeded his father to become President for Life, and life in my country became unbearable. One evil soldier tried to make an example of me in front of others to make us work harder and cut me badly. I was marked as ugly – an undesirable. I did have a strong body and strong will, and in a ragged boat with a sail made out of bedsheets and broomsticks, I made my way to south Florida, using only a cup to bail water.

"I found work on the docks in New Orleans, and that is where I met Serene. I flirted with her because she was beautiful, and as I had learned to believe, no woman wanted me because people deemed me ugly with my scar and my having a limited ability to speak English well. I did earn a high school diploma while going to night school. The day I met Serene I was showing off that I could dance. She could dance, I found out. She did not judge my looks. She saw goodness in me; she saw an intellect in me.

"She connected me to college students who schooled me. She enrolled me into Xavier University, a historically Black college, an HBCU. I was granted an exemption because of my late schooling and background, and I became an all-conference wrestler. I later became a high school PE teacher and have coached the school's wrestling team to many state titles.

"All I have achieved came about because I wanted to make her smile, and I did. In return, she helped me overcome. Once I made her smile, she let me show her about town in all the waves of parties going on, and then I took her for a balloon ride over the city. Although I was a younger man, she treated me as her equal in wanting love, if only for a while. She taught me how to find love in meaningful ways so I could inspire and cultivate relationships that flourish. Because of Serene, I met my wife. There were those who did not see her beauty either, but I learned that outer beauty is only skin deep; Serene helped me see. I saw in my wife a beautiful queen who stands tall, much like Serene was elevated. I have lived a satisfying life with my wife. I named my youngest daughter Serene May Perceval, and she now teaches at the same school and classroom where Serene was a teacher. I am blessed to be here to help her on her last journey."

I know I want to meet all the men burgundy-dressed who came to honor Serene. They were all talking to each other as if they were lost, friends.

I walk over to one of the men. "Hello sir, I am Blunile Rivers, the man who cared for Serene at my care facility."

"Hello, young man, my name is Earland Du Bois. I am glad you had the honor to care for her. Serene is someone who meant the world to me and still does even after her death. I was a lawyer at one time - pretty well known in certain circles. I was behind the scenes in the civil rights movement. I was in Memphis, just a block away when Martin Luther King was shot in 1968. The year before, I and several others invited him to come to Memphis. That same year, Serene and

I traveled from Memphis to Atlanta to hear him preach. We had a wonderful time while in Atlanta."

He is smiling at me, but it's as if he is somewhere else while he is smiling. At his age, he stands proudly upright, but his short steps are measured and tell of his advanced age. He had taken a few steps away but stopped and turns my way.

"I wish she was burying me instead of me watching her be buried. I lived my best years knowing what love is when I was near her. She needed to live forever. The world is a better place with her."

From Serene's Journal, I met this man; and now I meet her through his emotions and the love he still has for her.

Standing alone and away from people by at least fifty yards, a man smokes a pipe. I wonder, is he in Serene's journal? I walk my way over to him. His pipe aroma is sweet. He turns my way, and he is a tall, angular, handsome man with a perfectly groomed salt and pepper beard. He stood as if he were a ballroom dancer, seemingly ready to win a contest with his next steps.

"I apologize if my pipe has reached the nostrils of people."

"No, sir, not at all. It is a nice scent, but no, the breeze is calmly blowing the other way. I noticed you were one of the gentlemen helping to carry the casket. I am Blunile Rivers. I cared for Serene May the last year of her life while she was a resident at my care facility."

"Well, young sir, I am glad to meet anyone with whom my dear Serene has spent any amount of time. If you shared time and space with her, your life was enhanced.

"I am Amadore Booker. I met Serene at an age when men and women know they are adults. We were just past our mid 30s and doing, coming, and going to the places we wanted with no one's blessings wanted or needed. I was Pullman porter and living the life of Pullman porter, which meant I was free to come and go and see and do with whomever I chose. Serene was a professor at NYU, and her compensation for her greatness, which she demanded and deserved, allowed her to travel the world and come and go at her inclination.

"I had been a Pullman porter for Presidents Truman and Eisenhower, and once only for Kennedy. On my train, I was a porter for many stars: Louis Armstrong, Ella Fitzgerald, Lena Horne, Billie Holiday, Sam Cooke, and many others. I met Serene while I was a porter going from New York to DC on a regular short run."

"Mr. Booker, Serene played a lot of Sam Cooke's music and said she met him through a close friend. Might that be you?" I know it is him from Serene's journal.

"Yes, I did introduce them; that was a fun night for sure. Serene and I could not spend a lot of time together, but we became the best pen pals and met up whenever we could. She touched a part of me no other woman has been able to come close to. Even before hearing of her death, I missed everything about her, and it has been that way every day that I awake."

He and I walk back toward the still growing crowd, and Mr. Booker told me to make sure I meet the other men who escorted the casket.

"Hello sir, I'm Blunile Rivers. I was a caretaker of Ms. Serene May."

"Ah, okay, I am Austin Baylor. Right off the bat, I have a question of you, hoping you can help me."

"Yes, sir, what can I do for you:"

"This might sound strange but hear me out. I want a pair of Ms. May's shoes, and the older, the better."

"What?"

"Let me explain…Ms. May helped take my basic grade school skills at 50 years of age and elevated my education. She told me we were about the same age and I could learn no matter my age. I worked as a shoeshine man in the airport terminal, and I always polished her shoes or boots. Sometimes she would bring an extra pair, a new pair, and leave them with me to shine or put water protection on them and repair shoes if need be. I would have them ready for her whenever she came back.

"Ms. May always gave me $20 and sometimes $30 more than I charged, I would try to reject it politely, but she said every man or woman deserves a living wage – plus. Ms. May said it is her duty to show her pride in any man who puts forth his best effort. Ms. May inspired me, and I opened up to her about why I shined shoes. Early in life, I went to jail down South for being on the wrong side of town. At a time I should have been in school, I was working on a chain gang and had to fight to survive. At 30 years of age, I was released with maybe a sixth-grade education. I didn't know what to do other than to learn how to shine shoes.

"Ms. May took me into her housing compound, where she had small cottages adjacent to her main big house. She let me stay there rent-free. I went to school at night after my shoeshine shift. When she left town, she left food for me to cook. There were other men and women she housed and helped. She saw in me that I was smart and learned fast. Within two years, I took my GED and passed. After two more years of college, I soon owned a business teaching young men and women how to survive after incarceration, and that's all because of Ms. May. So the strange request to have a pair of her shoes is to put them in a case for others to see where I was at one time and that people will help you if you are willing to help yourself."

"Sir, I will make sure you receive a pair of Ms. May's shoes. Let us exchange information when the service is over."

It is almost time for the service to start, and I make my way over to the last man, or I should say he is making his way over to me.

"Hello, my name is CeCe Brown. I saw you talking to my friends. They say you are the one who made Ms. May's life comfortable for her the last year of her life."

"Blunile Rivers, sir, nice to meet you."

"Ms. May helped me right here in LA. I was a skycap at the airport, helping people with their luggage. She and I often spoke of world events, making me feel she appreciated my knowledge. I usually kept my schooling background off the table with almost everyone. Finally, one day, I let her know I was a Tuskegee Airmen and I had dreams to fly for major airlines. But at every point, I was denied. I owned a small airplane, and I took people out on tours – Black folks and people of color who wanted to go up in a small aircraft. I was teaching aviation to inner-city kids. I enjoyed life being a skycap for TWA, but they would never allow me to fly an airplane.

"Ms. May introduced me to a high-profile Black lawyer. The lawyer and his law firm went to TWA and said, you will hire this man or we'll file civil rights cases on top of cases. I became flight captain for twenty years. I expanded my airline school for underprivileged kids, and I put all my kids through college, and my sons and daughters all fly for major airlines. Ms. May's legacy is touching souls."

A few people read poems, with the service started, and her obituary was read by her nephew and niece. Serena's lawyer introduces a middle-aged woman who could pass for white but I assume she is a Black woman from her features and voice. Ms. Terrell Wells commands attention as soon as she said one sentence.

"Women's equality is for all, for the advancement and betterment of men and women. I learned this from the woman we are all here to honor. She helped me understand a woman can love a man with all her heart, but at the same time, she must love herself with the same energy.

"Many people want the hands of time to stop and go back, but Ms. Serene May wanted the hands of time to move forward and use yesterday as steps to get ahead for equality for all. The Eves - the first women on this Earth have grieved for man, for it is taught that if man falters, we all fail.

"Ms. Serene May educated me. I read her writings of times long before anyone crossed oceans; we walked the Motherland drawing maps to move within mazes of roadblocks. She taught there are paths, even if you must create them, to go over or under barriers. There was a point in my life I thought I was nothing to this world. Ms. Serene May taught me that I was the world, and that it was up to me to create a safe space.

"You see, I was born of a woman who did not believe she wanted me, I was passed around from family to friends, and at some point, I was raising myself only to survive by any means. I hated myself as I sold myself for less than a few dollars, or others sold me for less than cheap. I did not understand resistance and resilience. I did not know love. I did not know love was a coupling, a mating, a pairing, a union, a uniting to be felt inside one's soul and not just inside the body.

I begged for food or sold my body outside of the subway near the school where Ms. May taught people to be brilliant. One day, Ms. May and Mr. Amadore Booker, sitting right over there, approached me. As it had been, I thought they only wanted to buy me to have a good time. They took me to her place, and she had me bathe and gave me a choice to wear anything in her closet. I have to admit I had never worn silk undies, and they felt good." The memorial service audience all had a good chuckle. "They took me to a fine dining room, and from there, they took me shopping for clothes. Then they paid for a room for me in the same hotel they each had rooms at. They told me I had one month to make up my mind on what my world could or could not be. Each day Ms. May came to my room, and I went to her classroom with her and sat with what I thought were the most intelligent people I would ever be close to. This was NYU in New York; how could I be near these people when the weeks before I was begging from them?

"Each evening, either Mr. Booker or Ms. May or both took me to dinner, and the one question they would ask me, I had no answer to: 'What do I want my legacy to be? What do I want my journey to be?'

"They helped me find the answer. The answer I heard from them was, 'I will have made life better for others, and so they can do the same to have more complete lives long after I and them.'

"I stand in front of you with Ms. May, who was never loud, but she is shouting her legacy to all of us right now. That is why you are all here, and many more want to be here for this, I am sure.

"I stand before you as we're about to lay Ms. Serene May to rest. I became the Dean of Inclusion, Diversity, and Equity at serval universities, and currently, I have started charter schools nationwide for foster children. I have been happily married to an incredible man, and we have six adopted children who are all creating legacies of their own. I believe all who are here can say thank you, Serene May."

The memorial audience said, "Thank you, Serene May!" all simultaneously. People shook hands and hugged each other.

Ms. Terrell Wells had everyone mesmerized by her presentation of her life and what we all should do in our way of honoring Serene.

Then Serene's lawyer, Mr. Witherspoon, comes up to me and asks me to speak, saying that I was the last person to spend quality time with her and he wanted me to end the service. He knew it was last minute, but the person he wanted to end the service could not make it.

As I'm standing to do what I am asked, Mr. Witherspoon gives glowing praise for my facility and the people who work with the residents and all we do and how we do it. He is speaking of how I customize each life to be as close to each person's lifestyle. He tells how my facility needs to expand and have more business like ours to cater to all. Mr. Witherspoon cites, Ms. May loved each day under my care, and he noted that I was close to Serene, as close as any friend could be. Then he points to me to speak.

I am flushed and short of breath all of a sudden. I do not want to stand in front of all these people and start crying. I'm walking to the microphone stand behind the casket facing at least 200 people. I'm ill-prepared, but I know what is in my heart and head. I know I can speak about Serene.

"I want to start with something I read from Ms. Serene May, maybe written 70 or 80 years ago. Please excuse me as I read this passage on my phone. I keep the reading close by as it has become essential to my thinking.

Be mindful the world is steadily changing, and you are entitled to change your ways or path. When it comes to love, I feel it is best never to live anyone else's design, but like the person you chose to be and let the only judgments, conclusions and decrees come from you for you.

Always see and hear, feel and know them as,

They only wanted you

They only wanted the best for you

They did for you everything they could to protect you

Within that, they found themselves to be themselves to do the things that gave them the most pleasure in life

And that is they only wanted to be with you

For as long as you need

Then they support you to transform your being to stay or go and be blessed with the grace to return as it is best for you.

Be with someone you look forward to making decisions with. Be joyful when you make decisions with someone to become one through the toughest or best times. Think, if this world were yours and you wanted everyone to have a voice.

"I count my relationship with Ms. Serene May as singular; she has been my best friend: a teacher and believer and a listener with no judgments. She gave me unconditional love through her wisdom. I learned love conquers all. I gained control over hurt and can handle scorn if it should ever come. She never said to me, "You know better," but I heard her whisper, "This too shall pass."

"Now I look back to when she was near, and I smile. I know she is free at last, but close to my heart. Through her words, I know I can overcome time and time again, as it is not about how you practice your faith, it is about never turning away...no matter...no matter...it is about facing the winds of change and making change become the wind in my sails.

"I can hardly know what she meant to each of you, but I want to thank you for being in her life. From your experience with her, I am made better, and more is to come for the better for all of us because of Ms. Serene May."

CHAPTER

TWENTY FIVE

"My dear brother, you walk around here as if you are a mummy. Dear Ms. Serene May, she had a spirit life, a timeless love supreme where every moment mattered. You are sad, I understand; but in time, you must live to honor her. Maybe you should call your friend who set you up on a blind date and have them do it again."

I'm walking with my sister checking on each of our residents. I can't believe what she said about me going on another blind date when she was all against it the last time.

"Don't let your head spin off. I was trying to make you smile. You jerk your head like that when you still a bit beat up is not a good ting, my brother. What I want to say to you, let me know what I can do. How about you take a week off and fly to the islands? Go get some homemade cooking and maybe a potential wife to bring you some of dat love Ms. May made you 'tink about."

I don't respond. She doesn't know I have made plans to fly home to see my mother and her mother, or that I'm taking her with me. We can all use a different view. I will not be wife shopping. In two weeks, I'll be sitting at my mother's dining table eating her braised oxtails with rice and peas, plantains, stir-fried vegetables, and Jamaican beef patties and washing it all down with sodas – ginger beer.

We make it back to my office before I respond. She sits in my chair; I stand by the window and look out over the courtyard. Mr. Dell is playing chess against himself and, as always, some residents have picked sides on which Mr. Dell will win. Oddly, the black queen is down.

"Sherry, after knowing Serene and the woman she was, I know I can only be with that kind of woman, but in my age demographic. I'm not going anywhere in hopes of meeting a woman; when my time comes, she and I will find each other."

Sherry removes herself from my seat, and I plop down and give her a look to stop sitting in my chair.

"Blu, from the stories you shared with me from Ms. May's diary, she is one of a kind for sure. She was a creature of her times. If I could put you into a time machine, there is still no way for you to know if you would be the right man for her. So, my dear brother, you need to focus on these days and times. There may not be a woman of the fiber of Ms. May, but there are great women on this Earth. The one thing you might have missed from her diary is she adapted and evolved."

"No woman can ever be Serene; but her type of spirit walks on this Earth, and I'll wait. Though she did not speak often, she whispered inside me through her journal. Serene took me to places and educated my heart. Some of the journal narratives were accounts of her life, and for sure, there was fantasy, but even then, they were about love as she chronicled."

"Yes, my brother."

"Through her, I understand love is giving. It is not just a saying. I know more than before. Love will make one travel, move and sacrifice, defend and honor someone and give them freedom if it is the love they need.

"I read about great loves and relationships. Meeting a few of her suitors at the memorial service let me know there was never any bad blood left afterward; they all moved on with no negatives reasons. Eleven months, Serene was in my life. I don't want to take apart her room; it has a life of its own inside the walls where she took her last breath. I instructed everyone to leave her room alone for a while...please make sure. Serene's lawyer is making arrangements for her belongings. I'm going to ask him if I may have the journal. I may be asking a bit much though."

I show Sherry an email from Serene's lawyer following up that he will be here in about ten days to make arrangements for her belongings, but he will call to confirm; it might be days earlier. In the email, he stated that Serene compensated my facility well above what we charge, and she has also covered the bill of a few other residents who we give a discount to stay here. He placed money in our endowment program for people who we want to treat well even though they don't have the money that most of our residents have. He is also helping the couple who pulled me out of the river find housing.

I'm grateful to her for extending help to others. I know she loved me as an important man in her life. I have read the entire journal, and I think about the first words I heard her say, "Journey to Love." I'll wait until her lawyer comes asking about the journal, and I may ask for her albums.

Mr. Witherspoon is coming by today, a week earlier than I thought. We have some paperwork, and I like chatting with him. I'm sitting in Serene's room and will meet with him here. I had her clothes gathered up along with her small items, including her jewelry, accounted for and packed away. Her furniture is all as it was. I'm sitting across from a cerebral reflection of Serene sitting in her proper fashion. Smiling, I think about watching the sunset with her. I miss pouring her tea. Something interesting Serene would say to me, "Soon the day comes." One day, I had pulled my phone out and turned on the voice recorder as I recited a poem. I asked her to say, "Soon the day comes" when I pointed the phone in her direction. When I held the phone in her direction to test her, she had this little girl giggle. Now I have her voice saved for eternity; I even backed up the recordings on several drives and to the cloud.

I want to listen to myself talking to her as I look out the window, so I pull out my phone.

"Soon the day comes."

My friend

My lover

A friend she is

She is my friend

Being the opposite sex is good

But first, she is still my friend

A friend can be a lover

But a lover is not always a friend

A friend she is giving space

Keeping me in place

Helping me

Never demanding of me

She is my friend

Being sexy with me...well, okay

She does me well

Where is she

"Soon the day comes."

A friend she is

There is something different about her

She lets me be, or not be

She pushes me and pulls me

She doesn't force me

She energizes me

Empowers me

She's there for me

a friend she is

She is my friend

She is my lover

Where is she?

"Soon the day comes."

She is my rock

She is of solid ground

She prays for me as I lie down

She has risen every time I'm in need

She has opened her eyes from my pleas

I have faith in her faith

I hold on to her in dreams

Where is she?

"Soon the day comes."

As I cultivate

It is well she waits

As I learn

She is my earth, wind, and fire

She nurtures

I need

She sprinkles intellectual rain

She shows strength

I feel lifted

He has the best in care in her

She is a good woman,

A great friend she is

She is my lover

Where is she?

"Soon the day comes."

She always makes it right

My friend

My lover

Where is she?

"Soon the day comes."

As I listen to the recording, I stare out the window, but I see movement at the corner of my eye. My sister clears her throat at the same time I see her. Mr. Witherspoon is standing there along with my sister and Cassandra.

"Oh, excuse me, how long have you guys been standing there?"

"My brother, we have listened to you and Ms. May on your recording for some time."

"Mr. Rivers, I must say I am impressed and deeply touched by what I heard." Mr. Witherspoon said as he clapped his hands twice.

"I have her voice, and I listen to it occasionally, as she inspires and makes me feel better."

"I think in all my years of knowing Ms. May, I don't think I have any recording of her voice. It would greatly please me, if possible, for me to have a copy."

"Sure, no problem; and actually, I have a few requests of you."

Okay, I'm sure we can handle it all. I have a bunch of paperwork - do you want to do it here or in your office?"

Mr. Witherspoon steps forward, and I realize there is someone else in the room. Mr. Witherspoon is quite tall, and my sister and Cassandra are not short women, so they all blocked my view. Why are they all here anyway?

They all move left and right, and I see Serene. I think I'm looking at Serene. It has to be Serene, but she is younger.

"Excuse me, I heard my grandmother's voice, and I would like a copy too."

Sherry is on the verge of laughing, and Cassandra is tearing up.

"If you don't mind, please may I have a copy, and I loved your recital." Her voice is Serene's tone. I stand, unsure of what is happening.

"Mr. Blunile Rivers, meet Nefertiti May Adero. Nefertiti is the granddaughter of Serene." Mr. Witherspoon is pleased with his introduction, I can tell.

I wanted to speak, but as if I had run a 100-yard dash, I'm out of air.

"I understand you took great care of my grandmother, and I want to thank you."

I had seen pictures of Serene when she was maybe in the late 40s early 50s, and I'm looking at a carbon copy of her at that time.

"I'm lost for words. I did not know Serene had a granddaughter."

"Yes, I am her granddaughter, and she would be the first to tell you she had one flaw that stood out. My grandmother felt she never had the nurturing aptitude needed to be a mother or a grandmother. I would have loved to have been here for her last year on Earth, but she made it so that I did not know she was sick and that she would be leaving this Earth. That is the type of person she was.

"She knew that I was working with doctors with no borders on a ship, and she wanted me to stay at what I was doing. Mr. Witherspoon here..." she has a little irritation in her voice but also gives a little chuckle, "he has forwarded letters to me from my grandmother for the past year. He made it seem like she was traveling, but no, she was here with you. And, I understand under great care with all of you. For this, I am thankful, Mr. Rivers."

"It's been my utmost pleasure to be at your grandmother's service. She became my best friend." Cassandra lets out a little wail and turns and leaves the room. I think we all understand why.

"Serene taught me a lot, and she shared a lot with me, but she did not share that she had a granddaughter, I'm sorry to say. I do know about your mother and read of your mother's passing many years ago. Oh, and please call me Blu, spelled, B-L-U."

"Yeah, I was born as my mother was dying from the accident in Cairo, along with my father. My mother was pregnant, and she delivered me on her deathbed. My grandfather raised me as well, just like he supported my mother's life from birth. My mother, when she was a young girl, spent a lot of time traveling with my grandmother. The same for me when I was a teen, I traveled with my grandmother Serene, as I saw my grandmother frequently, but I lived with my grandfather. He passed ten years ago. They had the same arrangement they had when my mother was born.

"I had to let my grandmother know I wasn't happy about being away from her. I would have preferred to spend a whole lot more time in her life. She always promoted legacy, and she wanted me to start my life, get my life going, and do good things, so I missed out on her last year. But once again, I understand, she was in excellent hands here."

"Nefertiti, I have many questions I'd like to ask you when Mr. Witherspoon and I finish. Can you and I have maybe a couple of conversations? I have a lot on my mind."

"Mr. Rivers, I'm sure we can. I welcome your questions, and I have questions of you as well."

Mr. Witherspoon put his hand on my shoulder and smiled. "There is one thing I want to show you before we do any paperwork; actually it is a part of the paperwork. I want to take you outside to see something first, if you don't mind?"

I look to my sister, and she has her smirk-ish grin on her face. The three of us walk down the hall. I watch Nefertiti looking at the art we display.

"My grandmother loved it here; this is her style," Nefertiti says.

We step outside, and as I open the doors, there is my parking spot up front, but in my parking spot, there is a car. Parked in my parking spot is a greyish-blue British sportscar like James Bond's car. I had the blues every time I walked past my parking spot ever since my accident. I know the make and model, it is an Aston Martin DB5 convertible, and the top is down. I recognized the car as the one written about in Serene's Journal, once owned by her lover who passed away. This car is the one she drove up the coast and back from her sister and brother-in-law's on one of her last trips she took alone.

"Mr. Rivers, Ms. May made it quite clear that this car is to come to you. She felt awful that you lost your classic, and she loved riding with you in yours.

Riding with you refreshed memories of good times in her life. She had me take the car to experts and have it upgraded with the best safety equipment. As you can see, it has a safety roll cage; if ever, God-forbid, there is an accident, you will be safer. I have the paperwork to give you the title. Here are the keys.

My eyes stay glued more on Nefertiti than the car, although I'm happy to have the car. My heart, I can feel it pound with confusion. I knew Serene was a beautiful woman at 90 years old, but to see her granddaughter, and she's probably about the same age as me – 45 - I couldn't wait to talk to her. I want to know her.

"I can't wait to drive her."

"You called the car *her*; sounds like you should name her." Nefertiti has the same tone as her grandmother with a lightness in her voice.

We all laugh, but at this moment, I am thinking I should name the car. "Nefertiti, would like to go for a ride?"

"Yes."

TWENTY SIX

I'm nervous but encouraged to know I will learn more about Nefertiti and maybe more about Serene from another angle. We go back inside Blue Heaven. I head to my office. I want to make sure I have my car insurance in place and that is a matter of going online, "It should not be long," I tell Nefertiti. For the moment, Mr. Witherspoon and Nefertiti go back to Serene's room, and my sister goes off to check with housekeeping.

Ten minutes later, I'm ready to go and head to Serene's room to meet up with Nefertiti. As I pass the breakroom, I see Cassandra with Dr. Ferrnel from the hospital. I stop in the doorway, and because they are rather close, like close enough to inhale each other's exhale, they don't see me, but they should if their eyes peeled off each other.

"Hello Dr. Ferrnel, you are making a house call to see how I am doing?" I assume he is not.

"Ahm, no, but how are you feeling, Mr. Rivers?"

Cassandra's face shows wide-eyed embarrassment.

"Surprisingly, I feel hardly any pain and most of the soreness is gone." There is an awkward silence.

"He is here to see me. He brought me lunch."

"Oh, okay. I'll let you two get on with your visit." I'm smiling as I walk away.

I walk into Serene's room, and Nefertiti is sitting where her grandmother used to sit, and I feel like I am having a *Twilight Zone* moment of double vision of living in the moment but seeing in the past at the same time.

"Mr. Witherspoon, is it possible for you and me to finish up any details of business later this week? I want to take Serene's gift for a drive with Nefertiti."

"Absolutely. You two get going."

The sun gleams on the chrome of the 1965 Aston Martin DB5 as Nefertiti's fingertips glide along the front hood of the car as she walks around it toward me while I hold the door open for her. Maybe she is connecting to memories. As the space between us shortens, she speaks to me, but she is looking down.

"You were my grandmother's last connection, as I've been told. You experienced the last she had to give; moments I wished she and I could have shared, but she made sure I did my duty to add to a legacy. Will you take me to her? I'd like to visit her gravesite and say my final goodbye. I'm not sure I can do so alone."

Nefertiti speaks of needing closure. I sense seeing the headstone will give her that like Serene's journal allowed her to say goodbye to years long passed.

"She's beautiful, isn't she?" Nefertiti has beautiful hands that are rubbing on the polished saddle leather seats in the Aston Martin. "Mr. Witherspoon told me of your classic car that was ruined and so my grandmother wanted you to have this; it's only fitting for you to bring me, her granddaughter, to see her gravesite."

We watch Mr. Witherspoon wave and drive away.

My chest is heavy as I hold open the door for Nefertiti and stretch out my hand to usher her inside.

"Allow me to escort you to see your grandmother's resting place."

"Hopefully this is not too much of an imposition for you," her words are polite and gracious – just like her grandmother's – even in the midst of grief.

"Your grandmother was the best imposition I ever experienced."

Closing the door behind her, I hurry to the driver's side of the car. Easing behind the driver's seat, mixed feelings surround me. Nefertiti's eyes watch me with a smile. Fretfully, I don't know the operations of this unique classic Aston Martin with some welcomed upgrades like the ability to connect phone through Bluetooth and hear my playlist through the car's stereo system. I fiddle with each knob in the car to familiarize myself with all the functions. All the newness helps to hide my zillions of emotions that are drumming inside me about all that is in front and behind me.

"Do you mind if I play something for your grandmother as we drive?"

"Not at all. I think she would like that; I know I would."

I scroll through some of my favorite artists and decide to allow Donny Hathaway to soothe both of our souls. "For All We Know" begins to play, and from the first piano cord, Nefertiti closes her eyes and leans her head back. I allow her moment to take place, free from my interruption. With each crescendo accompanying the song's lyrics of, "Tomorrow was made for some...tomorrow may never come...for all we know," I see a light shining in a corner of the world of her darkness. She relaxes. She starts to accept the cycle of life.

With the melody still playing and the top down, as soon as I pull out onto the road her hair, which is pulled back and held in place only by her ears, begins to blow it's full length in the wind. It's the second most beautiful sight I have seen in the last few minutes; her face being the first.

Nefertiti breaks her silence by slightly turning in her seat in my direction. "My grandmother prepared me to know where the road leads, even though tomorrow is not promised, and as I ride next to you, I feel her. It's like you were a part of her, if that makes any sense. I hear her talking to me…'Life is to be lived without regrets, without second thoughts. Everything with a breath should breathe.' I can feel her. Can you?"

"I can. Your grandmother was a gift to us all. She was my patient, my friend, my mentor, and she healed me more than I could ever heal her. Her teachings continue to mend my soul, even now."

"She had that quality about her. Always leaving a mark, even without trying."

My playlist flips from Donny's catalog to Sade's. "Cherish the Day" begins to play.

"I love this song," she says, turning back in her seat so that she is facing forward, then she closes her eyes once again.

Watching the road in front of me, I hear the sweetest hum mixing with the wind. The sound is light and comes from under her breath, but it is soothing nonetheless.

Lost in her own world, Nefertiti begins to sing about air not being led astray. I listen as she gives a love song a new meaning, one of heritage instead of physicality. *Interpretation*…I know where she learned that. Serene's entry in 1948 comes to mind. Words written in blue stressed the importance of creating a vision that allowed interpretation to live.

"I cherish the day. I won't go astray. I won't be afraid." Power and self-reliance float from Nefertiti's lips to the sky, as if she is speaking directly to Serene.

"Your voice is beautiful," I say, reminding myself to keep my eyes on the road instead of on her.

"Thank you. But that is not of me, that is of God. Grandmother insisted most Black women can carry some sort of tune in a bucket; it's in our lineage. Our gift from God. It's naturally cultivated in us, and nature has no time or want for pretense."

Does she notice I'm smiling now? I remember those thoughts written by Serene. Like most things I took from Serene's wisdom, Nefertiti has hung on to life experiences she has not lived, but she has experienced vicariously through her grandmother.

"Do you mind if we stop for flowers? My grandmother had a love for them; it would be wrong for me to visit her without bringing them." I feel Nefertiti's hand on my forearm, she does that like her grandmother did to me often.

"Her love for flowers, I saw firsthand. I also learned that love was shared by your mother. You're right, we shouldn't arrive empty handed. As a matter of fact, let's also pick up something to eat and make your visit a real homegoing celebration."

"I'd like that. Less sad, less traditional...more carefree; just like the life she lived and like the life she gave me."

We stop at a tiny flower shop in Long Beach and as Nefertiti peruses the place, I ask for assistance. With the florist's help, we put together a unique arrangement of lilies, orchids, and a massive Russian Sunflower in the middle. After they are packaged, Nefertiti brings the arrangement close to her nose. I watch as she inhales their fragrance and the memories they represent.

From there, we head down the street to Roscoe's House of Chicken 'n Waffles and order our food to go.

"My grandmother brought me here to eat often, I miss down home ingredients."

We drive to Serene's gravesite. Her headstone is large and soft rose-colored. Under her name and the dates she walked the Earth is a picture of Serene chiseled into the granite. As Nefertiti bends over to touch it, she lowers herself, and I see her knees buckle a bit.

"Here, let me help you sit right here in front of her. Have a moment with your grandmother alone, and I will go get our food."

Lowering my head to give respect to both women, I walk to the car and retrieve the food. Sipping on my beverage, I view the passage of heritage taking place before me. Nefertiti is speaking to the tombstone as if her grandmother is standing in front of her. She allows me to hear the conversation. I imagine them smiling eye to eye. I imagine them hugging. I feel their love.

In my car, Nefertiti had sung about air exhaled by her grandmother; and although the air is thinner here at Serene's gravesite, her memory lingers.

"Thank you for bringing me here. Lifetimes of love and respect I needed to share with my grandmother. Having the strength of someone who cared for her by my side while I gave that love freely, gave me strength. I wanted to thank her for the life she lived and the ways she made it possible for me to live my life. The beauty of her character removed unspoken blemishes from mine. Her history gave meaning and purpose to my future. Full circle I had to come; thank you for helping me close the circle."

"Oftentimes, closure brings further enlightenment. Seeing you here, at her gravesite, and meeting Serene's heir – one I didn't know she had, is closure and enlightenment for me."

"How so?"

I chuckle a bit to myself and look downward, searching the ground for the ability to be vulnerable in my honesty.

"Together we pay homage to a woman and a life that continues to teach us how to express and embrace love. Your grandmother came to me as most of Blue Havens residents do. I opened up my facility to her in the same manner that I have done for all who end up calling it their home. Upon meeting her, I had no clue of the mark she would leave on my life. Each day she taught me something new; sometimes at the foot of wisdom being spoken, and sometimes through witnessing the grace embedded in her character. Before meeting Serene, I thought I was complete. I thought I was accomplished, and I had evidence of that success. What I did not realize is that I had a void in my soul. I was ignoring the fact that I have friends, family, and success, but what I do not have is love. Prior to meeting Serene, I had convinced myself that I couldn't miss what I never had.

But that is untrue. If you know 'of' something, you can miss the desire of having it for yourself.

"Your grandmother taught me what love is. She taught me that it is okay to have loved and to have lost. She gave my soul comfort to embrace being fragile to its need for love. I fell in love with the spirit in Serene's journal and how it detailed the woman she was."

"You read the journal, huh?" Her eyes connect with mine, her eyes show her approval. "That journal is an heirloom of our family's journeys. The tales of life and love connect three generations. Blue ink was owned by my grandmother, and green ink for my mother. My stories, I told in pencil so they could be changed and elaborated on as my years provided more substance. The fruit of three trees ripened through the pages of that leather binding.

"The Cairo entry is Sabine's story – my mother. I wrote it from what I knew to be true and what I imagined to be so. We can't rewrite history that is not our own, but we can construct our own understanding. That story is my version of parents I never knew."

Nefertiti's explanation of the different colored ink in the journal gives me further closure. Their heirloom gains value even though I already viewed it as priceless.

"Did you read all the journal contained?"

"I did. Each page spoke to my soul. Worlds untraveled by me were vividly revealed. Sensations were felt. Lessons were taught. I have to confess…looking in the face of a beautiful elderly woman whom I respected greatly, left me bemused in reading of her sexy adventures; but at the same time, I couldn't stop reading."

"Well, I have a confession on my grandmother's behalf. Her entry about the hot-air balloon was half her story and half inspired by me. Her Mardi Gras adventure did take place in the form of a young man bringing her out of her grief by making her speak to me, my mother, and all of our ancestors. The man held her, let her cry out her pain, and he sent her on her way to recovery. It was I who inspired my grandmother to take the memory to a more flavorful place. I shared with her my own personal story of being in a hot-air balloon over Northern Africa once and the exuberance I felt making love in that manner. Once I shared it, she added my experience to her own."

Inwardly, I know my thought should stay in my mind, but I can't help but ask, "Is your balloon man still in your life?" I search beyond her eyes as she answers.

"No. My heart has not found a place to rest yet. Most of all the lovemaking you read in the journal was written by me or assisted from my mind. My grandmother loved for me to be open about the touch of humans in the most passionate ways to be had. Funny…my grandmother and I were like two young girls giggling when we shared writing about sex.

"The ability to provide physical satisfaction alone has not quenched my thirst for someone who comforts every part of me…even my soul. I am still wanting, still needing. Maybe I am asking too much in wanting desire to be coupled with intellectual stimulation. Maybe my standards are too high in wanting soul-stirring conversations that force my heart to tell my body to surrender upon demand. Sex is sex, and I enjoy it just as much as the next man or woman, but I've yet to find the one who turns that act into love or legacy. At least in the manner I want. That's what I need. That is what I'm looking for.

"When it comes to matters of the heart, I'm probably seeking that which cannot be obtained. To be honest, my grandmother's journal, and the knowledge that love takes many forms, has given me patience. It has opened my eyes to knowing that I am free to be me. Happiness, like everything else in life, comes with expectations. When the right person comes along, they will meet all of my needs without force or pretense. I'm content on being patient. It's okay for me to search for someone who feels the same way I do. I want love to rescue me from myself, and until then, I remain content that one day, love will find me. With my grandmother's passing, in a way, life has been reset somehow. Maybe this time around, it will be right."

I digest Nefertiti's words as we ride up the coast from Serene's gravesite. I hit my playlist again and Donny Hathaway's "A Song for You" begins to play. I'm lost in his words, his thoughts, and in the totality of this day. In some way, I know I was in love with Serene in what she represented. Spending the day with her granddaughter has given way to a comfortable uncomfortableness I have not experienced before. Normally a structured person, the uncertainty I'm feeling in her presence is foreign, yet welcomed.

Could that be butterflies in my stomach? Felt from someone I don't know, yet feel as if I do?

She's laid back, far back, in the passenger seat of the Aston Martin. The new car and the woman are both exciting to me. With the top down, her hair swims carefree with the wind, yet again. Her feet are up and hanging out over the car door, and I admire her manicured toes as she sings in perfect harmony with Donny. Her pretty feet and the classic car are fitting of freedom. I find comfort in her feet being there. Comfort in Nefertiti being Nefertiti. I imagine myself being one of her grandmother's lovers from long ago. I sense that quirk in Serene's personality was cherished by them; an eccentric gesture they probably had to endure, just as I endure it from the unique woman sitting beside me. Beautiful personalities do eccentric things that bring them comfort.

Donny Hathaway's song is in final verse as I pull alongside the shorefront. I put the car in park, and we sit in silence as his words serenade the setting of the sun. Nefertiti joins in and hits soul-stirring notes along with Donny as if they are performing a duet. My heart applauds them both. The colorful reflection of hues of orange and yellow take place before our eyes, whispering the passage of time and the completion of a beautiful day. Donny holds the last notes of the lyrics "Singing this song to you" while ascending octaves with his last word.

After the serenade, I ask Nefertiti if she would like to take a walk on the beach. She put her shoes on, but once we walk on the sand, she pulls her shoes off again, and we walk hand in hand in the sand.

She looks at me. "I've been so many places in my life and time. Will you slow dance with me, please? Maybe it will help that I can stay in one place."

"Well, your grandmother said I was a pretty good dancer. Let's see if you agree."

I take her hand in mine and she begins to sing, "A Song for You" into my ear. Her voice, along with the slow rolling tide of the ocean, accompanies the rhythm behind the movement of our bodies pressed close.

Two souls, persuaded by the passion of generations of lovers, unite as we kiss with the sun retreating behind us on the horizon.

JOURNEY TO LOVE

We thank all for reading *Journey to Love*. Writing this book allowed us to look in the mirror of present-day existence and the experiences of those before us. We often read about history or were taught history through dates and times of historical figures or events. We wanted to share views through the lens of a woman who lived through nearly nine decades. We see how the times affected her as to finding love and holding onto or when see moved on in life. Serene May wanted to leave a legacy in how she offered her knowledge to help others and free the approaches, attitudes, and mentalities of those she came into contact with by having an open mind to wants and wishes and desires to push forward-thinking.

When we examine public figures in all eras, we have little firsthand knowledge of what went on in the background of their personal experiences. As such, we have taken some creative liberty in depicting certain events during those passages in time. The stories contained in *Journey of Love* are fictitious events stated from the prospective of fictitious characters. As an example of what we present in this book, Serene meets Amadore in New York City in 1963. We painted a fictional story of her meeting Sam Cooke through Amadore. While in Sam Cooke's dressing room, Serene finds the musician to be quite engaging, and a picture is taken of her sitting on the couch in his dressing room. Imagine Serene's possible thoughts of being between two handsome men, and one of them is Sam Cooke. Of course, Sam met many people backstage in his dressing room during his career; we took the liberty of placing the reader in one of those possible moments.

Rumor has it that Bobby Womack was a womanizer; we give the reader a glimpse at what might have happened between them during a short encounter where Bobby flirts with Serene May. Imagine being in a greasy spoon restaurant and Barack Obama walks in and asks to sit at the table because there was no other seat. Envision it is 1950, and upon entering an elevator, there is a chance encounter with Dorothy Dandridge on the same elevator. Maybe Dorothy is happy, sad, inebriated, or maybe even angry, and an invitation is extended for lunch or to come back to her hotel room for drinks and conversation.

Think of what it would have been like driving a taxi in 1940 and Joe Louis enters the taxi and he seems distraught. *Would you ask him what the problem is?* What if his response was, "I'm broke," or "My wife is leaving me," or "The mob wants me to throw a fight." Then, possibly, he might like your compassion and wants to keep talking, so you park the taxi and accept an invitation to come in his house and have a meal. At the same time as you are having dinner, the doorbell rings. You overhear, "Hey Champ, I have been missing you. Can I spend the night?" Joe Lois answers "Yes," and in walks a famous Hollywood starlit. While we know that Joe Louis was the Heavyweight Champion, we also only know of the rumors of his personal life.

In this book, we give homage to certain historical figures through invented interactions with Ms. Serene May. The historical mentions written in this book of possible scenarios give an idea of the *"Peoples History,"* of behind-the-scenes events. When we see a movie, many people may pass through; we see or hear them as the seconds and the extras. In *Journey to Love*, we wanted to bring to light the seconds and the extras.

ABOUT THE AUTHORS

Alvin Lloyd Alexander Horn, aka Alvin L.A. Horn, has lived and breathed the Northwest air and floated in all the nearby rivers and streams leading to the Pacific Ocean. Alvin's writings are all byproducts of his childhood environments and their subsequent travels. His Black American experiences in Seattle, aka The Emerald City, shine through his poetry, short stories, and novels. He states that growing up in the "liberal on the surface" Seattle lifestyle is grounded by interactions with Black people who had jobs and were not residents of stereotypical ghettos. He feels that his passion for writing was triggered by his mother sending him to the library when she placed him on restriction, often for daydreaming while in school. He also credits the librarian, the little gray-haired Jewish lady, a Holocaust Concentration Camp survivor. She introduced him to the likes of Richard Wright and Zora Neale Hurston. Upon reading the work of Nikki Giovanni, Alvin knew he wanted to be a writer of love stories and poetry.

Alvin also had a storied athletic career as an athlete, a coach, and a musician; the skills and talents, and knowledge gained from those backgrounds often shows up in his writings. Alvin played sports at the University of New Mexico. Alvin has worked in education, teaching life skills, poetry and creative writing, and history and working with at-risk youth. Alvin is a highly-acclaimed spoken word artist and the "2012 Billboard Award Winner of Best-Spoken Word." He has balanced his writing career alongside doing voice-overs for radio, TV, music, video, and movie productions, as well as acting.

Published Works:

2001 – *Poems from My Dresser Drawer*, the poem Trembling, the winner of Best Poem by, The Flava Coffee House Association

2006 – *Brush Strokes* - Romantic Blues Publishing - A fictional story of one's past painting the present and future through a romantic journey

2006 – AALA award for Best Romance Novel -Ebony Magazine - Top Ten Novel of the Year -Heart & Soul, Magazine - Best New Erotic Writer

2012 – *Perfect Circle*, published by Simon and Schuster Publishing, and Zane Imprint -released as the Hottest New Writer. Stalking, violence, and philandering in the Emerald City. The novel reached national bestseller status

2013 – *Pillow Talk in the Heat of the Night* (Peace in the Storm Publishing) an anthology of romantic stories

2014 – *One Safe Place*, published by Simon and Schuster Publishing and Zane Imprint.

Friends and foes, politicians and lovers intersect in love and crime in the Emerald City. The novel reached national bestseller status.

2015 – *The Soul of a Man 2:* Make Me Wanna' Holler, an anthology of essays concerning the Black man in America

2016 – The rerelease of *Brush Strokes* with an added short story, titled Desert Storm Lover, Romantic Blues Publishing

2017 - *Bad Before Good & Those In Between*, Romantic Blues Publishing

Mystery and suspense in Seattle along the streets of Beacon Hill and Rainer Valley

2019 – *Heart & Home*, Romantic Blues Publishing

A historical mystery and suspense fiction of Negro soldier from Seattle coming home from WW2.

You may visit the author at:

www.alvinhorn.com

www.facebook.com/alvinhorn

www.facebook.com/Alvin-LA-Horn-Literary-Artist

Instagram – alah57

https://twitter.com/alvinlahorn

You can hear his 2012 Billboard Award Winning CD at:

https://soundcloud.com/alvinhorn

Lorraine Elzia has always had an admiration for both the spoken and written word and has exercised that gregarious gift in various venues. She began her writing career when the first short story she had ever written was accepted for publication in the acclaimed *Chicken Soup for the Soul* series. Wanting to expand her gift of sharing stories with a relatable message, Lorraine became a contributing author in eight more anthologies before releasing her own debut novel. Having been bitten by the bug of weaving words, she then added editor and ghostwriter to her resume. Driven by determination of imaginative expression, Lorraine brings a creative and unique sculpting skill to the written word. As an in-demand editor, ghostwriter, and CEO of Aveeda Productions which offers literary services to self-published authors, Lorraine is consistently proving herself to be a breath of fresh air in the literary field and an aide for others to achieve their writing goals and dreams. In her ghostwriting capacity, she has penned stories for a dozen authors in genres ranging from religious to romance, erotica to Sci-fi, and urban fiction to autobiographies.

Lorraine is from Austin, Texas by way of Motown (Detroit, Michigan); her eclectic personality and life experiences include being an Army vet, a trained opera singer, a district court manager for over 25 years, a dispute resolution mediator, and an over nurturer of her family and friends. Lorraine considers herself to be a flower child growing wild who loves to travel while connecting with as many people as she can along the way. It is her desire that through the written word, delivered in different genres, she will be able to inspire, educate, and motivate others to see the beauty that resides within all people.

Published Works:

2005 – Mommy and Santa – *Chicken Soup for the Single Parent's Soul* (HCI Publishing) (Anthology)

2006 – The Death Penalty: Revenge, Retaliation, Or Retribution – *Surfacing: Phenomenal Women on Passion, Politics, and Purpose* (Outskirts Press) (Anthology)

2006 – Letters of Love – *Chicken Soup for the African American Woman's Soul* (Backlist, LLC) (Anthology)

2007 – Poem – Levitate – *Gumbo for the Soul: The Recipe For Literacy In The Black Community* (iUniverse) (Anthology)

2008 – Poem – Am I My Brother's Keeper – *Gumbo for the Soul: Here's our Child – Where's the Village* (iUniverse) (Anthology)

2008 – A Test of Faith – *The Triumph of My Soul* (Peace in the Storm Publishing) (Anthology)

2009 – *Mistress Memoirs* (Peace in the Storm Publishing) (Novel)

2009 – AALAS award for Break Out Author of the Year

2010 – NeeCee's Shine – *Gumbo for the Soul: Women of Honor* (iUniverse) (Anthology)

2010 – *Ask Nicely and I Might* (Peace in the Storm Publishing) (Novel)

2011 – AALAS award for Mystery Novel of the Year

2012 – *In the Heat of the Night* (Peace in the Storm Publishing) (Anthology)

2013 – *Pillow Talk in the Heat of the Night* (Peace in the Storm Publishing) (Anthology)

2021 – *Mistress Memoirs* (Revised and republished edition – Aveeda Productions) (Novel)

2021 – *Le Boudoir* (Aveeda Productions) (Novella)

2021 – *Ask Nicely and I Might* (revised and republished edition – Aveeda Productions) (Novel)

You may visit the author at:

Lorraineszone@gmail.com

Instagram – lorraineszone

www.Lorraineszone.com

www.Aveedaproductions.com

www.facebook.com/lorraineelzia

https://twitter.com/lorraineelzia

Footnotes – Tidbits

Mentioned in this book is *Alexandria Cornet – A Collection of Stories, Poems & Essays*. Alexandria Cornet is a pen name for Alvin L.A. Horn that is used, from time to time, for ghost writing and other writings.

History and or historical figures notations in the *Journey to Love*

1961 Ford Thunderbird

The Cotton Club

Lena Horne

Black Renaissance

Sidney Poitier

Jackie Robinson

The Negro Leagues

Althea Gibson

The Palmer House Hotel in Chicago in 1948

The Black Belt of Chicago

Jack the Ripper

Club DeLisa in Chicago in 1948

The Regal Theater in Chicago in 1948

Frank Sinatra

Red Saunders

Count Basie

Sun Ra

The Ink Spots

Sammy Davis, Jr

Lake Shore Drive

Wilma Rudolph

The Hotel Theresa on 125th Street in Harlem

Harvard and the slave trade

The Apollo Theater

Haight-Ashbury, 1967, Summer of Love

Golden Gate Bridge

Hippie Hill

Turtle Hill

Black Panthers

Jimi Hendrix

Apollo and Clytie, Greek Mythology

Grand View Park

Cairo

King Tutankhamun

Egyptian hieroglyphs

French Language

The Mena House

Museum of Cairo

Sphinx of Giza

Camel Market

1965 Pontiac convertible

Martin Luther King

Andrew Young

John Lewis

The Howard Johnson on Peachtree Street in 1967

Margaret Munnerlyn Mitchell, who wrote *Gone with the Wind*

Mason-Dixon Line

Vivian Dandridge – Dorothy Dandridge's sister

El-Hajj Malik el-Shabazz aka Malcolm X

Brown versus the Board of Education

Betty Davis

Ivan Dixon

Jim Crow

Trayvon Martin

Judy Garland

Marcus Garvey

1964 Aston Martin DB5 convertible

Roscoe's Chicken and Waffles

Highway 101 on the California coastline

Lagos and Benin Nigeria, Nairobi, Kenya, Palestine and Brooklyn and Egypt, Washington DC and New York

Bourbon Street Mardi Gras

Papa Doc' Duvalier – Haiti

Xavier University

HBCU

Pullman porter

Presidents Truman and Eisenhower, and Kennedy.

Louis Armstrong

Ella Fitzgerald

Billie Holiday

Music or musicians mentions in *Journey to Love*

"Going Out of My Head" sung by Little Anthony and the Imperials, 1964

"The First Time Ever I Saw Your Face" by Roberta Flack, 1972

"Our Ages or Our Hearts" sung by Roberta Flack, 1969

"Zoom" sung by The Commodores, 1976

"Fire and Rain" sung by Bobby Womack, 1971

"Saving My Love for You" sung by Nancy Wilson, 1967

"The Answer is You," "Meet Me on the Moon," and "I Don't Want to Lose You" sung by Phyllis Hyman

"Long John Blues" sung by Dinah Washington, 1948

"California Dreaming" sung by The Mamas and the Papas, 1965

"Sista Big Bones" sung by Anthony Hamilton, 2006

"What You Won't Do for Love" sung by Bobby Caldwell, 1978

"If You Think You're Lonely Now" sung by Bobby Womack, 1982

"Trouble of the World" sung by Mahalia Jackson, 1959

"We Shall Overcome."

"A Change Is Gonna Come," sung by Sam Cooke, 1964

"For Your Precious Love," sung by Jerry Butler and the Impressions, 1958

"Summer Madness" sung by Kool and the Gang, 1974

"Bye, Bye, Blackbird."

"Softly as the Morning Sunrise" sung by Abbey Lincoln, 1959

"Nothing Can Change this Love" sung by Sam Cooke, 1962

"Skylark" sung by Aretha Franklin, 1963

"The Answer is You" sung by Phyllis Hyman, 1979

"Do Me Baby," sung by Prince, 1981

"For All We Know" sung by Donny Hathaway, 1972

"Cherish the Day" sung by Sade, 1993

"A Song for You" sung by Donny Hathaway, 1971

Nat King Cole, Sam Cooke, Miles Davis, Dinah Washington, John Coltrane, Billy Ocean, Lena Horne, Fats Waller, Bobby Womack, The Valentinos, Jimi Hendrix

Movie or TV shows mentioned in *Journey to Love*

From the '70s TV show, *Good Times*, a young Janet Jackson was featured in several episodes.

The Twilight Zone from the '60s

Imitation of Life, 1959

The Spook Who Sat by the Door, 1973

In the Heat of the Night, 1967

Nothing but a Man, 1964

Made in the USA
Monee, IL
30 July 2021